GU00888879

ALL CATS ARE GREY

a dystopian thriller

Generation of Vipers Book 1

Also by K C Abbott

VIPER VENOM
~ stories to chill the blood ~
including a prequel to the
Generation of Vipers Series:
Birth of the Blues

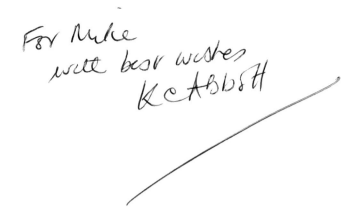

For Mike
with best wishes
KC ABBOTT

ALL CATS ARE GREY

a dystopian thriller

K C ABBOTT

Published in the United Kingdom
by GenVipers Press
https://kcabbott.com

All Cats Are Grey
~ a dystopian thriller ~

Copyright © K C Abbott 2015, 2017
First print edition 2019

ISBN-13 : 978-0-9957046-9-5
ISBN-10 : 0995704694

The right of K C Abbott to be identified as the author of this work
has been asserted by the author in accordance with the Copyright,
Designs and Patents Act 1988.

All rights reserved. No part of this publication may be reproduced,
stored in a retrieval system, or transmitted, in any form, or by any
means, electronic, mechanical, photocopying, recording or
otherwise, without the prior written permission of the publisher.

This book is a work of fiction. Names, characters, places and
incidents are the product of the author's imagination or have been
used fictitiously and are not to be construed as real. Any
resemblance to persons, living or dead, or to actual events, places or
organisations is entirely coincidental.

Requests to publish work from this book should be made to
kcabbott@kcabbott.com

Cover Design: jdsmith-design.com
Cover Image: Sergey Nivens/shutterstock.com/
Interior Formatting: K C Abbott

Dedicated

to those who provided technical and scientific advice on aspects of this story, and to those who believed in it during its long gestation.
Thank you all.

Table of Contents

In the dark, all cats are grey

ELLEN ASHE'S BUSINESS SANK without trace on the day the US dollar was abolished. Together, they had struggled against the tide. Now, together, they went down for the third time – and stayed down.

Ellen did not spare a thought for the millions across the water. Her prime concern was to avoid joining them: the outcasts, the dispossessed, and the hungry.

The world was again in turmoil, obsessed with yet another financial crisis. Nobody was likely to notice the collapse of a one-woman firm in this outpost on the edge of the habitable world. She might manage to worm her way into a deal that would keep her fed, at least for a while.

But not here in Greenland. Not in a province where she was known.

Ellen slumped deeper into her battered old leather chair, chewing at her bottom lip. She had carried on, totally alone, for more than two years now. It was so very hard. But at least she only had to make a survival plan for one.

She would have to create yet another new identity. And she would have to migrate once more. Even alone, her options were pretty limited, though. The tech squads might well catch up with her if she moved too close to the centre of things. If she wanted to stay free, to stay in control, she had to find a backwater where she might manage to outwit the watchers – a place where, one day, she might start up in business again.

Decision made, then.

She jumped to her feet and started to pack her possessions with brisk efficiency, ruthlessly discarding everything that related to her previous life. She prided herself on the fact that she had never been one to dither, even in the most difficult circumstances. And she always travelled light.

It would have to be London, after all.

• • • • •

The black-clad watcher stood motionless in front of the viewscreen. London, under a louring sky swollen with rain.

He cycled the screen through its targets one last time. Key London landmarks, predictably empty and grey. The maternity unit – a tiny handful of births, all female. European sister provinces, all battened down. American cities, some still besieged by starving crowds, most now cleared.

Progress.

The watcher's mouth stretched into a lean, cold smile.

"Mirror." The screen blanked and silvered. The man scanned his reflection for flaws. Too much skin between greatcoat collar and hat. He tugged it further down to shadow his eyes.

Then he stalked out into the fetid air of his city, under the clouds that could not rain.

ONE

THE IMMIGRATION HALL WAS huge and high-ceilinged, built for an earlier age when people came through in their tens of thousands. There were luminous arrows painted on the floor to direct new arrivals to the appropriate reception bot and enough automatic barriers to corral and control vast numbers. These days – with the sole exception of a shiny new propaganda screen, high on the wall – the hall reeked of neglect. The paint was peeling and the floor had not been swept. But the place still looked as it was meant to look – bland and unthreatening. Ellen was not fooled.

Once, she would have been able to conceal herself among crowds of newcomers, relying on her ordinary, unmemorable face to escape the notice of those around her. Other women prided themselves on being once seen, never forgotten. Ellen Ashe, once seen, was never remembered. It was a quality that had served her well each time she was forced to switch identities. She had easily morphed into Ellen Ashe when she fled from Ireland; now she was about to become someone else entirely. For London.

She would certainly need her skill today, for she was the last of only three arrivals, all females. That increased the risk, even though she had carefully chosen a day when the state's attention was elsewhere, focused on the celebrations for the Fiftieth Anniversary of the end of the Water Wars.

All but one of the reception desk screens were blank. She scanned the hall desperately, hoping that one of the others might blink into life. With two, she would have more scope for manipulation.

FOLLOW THE ARROWS STRAIGHT AHEAD. The voice of the barrier was cheap and tinny. It couldn't have been updated for decades. Not surprising, given how little use was made of this hall. The barrier repeated its instruction, more forcefully. *STRAIGHT AHEAD.* Ellen had no choice. No doubt its ability to inflict pain was still intact.

Hefting her holdall over one shoulder, she followed the woman ahead of her. The first arrival had finally been cleared and was making her way towards the exit at the far end. The second woman now stood in front of the reception bot, ready to lay her hand on the reader and answer the security questions that would flash up on the screen. Her voice was too low for her words to carry to Ellen, so she would be flying blind for this encounter. And it was a long time since she had dealt with London's security at first hand.

She lounged daringly against the barrier, idly tapping one toe against the tip of a yellow direction arrow. To the watchers, she had to look like a woman completely at ease, with nothing to hide. She told herself calmly, over and over, that it was true. It was one of the hypnotic techniques she often used and, normally, she would have had her body's responses totally under control within seconds. Mind control was vital if she was to fool the sensors. Without it, her body might betray her.

But that propaganda screen kept intruding. Someone had turned the sound up high, probably because of the grand anniversary parade, and the hall rang with martial music as thousands of uniformed women and men showed off their precision drill, turning and weaving in intricate patterns, as though they were dancers rather than killers. Distracting to the eye as well as the ear, Ellen decided sourly, trying to focus again on inward control. She didn't dare to turn her back on the propaganda screen. That would make her look suspicious, possibly rebellious. She would just have to apply all her mind-control skills to blotting it out.

It was not easy. When the richly coloured military pageant finally came to an end, the sound grew even louder as a tiny figure appeared beyond the crowds of dutifully clapping spectators. The President, of course. Or was it? He'd had so many death threats he was reputed to be afraid of his own shadow. On the other hand, this occasion was so important he probably hadn't dared to send a stand-in. He might be too young to have fought in the Water Wars, but he had a key ceremonial role at the parade – to assure the Old Ones that their "sacrifice" had not been forgotten.

At that subversive thought, Ellen's heart rate leapt uncontrollably. *Sacrifice,* indeed! Billions of innocent people had been culled in those wars. The Old Ones hadn't sacrificed a single life or a single cent. So few of them; but now, after fifty years of consolidating their power, and building their mega-corporations, they manipulated everything, directly or indirectly. Their wealth had ballooned, while most people were scrabbling to eat.

Her attention was caught yet again as the camera zoomed in to fill the screen with the platform party, all in gaudy toytown uniforms, decked with medals they had not earned with their own blood. No, not quite all, she realised. A single black-clad figure was carefully placed in the third row so that he was in shadow and almost invisible. Odd. And somehow sinister. Ellen shivered. Who on earth was he?

She shut her mind against the question and her own strange reaction. What mattered here was survival and getting past the security screening. She might be called forward at any moment. She dared to close her eyes, for just a few seconds. Then she took a long, deep breath and willed her heart rate to slow.

• • • • •

Anton jabbed a bony finger at the screen filling the end wall of the Jays' underground refuge and began to mutter even more angrily. His voice was starting to rise.

Jedda's head jerked up. She pushed a loose curl of hair behind her ear and frowned. She couldn't afford to allow Anton to wind everyone up. Not today, of all days. The anniversary was a major milestone, after all. For the Old Ones, fifty years in power was to be only the beginning.

And it surely would be, if freedom fighters like the Jays did not stop them.

Jedda glanced at the screen's brilliant colours, deliberately ignoring the contrast with the grey poverty they lived in. The Jays couldn't afford luxuries, or even comfort. As leader, she'd had to ensure that almost every cent was invested into the technology that gave her team their only edge. Living as they did, deep under London's streets, was certainly hard on the body. But what did comfort matter when the cause was freedom?

"We ought to be taking *action*," Anton insisted. "Against the President." Typical! Once he got his teeth into an argument, he wouldn't let it go. It could be maddening. And living on top of each other made it even worse.

Jedda answered as calmly as she could. "Remember, the president is only a puppet of the Old Ones. He knows they could get rid of him in a heartbeat. So he has to present them as the saviours of the planet. He can't afford to get on the wrong side of them. They've got far too much power."

"They've got far too much everything," Chrys put in quietly, with a grimace that twisted one corner of her thin mouth, distorting her flawless olive skin. Like Anton, she loathed everything about the Old Ones and their control.

Jedda needed to redirect her team's anger. She turned back to the screen. "Who do you reckon that is?" She pointed to a dark figure in the third row of VIPs.

"Don't know." Anton was just staring at the screen, shaking his head, his neat pony tail bouncing from side to side.

"Then find out," Jedda snapped. What was the matter with him? He was their technology wizard. If anyone could identify a distant image on a screen, it was Anton. But, these last few weeks, he hadn't been pulling his weight, even though they all knew their little group couldn't afford to carry passengers. She would give him one more chance – this chance – but if he failed them again, Jedda would have to replace him. As leader, she had to be ruthless, even if it meant sacrificing her friends.

Anton must have sensed something from Jedda's tone, for there was a faint reddening high on his ears. He tucked his chin down on to his chest and set to work.

Jedda focused on the strange, dark figure on the dais. What was it about him? She couldn't quite put her finger on it. Was it that he was wearing plain black? It did make him look very odd against all the colourful uniforms around him. He stood out like—

Anton swore suddenly.

Jedda spun round. Anton hardly ever swore. His ears weren't red any more. His cheeks were neon bright.

"It's K. It is! Jedda, he's decided to show himself at last."

Jedda gasped and repeated Anton's oath under her breath. They had been waiting more than two years for this. "Find out everything you can about him, Anton. Quickly. We'll never have another chance this good. Chrys, give him a hand."

Jedda turned back to the screen, as if she could ferret out the man's secrets by simply staring at that dark shape. "Viewscreen, zoom in. Repeat."

Even magnified, that shadowy figure remained a mystery. If he were not so tall, he would be completely hidden by those around him. And yet he was the second most powerful man in the province. Some said he was actually the first.

He was wearing a regulation black hat, pulled low, but Jedda thought she could see dark hair beneath it. His skin was so pale it was almost sickly. No wonder. When did K ever emerge into the daylight? Wasn't this the first time in years? So why had—?

The President began his address. K's head snapped up in the same instant. Jedda saw his eyes narrow as a shaft of light hit his face. "K's a Blue!"

"He can't be!" Chrys cried, looking up to check the screen. "You're seeing things, Jedda. Besides, he's the Controller. He couldn't possibly be a Blue."

Anton was too deeply involved in his wizardry to have heard a word.

Jedda stared and stared at the screen. In that split second, she had been so sure. And yet Chrys must be right. It was impossible to see any detail clearly. It must have been a trick of the light. No genetic inferior could ever get that close to real power.

The president's rabble-rousing speech dragged on. Eventually, it roared to a climax: "We rejoice in the genetic purity we now share. And we vow to remain vigilant against future contamination." Pause for a burst of cheering. "Disease – once the scourge of our lives – has been defeated. Life-spans are being extended, year upon year, and decade upon decade, under the wise direction of the Council of the Old Ones. We honour them and thank them for the long, healthy, and productive lives we have been granted and the ordered and stable society we now enjoy."

That was too much, even for Jedda. "The only people who'll live those long and healthy lives will be the Old Ones and their hangers-on," she snarled. "Most of us will be dead of starvation long before then."

"Not necessarily," Chrys said coolly. "We could always be shot."

Jedda was surprised into laughter. "Too true." She gestured at the viewscreen, now showing the platform party again. And K. "We should concentrate on the enemy we're actually trying to fight. He's the one I need to be able to second-guess." She shook her head in exasperation. What did K think of the Council's supreme power? Did it tie his hands much? Watching that black figure, frozen in its place, Jedda doubted it. The Old Ones took very little part in the day-to-day running of things any more, and rarely visited minor provinces like London. The president had their authority to wield ultimate power. K was only one step away.

But surely not if he was a Blue?

Anton's triumphant voice broke into Jedda's thoughts. "I've got him! The signal is much better than it appears on the screen. I even managed to use my DNA sniffer. Well..." he added a little sheepishly, "it did work for about half a second."

Jedda wasn't really listening. She turned away from the haunting black figure and forced herself to smile at Anton. "*Is* he a Blue?" The words were out before she could catch them.

Anton's dark eyes widened in shock. "*Blue?* K?" For the first time in their years of working together, Anton looked at Jedda with less than total respect. Then he dropped his gaze and said, simply, "Biometrics show him as genetically normal – Not-Blue."

Jedda nodded, trying to appear her usual, controlled self. A knot of worry settled in her gut. Whatever Anton had discovered, it did not explain what Jedda had seen.

Or had she?

• • • • •

The autobarrier spoke again. *FORWARD.*

Ellen strolled forward to stand in front of the screen. She was fully in control of her reactions now, though it had been a close-run thing. Without haste, she followed the instruction to place her right hand on the print reader, and then to look into the iris scanner. The machine moved seamlessly through its routine. She gave monosyllabic answers to the security questions. She was winning. She'd be through in a moment.

READ ALOUD THE WORDS BELOW.

Ellen's pulse began to drum in her ears. That was not part of the standard vetting procedure. Not unless they'd changed it in the last few hours.

Outwardly, she forced herself to maintain her usual calm. Machines were fallible. She had spent years outwitting them. Besides, her voice print matched all the other metrics she'd introduced into the London security system. Her new identity was watertight.

She read the required words in a low but clear voice. Her control was perfect. She didn't want to have to do this twice.

VOICE PRINT DOES NOT MATCH ID. REPEAT ALOUD THE WORDS BELOW.

"You have a malfunction," Ellen said in the sharp voice she used to instruct computers. "Send for a human supervisor."

VOICE PRINT DOES NOT MATCH ID. REPEAT ALOUD THE WORDS BELOW.

The barrier behind her was beginning to close in. Ellen sensed its menace at her back, but she would not turn. That would spell disaster. She focused all her attention on the screen. She needed a human now, someone she could control. "Malfunction. Call human supervisor," she said again.

MALFUNCTION OF RECEPTION SCREEN. SUPERVISOR. SUPERVISOR!

The autobarrier was still moving.

• • • • •

"Jedda! Quick! Come and look!" Anton was almost as excited as he'd been when he deciphered K's biometrics. He touched a button to bring the main screen alive again.

There was nothing odd about the immigration hall, as far as Jedda could see. It contained only one arrival, a rather ordinary-looking female, but that was perfectly normal, nowadays. Jedda frowned across at Anton.

"Look," he said again. He changed the angle of the camera he'd hacked into so that it showed more of the hall. "Somehow, that woman has beaten the automatic system. That's liveware walking across the hall."

Sure enough, at the far end of the vast hall, a small door had opened. A uniformed woman started across the floor, trying to push her cap down over untidy hair. She was yawning.

Jedda couldn't believe her eyes. The immigration system was old, but it was foolproof, wasn't it? No one had believed that human supervisors existed. Till now.

"Maybe it's a genuine malfunction?" Chrys suggested reasonably. "Those machines are pretty ancient."

"Nope." Anton was adamant. "I've hacked into them all in the last few months. Nothing wrong with any of them." He grinned briefly.

"Except that they're not Anton-proof?" Anton was clearly back on form. He really was the best in the business. Inwardly, Jedda breathed a sigh of relief. She wouldn't have to get rid of him after all. Her precious team could stay together.

"Watch." His voice was urgent again.

"Do we know who she is?" Jedda asked.

"We know who her ID *says* she is, but if she did create a malfunction, she's bound to be someone else entirely. Someone with astonishing skills. The reception system suspected that her voiceprint didn't match her other metrics. The barriers ought to have immobilised her by now."

"But she's still free," Chrys said in an awed whisper.

"How the *hell* is she doing it?" Anton sounded truly exasperated now.

All three watched, holding their breath. The uniformed woman was asking questions, but Anton's camera seemed unable to pick up the words.

"What's she saying, Anton?" Jedda snapped. *"Anton!"*

He switched to another sensor, but it was too late.

Behind the reception screen, the uniformed woman was entering the codes to shut the bot down. The unknown arrival was walking jauntily towards the exit.

"That's impossible!" Chrys gasped.

"No, it happened. And we need to know how," Anton said flatly. "She—"

"We'll worry about that later. Keep her in sight, Anton," Jedda ordered. "Whoever she is, I want to know exactly where she goes. We'll need to be able to find her again. To use her if we can. And if she decides to resist..." She shrugged. "Skills like hers are dangerous. We can't afford to allow K's people to get to her. If she refuses us, Chrys will have to deal with her. Permanently."

TWO

ELLEN'S GUT TOLD HER she was being watched.

She touched the computer sensor on her wrist, changing it to one of the specialist modes she had so carefully engineered beneath its cheap exterior. It confirmed what she already knew.

There was no point in looking behind her. There would be no one there for her to see. But someone was watching her, without a doubt, and had been following her every move from the immigration hall to the centre of the city. Someone had spotted her arrival, in spite of all her precautions. One slightly dodgy voiceprint wasn't enough to ring the state's alarm bells, surely? Especially since she'd covered it up so quickly. She hadn't made any more mistakes. She was sure of that. But something had made her a target, even in this backwater. Unfortunately, London had so many more sensors now that it was difficult for anyone to escape observation.

Difficult – but not impossible for a woman with sufficient skill.

Keeping her head bent, she hailed a passing electric streetbus. Almost everything about London had changed, except the tradition of painting buses red. It was old and dirty but it still drew up with silent precision, its door the regulation half metre from her feet. It was completely empty. It seemed that most of London was empty, now that the meltdown of the dollar had sparked off another financial crisis. A half-empty city meant fewer people who might be enemies, but also fewer people to hide behind.

The autodrive barked at her. *DESTINATION?*

Ellen stepped inside and made the sign for touch mode – she was wary of leaving a voiceprint on the bus's recorder, in case it was transferred before she could erase it. And no fingerprints either. She touched a fingernail to a random spot on the bus's map. Direction hardly mattered when it came to losing her pursuers; it was more a question of time and distance.

As the bus pulled smoothly away, Ellen slid her fingers under her sleeve to work her wrist computer by touch alone. The bus might be old, but its surveillance systems were probably state of the art. For the moment, only the camera at the front of the bus was focused on her, and she had ensured it was recording her nondescript back view. But in five seconds at most, the alternate camera at the rear would switch itself on and focus on her face.

Four. Three. Two.

Done it. The rear camera swivelled through ninety degrees and trained its lens uselessly on the street beyond the tinted windows.

Ellen pulled up her sleeve so that she could work faster. She couldn't afford to cut it so fine with the front camera, since it was already in operation. She needed to stop it from elevating and recording what she had done to its mate.

It took her several more seconds of frenzied work to make the forward camera do the full one-eighty and focus on the street ahead. But it was worth the effort. She had gained a little breathing space, and the thinking time she desperately needed.

Who could possibly want to target Ellen Ashe? Or Helen Birch, as her new ID proclaimed her to be? She had created Helen Birch to be no threat to anyone or anything, just a useless member of the London underclass, depending on state handouts to survive, one more Not-Blue female in a world with far too many of them.

Ellen moved along the bus to lean casually against the sidewall by the exit. One more touch on her wrist would spring the door open and stop the vehicle dead, so that she could disappear into the crowd.

If she could find any crowds big enough in a city newly turned in on itself and licking its wounds.

• • • • •

"Shit! I've lost her!"

At least Jedda wasn't around to hear his admission of failure.

Anton concentrated on trying to find a camera that could pick the target woman out of the crowds thronging New Piccadilly Circus. She must have sent that bus there deliberately, just as she had sabotaged its onboard cameras. She had chosen the one place in London where there was sure to be a decent-sized crowd today, apart from the parade square with all its safe, hand-picked spectators. The people watching the giant screen at New Piccadilly Circus were neither safe nor silent. They were milling about, confusing the swivelling sensors. Some were even daring to shout abuse as the president's speech was replayed above their heads.

The woman was nowhere to be seen. It seemed she had found a

way of disappearing.

Anton swore again. This extraordinary female was getting to him, in a big way. She had manipulated the immigration computers. OK, fine. Anton could have done that, no problem. She had dealt with the cameras on the bus. They were more recent technology than the immigration hall's, but not too difficult to fix. Anton could have done that, too. But could he have found a way of disappearing from New Piccadilly Circus under the noses of the most up-to-date sensors and cameras on the planet?

He was prepared to admit – at least to himself – that he wasn't sure on that one. He was beginning to wonder whether this elusive woman, calling herself Helen Birch, might actually be a better tech than he was.

Scary thought. Especially as Jedda was fired up to drain every last drop of knowledge from Helen Birch. What if the woman wanted to join them? What if Anton found himself surplus to requirements as a result?

You don't want to go there, Anton. Better to concentrate on finding her, and proving to Jedda that, however good that woman's skills may be, yours are better.

• • • • •

It was taking hours, during which Anton discovered that he wasn't the only one on Helen Birch's tail. K's resources had not been focused solely on the security for the parade. And now that it was over, his gaze had shifted.

Anton should have known. K was like a black spider at the centre of its web, feeling the tiniest tremble on every strand of its carefully spun gossamer. Even minor sabotage in the immigration hall would not have gone unnoticed. No doubt, the human supervisor had spent the intervening hours answering for her failings. No one knew how K extracted information, but everyone suspected it was not pleasant.

Jedda strolled in, with Chrys at her back. Perching on the dilapidated chair by Anton's desk, Jedda stretched out her long legs with a sigh. Anton could see that she was wriggling her toes inside her boots. Then she pushed her hair back off her face, a sure sign that she was worrying at something important. Normally she would let her curly hair fall forward to hide the jagged white scar by her ear.

Anton's update was brief. But when Jedda finally responded, she was more philosophical than he had expected. "Just goes to prove how important this Birch woman could be to us. She's clearly not in K's camp. Not with all that effort to evade his security. So she's half on our side already. All we need to do – all *you* need to do, Anton – is find her. She'll probably be glad of allies. No matter how good she is, it can't be easy to work alone."

Chrys had been frowning in silent thought. "Even a lone wolf has to sleep some time," she said slowly, practical as ever.

No one responded. Anton and Jedda both knew that, if Chrys had to eliminate Helen Birch, she would want to do it neatly and silently, while her victim was asleep. It was the way she preferred.

Anton's computer bleeped, an unusually strident, insistent sound.

"Yes! Got her!" There was an image on his screen, its focus so poor that it was difficult to identify whether the dark form was even human.

"Are you sure that's her?"

Anton beamed triumphantly at his leader. "Yup." It was time to play his trump card, he decided. Even Jedda wouldn't dismiss his skills after this. "Got a DNA signature." His DNA sniffer was working only intermittently, but it was much better than anything the other side possessed. So far. "It matches her Helen Birch ID. That's definitely her."

"Anton, how on earth did you—?"

Jedda waved Chrys's question aside. "Great work, Anton," she said brusquely, "but what about K's people? Are they still trailing her as well?"

Anton felt like a cock crowing from the top of a very big dunghill. He grinned even more. "She managed to lose them about an hour ago, according to my system. She's good. Better than anyone I've ever seen. She dropped an ID shadow on to another woman. Easy, of course, when you're average height and build, as Birch is. She almost fooled me while she was at it, but I've tweaked my systems to catch that sort of trick."

"You mean K's systems don't?" Disbelief showed in Jedda's face.

Anton shook his head. "It's people that matter, Jedda. Far more than systems. It's all down to the operator. You have to refocus the whole system to catch something that subtle. If you do it wrong, you could be totally screwed. None of K's minions would dare to risk that, even if they knew how. No, K's tech guy will be playing it safe, worrying about his own skin. It's what they all do."

"Ah, so K was using a man to track her? Interesting use of scarce resources."

"Men – some men – are easily distracted," Chrys said thoughtfully. "Not you, of course, Anton," she added. "But some of them. It can make things easier."

"What happens to K's man isn't our problem," Jedda said sharply, getting to her feet in a single, lithe movement and stretching her long limbs. Anton swallowed. Nothing at all average about Jedda. Rounded in all the right places, too.

"We need to grab the Birch female before K's systems catch up with her again," Jedda continued. "They're bound to, given all the resources he puts into them. Anton, get me the co-ordinates of her location. Alert us the minute there's even a hint that K's people are on her track. Chrys, you'll be with me. We're going to bring her in."

"Here? Are you sure it's safe?"

Jedda nodded. "It's your job to make sure she doesn't see or record anything she shouldn't. Understood?"

Chrys smiled.

• • • • •

The tiny sound broke the silence in the vast office. K looked up from his antique desk and frowned ferociously at the woman who had appeared through the main doorway.

"The immigration machine was corrupted beyond repair. And the supervisor… We tried everything but her memory seems to have been wiped." The section leader's voice cracked. She would not meet K's eyes.

Satisfactory. It was better when they were afraid.

"In other words," K said softly, silkily, "you've failed." He turned in his chair so that he faced his screen. "Computer—"

"No!" The word was almost a scream of panic. "No, K. There are other ways of finding out… Our tech will… We won't fail you."

K turned back and forced his body to relax slowly into his huge black chair. It gathered itself silently around him, obedient to its programmed role. He waited. The silence held its breath.

Finally, K raised one eyebrow at the quivering female opposite him. "Other ways? Really? Perhaps you would like to tell me *precisely* what they are?" He jabbed a long finger at the hard chair on the other side of the desk. "Now."

Very predictable, K concluded, as the woman began to lay out various tactics to secure their elusive quarry. But K said nothing. Not a word, not a single gesture, until the woman had finished her recital. Talking seemed to have calmed her a little. She had even stopped shivering.

Not satisfactory. Disposable creatures had to be kept on the back foot.

K allowed the silence to stretch between them again. The female was waiting for K's reaction. And her fear was mounting again. K could smell it. That was as it should be.

K did what he always did. Something unexpected.

Without a word, he rose and strode out of the room.

• • • • •

Jedda checked her comms implant and pulled her unruly hair back over her ear. She leaned over Anton's shoulder to get a quick glimpse of his tracker screen and the mystery female. Then she straightened and stretched. She had to be ready for action. It would be very soon.

"Target's moving at last. Going east." Anton's voice sounded incredibly loud through Jedda's receiver. Her skull was vibrating like a struck bell. She turned the sound level down several notches.

"OK. Final instructions." Jedda glanced over her shoulder for Chrys. She was in her usual place, fully armed and ready, two paces behind her leader's back. She had arrived without a sound.

"Let's not underestimate this female. She's a tech, and we have no idea what tricks she might use against us. She could be a warrior, too. Is she carrying any weapons, Anton?"

"Sensors didn't show any," he said, not raising his eyes from his screen. Jedda knew that was no guarantee of anything. This woman had outwitted the immigration systems; could she outwit Anton's, too?

Jedda checked the external viewer. It was getting dark early. The sky was battleship grey, and full of heavy rain clouds waiting to dump on any unprepared victim. The parade was long over now, so the jumped-up generals would not be caught out. She gave a choke of laughter, quickly swallowed, at the thought of little old men in sodden uniforms, freezing rain dripping on to their noses from the polished peaks of their caps. Pity it wouldn't happen.

"What is it?" Chrys hissed.

That whispered warning pulled Jedda up short. She shook her head angrily and motioned for silence. What on earth was she doing? Even with a seasoned fighter like Chrys at her back, she must take absolutely no chances.

Concentrate! You're responsible for this mission. And you, of all people, know how risky it is.

The slightest lapse could endanger them both. Weakness was

unprofessional. Especially in a leader.

She had been brought up to know better.

• • • • •

By the time Ellen caught the first glimpse of her goal, she had dropped ID shadows on three different women. That ought to be enough to fool any number of watchers, no matter how good. But she still felt uneasy.

She had learned long ago to trust her gut instincts. They were telling her that she was not safe. Not yet. Once she was inside…

She dare not risk starting to run. Although the streets were almost deserted, there were always hidden snooper devices. A running woman was bound to attract their attention. So she looked up at the leaden sky, shook her head as if worrying about being caught in the coming downpour, and quickened her stride so that she was hurrying, but not running. Not quite.

She rounded the last corner. There, at the end of the street, was the building she had chosen to serve as her London base until she could find a way to set up in business again. The tower was bigger than it had looked on screen in Greenland. More decrepit, too, at least on the outside. The expensive stone cladding was long gone, stripped off as high as the "recyclers" could reach with their makeshift scissorlifts. Only the very top of the tower bore any resemblance to what it had once been – a phallic symbol of wealth and power. Two hundred metres up, the letters FRANZ were still visible, incised deep into the stone, but fuzzy at the edges now, eaten away by weather and pollution.

The external details registered but she quickly thrust them deep into her memory. She was unlikely to need information about what lay above ground. She already had the rest. Before destroying her computer systems in Greenland, she had used them to uncover all the internal secrets of the Franz tower, to identify the best hideout, to set up what defences she could. Once inside, it would take only an hour or so to finish the tasks she had begun remotely. Soon, she and her refuge would be completely invisible to even the most sophisticated spy systems.

But in that hour, she could still be vulnerable.

With one last look up at the heavy sky, she moved nonchalantly into the lee of the building where the shadows would help to conceal her. Then she slipped round the corner from the main entrance to the side door she had chosen. As she expected, the top-of-the-range electronic lock was still intact. It might be good enough to keep the "recyclers" out, but not the probes from Ellen's Greenland systems.

A touch on her wrist computer transferred the pre-prepared codes; the lock was disabled. Another few seconds and she was inside, with the entrance relocked at her back, using her own, stronger encryption.

Silence. Darkness. Damp, musty air in her lungs and on her skin.

She needed an hour. The golden hour, medics called it, when they could save a life. Or the danger hour, when they could lose it?

She allowed herself to laugh into the darkness. She had no intention of losing.

Working swiftly, and by touch alone, she pulled her armoured bodysuit from the concealed compartment of her holdall and slipped it on. Much better already. She adjusted the integral headset.

"Miniglim," she said aloud. Obediently, the lights in the suit came on at the lowest possible level. No need for infrared here. She was alone in the building.

She slung the holdall on to her back and secured it. Then she touched her wrist once more. She needed voice mode on that, too. Her hands had to be free. Just in case. "Head-up of Franz plan." The ground plan of the building appeared on her headset display. She had memorised it before she left for London. But she was taking no chances.

The weapon slid into her palm like a lover's caressing fingers. Her final insurance. She smiled. Better still.

Her hour was ticking away. She started for the stairs.

THREE

JEDDA AND CHRYS WERE hurrying through the narrow deserted streets. After the stale atmosphere of the bunker, the winter air fizzed deliciously on Jedda's tongue. But here, outside their hidden refuge, everything was a danger.

Anton's voice came through their implants again. "Target's moving now. Quite fast. Keep on your current bearing."

They speeded up automatically.

"About six hundred metres ahead of you now. You're gaining on her."

"Wha—?" Jedda fell her length on the slimy path. All the breath was knocked out of her.

"Alpha? What's happening?" Anton again.

Chrys was already crouching beside her, weapon in hand, scanning for attackers.

Jedda pushed herself up and wiped her palms down her dark grey trousers. The green gunge melded instantly with the cloth. "I'm OK. I tripped. Careless of me." She pointed to a curl of root on the ground. Quite small. Inanimate. Not threatening at all. "Come on. We're losing time."

After another two hundred metres, Jedda called for an update.

Anton's voice rang in her head immediately. "Target's stopped. Looks like she's going into what's left of the Franz tower. No sign of the opposition yet. You need to get to her before she's put up her defences."

And before K's thugs arrived.

Jedda and Chrys exchanged a look and started to race down a dark alley. Too bad if they were seen by the watchers. Only the target mattered now. "Control, guide us in," Jedda messaged. "We need to take her from behind if we can."

"Roger." A pause. One second. Two. "Next right. Then second left." He was guiding them around the sensors.

They speeded up even more, following his complex directions

19

without question. It took them less than three minutes to arrive at the far side of the ruined Franz building, once the headquarters of a worldwide empire. But it was taking precious, frustrating minutes for Anton to deal with the incredibly complex locks.

"Target is moving down. Southwest section." A short pause. Then, "Target in sub-basement. By corner walls. Movement stopped."

"No chance of taking her from behind," Jedda said.

Chrys nodded agreement.

"Have to be from two sides at once then," Jedda decided.

Chrys simply weighed her weapon in her hand. She was ready.

"Locks disabled. You're in."

At last! "Control, two routes down. One-eighty degrees apart. Quick as you can."

"Wilco. Separate channels."

Anton's directions came fast. Jedda had to concentrate hard to follow them. He sent her doubling and twisting through half-broken staircases and down tunnels built for squat scuttling machines. In the open areas, her autolights reflected off stinking black pools. What dangers were they hiding?

Long years of training kicked in. She was even more wary now. She leapt over an ominous-looking pool and raced on. Her heart was pounding. Not fear. Excitement. This was what she was born to do.

Chrys would arrive by her own route. They would approach the target from opposite sides. Anton would disable any defences the woman might have set up.

In the end, it would come down to a straight fight. One target female, against two proven warriors. Pretty good odds.

Jedda bit back a smile and kept running. This was going to be fun.

$$\bullet \bullet \bullet \bullet \bullet$$

K stood in front of the huge viewscreen, watching the changing images. Still nothing. London looked almost deserted. As darkness fell, it had started to pour with rain. Even the scavengers had crawled back into their holes.

The door opened behind him, but he did not turn.

"K?"

It was Linden, K's second-in-command. K continued to gaze at the screen, waiting for the man's report. Had someone, somewhere, discovered a new clue to the fugitive's whereabouts? Unlikely. Anything of importance would have been reported first to the central systems here in K's office. Everything ran from here. Information was crucial – followed by analysis, decision, and action. K was sure that his was the only way to keep control.

"K, can't we stop the rain?"

K turned at that. Linden was standing at the far side of the room. Unlike the others who entered here, he was not afraid. As K's number two, he understood what London Central did and why. Some of it, at least. One day, when Linden was older, wiser, and a great deal more ruthless, he might be ready to take over his own province. His grandfather would like that. And since his grandfather sat on the Council of the Old Ones, it would probably come to pass, whether Linden made the grade or not.

Nonetheless, K had to admit that the young man had talent. A first-class warrior, and brains, too. Far too idealistic, unfortunately, in spite of his aristocratic grandfather's murky example. But idealism could be made to fade. It was K's job to ensure Linden gained the sort of cold-blooded experience that would deaden even the most upright soul.

K shook his head. "We stopped the rain for the parade, because the Council insisted. That's enough." He shrugged dismissively. What did it matter if the weather was foul? The hunt was bound to be over soon. The target was only one lone woman.

Linden looked puzzled. The frown sat rather oddly on the breadth of his smoothly handsome face. "But the experimental smell implants don't work well when there's so much water about. I know the techs will overcome that – eventually – but right now, it's giving our search packs a real problem."

K walked over to his chair and sat down. For Linden, he was prepared to explain. Linden had to learn. "Yes, drier weather would make the hunt easier. And certainly less difficult for our hounds. But it's a diversion of scarce resources that we can't afford. Haven't you looked at the costs of weather warping?"

Linden grimaced and shook his head. Accounting was clearly not his thing.

"Then do so. Soon. You need to understand that cost is an essential part of our job. For example, if we had unlimited funds, we could implant all the world's population and set up systems to monitor their every move. We'd have absolute control. But we don't have the resources. The earth itself no longer has the resources for that size of operation. So we have to make judgements about what we can and can't afford. And, as a result, our control is… Shall we say, it's less perfect than we would wish?"

Linden gave a bark of laughter. It sounded more like shock than amusement, but he responded without missing a beat. "It's certainly less than perfect at the moment, K. We still haven't found any signs of that female who arrived earlier."

"No traces at all?" K snapped. Instantly, he damped down his physical reactions, making his face expressionless. Others must not be able to tell what he was thinking or feeling. That impassive mask was part of his myth.

But, underneath, he was starting to worry. Others might dismiss the incident as merely a minor technical glitch in an antiquated immigration hall, but K knew better. It was no fluke that the woman from Greenland had beaten his systems. She was a manipulator, with dangerous skills. She had to be found; and "encouraged" to serve the state. Or eliminated.

"No, nothing," Linden said, shaking his head so hard that his fair hair flopped over his eyes. Safe, dark brown eyes. He pushed his hair back with an impatient, boyish gesture. "Our so-called hounds can't be hunting hard enough. I'll go out with the women myself, make sure they're not missing any leads."

"No. Your place is here at HQ. Get the pack leader in. Tell her exactly what will happen to her if she fails to find the target. I guarantee she'll try much harder." He paused, assessing Linden's change of expression. Distaste, predictably. Linden was always too soft on women. Yet another character defect to be eliminated, if the man was ever to make the grade.

"You'll have to convince her that your threats are real, of course," K added smoothly. "Think you can actually do that?"

· · · · ·

Just before she emerged into the sub-basement, Jedda stopped for a second. She switched her lights to infrared and pulled her goggles down over her eyes. Then she turned off her comms implant. She couldn't afford distractions. She had to see without being seen. And to move in total silence.

In the far corner, there was a heat source surrounded by cold, blank walls. A single, human figure. Not Chrys. She was coming from the opposite direction. This had to be their target.

The woman had her lights on miniglim. So she wasn't expecting company. Good. She was in for a surprise.

Jedda checked her weapon again. Yes, it was still on default – minor damage only. They needed this woman alive and functioning.

Jedda began to move, testing each step before transferring her weight.

The unknown woman was moving rapidly about in her corner, bending down to the floor and then moving on again. What on earth was she doing? Setting up sensors, maybe? Or booby-traps? Impossible to tell using infrared from this distance.

Jedda needed to get much closer. She had to know what she was up against. She would have only one shot.

Another ten metres. She stopped, sighted. Still too far for a low-intensity shot against a moving target. And what on earth had happened to Chrys? Jedda spent precious seconds scanning the area. No other heat signature anywhere. Chrys hadn't reached this floor yet. Jedda was on her own.

Twenty metres more and she could fire.

She continued to creep forward. Halfway to her goal, she pushed up the night vision goggles. The other woman's miniglims were enough to see by. She had almost finished setting up her ring of devices on the floor. Jedda had no idea what they were, but they looked dangerous. Too dangerous to let her finish.

Jedda was still five metres outside ideal crippleshot range. She sighted and fired.

The target staggered back a step but didn't fall. The miniglims went out.

Jedda was blind in the dark. Instantly, she sprang away and dropped to the floor. She could be the target now.

She hauled down the infrared goggles just in time to see the floor splinter where she had been standing. Damn Anton's sensors! The woman was armed after all.

Jedda slithered towards the wall. It was blank. No cover at all. Did the woman have infrared? Could she see anything? If so, Jedda would be in plain sight. And at this range Jedda's light body armour wouldn't stop a lethal zapshot.

Chrys! Where are you?

Useless. Thoughts couldn't transmit like spoken words. And speaking would betray Chrys's existence.

"Stay where you are!" The woman's weapon was pointing straight at Jedda. But Birch had no infrared goggles. She was guessing. She must be.

Jedda sprang to her feet and danced two steps sideways.

The weapon followed her. "I told you to stay still. One more step and I shoot."

The Birch woman could see in the dark.

Jedda froze, her mind racing. It was stalemate. They both had weapons. They could both see. Either of them could win now.

The woman took two deliberate steps towards Jedda. Her weapon didn't waver a fraction from its target. "You think we're equal, don't you?" She came another step closer. She was well within crippleshot range now. "You're wrong," she said flatly.

Jedda moved her weapon so that it was pointing directly at the woman's heart.

Birch laughed sharply. "Yours is on maim, mine is on kill. You think that's equal?"

"This close, a crippler to the heart can be lethal," Jedda retorted.

"Not through my body armour."

For a split second, Jedda was almost floored. Birch's form-fitting suit looked nothing at all like body armour. But it explained why Jedda's first dropshot had failed.

"Whereas yours can't stop a killshot. At this range, nothing can." The woman took another step towards Jedda. She held out her free hand. "I'll take your weapon." Her voice was low and soft. Commanding somehow. Her strange, compelling eyes were staring into Jedda's.

Jedda's hand began to move. Almost by itself. What the hell…?

She forced herself to look beyond those staring eyes, over the woman's shoulder and into the darkness. Her mind slipped back into gear. She straightened her spine and tightened her grip. "No," she said calmly. "I think I'd rather try my luck against your fancy armour. It may not be *quite* as good as you think at such close range. Shall we see?"

Birch backed off a step. Straight into Chrys. And, in a second, Chrys's weapon was pressed against the woman's unprotected throat. "Mine is set on kill, too," Chrys lied silkily into her captive's ear.

Jedda lunged forward to grab the woman's weapon. She grinned at Chrys. "What kept you?"

Chrys shrugged. She used her free hand to pinion the woman's arms behind her back so that Jedda could search for any more weapons in that slinky suit. Nothing. Apart from a wrist computer that Jedda pocketed.

"Right," Jedda began crisply. "We're going for a little walk. All three of us. But first I want some information. Who are you?"

The woman said nothing. Chrys pressed her weapon a little harder. The woman raised her chin and stared defiantly at Jedda.

"OK. Let me tell you. You say your name is Helen Birch. You arrived today from Greenland. You screwed up the systems in the immigration hall. Right so far?"

Helen Birch said nothing. Her eyes were still fixed on Jedda's face. But Jedda wasn't going to make the mistake of looking back into those eyes. Once was enough.

Chrys made to push up her goggles and switch to miniglims.

"No!" Jedda ordered. "We stay with infrared." She would explain later, once the Birch woman was safely locked away. Besides, Jedda's theory might be wrong. She doubted it, though. Nothing else fitted the facts.

She turned back to the prisoner and trained the woman's own weapon on her bare throat. "You don't want to co-operate?" Jedda asked pleasantly. "Fine by us. We'll leave you to K's…er…tender mercies. I imagine his people will be here quite soon." She nodded to Chrys and gestured to the devices on the floor and the open holdall by the wall. "Collect up her stuff. And take that suit off her. We'll take it all with us." Chrys almost smiled in response.

"Wait. Surely we can find a—?"

"No time for negotiations. Decide. You come with us – willingly – right now. Or we strip you and leave you to K." Out of the corner of her eye, Jedda saw that Chrys had finished filling the holdall. "You have five seconds to choose. One. Two—"

"I'll come with you."

"Very wise. Take off that suit."

"No!"

Jedda raised the weapon a fraction. "Take it off. You're not going out there better protected than we are. If you try to escape, I want to be sure I can shoot you."

The woman's jaw worked. She shrugged and stripped off the suit. She was wearing her ordinary travelling clothes underneath. No body armour that Jedda could see though Chrys searched her anyway. At Jedda's nod, Chrys grabbed the armoured suit and bundled it into the holdall. It took up hardly any space at all.

"We leave now." Jedda motioned to the woman to follow Chrys. Jedda tucked herself in at the rear, her weapon at the ready, and turned her comms back on. "Control? We're three. Coming out now." She chose her words with care. She wanted the woman to hear that much, to know she would be watched. But no names.

"Street level clear." Anton's welcome voice in Jedda's head. "But not for long. Get a move on. There's heavy rain."

"Roger. Street level in four minutes."

Chrys had already broken into her easy half-run. "Get after her, Birch," Jedda ordered. "Keep up, or we can still leave you behind for K."

They reached street level in just over three minutes. Chrys tore off her goggles and reached for the door lock.

Jedda had to say something now. "Walk arm in arm. You're hurrying to get out of the rain. Don't look each other in the face."

Chrys's eyebrows shot up. Then she read Jedda's expression and nodded.

"Birch, don't try anything. If you do, my companion will shoot you. And remember, I'm right behind you both. With *your* weapon, set on kill."

Chrys pushed the door open. Arm in arm, the two women scurried out into the rain. Jedda hung back for a moment. "Control. Warn Bravo not to look into Birch's eyes. Tell her I'll catch up with them in five minutes max. There's something I have to do."

• • • • •

The hunt was out in force at last. K stood watching their slow progress on the viewscreen. Not good enough. Not by a long way. Future hunts had better be sharper, rain or no rain. Still, it was only a matter of time now. The fugitive had gone to ground in the Franz building. Street sensors had finally confirmed it.

He switched the picture to the Franz tower. The streets around it were deserted. Floods of churning water were trying to push past the filth that dammed the gutters and the driving rain was bouncing high off broken paving stones. Foul weather. But the hounds would arrive soon. Once inside the building, away from the wet, the hound-pack women would soon sniff her out.

And then he saw it. A square white blotch by the main door.

He touched the screen. "Viewscreen, zoom in."

A square white blotch with words on it. *"You can stop looking now. We have her."* And something else, scrawled in the bottom corner.

"Viewscreen off." He didn't need to zoom in closer to see what was on that common white card. He knew already. A crude sketch of a bold, sharp-eyed bird.

A jay. A *blue* jay.

Battle had been joined again. And this time, it seemed he had lost.

He stared at the blank screen. He should have stopped the rain.

FOUR

ELLEN LET HER BODY slump on to the bench in the bare, windowless cell. It could have been worse. The two women could easily have killed her. Or let K have her.

Thoughts of the state and its malign power still made her shudder, but she managed to suppress it this time. Her captors would see no hint of fear, however good the resolution on their sensors. She needed to ensure it stayed that way.

She let her head drift back until it was supported by the rough, damp wall. Then she let out a long breath. Although she had checked every inch of the cell once already, she let her gaze roam over the walls, the ceiling, the floor. No sign of the sensors, but they were bound to be microscopically small. Impossible to find. No sign of anything at all that she could use to help her escape.

She was wearing nothing but an ankle-length shift. That silent warrior with the thin-lipped smile had stripped off all Ellen's clothing and searched every possible hiding place on her body. The woman had been deft and very thorough. She had combed through all Ellen's hair. She had even found the tiny computer hidden between Ellen's teeth.

Ellen had nothing left. Except her own face-to-face power over human beings, the power she had been working to perfect since her childhood in the wilds of Ireland. In Greenland, she'd managed to keep it hidden, knowing it would make her a target if it were discovered. But in the immigration hall, she'd had no choice but to use it on the supervisor, since it was that, or arrest.

It all seemed an age ago now.

She closed her eyes and forced her shoulders to relax. Her power might not be of much use here. That was her own fault, too. She shouldn't have tried to use hypnosis against an opponent with a weapon. And she should have realised that infrared goggles would reduce the impact.

Stupid, stupid! Why hadn't she simply killed her attacker? She shouldn't have let anything get in the way of her own survival. It didn't matter how recklessly brave the woman was. That tiny spark of admiration had been Ellen's downfall.

From now on, she would focus purely on self-preservation. It was the only logical approach. Cold, ruthless calculation had saved Ellen for nearly three years now, ever since Grant had begun to suspect the secret police were closing in. He'd insisted she escape to her new identity in Greenland. He simply wanted her safe, he said. From there, she'd had to watch, alone and impotent, as he was betrayed and arrested. And finally executed. He had trusted too much. He had refused to learn to fight really dirty. His integrity was part of his character, and part of the reason she had loved him so much. But those all-too-human qualities had made him vulnerable. Ellen must not make the same mistakes.

The leader here – whatever her name was – knew the risks now. She was shrewd enough to have worked out what had happened in their Franz tower confrontation. She would ensure that none of her people allowed themselves to look directly into Ellen's eyes. There would be no hypnosis on these people.

Unless Ellen could trick them somehow? Direct their attention elsewhere, like a conjurer, so they would forget what she could do? Given long enough to overpower just one of them, she could get out of this hellhole.

She groaned inwardly. It wouldn't work. They were bound to come after her, and they might be clever enough to catch her again.

No. If she did manage to escape, she couldn't afford to leave any of them alive.

· · · · ·

The close-up of the prisoner's face filled the whole viewscreen.

Anton gasped and swore vehemently. "She's a Blue! Jedda, you must have been mad to bring her here. Think what she could—"

"She's *not* a Blue. Look again. Carefully. Her eyes are hazel. That's a tinge of green you're seeing, not blue."

"Pretty much the same thing. Besides, it could be an illusion."

"What's up with you, Anton? What's happened to your famous rational brain? Have you fried it in one of those crazy experiments of yours?" Anton said nothing. "Birch is Not-Blue," Jedda said flatly. "She's dangerous. But not because she's a Blue."

"We can't take the risk," he said stubbornly. "You could be wrong."

"Anton, you know there's no risk from being near a Blue. It's not infectious. They *say* there's a risk if you—"

"Fuck her?" He spat the words out. "Fat chance. Not a filthy Blue."

Jedda ground her teeth. "It's not as if she could turn us into Blues. Blues are born that way. Defective genes *aren't* catching." Jedda heard herself beginning to sound exasperated. But she knew Anton wasn't rational when it came to Blues. She took a deep breath. Then another. "For the last time – the woman's *not* a Blue, anyway."

Anton snorted.

Jedda's hair had fallen over her eyes. She pushed it back impatiently. "You know, Anton, I hadn't realised just how prejudiced you are."

"If you'd grown up with as many Blues around as I did, you'd be prejudiced, too," Anton growled.

"If I'd grown up with as many Blues around as you did, I'd know the difference between blue and green," she bit back.

"But—"

"Enough. End of discussion. Helen Birch does not have blue eyes. She is not a Blue. Don't treat her as if she were. That's an order, Anton." She marched across to her station and sat down. "Time to get back to work," she said, in something more like her normal voice. "I need your report on all that woman's stuff. Soon as you can." She kept her eyes on her screen, but she heard him cross the floor and pull out his chair with the high-pitched scrape that always made her nerves jangle.

Silence followed. Jedda's breathing slowed. Anton was back at work.

· · · · ·

Jedda was yawning as she walked down the corridor to central control carrying her mug of coffee. She didn't care whether it tasted like the real thing or not. Without a large dose of caffeine, she couldn't get going in the mornings. Especially not this early.

She would swallow her caffeine, check the external sensors, and look in on the prisoner. Perhaps the woman would be easier to deal with after a night on that hard bunk? Perhaps she would—?

Jedda stopped dead in the doorway. "Anton! What are you—? Have you been here all night?"

Anton rose, looking a little sheepish. And very dishevelled. His ponytail had come undone. Some of his hair was standing on end as if he had been running his hands through it for hours.

"Got involved. Forgot the time," he mumbled. "But look what I've discovered! Jedda, this stuff is fantastic. See for yourself!" He held up the armoured bodysuit. It was draped over his arm like a sheer silk scarf.

Jedda touched it gingerly. Then she took it from him. It weighed almost nothing. "I don't understand how something as light as this could stop a crippleshot." She shook her head in disbelief.

"Well, I've tested it, and it does. What's more, it will stop a killshot, too, even at pretty close range."

"But she told me that nothing could— Oh." The Birch woman had lied to Jedda about what her armour could do. Odd. Why on earth would she do that? What did she have to gain?

Anton was not listening. He was still raving about the properties of the strange bodysuit. "Amazing material. Never seen anything like it. K doesn't have this or we'd have seen it by now. This is totally new. If we all had this, we'd be invulnerable."

Jedda swallowed a laugh. "Not quite invulnerable, Anton," she said. "The woman was wearing it when Chrys and I captured her. Remember?" She took a long swig of her coffee and sighed with pleasure as she put the mug down. Much better. "Though I admit it would certainly be a help," she admitted, with a smile. Anton had worked for hours on this. His dedication deserved to be acknowledged. "You're doing a great job. What else have you found out?"

The list of Anton's discoveries came tumbling out. The integral headset of the bodysuit could provide infrared images, without goggles. The headset display was so thin and delicate, it was almost invisible. The computer from the woman's teeth was the latest in nanotechnology, minuscule, but immensely powerful. Mind controlled, of course. There was no better way, according to Anton.

"What about the things she was putting down on the floor? Were they booby traps?"

"Um." Anton's face fell. "I'm...er...still working on them. Nothing so far. But I don't think they're booby traps. Sensors, maybe. I'll know more in a few hours. I'll—"

"You'll go and get a few hours' sleep, Anton." Jedda put an arm round his shoulders to soften her sharp instruction. "You're exhausted. You'll work much better when you've rested for a while."

"But—"

She pushed him in the direction of the door. "See you later, Anton. Sleep well."

His shoulders slumped. He really was exhausted. Now the adrenalin of discovery had worn off a bit, he would be feeling it. He smiled wearily at Jedda and made for the door to the corridor and the sleeping cells beyond.

"Phew!" Jedda weighed the bodysuit in her hands and threw it over a chair. Supple and featherlight, it settled like a velvet cloak on a courtesan's shoulders. Jedda didn't begin to understand how it could be as strong as Anton said. And what about the rest of Birch's stuff? Anton was clearly envious of the woman's skill. He was assuming, of course, that Helen Birch had engineered all these marvels. Had she?

Only one way to find out.

Jedda swigged down the last of her coffee, dumped the mug at her own workstation, and strode off down the corridor to the holding cell.

Outside the locked door, she stopped. Impulsive leaders didn't last long, especially against opponents as sharp as Helen Birch. Jedda's predecessor had been reckless. In the end, it had cost him his own life, and the lives of all his attack team. Now there were only the three of them left.

Too few to be really effective, but she could never give up the fight for freedom. Her parents had died for the cause. They had passed the torch to her and she had accepted it willingly. She would never let it go out.

Jedda leant against the wall and let out a long breath, allowing her body to slide down the rough surface until she was sitting cross-legged on the uneven floor.

Time to think, Jedda! And to plan. Even one-on-one needs a plan.

She knew what she was going to do. But she hadn't worked out quite how. No point in consulting Anton and Chrys. This was a leader's decision. Besides, Anton would have a fit. Chrys would go along with it – probably – because loyalty to the leader was part of her code.

Even if the leader was doing something so dangerous that it could be the end of them all.

• • • • •

Ellen pulled the blanket more closely round her shoulders and hugged her knees. It was not exactly freezing in this bare cell, though it was far from comfortable. She had caught a glimpse of her captors' sleeping quarters on the way in. Their bunks might be slightly softer, and they might have a few more blankets against the cold, but it looked to be a pretty spartan existence.

She had not slept much, partly because of the hard bunk, and partly because of... Oh, everything else. Being a prisoner again. Being powerless.

And being so very alone.

She had come a long way since she'd lost Grant, and much of it was downhill. It seemed a lifetime since they had been together, meeting in secret, evading state surveillance by ever more extraordinary tricks. When Grant and Ellen's years of working side by side had finally begun to blossom into something deeper, he'd insisted they take precautions. He said it was because his tech company was a target, because the state would use any means to steal his secrets. If Ellen were known to be his lover, the state could grab her, and use her to get to him. He wouldn't allow that to happen. So he helped her to hone the fighting skills she'd learned in the backstreets. Turning her into a warrior was not enough, though. He'd insisted she set up a company of her own in Ireland, and a secret backup in Greenland. Then, once her escape route was secure, he engineered a very public rift between them. And fired her.

As far as the world knew, she simply stormed out and they never spoke again.

Ellen had been sure his fears were over the top. She couldn't really believe she was in danger or that either of them was vulnerable. They were technocrats and entrepreneurs, after all, the kind of wealth-creators that the state was desperate to encourage. But she hadn't known, then, about Grant's secret life and the risks he was taking, every single day, as leader of a guerrilla band. For her, their secret affair seemed more of a challenge than a threat; they could hardly ever be together, but she gloried in the thrill of every stolen hour, while her blood pounded in her veins and her nerves sparked like shooting stars.

She had revelled defiantly in the luxuries they indulged in: rare wines and – even rarer – real food, shared in front of fragrant applewood fires. Those poignant memories were vivid even now: salty forbidden caviare, sweet creamy butter, with the surprising crunch of Melba toast. And the taste of Grant's lips in the kisses that followed and carried them on to glorious lovemaking, skin caressing skin, flesh joined with burning flesh. Once, they had shared a huge bed with chocolate brown satin sheets so shiny that she had slithered out on to the carpet. She had been laughing so much she could hardly breathe. Then the laughter had melted into desire as she pulled Grant down beside her, to make love – fast, hard, heart-stopping – naked on the floor.

The memory of the love, and the laughter, seared her like a brand from that long-ago fire. She wrapped her arms around her middle, rocked back and forward for a moment, and forced the pain into submission. It was over. Grant was dead. She was alone, and she had to continue to survive. One day at a time. What else was there?

She thought she heard movement outside her cell door. Perhaps some thoughtful person was bringing her breakfast? She had eaten nothing since leaving Greenland and she was starving hungry. In this set-up, the food would be nothing special, but she was used to that. Over the years, she'd had everything from banquets to beetles. She fervently hoped it would not be beetles again.

She set her expression to bland and waited for the door to open.

Nothing. No movement, no noise. And yet she knew she had not imagined it. There was someone outside, waiting. Waiting for what?

For information, of course. But who on earth were these people?

More than once, Ellen had been dragged into state prisons, to face police interrogators, usually because they thought her company was not doing enough to assist the state. She had always known precisely what she was dealing with – mere foot-soldiers, ruthless but simple-minded – and she had always been able to manipulate them into releasing her. But these women were not state agents, not unless their acting ability was brilliant. These women were just as ruthless, but they were also smart, possibly even smart enough to overcome the best of Ellen's tricks. If so—

Her palms were starting to sweat. Moving cautiously under the concealing blanket, she wiped them dry on her shift.

The door opened. The nameless leader walked in alone. She was tall, with a warrior's presence, alert and wary. Dangerous. She did not appear to be armed, but her silent companion was probably waiting outside. Nameless closed the door and leant one shoulder against it. "Sleep well?" she asked brightly. She might have been a Council hostess enquiring after a house guest.

Ellen said nothing.

Nameless raised her eyebrows and shrugged. "I'll take that as a no. Don't worry, you'll get used to it once you've been here a while."

"I wasn't planning on staying," Ellen snarled, goaded into speech.

"Oh, but you will," the other woman replied smoothly. "You're a fugitive. You need us, Helen Birch."

Ellen clenched her teeth. She didn't need anyone any more. It was these people who needed her, for her technical skill. They were not going to get it.

"So, here's my offer," Nameless continued with a cold smile. "Join us, Helen Birch. Help us to fight K and his state machine. Fight for freedom."

Ellen snorted. "Not exactly the *best* offer I've ever had. What's in it for me?"

"Your life?"

Ellen glanced up into the other woman's face. Her striking features were not beautiful, just strong. And her fierce frown and the stubborn set of her jaw told Ellen that this was no idle threat. If Ellen refused to co-operate, she would die here, deep below the pitiless streets of London.

The odds were stacked against her but she knew she could find a way to beat them. Even alone. She would escape and make a new life for herself. By herself. She'd done it before, hadn't she? Ellen Ashe should not let herself be bested by this tiny group of would-be Robin Hoods! Romantic they might be, but their struggle would be futile in the long run, for the state was always too strong to be beaten. Bad Prince John had become King John in the end. And where was Robin Hood then?

Decision made, she began to assess her enemy more carefully. As she should have done from the start.

Unlike Ellen, Nameless looked anything but average. Younger than Ellen, too. She might even be as young as she looked, for she still had that attractive sheen of idealism that could lift spirits and inspire sacrifice. Yes, clearly a remarkable young warrior.

The battle starts here and now. With every carefully chosen word. Ellen's pulse was already beginning to race in the old way at the mere thought of fighting and outwitting a worthy opponent.

She forced herself to relax against the rough wall. Even through the blanket, the damp seeped into her limbs. "My life?" She allowed herself a world-weary smile. "Yes, I see. And, in exchange, you want what, precisely?"

"Why did you lie to me about what that suit of yours could do?"

That was the last question Ellen had expected, even from an adversary as sharp as this one. "Why should I tell you the truth?" she retorted, after a moment. "It pays to keep an opponent guessing, especially when she's pointing a weapon at your heart."

Nameless paused, digesting that. Then she almost laughed. "Yes, very clever. I'll grant you that. You were hoping to escape, of course. You knew I would try a long-range killshot rather than chase after you and risk being shot myself. You were relying on that fancy suit to get you away from us."

Ellen tried to look smug, though none of it was true. She had lied automatically, because lying came as second nature to her. Nameless was endowing her with far too much foresight and calculation. Though from now on, Ellen would have to have both.

"Better not try to escape now," Nameless said. "Remember, we've got your suit and the rest of your kit as well. You wouldn't get far in the shapeless sack you're wearing. And it's no protection at all, even against a crippleshot."

Ellen said nothing, waiting.

"I suppose you'd like some time to think about my offer?"

"What I'd like is something to eat."

Nameless laughed, for real this time. "OK. That, too. But I'll be back later for your answer. Enjoy your breakfast." She pulled open the heavy metal door and started to leave.

Ellen waited until the door began to close again. "Don't you have a name?"

The younger woman stopped, and turned back. She narrowed her eyes and put her head on one side to scrutinise her prisoner. An impressive pose, except that some of her hair fell over her eyes and she had to push it out of the way.

Before Nameless could get a word out, Ellen said, "You probably prefer to use something descriptive. Warrior Queen, perhaps?" It was a childish jibe, but Ellen relished the flash of reaction in the other woman's eyes. Even a minor hit could be useful in their continuing struggle.

"I have a name. If you join us, you'll find out what it is. If you refuse, you'll be a nameless corpse at the hands of a nameless assassin. It's tidier that way, we always think." She flashed a broad smile and disappeared into the corridor, pulling the door behind her. Silence. Then the electronic lock engaged with a loud click and two old-fashioned metal bolts were shot home.

Ellen was alone. She had lost that round. And the clock was ticking.

FIVE

JEDDA GLANCED AROUND TO make sure she was alone. The corridor was empty and silent, apart from the low hum of their makeshift air circulation system. She slumped back against the wall opposite the locked door and let her face muscles relax for the first time since she had gone into the prisoner's cell. Sighing out a long breath, she shut her eyes against the garish light and swallowed hard, in an attempt to get some moisture into her dry mouth. Being leader was so hard. Always with the team, always working for the team, but always alone.

She had taken the decision. And she knew what she had done was right. But she worried about how it would turn out. The Birch woman was tough and resourceful. She had shown it in the Franz building and she was showing it again here, even with the odds stacked against her. She must accept the offer in the end. Surely no one would meekly choose death?

No point in wasting time over that. In a few hours' time, they would find out what the prisoner had decided. In the meantime, Jedda had more important, practical tasks to carry out, to hold the fort while Anton slept.

Once the team was assembled again, she would have to tell them.

• • • • •

Anton had spruced himself up again after his enforced rest. He no longer looked exhausted. In fact, he looked sharper than usual, even eager. Jedda suspected he was very keen to get at the Birch woman, or at least at her technology.

"Did Birch say anything when you took in her food, Chrys?" Jedda had decided on a neutral opening. In a moment, things might get explosive.

Chrys shook her head.

"Not surprised. She doesn't say much at all." Jedda took a deep breath and turned to Anton. The opposition and the argument would come from him. "I've asked her to join the group. She's thinking about it."

Out of the corner of her eye, Jedda saw shock on Chrys's face.

"You're out of your mind, Jedda!" Anton's dark eyes were blazing and his ears were bright red. "We can't possibly trust a woman like that. I know we're short-handed since Jay— We could do with expanding the team, but not at any price."

"We could do with her skills, Anton. That bodysuit, for example."

"I can get to the bottom of her technology. I just need a bit more time."

"No. That could take ages. We've got better things for you to do. If she joins us, she'll share. You can work together, build on both your skills. It's the obvious solution."

Anton snorted. "If she joins us, it'll be because she has no choice. I wouldn't want to turn my back on her. Given half a chance, she's bound to betray us."

"Why would she? After all, she's a fugitive, too. She must know she can't bargain with K. He never sticks to his side of anything. He would scoop us up, sure, but he'd take her as well. She daren't let him find her. If he does, she's dead meat. She *needs* us. And we need another warrior for the group, never mind her tech skills."

"I vote we extract her information and dispose of her. Anything else is too risky."

"I wouldn't bet on getting anything out of her, Anton," Jedda said sharply. "She has mind control skills. She'd have used them on me in the Franz building, if I hadn't had the IR goggles. I'm pretty sure that's how she managed the immigration business, too. She insisted on dealing with liveware, remember?"

"But she—"

"No. You don't get a vote here. It's the leader's decision."

"She's already got us at each other's throats," Chrys put in quietly. "Is that a good trade-off? I agree it's your decision, Jedda, but Anton is right about one thing. You'll always have to be watching your back."

"I've always relied on you to do that, Chrys." To Jedda's surprise, Chrys suddenly looked a little uncomfortable, as if Jedda had questioned her loyalty.

This was becoming really difficult.

Jedda changed tack. "Look, you both admit we need more people. We've barely been able to function since Jay got the away team killed." She swallowed the rage that always filled her when she thought about her predecessor's decision to mount that suicidal raid. Everyone had been killed, including the leader himself. As the number two, Jedda had watched the slaughter from base control and had been left to pick up the pieces. It reminded her, as nothing else could, that leaders' decisions were not always right. She needed to take her team with her.

"I've contacted some of the other groups, to ask for reinforcements. The European groups are all stretched to the limit, just like us. A couple of the South American groups have promised to do their best, but it will take ages for anyone to get here. Travel is in chaos over there since the US dollar went down the pan and barter doesn't get you very far. Besides, K's immigration people will be keeping an even closer watch now. Our people will have to be doubly careful when they do make it across the pond." She waited. No one spoke.

Jedda reached out to put a hand on Anton's arm. "I know she's dangerous. And I'm not suggesting we actually trust her. But we can use her. With care. Just for a while. Just until the South American people get here. If she proves her worth, we can decide whether to keep her with us." Jedda shrugged. "If not, Chrys can deal with her."

"We'd have to change the rotas," Chrys said, in her practical way. "To ensure she was never alone with any of us, in case she started playing her mind games."

"No need," Anton put in quickly, with a flashing grin. "I've got tech skills too, you know. If I analyse what she's doing, I can make us all contacts that will screen out her clever tricks, better than the IR goggles did. I can't protect us against a physical attack, though. She *is* a warrior, isn't she?"

Chrys's mouth twisted as she nodded.

"Right," Jedda said. They were all agreed. They were a team again. "Anton will prepare the contact lenses. Chrys will make sure Birch is locked in her sleeping cell at night. We'll all take care that she doesn't lay a finger on a weapon, unless we've taken her with us on an away mission. Understood?"

"Understood. But she doesn't touch any computers unless I'm there to watch her," Anton added. He was frowning. "She could sabotage things in seconds."

The two women nodded. "Right, I'd better find out what she's decided," Jedda said. "You never know, she may turn me down. She didn't seem to have much to live for. Never seen such bleak eyes. As if she were a thousand years old." She turned to go.

"One thing, Jedda."

She spun back to face Anton.

"What was the point of baiting the state with the Jay symbol again? We haven't used it since Jay died. And now K'll be after us again, worse than ever."

"Jedda, you didn't—?" Chrys began, looking concerned.

Jedda cut her off with a gesture. "I left it at the Franz building. Quite deliberately. It's time to confront K again, before he gets too strong for us. He needs to be kept on edge, like he was when Jay and the full team were active. K never found out that Jay himself was among the dead, so he'll assume the real Jay is still alive and has returned to plague him. And he'll worry. He knows the ordinary people out there will always rally to support the Jay. For them, we're like Robin Hood, or the Scarlet Pimpernel. Only those guys weren't real, and we are."

"Jedda's right," Chrys said. "It should still work. And J is for Jedda, as well as Jay. K's always been afraid that the Jay could start a rebellion."

"Some rebellion, with just three of us," Anton muttered.

"Four," Jedda said firmly, and strode out before he could say another word.

· · · · ·

Ellen put the plate on the floor and pushed it towards the door with her bare toe. Not bad food, considering. At least there was enough to stop her stomach growling.

Nameless would be back soon, expecting an answer.

It was all a charade. There could be only one answer. Ellen might have precious little reason to live, but she had even less reason to die, in spite of everything. If she was going to die, she wanted it to be in the heat of battle – quick and clean. Execution was sometimes quick, but it was never clean. And it was demeaning. Grant's body had been almost unrecognisable when the security police had finished with him and thrown him out into the public square. It was what the Council's killers liked to do to subversives, as a lesson to others who might dare to think rebellious thoughts. The silent assassin here wouldn't be in the Council's pay, but she was probably no different.

If I accept their offer, I'll be working alongside a woman who hopes to kill me.

The thought sent a shiver through her, but it lasted only a split second. Ellen knew she had more skills than a mere assassin could ever have. Killers could be beaten by guile as well as brute force and weaponry. Even when the odds were three to one.

The metal bolts scraped out of their sockets. Nameless was back for her answer. And Ellen was ready.

· · · · ·

Linden entered K's office and closed the door quietly behind him. "Pell is outside. She says you sent for her. You intend to debrief her yourself?" He was not quite managing to keep the resentment out of his voice. He had cause for his irritation, of course, but he was much too easy to read. Something else Linden needed to work on.

K nodded. Normally, it would have been Linden's job to debrief Pell, the leader of London Central's chief pack of hounds. But Pell, with the latest experimental canine implants allied to a sharp, if unimaginative, human brain, had sniffed her way all over that deserted building. She might remember some minor detail that could make all the difference between catching the Jay and failing again.

When it was a matter of survival, K trusted no judgement but his own.

"As you wish. I'll send her in." Linden turned to leave.

"No. You're in charge of the hound packs. You need to hear this. Especially if changes are required." K did not need to remind Linden that the hounds had failed to run their quarry to earth. Or that their failure reflected badly on Linden himself.

K sat down behind his desk and waved Linden to one of the hard chairs opposite. "Computer, send Pell into my office."

Pell entered immediately, scanning the room to judge what she was up against for this first face-to-face encounter with K. She looked like a surprisingly ordinary piece of female liveware, dressed in drab brown overalls and boots, and with her brindle-coloured hair cropped very short. But when K scrutinised her more closely, he saw that her cheeks were slightly wider than a normal woman's, and that her nostrils were large. She held herself proudly erect and clearly knew her own worth. Her dark eyes were bright, too, and watchful. K fancied it would not be easy to unnerve her.

He did not invite her to sit. He simply beckoned her across to his desk and relaxed back into his black chair, staring up at her face. "Report," he said sharply.

"The pack searched the building and the streets around. Scent traces of three females inside the building, operating separately and together. Most traces were in the southwest corner of the sub-basement. Weapons had been discharged there, but no sign of any liveware damage. Apart from scent traces, no evidence at all. They took everything with them." She returned K's stare boldly, waiting for his verdict.

"What did you deduce about these females?"

Pell's eyes widened a fraction. "They opened sophisticated computer locks. They knew the layout. They had the kit to operate in the dark. Once inside, they were quick and careful. Professionals."

"And outside?"

"One arrived alone. The other two arrived together, later. All three used the same entry door."

"Which means that you have no outside information apart from what you gleaned in the sheltered area around the building itself?" K said coldly.

Pell shuffled her boots a fraction, but her confident expression did not vary. "No, none. The streets were like rivers. Our implants barely register anything in so much water. I've asked for the next upgrades to be fast tracked, but I'm told it's low priority."

It was a diversion of engineering resources that London Central could not afford. Other projects had to take priority. In any case, techs in Warsaw Central were supposed to be working on the upgrades. Supposed to be. K would say nothing about that to Pell or Linden until he saw some solid results.

"You and your pack have banked the IDs of the three women?"

"Yes, sir. Priority order from the Director." She glanced apologetically at Linden for a second. "Everyone recorded their scents on the spot."

"As soon as the weather improves, I want your pack to start scouring London for those scents. At the first sniff of anything, you report direct to me. Understood?"

Pell nodded. Out of the corner of his eye, K saw that Linden was looking increasingly angry at having his authority usurped. Too bad. Linden's injured feelings were much less important than preserving order and stability.

At K's nod of dismissal, Pell left even more quickly than she had arrived. She would be in no doubt about the importance of producing results, and soon.

K needed to know where those Jay women were hiding so that he could seize them before they began another public campaign to undermine the state. The underclass had rallied to the Jay once before, but it was ages ago and the rebels had been successfully cut down. If this was the same group of terrorists, led by the same man, where had they been all this time? And why had they resurfaced *now*?

Linden got to his feet. He said nothing, but his annoyance was not very well hidden.

"Make sure the search for those women is the pack's first priority, Linden. Keep them at it. Use threats if you have to."

"Do you want daily reports?"

"No. That's your job. You're in charge of the hounds. Just make sure they let me know when the women have been traced."

"And what happens then?"

"We'll send the pack in to take them. You will lead the raid. But not until I have reviewed all the information we have, and agreed your plan of action. We've already lost these females once. It is *not* to happen again."

Linden swallowed. Then he lifted his chin and looked at K with narrowed eyes. He was down, but far from out. "What about the Jay?"

K kept his features impassive. "What about him?"

"You saw the sign?" When K nodded, Linden went on, "I destroyed it, of course. There was only one, this time. I don't think anyone will have seen it because the rain had emptied the streets. But if the Jay's back, we've got a major problem."

"That sign was planted by one of those women. Either the Jay is using them, or they are using his old legend to stir up rebellion. So concentrate on the women. We'll extract the truth of everything – including the Jay – once we've got them safely shackled in our cells. Anything else?"

Linden shook his head and marched out of the office without looking back.

K stared at the closed door and deliberately allowed his fingers to drum on the arm of his chair while he considered the problem that was Linden. The man seemed to be getting restive. He'd had the trappings of power much too early, thanks to his grandfather. Other men had to earn their promotions, moving from province to province, proving their worth at every step of the way, as K himself had done. But during Linden's gilded progress, he had not had to learn to accept criticism. He did not take well to it, especially from K. Still, one successful raid could set Linden back on an even keel. Until the next time he found himself suffering from a bruised ego.

If the raid was unsuccessful, the bruises to his ego would be immediate and very painful. It was K's duty to see to that, in spite of the interfering grandfather.

K returned to what he had been working on before Pell and Linden arrived. While the hounds were off on the hunt, K could concentrate on trying to get the Council to address the huge imbalance between women and men. It was a major problem, and getting rapidly worse. Over the decades, fewer and fewer Not-Blue males had been born. Now there were almost none, even in the lab.

The Old Ones were to blame, though no one dared to say so. They had triumphed in the Water Wars by exploding Y-dust bombs, showering whole nations with a carefully engineered virus that attacked young males through the very thing that made them men – the Y-chromosome. Nearly all of the enemy's young soldiers had died of the new bug; some of their older men survived, but most became sick and infertile. A simple matter for the Old Ones to send in their own armies – previously vaccinated against the Y-bug, naturally – to cull everyone who was left. Lands were emptied. Billions died.

It had been necessary in order to save the planet. Everyone knew that.

For years after, while the Council consolidated its power, the world had peace, and relative prosperity. The remaining men were immune to the Y-bug, and were hugely grateful to the Council for its foresight in creating that ultra-powerful vaccine. Soon most people – stupid people – were convinced that the Y-bug had died out altogether.

It hadn't, of course. Predictably, the Y-bug lived on in animals and mutated. When it eventually came back to attack humans, nothing could stop it. Generations of the Council's own young men were lost, while scientists struggled to catch up with the changes in the virus and to update the old, useless vaccine. Old men died, too. And the few who survived were rarely capable of fathering children to replace their sons and grandsons. The world was looking into the abyss.

In the end, the solution was not a vaccine at all. But it changed everything.

Almost everything.

Nowadays, Not-Blues were routinely injected with nanobots to eliminate viruses and clean out the body's own defective cells. These worker-bots, toiling constantly inside the body like bees in a hive, were seen as a miracle cure. They were abolishing disease, including the Y-bug, and halting the normal ageing processes. Now, Not-Blues should expect to live, in strong, healthy, youthful bodies, for hundreds of years. It hadn't happened yet, of course, but it was clearly what the surviving Council members intended for themselves. For them, almost eternal life – and power – beckoned. Death was being swept away.

Yet new life had not returned. The nanobots had failed to recreate men's ability to make potent sperm. The amount of viable sperm in the banks was now vanishingly small and was not being replenished fast enough. The few women who were licensed to breed almost always had daughters – at least a hundred females were born to every single male. The imbalance was getting worse and worse.

In spite of K's repeated attempts to persuade the Council, it refused to make the problem a world priority. Soon, everyone would live for centuries, they said, so it did not matter if a generation or two went missing. The earth's depleted resources would recover better if world population was kept low. Eventually, a better worker-bot would be devised and the sperm problem would go away.

K suspected that the Council was none too keen to find the solution. Bands of young, strong men could easily become a threat if they were kept from power. Women were generally easier to control. Though, even there, the Council was taking no chances. Its latest world priority project was to develop special conditioning programmes to keep women docile and obedient.

Those Jay women were certainly not docile.

Was that the future? Groups of warrior women trying to bring down the state?

He would not allow it to happen. He would make an example of those three – and of any others who dared to challenge order and stability. And he would find a way, somehow, of getting the infertility research restarted. The state needed to keep dangerous young women in check. For that, the state needed young men.

SIX

ELLEN LOLLED AGAINST THE wall once more, hugging her knees. The blanket sat round her shoulders, exactly as it had before. She was ready for battle. She knew she had too few weapons to win this round – besides, what mattered was winning the long war between Ellen and her captors, not just one minor skirmish – but it might unnerve her opponent if Ellen seemed to have been immobile for hours.

Nameless pushed open the cell door and stepped inside. "Decision time." Then she saw Ellen's pose and her jaw clenched. "Well?" she barked.

The woman was letting her irritation show. So she had less than perfect control. Good. Ellen allowed the corner of her mouth to curl up a fraction, as if she were trying to hide a smile. Nameless was bound to notice it. And worry.

Nameless booted the door closed at her back and leaned one shoulder against it. She simply folded her arms and waited. Pity. She must realise she had made a mistake. She was too sharp to make another.

The silence stretched between them like quivering wire, ready to snap. Nameless risked one brief look into Ellen's eyes and then dropped her gaze to the bunk where Ellen's bare feet were poking out from under her shift. They were blue.

It reminded Ellen, starkly, of just how cold she was. In a moment, she would start to shiver. That would signal weakness. To divert her senses, she pushed herself off the wall, closed her eyes and rolled her shoulders as if to ease cramped muscles. She let out a long breath, making it sound like a sigh of pleasure. "Much better," she drawled. "Cold gets into the bones." She glanced round the empty cell as if it were a room for hire. "Is this the best you can do?"

Nameless did not move, though her gaze travelled up Ellen's body towards her face. It stopped at Ellen's mouth. Ah. So her captors still had no sure defence against hypnosis. That was precious information. Another potential edge.

"I ask the questions. You answer," Nameless said flatly. "A simple yes or no will do. You have ten seconds."

Ellen's lips tightened automatically. She hated to yield. Was she stubborn enough to sign her own death warrant? To prove a point?

With one second to go, Ellen forced herself to speak. "We both know I have no choice." Her voice came out colourless and harsh.

"So you are joining us?"

Ellen's lips tightened again. She nodded. It was all she could bring herself to do.

"And the price?" Nameless added smoothly.

"What price?"

Nameless relaxed against the door and let herself smile slowly. Not exactly triumph, but smug satisfaction, clearly sure she was back on top. "You need to give us something we can use against you if you try to betray us. Call it a hostage for your good behaviour."

Ellen took another deep breath and sighed it out. She forced some of the tension out of her jaw, but all the while, her mind was racing as she weighed up her options. "I see," she said slowly. For a second, she chewed at her lower lip. *Give them something they'll value at more than its real worth. Something that's too difficult for them to handle.* "Mind control. It works on any liveware. Will you take that?"

"Only if we can use it on you," Nameless retorted instantly. "And we can't, can we?" she added, making sure her sarcasm showed.

Ellen cursed her own stupidity. *Think before you speak, Ellen! Don't underestimate this woman. She's a proven leader. Leaders who make careless mistakes don't survive.*

"Try again. Something worth your life this time."

Ellen swung her bare feet to the floor and stood up, almost toe to toe with her opponent. Another mistake. She'd forgotten Nameless was almost half a head taller.

"Don't do anything stupid," the woman said quietly, transferring her weight on to the balls of her feet, ready to meet an attack. She touched her hand to her weapon.

Ellen forced herself to stand her ground. "If I pay your price, do I get my clothes back?"

Her opponent's eyes widened in surprise, but she shook her head slowly, playing for time. One more point to Ellen. Then, "Nope.

You get the clothes we provide." Nameless laughed, but it was forced. "You won't freeze. Or starve. But you do have to pay." She relaxed a little, confident of her power, waiting.

Ellen stared into her face, but Nameless would not meet her eyes. There had to be a way of getting to her. Ah, yes. "You've been watching me, you and your people. And you stole all my kit. So *you* tell me – what price do *you* want for my life?"

It worked. Nameless couldn't answer. Because she wasn't savvy enough about technology to be able to choose.

Ellen lifted her chin and pursed her lips. She was trying to look like a Victorian governess, waiting for an admission of wrongdoing from a hapless charge. Effortlessly superior. It felt right.

After barely a few seconds, Nameless came back, fighting. "You're prepared to give us anything we choose, in return for your life?"

"Any *single* thing you choose, yes." That would leave Ellen plenty of technical wizardry to use against them when she was ready to escape. And ready to kill them all.

"And you will join our group, join the fight for freedom?"

"That makes two things, not one," Ellen snapped.

"That's the offer. Take it or leave it. You're not in a position to bargain."

No, she wasn't. She swallowed hard. "OK. It's a deal. I'll join your resistance group and I'll let you in on one of my technical secrets. Your choice. But you only get one." She stuck out her hand to shake on the deal.

Nameless looked down at the outstretched hand. It was rock steady, Ellen noticed with satisfaction, but the flesh was blue and shrivelled.

"I'll fetch you some clothes." Nameless marched out without making any move to acknowledge their bargain.

She probably intends to weasel out of it, just as I do. Ellen sank down onto the bunk so that she could peel her feet off the freezing floor. She needed to concentrate on tactics. She would be up against the whole group soon, she reckoned. How many were there? Those two warrior women, of course, and at least one tech, gender unknown. Soon she'd find out if there were more. And she would have to watch her every word.

She focused her mind inwards, starting to repeat the hypnotic words that would ensure her body did not betray her.

The cell door crashed open again before she had managed to

establish total control. Nameless threw a bundle of clothes on to the bunk, followed by a pair of thick-soled boots. Ellen looked longingly at them. It would be bliss to have such a stout barrier between her bare feet and the icy floor.

"Get dressed. Then we'll decide exactly what we want from you."

Ellen waited for Nameless to leave, but Nameless pushed the door closed and leant her back against it. She might appear to be staring at the blank wall, but she was surreptitiously watching Ellen all the time. No hint of sexual desire – Ellen could have used that for leverage – just a cold, calculated manoeuvre. Ellen was being forced to accept that she was totally in her captors' power, that she had nothing, not even her own body, that she could keep for herself.

Ellen didn't waste time or words. She swung her feet back to the floor and stood up, never for a moment taking her eyes from her opponent's face. In a single smooth movement, she seized the hem of the shift, drew it up over her body and threw it aside. For ten, fifteen, twenty seconds, she stood motionless, proudly naked, staring at the woman who did not dare to look into her eyes.

It was a victory. Of sorts.

• • • • •

"They'll be here soon," Chrys said, checking her weapon. "Jedda won't allow the woman time to collect her wits. We need to be ready."

"I *am* ready." Anton kept his eyes glued to the figures flashing across his screen. That armoured suit was finally beginning to give up its secrets. It only needed—

"Better to be standing up. You don't want her looking down on you."

"What?" Anton spun his chair round. Chrys had that knowing half-smile again, the one that made him want to wipe it off her face. It said that he was only a tech, that he didn't have a clue about fighting, even with words. And it wasn't true! Anton was not a trained warrior like Chrys and Jedda, but he could fight when he had to. Otherwise he'd never have survived as a Not-Blue in a commune of Blues.

"I suggest we stand shoulder to shoulder, over here," Chrys said patiently, "so that we're facing them when they come in. It'll make us look stronger. And united."

Anton heard footsteps. More than one set. Without another word, he took his place at Chrys's side.

The prisoner appeared first. Jedda was a couple of careful paces behind. Jedda smiled and nodded briefly when she saw Chrys and Anton ranged together, but her face became ice cold again before she moved into the captive's eye line. Trust Jedda to look the part of the hardened killer.

"Right. Our *guest* has agreed to join us and to share her skills with us."

"Skill. Singular. That was the deal."

Jedda ignored the woman's surly words. "We'll start with introductions, I think, since we'll all be working together. This is Chrys. And Anton." Anton nodded automatically. Chrys, he realised too late, hadn't moved a hair.

Jedda turned back to the prisoner. "And you?" The woman said nothing. "Your name isn't actually Helen Birch, is it?" Jedda said flatly. "Come on. Give."

The woman raised her chin proudly. "Ellen."

"Ellen what?"

"Just Ellen. Same as *just* Chrys, and *just* Anton."

She was a tough one, right enough. A warrior, a tech, and a woman with guts. The kind who would keep pushing, even if it meant pushing her head into a noose.

Jedda laughed. It sounded harsh but it was real, Anton knew. Jedda valued courage, in herself and in others. She would respect this woman for that.

"And what about you?" Ellen rounded on Jedda. "You *do* have a name, do you?"

"I'm Jedda. Also called Jay," she said, smoothly adding the lie. "You may have heard of me."

Ellen paused, apparently racking her brains. She shook her head as if mystified. "Nope. Can't say that I have. Are you supposed to be famous or something?"

Anton had to bite his lip hard to stop himself from laughing. Watching these two sparring was going to be fun. Until it became lethal.

· · · · ·

Nameless— No, Ellen reminded herself, the name was Jedda. Jedda was certainly impressive. She took control by walking into a room. A born leader, clearly. Not sharp enough to have noticed that her tech guy was trying not to laugh, though. Ellen banked that piece of information. The two warriors – Jedda and Chrys – probably had no sense of humour at all. Killers didn't, in Ellen's experience. But there might be a chance of some kind of rapport with Anton. Over shared tech experiments? Or something more intimate, perhaps? It was difficult to tell on first meeting, but he *looked* like a hetero.

Jedda grabbed the back of a chair and dragged it out. The bare metal feet screeched across the floor. Ellen couldn't prevent herself from wincing as the sound lanced down her backbone. No one else reacted. Must be used to it.

"Sit," Jedda commanded.

Good tactics, Ellen's inner voice commented, in a strangely detached way, as if she weren't facing death at any moment. *The odds are already three against one, and I'll be sitting down while they all loom over me. It makes hypnosis almost impossible, too. Yup. This is a clever, dangerous team. Not to be underestimated. Even if there are only three of them.*

Ellen sat down and clasped her hands loosely in her lap. The borrowed jacket was too tight across her back. The trousers were little better. Not enough freedom of movement for effective fighting.

Did these three think of *everything*?

Jedda moved to stand directly in front of Ellen. Anton ranged himself at her left shoulder. Chrys moved out of Ellen's eye line, but Ellen could feel that threatening presence at her back; the hairs were standing up on her neck.

"Ellen has agreed to share one of her tech secrets with us," Jedda began. "You've assessed all her kit, Anton. Your choice." Jedda didn't even glance at the man beside her. Did she trust him to the point where she would allow an underling to make such a crucial decision?

It seemed she did, for Anton nodded eagerly and moved half a step forward. Ellen stared up into his face, but he avoided her eyes. Pity.

"Nice little haul we got with you," Anton began.

He was failing to keep the excitement out of his voice. He must have felt like a child let loose in a toy shop when he saw the contents of Ellen's holdall. But had he sussed out how the toys worked? Or even what they were for?

"All your own work, are they?" His tone had changed to a mixture of envy and disbelief. Pathetically easy to read.

Ellen did not allow herself to smile. Instead, she transferred her gaze to the floor so that she would give absolutely nothing away. "Not part of the deal," she retorted, deliberately needling him. "You get to choose one bit of kit. I tell you how it works. That's all you get."

"You're assuming I haven't worked it all out already."

"Bull's-eye! Give the boy top marks for insight."

Ellen heard a quick intake of breath behind her and instantly regretted her words. Not because of Chrys, but because of Anton. He was the only one who might be a potential ally. Ellen certainly wouldn't make allies with that kind of nasty point scoring.

She glanced up just in time to see Anton lift his chin and narrow his eyes. She was in for a battle of wills now, and it was her own fault. Stupid! She had promised herself she'd stay in control, and she'd failed miserably.

Anton's voice was suddenly deeper, with a raw edge to it. "Don't underestimate what we do here, Ellen. You're not the only one who can develop new ideas. How d'you think we got to you before K's hounds did?"

That really was a bull's-eye, but Ellen forced her body not to react at all. She said nothing. He needed to hit back. Let him win one. Let him think they were equal. She had no idea how he'd managed to see through all the false trails she'd laid and she couldn't afford to divert her energies into trying to work it out. For now, she must keep focused. Anton had probably just been lucky.

"You don't know how we did it," he went on, more confident now. "And you won't find out, either. This deal cuts both ways. If you won't share, neither will we."

Ellen took a deep breath. *Calm. Careful. Focus!* "I will share one piece of kit, as I agreed. For that, I get to stay alive. I'm not expecting you to share your skills with me. I don't steal from other people. I do my own development work."

Anton laughed. It was only a little forced. "Didn't work too well in the immigration hall, did it? You screwed up. If you hadn't been able to hypnotise that dozy human supervisor, they'd have caught you."

It was a punch to the gut. For a second, Ellen couldn't breathe. He was right. Ellen *had* failed there. And cocky Anton knew all about it. Somehow.

Jedda touched her knuckles to the back of Anton's arm in a clear warning. He gritted his teeth and the top of his ears reddened a fraction. But he didn't stop crowing. "Admit it, Ellen. You're not nearly as clever as you'd like us to believe, are you?"

Ellen blinked hard. She needed every last ounce of her control to choke down the fury welling up inside her. *Step back, Ellen. You MUST resist the urge to respond in kind.* "No one is perfect, Anton," she said finally, surprising herself with how conciliatory she could sound. "Not me, not you, not even Jedda here. I could have killed her yesterday. She knows she's lucky I didn't. You have tech skills. I have tech skills. Not perfect, not the same, but we're probably equal, I'd say."

"If you worked together, shared, you'd be even better," Jedda said in a matter-of-fact way. "Both of you would benefit."

"We'll stick to the deal," Ellen said instantly. No compromises. Not with people who really wanted her dead. "One item only. Well, Anton? Which one do you want?"

Anton was silent for a moment, clearly struggling. Ellen felt a flutter of triumph as the tables were turned on him. His ears had gone even redder. He clearly didn't understand what he had. Any moment now, he would have to admit he was fallible.

Ellen waited, staring up at him. It was her turn now.

To her surprise, he said nothing. With a snort of anger, he strode across the bleak room and bent to the floor behind one of the workstations. When he stood up again, he had one of Ellen's devices in his hand. "This one," he spat.

And threw it at her.

SEVEN

ELLEN FIELDED IT AUTOMATICALLY, with a warrior's reflexes.

Jedda knew it was time to intervene. Anton's desire to be top dog was getting the better of his common sense. He had just betrayed the fact that they knew Ellen's device was not a bomb. Did that matter? Maybe. Maybe not.

"As you'll have guessed, we already know quite a lot about this little bit of kit of yours," Jedda said, deciding on the spur of the moment to make the most of Anton's slip. "So, tell us exactly how it works."

"This is the one you want?" Ellen widened her eyes like an innocent child.

Jedda nodded quickly and looked away. By tomorrow they'd have the special contact lenses. Then they'd be able to take on this extraordinary woman, face to face.

"Fair enough." Ellen relaxed into her chair and turned the device caressingly in her hands. "It's a screening system. Place a series of these round an object, or a person, and they become invisible and undetectable. By any existing detection device."

"I don't believe it!"

"Hear her out, Anton," Jedda ordered. What was it with him? He was reacting like a child, not a grown man.

"By *any* existing detector," Ellen said again. "If you'd arrived five minutes later yesterday, you would have found nothing at all in that basement."

"But that's not—"

"We'll be the judge of that," Jedda said quickly, interrupting Anton's outburst, "when you've explained to us exactly how it works. Anton will organise a proper test. For your sake, I hope it does what you say it does."

Ellen shrugged. "You'll see," she said easily, before launching into an extremely complicated description of the inner workings of her device. Jedda prided herself on keeping up with technology, but after about five minutes, she was lost. Anton, however, was fascinated. He even sat down next to Ellen to urge her on.

As if they were part of the same team, working together.

Jedda pulled the infrared goggles from her pocket and forced them into Anton's hand. A reminder that needed no words.

He didn't get up, but he did put on the goggles. No matter how absorbed he became, he would be beyond Ellen's powers of hypnosis. But what other powers might this extraordinary woman have?

• • • • •

Chrys moved silently across to join Jedda at her workstation. Anton was still quizzing Ellen about the detailed workings of her device. They had both become quite animated as they delved deeper and deeper. But Chrys dare not relax her guard. Jedda was relying on Chrys to keep them all safe from whatever this woman could do.

One quick sideways glance at Jedda's screen and Chrys went back to watching the captive. "Are you planning something there?" Chrys said carefully, without turning from her task. Jedda was watching a live feed from the New Thames Barrier, the one that had been thrown up so hastily after the original was overwhelmed by tidal surges. Chrys had been saying for months that the Barrier was a prime target. Anything built at that speed was bound to have weak spots and it would be a huge win for the Jays, even if they couldn't destroy it completely. Maybe Jedda was coming round to the idea at last?

"Not yet," Jedda murmured. "But I want you to do a recce. Now would be a good time, I reckon, while the rain is still pelting down."

That made sense. A hooded figure would not look out of place and the cameras' view would be slightly distorted by the rain. Fewer people to hide among, though. But on balance, the timing was good.

Jedda dropped her voice even more. "I want you to take Ellen with you."

Chrys flinched.

"Yes, I know. I do understand what I'm asking you to take on," Jedda said, in that open reassuring tone she shared only with Chrys.

The trust between them was special, and Chrys valued it above everything. Jedda did confide in Chrys, some of the time, though not when she was struggling with her responsibilities as leader. Jedda clearly felt she had to fight those demons by herself. Given her family background, it wasn't really surprising, but Chrys intended to keep trying to help lighten Jedda's burdens.

"We need to get a handle on her fighting skills and you're far and away the best of us for that." Jedda was being generous in her praise. She was almost as good as Chrys at hand-to-hand combat and even better at the planning side of operations.

Chrys felt her cheeks colouring and was glad that she still had her back to Jedda.

"Take her with you as another pair of eyes and ears," Jedda went on, murmuring close to Chrys's ear now. "Get her to do an assessment of the defences, the possible weaknesses. Then you'll be able to judge whether she knows how to mount an attack. Check out her skill at blending into the background, too. OK?"

Chrys didn't like it, but Jedda's assessment was right on the nail, as usual. The Jays needed to find out what Ellen could really do. Chrys nodded. "Now?"

"I want you to get there as it's getting dark. The rain isn't going to stop until midnight, according to the computer."

"Not unless K goes in for weather warping again," Chrys muttered.

Jedda laughed. Surprised, Anton and Ellen stopped in mid-sentence and turned towards the sound, but Jedda was too canny to share. She simply shook her head at them. "Are you about finished impressing each other with your jargon?" she asked evenly. "I need you in ten minutes. I've got a task for Ellen, now she's one of us."

Ellen stiffened almost imperceptibly. She clearly didn't like the implications of that. Chrys allowed herself to smile across at the woman. She was in for a nasty shock. Doing a risky recce on the Barrier was not even the half of it.

• • • • •

Ellen got up and pulled the waistband of the too-tight trousers into place. "We've done all we need to do. Anton has more than enough now to run the trial you're so set on. You'll find that it works. Just as I said."

Jedda ignored the sarcasm. "Chrys is going out on a recce. I want you to go with her, give her a hand."

Ellen was not naïve enough to believe that. It was another test.

But it might also be a chance to escape! Ellen would have to leave her kit behind, but she could always construct some more. Getting away from these maniacs was worth any risk. Sooner or later, K would reel them in, like hooked fish, and Ellen was determined not to be part of his catch. For that, she needed to be shot of them all.

Ellen knew she must not seem too eager to get out of the bunker. "Why should I?" She was impressed by how surly she sounded.

Jedda smiled. After a second, the smile broadened into a self-satisfied grin. "Because you think it might give you a chance to escape."

Oh.

Behind Ellen, Anton chortled. He was crowing again.

"I agreed to join you," Ellen protested. But it was half-hearted.

"You did," Jedda said, still smiling, "but you didn't put a time limit on it. Five years, five weeks, five minutes?"

Ellen said nothing. She needed to think. They were so sure of themselves. They must have a trick up their sleeve that she hadn't spotted. So what was it?

Jedda was staring pointedly at Ellen's jacket and the tight bodysuit beneath.

The penny dropped. "Very smart," Ellen said with a nod of appreciation. "A tracker, I assume? One that I won't find even if I shred these clothes of yours?" It was Chrys who smiled this time. But surely Ellen could overpower a lone warrior, take her clothes? She'd walk across London stark naked if it would buy her freedom.

"Don't try it," Jedda said, as if she were reading Ellen's mind. "You'd be wasting your time. And ditching your clothes..." She let the words hang, menacingly.

No wonder they'd insisted she wear what they'd provided. Not just a tracker or two, but a booby-trap as well. If Ellen stripped off the clothes she was wearing, she would end up free. But a corpse.

She had lost this round. Big time.

Maybe she had lost more than a round? Self-doubt tried to settle in the pit of her stomach. She fought it with vicious mind control. Finally, she squared her shoulders and turned to Chrys. "OK. So I don't have a choice. What do you need me to do?"

• • • • •

The new barrier was pretty impressive. Not at all what Ellen expected. She remembered vividly discussing it with Grant when they were lying together, sated, snuggled like spoons, with only the sheen of drying sweat between them. It had been such a strange thing for lovers to talk about, but Grant was obsessed by it, returning to it again and again in their last few snatched meetings. Once he'd begun to confide in her, he used her as a sounding board. He said the Barrier was a "lash-up", and bound to be vulnerable. He said it showed how desperate the Old Ones were to hang on to

London even though the real centre of power had moved far to the east.

Ellen tried to focus solely on what Grant had said about the Barrier. But the mere thought of them together had started that warm melting glow, deep in her belly. Even after all this time. Perhaps she should give in to the feelings, give up on life, let the memories of love and longing have their way? It wouldn't be so hard, after all. Just strip off every stitch of clothing and wait for the warm embrace of oblivion.

"Ellen! Don't just stand there!" Chrys's hissed words cut into Ellen like a knife thrust. This was real. Perhaps it was even what Grant would have wanted her to do?

She allowed herself to cling to that new thought for two long seconds before she locked it away and returned to the realms of cold logic. Feelings made her vulnerable. She could not afford them.

• • • • •

CONTACT!

"Computer, detailed report," K barked. "Visuals on screen."

TWO FEMALES, SUSPICIOUS BEHAVIOUR, THAMES BARRIER AREA. TERRORIST PROBABILITY, FIFTY-FIVE PERCENT.

The computer had very little information to go on, K supposed, but spuriously accurate fifty-something percentages were worse than useless. A top-notch system would be able to identify terrorists with better than ninety percent accuracy. This system was getting old – not in that league. Might as well have said "maybe they are, maybe they aren't."

The viewscreen picture was blurred by the steady downpour. Two figures shrouded and hooded against the weather. One of them was standing stock still, and she seemed to be staring at the Barrier as if she had never seen it before. Perhaps she was new to London? Perhaps she was the one who had—?

At that moment, the second dark figure took two quick paces out of the shadows and pulled the staring figure into the gloom. She said something, too, but the words were inaudible under the drumbeat of the rain.

That was better than fifty-five percent! "Computer, get the nearest pack out to the Barrier and bring those women in. I want them both alive. And able to talk."

• • • • •

"What kind of a warrior *are* you?" Chrys grabbed Ellen's sleeve and pulled her roughly towards the shadow of an overhanging building.

"Do you *want* to make us a target?" Chrys touched her concealed weapon. "If you've got some mad impulse to get us both killed, forget it. I'll kill you first myself!"

"Sorry," Ellen mumbled. And she really was. If her momentary lapse of concentration had been spotted by the watchers, it could cost them both their lives.

Just when she had realised she wasn't ready to die.

Chrys ignored the apology and concentrated on the mission. "Right. Make an assessment of the Barrier. We're looking for points to attack. Destruction if possible. Long-term damage, if not."

"Explosives?"

"Yes, but don't discard other means. If you can think of any."

Ellen ignored the jibe and concentrated on the huge barrier, gleaming proudly even through the rain. The Thames itself was grey and choppy, without reflections, hiding its destructive power as a black hole hides light. Ellen remembered how much smaller the old barrier had been, with polished silver housings stretched across down-river like the hoods of medieval cradles. But the combination of higher sea levels and tidal surges had drowned the cradles and almost finished the city. London had taken years to recover. In the end, it was sheer stubbornness that did it, for the remaining people would not be beaten by mere water and refused to move away. The Blitz spirit, they called it, harking back to something none of them could possibly have experienced.

The new barrier was further up-river, and bigger, higher and much more robust than its predecessor, even if it was a "lash-up". The Council had decreed that protecting London was far more important than trade, so the new barrier had been thrown up without any real provision for shipping. Smaller ships could still get through, though, and that might be a weakness. It was certainly one possible way of getting on to the structure without being detected.

Ellen banked that thought and kept on scanning the barrier. The steel superstructure was sunk into massive stone and nucrete pillars on the river bed. Even for such an important structure, expensive concrete had been out of the question. So there might be a weakness. She'd need to get closer to see how well the two parts were married together. And destruction would need co-ordinated explosions at several separate points. Not easy. Still—

A shout from behind them. Ellen spun round. They'd been spotted! A bunch of K's thugs was charging towards them.

Chrys had already dropped to a crouch, weapon in hand. A split second later, she fired. The squad leader fell. The others slowed.

Ellen reached automatically for her weapon. *Sod it! I've nothing to fight with!*

"Here!" From nowhere, Chrys produced a second weapon and tossed it to Ellen. Then Chrys fired again, taking down another of the thugs. In the same instant, she barked, "Control! Distraction would be good. Now!"

Ellen sighted and fired. A kill! Then another. It was like a turkey shoot. Why weren't they returning fire?

"Get my back!" Chrys yelled. "They want us alive."

The two women crouched back to back. Behind Ellen, Chrys fired again. A scream of pain echoed off the walls. On Ellen's side, there was nothing to shoot at.

Yes, there was. A much larger squad had rounded the far corner. Too late for a decent pincer movement, but nasty odds for just two fighters. Chrys was right. Distraction really would be good. Right now.

Ellen shot the leading squad member who crashed to the ground. Two others fell over the body. Good tactics. That squad was too close together. Ellen aimed again, picking off a hound in the middle. Another pile up.

"Odds improving my side," she gasped. "How about you?"

"Get ready to run. On my command." Chrys fired again. This time Ellen heard opposing fire. The first squad was close enough for crippleshots.

Ellen's squad was not. She picked off two more hounds in quick succession. But now a third squad was coming round the same corner, weapons drawn. She couldn't fire fast enough to deal with them all.

"Now! Follow me!" Chrys doubled across the open space towards a dark alley directly opposite the river, shooting as she ran. Ellen followed, dodging and weaving to avoid the crippleshot brigade. She picked off a couple of them, then fired back at the second squad to keep them cowed.

"Down!" Chrys yelled, dropping on to her belly in the lee of a building.

Ellen did the same. Only just in time. Squad three had started firing volleys of shots, mowing down everything in front of them with murderous efficiency. Squads one and two collected it all. In the front. In the back. It didn't seem to matter. And it didn't make any sense.

"Move, woman!" Chrys was crawling towards the corner of the alley. In a few metres, she'd have the bulk of the stone building between her and their attackers.

Ellen didn't look back. Together the two women slithered through the puddled, stinking slime. The zing of death echoed above and behind them.

And then they were clear. Clear, but not safe. Not yet.

"Let's see how fit you are," Chrys gasped out, pushing herself to her feet and starting to sprint down the alley. "Control, we need you to guide us in."

Ellen started after her. What choice did she have? Anton's bony finger was still on her destruct button.

EIGHT

"SHE'S FIT. AND SHE'S shit-hot with a weapon." Chrys didn't need to pull her punches when she and Jedda were alone. And Jedda needed the unvarnished truth about Ellen.

"Better than you?" Jedda asked, with the hint of a smile.

Chrys smiled back. They could both afford to smile now that the op was over. But it had been a close-run thing. "Not from what I saw," Chrys said, brutally honest. "But the weapon was unfamiliar. It wasn't a fair test."

Jedda gave a snort of laughter. "You're generous. Considering."

"She had my back. Without her, one of the squads would have taken me down."

"She could say the same for you."

"We'd both have been mincemeat if it hadn't been for Anton. If that was a spur-of-the-moment move, it was brilliant. And lightning fast."

Jedda shook her head. "It was pre-planned. But I'd been hoping to save it for a bigger prize, to take out lots more of them. K's bound to make sure we can't interfere with squad comms so easily in future. He'll start some kind of new code system, probably, so that they know our instructions are fake."

"Well, I have faith in Anton," Chrys said, with feeling. She owed him now, and so did Ellen. Anton, being Anton, would be looking to collect. Probably with one of his evil practical jokes, and at the most inconvenient time. "I'm sure he'll be able to find a way of hacking in."

Jedda clearly was not convinced. "Once the squads have better recognition systems, they won't shoot each other, no matter what instructions we give them. It worked this time because squads one and two could have been exactly what we said they were – terrorists in stolen uniforms. It won't work twice."

No point in arguing with that. "What do you think will happen to the killer squad?" Chrys asked. It shouldn't be bothering her, but it was. They still called it "friendly fire", accidentally killing your own side. Mistakes always happened in the fog of war. But it was something she dreaded.

"Nothing much," Jedda said with a shrug. "K will soon work out how we did it. The third squad weren't to blame. He'll interrogate them, I assume—" Jedda grimaced "—but they'll probably be put back on the streets afterwards. If they're still fit for duty when he's finished with them…"

A tiny shiver trickled down Chrys's spine.

"And the dead will be written off. As usual." For a second, Jedda's gaze was unfocused. She seemed to be seeing beyond the blank wall of the tiny cell that was her only truly private space. Then she added, in a strange, tight voice, "K fills his squads with women who are expendable. They die for him. And their families are lucky if they get a body to grieve over."

Don't let her go there! Chrys's inner voice was insistent. *Get her thinking about something else, something mundane.* "How do you rate Ellen's recce report?" she asked quickly. Too late, she remembered that Jedda rarely discussed one team member's shortcomings with another. Her way was to give it to the person straight, face to face.

"Not bad for someone new to London. And she *was* …er… interrupted before she'd finished." Jedda grinned, even though they both knew it was a pretty poor joke.

Chrys laughed, relishing the lighter atmosphere. And the fact that Jedda was prepared to share. Of course, Ellen was not really a member of the team.

"She wants to go back again, for another, longer look. To assess the maximum size of ship that can go through, she says, and how many pillars we'd need to take out to destroy the whole thing. She seems thorough. And thoughtful." Jedda's slight emphasis showed she approved. Jedda herself was always thoughtful about plans. And about people. It was one of the qualities that marked her out for leadership.

"So what will you—?" Chrys broke off. Wrong kind of question to the leader. "Do you want me to do anything more with her?" That was better.

Jedda pushed her hair back behind her ear. She was frowning slightly. When she eventually spoke, it was as if she were thinking aloud. "We've got to find a way of living with her, so she's not a danger to any of us. And we've got to milk her for information.

Anton finished testing that invisible curtain of hers while you were drying off. It seems to work. In the lab, at least. Amazing technology, like nothing we've ever seen. So we have to find out about all the other clever ideas she's got tucked away in that cunning brain of hers."

Chrys nodded. Ellen sounded even more dangerous than they'd feared.

"Anton is going to be busy on the tech side, so you're going to have to be her main jailer. Sorry, Chrys. It's a rotten job."

Chrys shrugged. It went with the territory. "No problem. Where is she now?"

"Locked in her cell. Anton has rigged the destruct mechanism so that she can cope with being here in the bunker. She had to undress and shower. She was even filthier and wetter than you. And she stank to high heaven."

They both had, Chrys knew. Chrys had been able to throw off her slime-covered outer layer as soon as she reached the bunker. Ellen had been afraid to dump even a stitch of hers. For good reason, then, but not any more. "Once she's got her clothes off, she'll comb through them for the tracker. And the destruct switch."

Jedda shook her head. "She won't find them." That issue was clearly closed.

Jedda turned to the locker in the corner of the cell and pulled out a small packet. "Here. Your contacts. They'll protect you against Ellen's hypnotism. We'll all be wearing them, but you'll need them most. Jailers are always the most vulnerable."

Chrys had absolutely no intention of being vulnerable to a woman like Ellen. But she said nothing about that. Instead, she peered into the package and said lightly, "Anton really has been burning the midnight oil, hasn't he?"

· · · · ·

Ellen threw the last of her clothing on to the floor with a grimace. She had searched through it all, almost thread by thread, but she had found only what she was sure Anton intended her to find – a fairly crude tracker device in the seam of her bra. It was too obvious a place to hide it. Bound to be more. But where? And then there was the bomb, or whatever else he had devised as her mode of execution. How could a bomb be totally invisible?

She sighed and leaned one shoulder against the cold metal door. They had given her a couple of pillows, and extra blankets. Signs of acceptance? Not while she was being kept locked in a cell. She was back wearing the ankle length shift – she had nothing else to wear – but at least she was clean while she waited for her clothes to absorb all the filth and renew themselves. As soon as they were dry, she would be able to put them back on and they would be pristine.

But still able to kill her!

The Jays must have laughed as they watched Ellen vainly trying to find Anton's devices. He would be crowing again, no doubt. Unless…

Unless there was NO bomb!

The idea was so huge it took her breath away. What if it was all a gigantic bluff? Maybe she hadn't found it because there was nothing there to find?

She sat down on the bunk with a bump, totally overwhelmed by her insight. Barely a second later, she plummeted back to earth. She could only discover the truth by calling their bluff. And if there was a bomb, her gamble would be terminal. *Think again, Ellen! Think smarter!*

They were three against one and – she had to admit it – they were better than good. They were a really crack team. Unlike almost everyone in this stinking rathole of a world, these people weren't just out for themselves. They were professional, devoted to their cause, brilliantly led. They supported each other. No one was alone.

But Grant and his team had been all those things, too. And what had happened to them? Every one of them dead, horribly, except Ellen. And that was only because Ellen had not been allowed to be part of his team. She'd been Grant's diversion, his escape into carefree fantasy-land. He had gone to incredible lengths to ensure that no one knew about her. And that she learned very little about his terrorist activities.

He protected me. Just as he swore he would. They tortured him but he never gave me up to them. Whatever else he told them, he didn't betray me. If he had, I would have been dead long ago, with all the rest.

He really did love me. He must have. Just as he swore he did.

Love was not enough. Idealism was not enough, either. The state was too powerful for anyone to win more than a few minor skirmishes. In the end, the state always got its way. Jedda's team would be no different from Grant's. They would all die in the end. If Ellen threw in her lot with Jedda, she would die as well. And for what? A few weeks of companionship, a bit of human warmth, a shared joke or two?

She dare not trust them. Idealism was for the birds. Only survival mattered.

She closed her eyes and began to chew her bottom lip. Eventually, she chewed too hard and tasted the metallic tang of blood. Plus a tiny prick of pain. Pain was good. It reminded her she was alive.

She intended to stay that way. And free. And alone. So she really had only one solution here. It would take time, and patience. She would never be able to drop her guard. She would have to give more than she had intended, too, but the ultimate prize was probably worth the price. And there would be rewards in the meantime – like being able to sleep sound, knowing that someone else was on watch.

Now that *was* a prize worth winning.

Ellen laughed out loud and then found herself wondering what the watchers would make of it.

I don't care! I'm going to survive and be free of you all, sooner or later. And if you try to stand in my way, you'll lose. I guarantee it. Nothing matters to me now. I would sacrifice anyone – ANYONE – to buy my freedom.

• • • • •

It was time to confront Ellen again. She was beginning to look much too relaxed, in spite of the kill device. She had dressed without a protest as soon as her clothes were dry, and now she was lying nonchalantly on her bunk, booted feet on the blanket and hands clasped behind her head. As if she had not a care in the world.

Jedda pinged the lock and drew back the bolts. Ellen didn't move a muscle when Jedda entered the cell and pushed the door closed.

"Feeling better?"

Ellen still didn't move but she did speak. "Cleaner, yes."

"I have a proposition to put to you," Jedda said quietly. "Want to hear it?"

In reply, Ellen sat up in a single smooth movement, using only the strength of her stomach muscles. "I'm listening."

She was also staring into Jedda's eyes but, this time, it would have no effect. Jedda saw the moment when realisation dawned, even though Ellen did her best to hide her disappointment. "We're holding all the aces, you know," Jedda went on, in the same reasonable voice. "Hypnosis won't work on us. We're unravelling the secrets of all your kit. If you try to escape, you'll die. Quite nastily. Best to know that at the outset."

"Thanks. Kind of you to let me know."

Jedda sucked in her bottom lip to stop herself from smiling. Ellen's courage was remarkable. Could Jedda show as much in the same situation? Bad question. Jedda wasn't about to find out. She was *not* going to get caught.

Ellen was still staring, still immobile.

"You've seen that our team is short-handed," Jedda said simply. No point in denying an obvious truth. "You have skills we could use, both as a warrior and as a tech. We want you to join us. *Really* join us. Become one of the Jays. Work with us to help overthrow London Central."

"Overthrow Lond—!" The expression on Ellen's face was shock mixed with disbelief. "You don't believe in doing things by halves, do you?"

"And you don't believe in doing things for anyone but yourself," Jedda retorted. "Do you?"

Silence. But all the colour had drained from Ellen's face.

Jedda waited a full five seconds for the message to sink in. "So…will you join us? For real?"

The response was slow and barely a whisper. "Yes. Yes, I will join you."

NINE

K STOPPED PACING. IT betrayed the fact that he was not fully in control and he would not allow anyone to suspect that. Linden could walk in on him any moment. The man was already ten minutes late.

K forced himself to sit calmly behind his desk to consider his next steps. He'd lost another round to the Jays. First the capture of that Greenland woman; then a major shoot-out in broad daylight! Just two women – two! – against three of his best hunting packs, and both the women had got away without a scratch. One of the two was almost certainly the fugitive from Greenland. Pell had picked up a tiny whiff of her scent by the wall of a building, one of the few places where the ground was not running like a river. Pell was good – much better than any of the rest of her pack – even though her experimental smell implant was only a crude local stopgap. If K could get hold of a proper upgraded version and give it to Pell…

He made a mental note to chase up progress in Warsaw Central's tech labs.

Back to the problem of the Jays. He realised he was drumming his fingers on the desk, without meaning to. Had he ever done that before, when he was alone? It was a tic he used deliberately when he was trying to unnerve an underling, of course, but not unconsciously, surely? Just in case, he put one hand flat on the arm of his chair, curling his fingers round the supple old leather, and put the other hand in his pocket.

Jay himself, the leader of the terrorists, had not made an appearance yet. Only women so far. Would Jay lead a third sortie? Whoever led it – and K was absolutely convinced that it would come soon – it must *not* be successful. The Council had not been briefed about the minor matter of the disappearance of the Greenland woman, but K had been unable to cover up the street fight and the deaths of more than half the hounds. The Council took a serious view of anything that suggested state control was less than complete. The loss of the pack members was barely a note in the margin, but interference with frontline comms and redirection of foot soldiers was enough to make some Council members focus closely on London.

The Council did not know about the return of the Jay. It had to stay that way.

The danger was Linden. What if he told his grandfather about the Greenland woman? Or dropped some other information, without meaning to? It hadn't happened so far, or K would have felt the repercussions by now, but it was an ever-present risk. K needed to detach Linden from his grandfather and ensure that the younger man's careless tongue could not wag.

Or, even better, ensure that Linden was in the firing line of the Council's wrath. Yes. That would do it. It was high time that pampered brat learned the reality of running a province and the importance of always keeping plans and information to himself. Risks for Linden would niggle at his grandfather, too, and make the old man less confident, which might help to undermine his standing with the rest of the Council. For the last few years, Linden's grandfather had been much too successful. Some of the Council thought he was infallible.

No one was infallible. That second encounter with the Jays had proved it.

LINDEN HAS ARRIVED. The computer's tinny voice.

K took a deep breath, relaxed his shoulders and leaned back into his chair. "Computer, send Linden in." K's fingers were still safely flat on the arm.

Linden had lost his usual jaunty confidence. He closed the door behind him with exaggerated care. He launched into speech before he had even turned round. "The hounds are in turmoil, K. Never known such losses before. Some of Pell's pack want to take the bodies home to the families."

K tensed. "Your report said that none of Pell's pack was killed," he said brusquely.

"They weren't. But some of her women had friends in the other packs. They're all in shock. Grieving."

K noted that Linden's face was drawn, as if he were sharing their grief. Typical! The man was a wimp with no stomach for the kind of work that had to be done. By rights, he should never make it to Controller rank. Not enough backbone. "And what was your response to this unprecedented request for burial leave?" K enquired tartly.

Linden's jaw worked. He began to look guilty. "I...er...I told Pell that no one could be spared from duty. If the women wanted to do anything, they'd have to do it in their own time."

"You're allowing them *private* time? Now, when we're two half-packs down?"

Linden would not meet K's eyes. "No. No, of course not," he said, too quickly. "It was just a way of...er...damping down their emotional reactions. I'll— I've made sure they're all on round-the-clock shifts. Dosed with No-Sleep. And constant patrolling will keep their emotions in check."

K relaxed again. The message was finally sinking in. "Have you spent all day with them?" he asked, allowing himself to sound mollified.

"First at the scene, and then back at the barracks, once we'd recovered all the bodies. A couple of Pell's hounds supervised the cleaning up at the Barrier. It didn't take too long. Most of the blood had been diluted by the rain."

K nodded. "There was no indication that those two fighters were the Jay's people?"

"There was no calling card this time, no. But Pell got a—"

K stopped Linden with an impatient gesture. "I've already seen Pell's report. She identified the Greenland woman. That was good work on her part. Tell her."

"I already have."

"Tell her from *me*."

"Oh. Yes. I see."

"So..." K put his elbows on the desk and rested his chin on steepled fingers. "We've had two operations run by the Jay, both of them disastrous from our point of view. What do you propose we do?" He waved Linden to one of the hard chairs.

Linden pulled it a lot further away from the desk before he sat down. There was tension in his shoulders and his hands were clutching his knees as he leaned forward. He had clearly been thinking quite hard about their problem, but he was nervous about sharing his conclusions. "I think we can't afford to wait for a third attack. We need to go on the offensive, find the Jay, bring him in. His women as well, of course."

K almost smiled. He had expected to have to force this mission onto Linden, but it seemed that the younger man was eager for it. Did he feel a need to prove himself? To his grandfather, perhaps? Which reminded K...

"You know, I hope, how important it is that there should be no rumours – not even a whisper – about the return of the Jay? It is not to be mentioned in any report. *Not to anyone.* Who knows apart from the two of us?"

"No one. I destroyed the sign at the Franz building before Pell saw it."

"Good. What about your plans to raid the Jay's hideout?"

"We haven't pinpointed it yet. But I set up the raiding party immediately after our last meeting. It will be ready to go as soon we identify the target. We— That is—"

K waited while Linden struggled to catch up with the new reality.

"The raiding party will need to be reconfigured, of course, to take account of our losses." He nodded, trying to emphasise how he had everything under control. One strand of his unruly hair flopped into his eye. He winced and brushed it away impatiently. "I was planning to get on to that as soon as I'd finished my report here."

"Good," K repeated blandly. "I'm putting you in sole charge of the hunt for the Greenland woman. Helen Birch, as she calls herself."

"K, that's fantastic. I—"

K continued without a pause. "You have Pell's pack, plus two new packs I'm assigning to you. Get them all out on the ground and *find that woman!* It's clear she's gone over to the Jay, so when you find her, you'll find him as well. I don't care how hard you drive the packs. This is priority one. You have to arrest Jay and all his people before they can mount another op. You are to bring them in alive. Do you understand?"

Linden had gone pale – not surprising with that amount of responsibility on his shoulders – but he looked remarkably resolute. "If I flood the streets with hounds, the Jay will keep his people out of sight. So even if it takes a while to pin them down, we should be safe from another surface attack."

"Not good enough," K snapped. "Think about it, Linden! How did they escape from that last ambush? Comms. They hacked into our most secure comms. They can do us major damage without being out on the streets."

"I've changed the operating procedures," Linden protested. "They won't be able to do that again."

"No," K replied coldly. "And they won't even try. It will be something totally different next time. I think you're in danger of underestimating these people."

Linden stiffened. There was a tiny hint of red on his neck. "I fully intend to deliver the Jay and every last one of his team to the cells. Within the week," he added proudly, volunteering his head for K's dangling noose.

"I see. Have you told your grandfather that?" K asked softly.

"No. No one knows except us. I told you that." Under K's stern gaze, Linden's sudden bravado seemed to evaporate. "I...er...I thought it would be better to surprise the old man. After the op was all over and tied up."

Not so naïve after all, K decided. "Very wise," he said, nodding. "Keep the mission on a need-to-know basis: you, me, and – only if you absolutely have to – Pell. I'll expect daily reports, but the tactics are basically down to you. Take all the resources you need. Even a fourth pack if you have to."

Linden swallowed a gasp. "That would leave almost no one for special ops."

"It goes to show how important this is. I'm trusting you with a vital mission, Linden. If you succeed, it could make your career." K didn't add the obvious rider and Linden seemed to be so overwhelmed that he failed to notice the downside.

K smiled then. "Anything else?"

Linden hesitated a second before saying, "Is there really no way to stop the rain?"

• • • • •

The Jays were holding a council of war, sitting together in the control centre of the bunker. Everyone had to take part, Jedda had decreed; they would rely on Anton's external sensors to warn of any dangers.

"I'm going to bring Ellen in as well," Jedda said flatly.

Anton sucked in a noisy breath but no words came out.

Chrys knew better than to intervene before Jedda had finished.

"But before I do, we need to get the ground rules clear."

This time, Chrys nodded. Practical detail was one of her strengths. She could contribute here.

"You're not planning to give her the run of the place, are you?" Anton protested. "She's not to be trusted, Jedda, she—"

Jedda raised a hand for silence.

Anton subsided. His shoulders slumped, making him look like a slightly rumpled sack. For some reason, he had chosen to wear an orange bandana round his head today, as if announcing that he was about to go into action. It announced that he knew nothing about real action. Orange and camouflage were not good bedfellows.

"These are the rules I propose." Jedda began to count off on her fingers. "One: Ellen is never to be left alone, except when she's locked in her cell." Jedda ignored Anton's sigh of relief. "Two: the destruct device in Ellen's clothing will become fully automatic whenever she leaves the bunker. We will not hide that from her, though she will expect nothing else. Three: Ellen is to be treated with courtesy, otherwise. She has said she will be a full member of the team. We have no grounds for doubting her."

"Yet," Anton put in, with a snort of disbelief.

"Four: Ellen will be given a chance to prove her loyalty to us. If she does so, we will accept her as a full team member, and rules one and two will be dropped. Any questions?" She turned first to Chrys.

"Not sure how Ellen can prove her loyalty to us while she's wearing an active destruct device. She's bound to stick with us as long as Anton has his finger on the trigger. She can only prove she's loyal if we give her a real chance not to be."

Jedda smiled. "Spot on, Chrys. I'd thought of that, too. She *will* get a real chance – I can't deny her that – but it won't involve any risk to the rest of us. It needs a special set of circumstances, but it can be made to work."

"What can?"

"My plan, Anton," Jedda said, still smiling a little smugly. "Needs special external circumstances, as I said. I'll share it when the time comes."

Typical Jedda, Chrys thought. *Always keeps her ideas close to her chest so she can adapt as she goes along. It will be a good plan, though. Jedda's plans always are.*

"Anton?"

"I don't like it, Jedda, but you already know that. Ellen will never be one of us. She'd see us all in hell first."

"You don't trust her. Yup. Got that message. But have you any specific objections to the rules I'm proposing?"

"Um...no."

"Including rule three? Treating her with courtesy?"

"I'm not a complete idiot, Jedda," Anton retorted. "I can bite my tongue when I have to. And even I can see that she'll never come over to us if we don't treat her better than we have so far."

"Fine. Thanks. It's agreed, then. We give Ellen a real chance. Good. I'll go and fetch her."

Chrys stepped forward. "Shouldn't I go?" She was the appointed jailer, after all.

Jedda shook her head. "Thanks, Chrys, but I want to do this myself. I need to lay out the ground rules for her in private. She has to agree to be courteous to all of us, remember. Even Anton." She chuckled at that, and was still chuckling as she walked off into the corridor.

"She's too straight," Anton muttered as soon as Jedda was out of earshot. "Her parents have a lot to answer for. One day her sense of honour will be the death of her."

"Her parents made her the leader she is." Chrys had never allowed anyone to criticise Jedda, even when she was only Jay's deputy. "They set her a fine example. If you think she's making a mistake, tell her to her face!"

"I *have* told her. She refuses to listen."

"Because she's sure you're wrong. And, for what it's worth, I agree with her. We'll get far more out of Ellen if she's a full team member than if she's a surly prisoner."

"Yes, I suppose…"

"And, don't forget, I've seen her fight. It's quite a combination, a warrior who can do all the tech stuff as well." The look on Anton's face stopped Chrys in her tracks. She might as well have accused him of cowardice. "Anton…"

"Forget it," he said gruffly. "I've never pretended to be a warrior. But I *am* the best when it comes to tech."

Chrys said nothing. Having seen some of Ellen's amazing inventions, Chrys reckoned Anton would have his work cut out to make good on that boast.

The rather awkward silence was broken by the arrival of Ellen, followed by Jedda. Whatever Jedda *said* about treating Ellen with courtesy, it didn't include giving her a chance to attack from behind. Chrys, the seasoned warrior, smiled inwardly. It was what she would have done, too.

"I've laid out the ground rules for Ellen and she accepts them." Jedda waved Ellen to a seat between Anton and Chrys. "Ellen?"

"Agreed. But I have a question. Does the courtesy rule extend to not blowing me up?" Her voice was low and incredibly polite. She could have been asking someone to pass the salt at a society dinner table.

Jedda laughed, but Chrys knew she was not amused. "We wouldn't do it for fun, Ellen," Jedda said. "Only if you give us cause. And then, *you'd* be the one who'd broken the rules, wouldn't you?"

Ellen shrugged. "Fair enough. Provided Anton buys in to that as well."

"I don't like you, Ellen, and I don't trust you," Anton said, "but I'm part of this team and I abide by the rules we've all agreed. I won't pull the trigger unless you betray us. But if you do, I won't hesitate. In fact, I'll enjoy it."

Ellen took a deep breath. "Right. Rule three. Mutual courtesy. Got it."

Jedda threw a black look at Anton. "Enough. We have business to discuss. I want to activate one of the alternate bunkers. With Ellen's invisible curtain device, we'll be able to run more than one without having to leave someone behind to guard it."

"You're expecting this bunker to be raided?" Ellen asked.

"I'm expecting K to use every trick he can think of," Jedda replied. "Viewscreen, image of K."

The close-up from the anniversary parade filled the wall. Menacing. Monochrome. *Different.* Chrys thought that Ellen shivered.

"We've beaten him twice and he'll be smarting," Jedda went on, apparently unaffected by the sight of the enemy. "He likes to think he's invincible. More to the point, he likes the Council to think it. He'll be wanting to score a victory by snatching you, Ellen. So it pays to have a spare bolthole. And a Plan B."

"When do we start?"

"As soon as it's light. Ellen, get all your devices ready. Prepare enough to cloak quite a large space. I'll give you the floor plans. Anton, you're responsible for packing all the other tech and comms equipment for the new bunker. Chrys, you're on weapons and body armour. You both know the routine." She glanced round, assessing them all, looking for problems. No one else spoke. "Right. Get started on your preparations now. I'll work with you, Ellen, but I'll be round to check progress with Anton and Chrys later. Everything is to be ready to roll by 0200 so we can get our heads down. I want everyone to have at least four hours' sleep before we start out."

Silence. Chrys and Anton nodded.

Jedda smiled round encouragingly. "Any questions?"

TEN

JEDDA LOOKED ROUND AT the new bunker. Not bad, all things considered. They'd managed to bring over the kit they needed just before first light. They hadn't been spotted. For once, the foolproof weather forecast had been wrong. The rain was still pelting down, even now. She was glad of it. The dreadful weather had provided much needed cover.

It had taken hours, but all the kit was installed, and working. First time, too, most of it, which was unusual. Anton's most sensitive machines often threw a strop and refused to function after being moved. This time, they had all behaved. If she hadn't known better, Jedda would have said that Anton's kit was determined to show Ellen just how good he was!

This bunker would be OK as a fallback, but not for normal operations. It was freezing cold and a bit damp which would upset some of Anton's systems. It would need a lot of work to bring the air circulation system up to scratch. Most important, it was much too cramped. No real living or sleeping space, just the command centre with the computers and the weapons. They'd have to squeeze their way between the closely packed machines. Bound to cause accidents, especially in an emergency. But what choice did they have? All the layout decisions had been driven by the needs of Ellen's invisible curtain. She didn't have enough individual devices to curtain a larger space.

That would have to be fixed. As a priority.

"Ellen, how long to double the number of devices we have here? We need at least twice this space. It isn't big enough for long-term operations."

Ellen was kneeling down on the floor by one of her devices, apparently calibrating it in some way. She didn't look up or turn. "It's not the length of the perimeter that matters. Numbers depend on the cubic space they enclose."

Jedda wanted to kick herself for making such a basic mistake.

"OK. You tell me." She kept her tone even, but strong. "We need much more space, or it won't be viable for more than a day at a time. How many devices? How long do you need?"

Ellen sat back on her heels and took her time stretching her back and rolling her shoulders. "It'd be a damn sight more comfortable if these clothes weren't so tight," she said, with feeling. She was determined to make her point.

Jedda ignored that, waiting.

"Numbers will depend on how secure you— er, we want to be. And that depends on just how sophisticated the opposition's detector devices are. Anyone know?" She threw a malevolent glance at Anton who had just finished setting up the last of his kit.

"They won't have dealt with anything like this." There was grudging admiration in Anton's voice. "There's nothing like it in the province."

"Doesn't mean we're fireproof," Ellen retorted. "Parts of these devices are common to a lot of systems. I need to know what we're up against, so I can decide how tight to go on security. Can't you even tell me that much?"

Jedda intervened before Anton could respond in kind. "May I remind you – both of you – of rule three? The courtesy that we all agreed to?" She took a step towards Ellen and frowned down at her. "That includes you, Ellen."

"Yeah, right." It was a barely audible mutter.

"And in that 'spirit of co-operation', I should say that no one knows how K's systems will respond to this. What about probing them, to see how they'd react? Anton? Ellen? Maybe a curtain device somewhere else, somewhere K's people will come across it? To watch what they do, how much they discover?"

"Risky." That was Anton.

"Too risky." Ellen was agreeing with Anton, for once. "If K gets his hands on one of these, he'll be able to set up countermeasures. We'd lose our advantage. We can't take the chance." She put her hands to the small of her back, as if she was in pain. But it was clearly a ruse. A second later, she rose to her feet in one fluid movement.

Jedda registered Ellen's manoeuvrings but chose to ignore them. She'd deal with the woman later. Bunker security was what mattered for the moment.

She considered for a moment longer. "OK. Here's what we're going to do. Ellen, you're to start building more curtain devices, as quickly as you can. Anton, you'll help her." She pretended not to hear Ellen's snort of disapproval. Jedda strode across the floor, through the ring of devices, until she was standing by the pillar at the far end of the main space. It would extend the existing bunker by as much again, plus another two small rooms.

She smacked the pillar with the flat of her bare hand. "Your task is to take the curtain to here." She raised her hand to silence their instant protests. "Do it in stages if you have to. But do it. Plan B only works if this place can be as secure, and as usable, as the bunker we already have." Jedda narrowed her eyes at Ellen, daring her to object.

For a long moment, Ellen held that stare. Eventually, she shrugged. "You're the boss. It'll be trial and error, though." She glanced over at Anton, who was looking mutinous. "Particularly error, I expect."

"For the last time, will you—"

"OK, Jedda. OK. Rule three. Yes, fine. I'll teach Anton how to make the devices. In a couple of days – with luck – I'll be able to tell you how long it will take."

Jedda nodded, satisfied for now, and came back to join them. "Good. Now, if you've finished setting up, can we test this thing? We can't leave here until we're sure it's a hundred percent reliable. Last thing we need is for K's goons to capture our kit." She gestured towards the piles of equipment.

Anton ran a hand through his hair. He had gone very pale. It seemed he'd finally realised the implications of leaving this bunker totally unmanned, trusting to a device that might not be K-proof. "I think I'll…" he began. "There are some things I always keep by me. No need to leave a set here. If we need to leave the main bunker, I can bring them with me."

"If we need to leave the main bunker, we'll barely have time to set the self-destruct," Jedda said sternly. "We can't afford to end up without essential kit, Anton."

"We won't be," he said stubbornly. "I'll keep the spare set packed up, ready to grab. Better that than…" He eyed the line of curtain devices with mistrust.

"We'll settle this now, once and for all. Anton, you keep saying your detection kit is as good as anything K has. And you're the one who has doubts about how Ellen's kit will work in the field. So prove which one of you is right. Get outside the curtain and show me what K could do against this device. Be as devious as you like."

She turned to Ellen. "You have three minutes. Then run the test."

"Jedda!"

It was Chrys. At the gallop.

Trouble. But how bad?

Chrys was streaking across the bare nucrete floor towards them. "K's thugs," she gasped out. "Small squad. Five minutes away. Could be coming here."

Jedda didn't waste time on questions. She drew her weapon. "Everyone behind the curtain line and cut the lights," she ordered. "Infrared goggles. Weapons on kill. We need absolute silence. And no one moves even a hair."

The others nodded but she was already on to her next instruction. "Ellen, this is your test. For real. Show us what you can do."

• • • • •

Pell and her pack were setting a bruising pace through the driving rain, but Linden was able to match them without difficulty. Since the pack were all seasoned warriors, that made him feel a tiny bit smug. He was a warrior, too, though not in Pell's league. Still, he prided himself on his fitness. He worked really hard to achieve it, and his regular sessions on the range ensured that he remained a crack shot with a weapon. On that score, he might even be a match for Pell.

To Linden's surprise, his grandfather had commented on his physical prowess just the previous day. Linden had never imagined that a man as eminent as his grandfather – a busy member of Council who travelled a lot – would know about such things. The old man not only knew, he encouraged it. He was so complimentary that Linden glowed with pride for hours afterwards. Senior officials in the Council's provinces, grandfather said, should be able to turn their hand to almost anything. Including combat.

Could K fight? Would he even be able to keep pace with Pell? Linden doubted that K took any exercise at all. The man always seemed to sit in his lair. Controlling. He probably could not handle a weapon either, Linden decided, feeling that glow again. K always used packs like Pell's to do his dirty work.

Pell stopped dead. The whole pack stopped with her, as if by telepathy. Linden, at the rear, almost collided with the hound in front.

Concentrate, you idiot!

Pell raised her head and sniffed the air. "One of the women has been here." She nodded to the ramshackle old building to their left.

"In the shadow there, where it's not quite so wet. Anyone else get it?"

The pack shook their heads. Not surprising, really. Pell's experimental implant was good, but it was a one-off. What's more, she had spent hours honing her skills to make it even more effective. She was utterly dedicated.

"I get only one woman." Pell looked round at her pack, and finally rested her gaze on Linden. "No way of knowing if she's still inside. Don't know how many we'd be up against, either. We have a choice. We go in now before it gets dark or we call for reinforcements. And wait. That would probably be sensible. After all, we're only a small group. Just five – six, if you take over, Linden."

"You're the pack leader, Pell. You decide what to do."

Pell's expression changed to cynicism, laced with contempt. Her lips thinned, as if she were trying to stop herself from saying something dangerously insulting.

"I am *not* a coward," Linden spat indignantly. "I'll be happy to join your team, but you're the one with all the leadership experience, Pell, not me. I do outrank you, but I won't push you out of your proper role. You lead. I'll follow your instructions."

Pell beamed. The rest of the pack murmured approvingly. Their sudden warmth towards him was almost strong enough to touch. It made him glad he had done it.

Pell stared up at the building, assessing it carefully. "Quite a height. That means the foundations will be solid. And deep. That's almost certainly where our target will be, if she's in there at all."

She looked round at her pack, fixing each one in turn with her steady gaze. Then she nodded, satisfied. "OK. This is what we do. We'll go down in single file. I'll lead so I can follow the scent trail. Linden will be number five. Delta will bring up the rear, as normal. We don't know what we're going to find or what the inside of the building looks like. So we need to be ultra careful. If we find we're really outnumbered, we'll retreat and call for reinforcements. Understood?"

They all nodded, including Linden.

"Right. Weapons on kill."

"No!"

"No?" Pell stared hard at Linden. "I thought you said *I* was leading this op?"

"Yes. You are." He shrugged apologetically. "But K's orders are absolute. He wants these women alive. He wants to find out exactly what the J— exactly what these renegades are planning, how many there are, where they're hiding. You know what K is like. We don't have a choice," he finished, conscious of how lame his explanation sounded, but grateful that he'd managed to avoid saying the Jay's name out loud.

After a few seconds, Pell agreed, though with obvious reluctance. "Weapons on default, then," she ordered. "Now, let's be clear. This puts us at a further disadvantage. We need this building to have lots of internal walls, so we can get close without being seen. If the basement is one big open space, we won't have a hope of getting within crippleshot range. We'll have to abandon the op. And we will. No heroics. Not from *anyone*. Do I make myself clear?" The expressions on their faces showed that her message had gone home.

Weapons drawn, the pack lined up in silence. Linden checked to ensure that his own weapon was on default and slid into his place at number five, ahead of Delta.

With one final check of her team, Pell bent to a sort of half-crouch and started towards the entrance to the building. Since the pack copied her every move, Linden tried to do the same. Within minutes, his back was aching. So much for the fitness he was so proud of. He'd have to go back to the gym, and work much harder.

Pell led her team into the dull grey building. Inside, it was dark, but the pack members seemed to be able to adjust very quickly. They didn't use any kind of aid and they didn't slow down, not even a fraction.

Linden hauled on his infrared goggles and tried to keep up without falling over the rubble that was strewn everywhere. The goggles were not much help – the only real heat signals were from the pack members ahead of him. He was grateful for Delta's guiding hand on his arm.

The building was a filthy, decrepit maze. Linden wondered how it was still standing. There were fallen beams and dark pools of water that were probably eating away at the building's fabric. But the stairs were less damaged, and passable, with care.

Following the elusive scent, Pell led the pack through passages and down several flights of stairs, hugging the wall to avoid the obstacles. Suddenly, she stopped.

Delta's hand gripped Linden's arm for a second so that he stopped too. Everyone froze in their place. They were at the end of another passageway. Where did it lead? Pell was silently sniffing the air.

Even Linden could tell that the air here was different. They were on the edge of a much bigger space. It felt… ominous.

Pell motioned to her team to stay back. She moved cautiously out towards the space. Into the unknown.

Everyone waited. Silence. No movement. No scents.

Nothing.

Then the basement was flooded with light. Pell had turned on her torch and was panning it across the space between them. Behind her, the darkness was impenetrable.

She shook her head. "They were here. At least two of them. Not more than an hour ago. Maybe less." She took a deep breath and sighed it out. Disappointment. And frustration. Then she turned round and shone her torch into the space behind her. The light caught on the pillars that were holding up the roof.

Apart from the pillars, the huge space was completely empty.

• • • • •

Jedda watched from behind the safety of the curtain as the squad members came out from the shadows. Not many at all. Not surprising really, after their huge losses at the Barrier. That battle had improved the odds for the Jays in a very satisfying way.

There was a man among them! Now, that *was* surprising. Jedda studied him with care. Well-muscled, young-looking, carried himself as if he knew what he was doing. Looked as if he knew how to handle a weapon, too. But why was he here? He clearly wasn't the leader and K hardly ever risked the few male resources he had.

Jedda parked that question for later. Things were happening. The leader was walking slowly out towards the centre of the basement, her head swaying from side to side. What on earth was she doing?

Suddenly, everything speeded up. The leader loped across to the pillar where Jedda had been standing only minutes before. The woman put her face to it. Very close. Her nose was almost flattened into the nucrete. "One target put her hand here," she yelled. "Not long ago."

What? This couldn't be happening. Jedda knew she had left no visible trace there. She'd only touched the pillar for a second. But the team leader seemed to know exactly what Jedda had done. How? It was impossible!

The leader had turned away from the pillar now. Jedda could see the woman's face in stark profile as her team gathered round. They stretched their necks towards the pillar. "I've got it now," said one triumphantly. "Faint. But a clear trace."

Trace? Faint? Jedda's blood ran cold. *Nose to the nucrete.* It ought to be impossible. But the hollow feeling in her gut told her that her guess was right. These women were sniffing out their prey.

The squad leader straightened and wrinkled her nose. Deliberately making her point. Almost as if she sensed Jedda was watching. "It's strong enough here. You should all be able to smell it."

Jedda's gut clenched even tighter. The Jays thought they had answers to everything. They could hide from electronic detectors. But not from this. Not when the pursuers were on the spot, sniffing out the Jays. The curtain gave the bunker invisibility but no physical protection. What if the women ignored what their eyes were telling them and followed their noses? They could easily cross the curtain, and then—

It was too big a risk. She had to stop them.

She jerked her head to Chrys, who nodded. Then Jedda signed to the others to stay where they were. Two should be enough.

Jedda slid out through the curtain, dropped to the floor and slithered along the wall in the darkness. Chrys followed. Within seconds, both Jays were in the furthest corner of the basement, their backs to the wall.

"Contact!" One of the squad had spotted them.

Jedda gritted her teeth and tightened her grip on her weapon. Yup. Things really were going to start hotting up.

Any moment now.

ELEVEN

THE TORCH WENT OUT. Darkness.

The man had been the only one in the squad wearing infrared goggles. Did the women have internal night vision as well as superscent? Jedda wouldn't bet against it.

She signed urgently to Chrys. Pincer movement. They'd used it often before.

Not much cover on this floor, apart from the pillars. Jedda launched herself forward and to the left, just as the shooting began. Firing back rapidly, she zigzagged across the floor and threw herself to the ground behind the nearest pillar.

At the far end, a sharp cry of pain, quickly stifled. One down. Five to go. The Jays were lucky. So far.

Chrys had made it to her pillar, much further down. An ideal position. Jedda needed to move one more pillar closer on her side. Then, when the enemy moved forward to attack, they'd be caught in the crossfire.

Jedda risked another quick look. One of the women was dragging away their fallen comrade. The rest – just four now – were advancing slowly in a tight group. The leader, at the front, was firing from a weapon in each hand. In spite of her solid body armour, leading made her vulnerable. To the right shot.

The squad leader was yelling to make herself heard above the volleys of shots. "Give yourselves up. You're outnumbered. Surrender. Or you'll die here."

Jedda stuck her weapon round the pillar and fired a burst. No luck this time.

At the same moment, Chrys signalled urgently from the far pillar. Jedda *had* to get to that next pillar before the enemy came any closer. If she didn't, Chrys would be exposed.

The enemy would know that. They would be expecting Jedda to move.

Jedda signalled to Chrys for covering fire. Attack was their only option. The enemy knew it, but Jedda might still catch them out. She fired off a volley into the ceiling over the squad's heads. Immediately, chunks of masonry starting falling on the tight enemy formation below. The group scattered to avoid them. Bent almost double, Jedda raced towards her goal, ducking and weaving.

The enemy quickly recovered. More shots sprayed round the basement. One burned past Jedda's ear. Another thumped into the floor by her feet, spraying nucrete fragments in a wide arc. One hit Jedda's goggles. The lens shattered instantly.

She cried out.

• • • • •

Crouching behind the invisible curtain, Ellen saw Anton tense, preparing to go and join the fight. She reached out to grip his forearm, squeezing hard enough to cause pain. She shook her head vehemently at him. Jedda had deliberately split the team. Ellen and Anton were to defend the curtain, and the vital kit hidden behind it.

For a second, Anton looked as if he would shake off Ellen's restraining hand, and storm out to join Jedda. But Ellen spun him round and forced him to focus on his precious kit. He subsided enough for her to release him. His rational brain had overcome his gut response. He knew he had to defend the bunker. And so did she.

She needed a weapon.

She held out her hand, palm up.

Anton glanced towards the curtain. No need. The sound of firing was echoing off the walls, even louder than before. Jedda and Chrys were outnumbered. Jedda might have been hit. They could both be taken down. At any moment.

Anton slapped a spare weapon into Ellen's hand.

Her reactions were automatic. She had to lead here. She pushed Anton to the back to defend their secrets. To destroy them, if the fight was lost. She took the forward position herself.

She crouched down, readying her weapon. The blood was pounding in her ears. She was not afraid. She was fighting for… something. She felt alive again.

• • • • •

It took a full twenty seconds for Jedda to recover her wits. Stupid! The enemy could have been on her. Without Chrys's sustained volleys, they would have been.

Jedda's eye was undamaged, thanks to Anton's contacts. With only one infrared lens, though, her vision was not great. Time to finish this! She squinted round her new pillar. The squad leader had dropped to all fours. Madness. How could she shoot from there? And she was doing that strange swaying with her head again.

Suddenly, Jedda's heart was in her mouth. What if the woman could sniff out—?

"To me!" the leader yelled, clearly excited. The excitement of discovery?

Jedda held her breath to steady her hand. She closed one eye. Sighted through her remaining lens. She needed a precision shot.

"Linden, there's more of—"

Jedda fired. The words stopped in the leader's throat as she fell. A single gasp of pain. Then a gurgle.

The man threw himself forward to shield his leader. He had a weapon in each hand, but he was not firing. He dropped to one knee to check the body. "She's alive."

Jedda had missed her kill. *Damn and double damn!*

"Get her out of here, you two," he ordered. "I'll hold them off."

Behind him, the two women holstered their weapons and started to drag the body along the floor. Occasionally, it gurgled.

The man stood up again and began to shoot.

He was insane. Two warriors against him and he wasn't even trying to make himself a smaller target. Body armour, of course, but if Jedda sighted carefully…

She tried a quick head shot. It missed.

The man kept firing.

The squad members had almost got the body clear of the basement. "We're out, Linden," one of them called. "Save yourself."

He didn't move. Just kept shooting, right and left, keeping both Jedda and Chrys pinned behind their pillars.

Jedda sighted for another head shot.

In the same moment, Chrys fired a volley into the ceiling above him. A huge piece of grey nucrete came loose and hung for a second, trying to pull free.

It should have killed him. But a shouted warning from his team saved him. He jumped aside just in time, though the block still hit him on the shoulder. One of his weapons fell to the ground and skittered away. He swore loudly. Then, with a last defiant volley, he spun round and raced for safety.

The Jays fired after him. Useless. He could duck and weave just as well as Jedda. In seconds he had disappeared.

Jedda and Chrys held their positions. Too risky to move before they were sure the enemy had really gone.

In the sudden silence, their ears were still ringing with the sound of constant firing. Finally, Jedda judged it was safe. She stood up and came out into the open. She crossed to where the man had stood, insanely defying the odds. Blood. Lots of it. "I missed." She shook her head. "Should have killed her outright. I just grazed the side of her throat, I think. Nasty enough with a killshot. She may still die."

Chrys bent to retrieve the man's lost weapon. She looked at it, and caught her breath. "Set on default."

"What?"

"Crippleshots. No wonder they came off so badly. They weren't really trying."

Jedda groaned. "They were trying all right – to take us alive. So K really is frightened of the Jay." She nodded to herself. "Actually, we can use that."

She strode across to the invisible curtain, switching on her torch as she went, and ripping off the broken goggles with a sigh of relief.

She stepped across the curtain. Facing her was Ellen, and a weapon set on kill.

"Put it down, Ellen," Jedda said wearily. "We've got better things to do. Like getting you and your precious curtain out of here before K's reinforcements arrive."

• • • • •

In a matter of minutes, everything of value had been stripped out of the alternate bunker. It took longer to get back to their HQ, burdened as they were. But by using Anton's portable detection devices, they made it without meeting any more of K's thugs. The gathering darkness helped.

"Be thankful you two killed so many of them at the barrier," Jedda said as they finished stowing their gear in the main command centre. "K would have flooded the area with goons if he had them. And we'd have been pushed to get back here in one piece." She smiled at Chrys. And then, tightly, at Ellen.

They knew about the scenting. Now, she had to tell them the rest. Unfair not to.

"I think the squad leader's sense of smell was special." Jedda was trying to keep the worry out of her voice. She wasn't sure she was succeeding. The Jays had worked so hard to develop countermeasures against sophisticated detectors. And they had succeeded. But smell was basic. Primitive. How could they combat that? If it hadn't been for the continuing rain… She ground her teeth.

Don't go there, Jedda!

"You dealt with her pretty effectively," Anton said, bent over his screen. He was checking the outside sensors, obsessively. "She won't be able to speak for a while."

"She'll be able to write," Jedda said bitterly.

Anton shrugged. "Only if she lives. K usually disposes of badly wounded soldiers. At least, that's what people say."

He was missing the point. "I think she may have sniffed out that you two were behind the curtain."

"It doesn't matter if K finds out that we were all there." It was the first time Ellen had spoken since she'd grounded her weapon, back in the basement. She sounded strangely subdued. "He'll assume we were behind a wall, or on another floor, or something. That woman might simply have picked up our traces from her side of the curtain. After all, Anton and I had both been out there. But if she could tell we were actually *there* in the basement – invisible – behind some kind of veil… Once the curtain is known to exist, it loses most of its value."

Jedda didn't trust Ellen an inch, but she felt a momentary sympathy for her. Ellen's amazing invention had probably been devalued by a development coming completely out of left field.

Chrys broke the taut silence. "So now we know why the goon-squads were suddenly nicknamed 'packs of hounds'." She grimaced.

"Yes." Jedda swallowed a curse. She had forgotten about that nickname. K's people might as well have hung out a banner announcing their latest discovery. How could she have missed something so obvious? She was an idiot! She had put her whole team at risk. By underestimating K. Mistakes like that were usually fatal.

"It wasn't your fault, Jedda," Chrys said quickly. After so many years, they could almost read each other's minds. "No one made the connection. We *all* failed."

"I—"

Anton interrupted them. "Ellen was the one who failed. She said her invisible curtain was detection proof. And it isn't." He raised his eyebrows and nodded his head to emphasise his point, like an academic lecturing students. The donnish effect was spoiled when his pony tail came undone and his hair flopped over his ears.

"You weren't listening, Anton," Ellen bit back. "I said it was undetectable by any existing detection device. What that pack leader had was not a *device*."

"Angels on pinheads," Anton muttered.

"And *your* assessment of K's foot soldiers was totally accurate, was it?"

"Oh, stop squabbling like children," Jedda snarled, exasperated. "What matters is where we go from here."

Anton shrank a little. Ellen raised her chin defiantly. She clearly thought she had won that round.

"Right. Council of war." Jedda gestured to the others to gather round. "We have to plan for the worst. So let's assume K knows we have a cloaking device that can't be penetrated by his electronic snoopers. And also that, if his hounds can get close enough, they can detect us behind it, using their scenting skills. What will he do? And what can we do to counter him?"

Chrys was the first to speak. "He'll send out all the hounds he has in order to find where we are holed up. He'll want to capture us. *And* the curtain device. But he's short-handed. And it's still raining. Both are real problems for him." She paused, thinking. "He may try weather-warping. If he stopped the rain…"

"It was his weather-warping that started it," Anton said, sounding more like his normal self. "I'm pretty sure he used it for the anniversary parade. Once it's switched off again, the weather often goes haywire. Sometimes for weeks. I reckon that's what's happening now. He'd be mad to go for weather-warping again so soon."

Jedda digested that. It explained quite a lot. "OK. If Anton is right, K is unlikely to stop the rain. That'll help us, in the short term. Chrys? You were saying?"

"He's very short of foot-soldiers. He'll need to build up his hound-packs. He may even bring in reinforcements from other provinces."

"Unlikely." Ellen seemed very sure of herself. "That would be an admission of weakness to the Council. Everyone knows K doesn't do weak."

Chrys laughed. It helped to release the tension in all of them.

Jedda smiled round at the group. They were beginning to make progress at last. "OK. Let's focus on this smell thing. Ellen, what's your take on it?"

"The leader was much better at it than the rest of the squad. She was having a go at them, because she could smell the trace of Jedda's palm print and the others couldn't. We heard her, remember? It's probably very new. May even be unreliable, though we daren't assume that. But it's probably safe to assume that K will need time to train up a large group that's as skilled as that leader was. And she won't be back in action for a while. If ever."

"Hmm. Countermeasures?"

"No obvious ones. I'll need to think about that."

Jedda wondered whether Ellen was holding back. It would be in character. She'd done well at the other bunker, but she still wasn't prepared to become a full-on member of the Jays. Maybe—

"*I've* thought about it," Anton put in, sounding pleased with himself for being ahead of Ellen. "Standard technology won't help us here. Smell is about as basic as things get. So we have to be basic, too." He paused and looked round at them all.

Jedda decided to humour him. "Another one of your off-the-wall ideas, Anton? I'm prepared to give anything a try. So, what is it?"

"We have to give them what they want. Scent patterns." He grinned at their obvious incomprehension. "Don't you see? We'll— I'll engineer nanobots that generate random scent patterns for each of us. I can probably make the patterns change at least every twenty-four hours or so. K's hounds would have so many different scents to process, they wouldn't know which to follow."

"That's brilliant, Anton. But…er…complicated? Are you sure you can do it?"

"As sure as I can be at this stage, Jedda. I should be able to re-engineer some of the anti-disease nanobots that we've all got in our bloodstream already."

"How soon?"

Anton laughed and shook his head. "You don't change, do you, Jedda? Always pushing for results. By yesterday."

"How long?" she repeated.

"Well now, how long is a piece of string?" He gestured with his hands, stretching an invisible piece of elastic. He was grinning.

"Anton…"

"OK, Jedda. Keep your hair on. I'll try to do it before the rain stops. Let's hope that K's little weather experiment has screwed things up for a good long while."

• • • • •

Ellen was back in her cell. *Locked* in her cell.

So much for being a member of the team! She was still a prisoner. And her clothes were still booby-trapped to ensure she couldn't escape.

She lay back on her bunk with her hands behind her head and

gazed up at the ceiling. It was almost as ramshackle as the one Jedda had brought down on the enemy's heads. Ellen narrowed her eyes to examine this one more closely. Old, but not too many cracks. Safe enough, she decided, provided no one fired shots into it.

Stop it, Ellen. You're focusing on side-issues in order to avoid the real one.

The real one was stark enough. The Jays were still ready to kill her, but she had been prepared to fight for them.

Why? It made no sense.

Well… Maybe a little sense. She'd been fighting to defend her invisible curtain. It was valuable technology, and she really, really didn't want the state to get hold of it. If the three Jays had been killed, Ellen might even have been able to get away. And without Anton's finger on the trigger, she might have got rid of the booby-trap, too.

She took a deep breath and finally faced the truth. She had been caught up in the moment, adrenalin pumping. She'd felt part of something, in a way she hadn't for years. Something worthwhile. In spite of the real danger of dying, she had relished it.

Given half a chance, she would have been outside the curtain, standing alongside Jedda and Chrys, helping them to take the fight to the enemy.

But that was then. This was now, locked in a cell. A prisoner. Mistrusted by everyone.

She had learnt a valuable lesson. She was still on her own.

TWELVE

K WAS FURIOUS, PACING his office like a demented beast in an old-fashioned zoo. For once, his display of temper was not an act. Linden was sure of that.

Perversely, Linden felt more comfortable facing the man when he was not hiding behind that infernal mask of control he usually assumed. It really helped, too, that Linden had just been in combat, while K had not. It evened things up, somehow.

Linden was feeling very proud of what he had done. He hadn't captured the enemy women, but he *had* done the most important thing – he had saved Pell. She was going to survive, though she was in a coma. His injured shoulder was black with bruises, but it looked much worse than it really was. The medics had taped him up and even given him a sling to wear. He had taken *that* off again this morning. He would not show weakness in front of K.

"Precisely *what* did you think you were doing, Linden?"

"My duty, K," Linden responded promptly. "Trying to bring in the Jay women alive. Those *were* your orders."

"Yes, and you had two of the women in your sights. You lost them because you split your forces to save the wounded. What have you to say for yourself?"

The first split had been Pell's doing, but Linden would not hide behind that. *Never apologise, never explain.* That was his grandfather's motto. But K was Linden's boss, so... "I took over when Pell was hit. I split the team to get her to safety."

"Misplaced chivalry," K spat. "Why not just get on with the mission?"

Linden blinked, stunned. He should have abandoned Pell? Or, worse, killed her? Linden had heard the rumours about K's cold-blooded approach, but he had not believed them. Would this man really kill off his own wounded because they were holding up his plans?

Linden could never – ever – do such a thing. Chivalry was part of his code. Had been, even since…

Not very chivalrous, Linden. His dead mother – the mother he had loved beyond any living soul – had used those words to him, long ago. He had been sparring against a much smaller, weaker female. He had tricked the girl into thinking the bout was over, an honourable draw. The moment she dropped her guard, he had used his adolescent male strength to overcome her. But when he looked to his mother for approval of his win, he found only disgust. A real man, she said, did not cheat to win. A real man, a chivalrous man, did not take advantage of women, or the weak. A real man protected them. She was disappointed that her only son was not such a man.

Linden had spent years trying to live up to her standards. And he had made them his own.

Now, his brain began to race. Clearly no point in telling K that he had saved Pell because it was the right thing to do. Or that comrades fought better together when they looked out for each other. Only something stark and practical would do for K.

Yes. Got it!

"Pell is the only hound in London province with your experimental smell implant and the knowledge to use it. If she died, we would have to start again, from scratch. We'd lose all her experience. If she's restored to health, we can use her. Even if she's not fit enough for frontline duty, we can use her to train others." Privately, Linden was sure Pell would never make it back to active service. It was a great loss.

His response seemed to have made K stop and think. That was a first. "London province *needs* Pell," Linden said, driving his point home.

"I'll grant you she is useful. But I'm not convinced she's worth the loss of both those Jay women." K stopped pacing and sank into his black chair. For several seconds he sat totally immobile. Then he smiled knowingly. "You're not forgetting that you promised me those women within a week? Tomorrow, I think you'll find, is day three."

Linden felt the blood drain from his cheeks. He'd been a fool to make that boast. K now had the means to lever Linden out of his position. And Linden himself had stupidly provided it. He'd behaved like a spoiled brat instead of a grown man.

Nothing to be done. He'd made a commitment and now, to save himself, he was going to have to deliver on it. He was not rash enough to repeat it, though. "You said I could have more resources,

K. Does that still stand?"

"Yes." K leant back in his chair and closed his eyes.

Linden wasn't fooled. He persisted. "And they have to be delivered alive?"

K's eyes snapped open. "Yes. All of them. Especially the Greenland one. She has special skills. She's going to help us a great deal. Eventually."

There was nothing more for Linden to say. K was counting down towards Linden's disgrace. If that happened, Linden's grandfather would be damaged, too. Not much, perhaps, but enough to cause a deep rift between Linden and the old man. Linden didn't much fancy the idea of earning his keep as a lowly minion in K's control factory. Without his grandfather's patronage, that might be all that was left to him.

"I'll report when I have something." Linden turned for the door without waiting for a response.

He got one, just the same. "See that you do."

K narrowed his eyes, watching Linden's back as he went out. Something about him had changed. Something so subtle that K could not quite put his finger on it. Perhaps it was just the normal post-combat high? Pell's team had one dead and one seriously wounded; Linden had come out unscathed, even a bit of a hero to the troops.

Ah, yes! That must be it. He was basking in hero-worship.

It would not last long.

• • • • •

Jedda padded down the corridor in the half-light. She was enjoying the silence and solitude, though not the cold. She had put on several extra layers before she came on watch at midnight. And still the cold was getting to her. She wrapped the fingers of both hands more tightly round her steaming mug of coffee. She drank too much of it. She knew that. But without regular boosts of caffeine, she would not be alert enough to stay ahead of the game. She never had enough time to sleep properly, and her eating habits were a joke among the Jays. She chuckled and shrugged away that thought. *Oops.* Her coffee slopped over the side of the mug.

Ever the careful leader, she dropped to one knee and allowed the pool of coffee to soak into her trousers. In minutes, the material would absorb it and be clean again. More important, there would be no risk of someone slipping on the spilt liquid.

She checked her wrist computer as she got to her feet. Nothing worrying on any of the external sensors. The blessed rain was still beating down, washing away any betraying scents in rivers of gluey mud. K's hounds could not sniff out any traces of the Jays' main hideout until it stopped. And there would be no new traces for them to follow. Not if Anton's plan succeeded.

He had been working on engineering his scent-pattern bots for two solid days now. He had kept himself going by swallowing No-Sleep pills, but the drug did not suit him at all. He said it kept him on high alert but took the edge off his creative instincts. Jedda was not surprised. It was a battlefield drug, designed to keep soldiers fighting for days on end, without sleep or even rest. It ensured they were fit to follow orders. Foot-soldiers did not need to be creative. They needed to be ready to kill. Or to die.

Since the rain was still giving them breathing space, Jedda had ordered Anton to take the antidote and get his head down for some real sleep. She fervently hoped she had made the right decision. Anton said he was close. Great. But he could not say how much longer he needed. His silly joke had been right. *How long is a piece of string?*

There was nothing more Jedda could do. She had ensured none of the Jays went outside HQ, even in the rain. She was not going to push her luck on the scent front. No doubt K was pressurising his lab techs for instant improvements for the hounds. He just needed one lucky break and—

Jedda shut down that train of thought. It was a skill she had taught herself early on. A leader had to be able to assess the risks facing her team, but it was a waste of time and energy to worry about what-ifs like luck.

The door to the command centre was closed. Odd. She had left it open when she went for coffee.

Her senses prickled a warning.

Without a sound, she set her mug down and drew her weapon. She checked her call button with her free hand. Even if she was overpowered, she would have time to sound the alarm. Chrys would respond in seconds.

One. Two. Three.

She flung the heavy door open and leapt through the gap, weapon at the ready, finger itchy on the trigger.

"Anton! What the hell—?"

He was sitting at his station when he should have been sound asleep. He looked dreadful – grey and drained, hair all over the place. But his eyes were alive. Dancing. With excitement?

At the sound of her arrival, his ears turned bright red.

Jedda raced round the desks. As she reached him, his screen cleared.

She waved her weapon in his face. "I could have shot you, you idiot. What are you doing here?"

"Working," he muttered, avoiding her eyes. He nodded at his screen. It was full of figures and graphs.

Jedda bit back the sharp words on the tip of her tongue. Let him read the anger in her face for himself. She gestured impatiently towards the door.

With a shrug of resignation, he turned back to his screen and shut it down. Then he shuffled out of the room without a word. His body was drooping. From exhaustion.

Jedda stowed her weapon away and stared thoughtfully at Anton's dead screen for several minutes. She lacked the skills to get behind his security and recreate what he had really been doing when she came in. If she challenged him, he would say she had simply caught the end of a screen refresh, part of his research.

But it could not have been research. There was nothing wrong with Jedda's eyesight. It had been only a split second, but she was sure she had glimpsed the inside of someone's living quarters. Rather attractive quarters, too. Much more comfortable than anything the Jays had access to.

She went over it in her mind while she fetched her mug from the corridor and settled herself at her own workstation to cycle through all the cameras. Outside, the streets were deserted. No sign of any patrols. Certainly no civilians in this poor rundown part of the city. Inside, the sensors registered nothing out of the ordinary. Ellen was safely locked in her cell. From her breathing, she really was sound asleep.

By now, Anton would be asleep, too. So Jedda was on her own.

She swigged down the last of her coffee and checked her screen yet again. Nothing. She could afford to put the alarms to fully automatic. She would be warned soon enough if anything happened.

She sighed out a long breath and slid across to Chrys's empty station. The screen sprang to life at her touch.

"Computer, find—" Mid-instruction, she stopped. She got up and went to the door, dragging it shut, so the noise would not disturb anyone else. She really wanted to be alone. She had had no time to herself since before the mission to the alternate bunker. She might not get another chance for days. She had to take it now.

For this.

"Computer search," she ordered, sitting back down at Chrys's station. "Target – human male. Apparent age, mid to late twenties. Location – London. Warrior skills. Probably state employee." She paused, marshalling her memories, assessing them. "Description – hair fair, skin light, eyes dark, height about one metre eighty to one eighty-five. Build medium. In good physical shape." Excellent physical shape, in fact.

SEARCHING...

No point in mentioning insane heroics. That would not compute.

The computer was taking an age to produce anything. Jedda realised she was holding her breath. What was she doing that for? She automatically began the relaxation techniques that she had learned as a child. She exhaled slowly and deliberately, and forced her knotted stomach muscles to unravel. With the next long breath, she realised she had left out the killer fact.

"Target may be using the name Linden."

• • • • •

SEARCH COMPLETED.

At last! "Report on screen." Only one male matched Jedda's description, and "Linden", it turned out, was his real name. She scanned through the physical description. She'd had it right to within a couple of centimetres. What she needed now was—

Even swear words failed her when she saw what the computer had dug up.

OCCUPATION: STATE EMPLOYEE. AGE: 27. POSITION: DIRECTOR, ENFORCEMENT & EXTERNAL OPERATIONS, LONDON, REPORTING TO CONTROLLER, LONDON CENTRAL.

Linden was no mere warrior. His job was to run all those hound packs for K. Plus anything else K needed done in order to keep the populace properly cowed and obedient. He was clearly K's right-hand man. Suppressor-in-chief. Possibly even torturer-in-chief. Jedda felt rather sick.

NEXT OF KIN: GRANDFATHER, BARON JAGO MARUJN, SENIOR MEMBER OF COUNCIL.

Now, Jedda could hardly breathe. No wonder Linden had made it to be K's number two before he was even thirty years old. It helped that he was a man, of course. But, most of all, it must have helped that his grandfather was one of the Old Ones. Nepotism was alive and well and living in London Central.

An odd thought struck her. Why did Linden have a grandfather but no parents?

"Computer. Report on parents of target."

PARENTS OF TARGET DECEASED. FURTHER INFORMATION NOT ACCESSIBLE.

Parents deceased. Many of that generation were dead in the wars and rebellions, including Jedda's own parents. But if the computer could not access the records, they must have been sealed. Why? Was there something to hide? Or was it that someone as prominent and powerful as the Baron liked to keep his family sorrows private? Jedda decided to get Anton to probe further, though not until the scent-pattern bots were ready to go. Linden was low priority by comparison.

There were some things she could do herself, without Anton's wizardry. "Computer search. Background on Baron Jago Marujn."

SEARCHING...

Jedda read the computer's report with increasing alarm. The Baron would be a seriously dangerous man to have as an enemy. He was ruthless in the pursuit of power, apparently for its own sake. He had amassed a vast fortune, with luxury homes in every remaining habitable province. If he could not get what he wanted legitimately, via the formal Council route, he used his wealth to fund less "reputable" avenues of action. Or so it was rumoured. However, there was not a shred of hard evidence that the Baron had ever committed a crime of any kind.

Jedda sat back from the screen and grimaced. A man like that was never directly linked to anything illegal. Evidence, even living, breathing evidence, had a habit of going missing. She ran her hands over her face. Her gut was telling her that she should not be diverted into pursuing Linden and his sinister grandfather. Personal vendettas led to a loss of objectivity. She could not afford that.

"Computer. Delete all searches on Linden and Baron Marujn."

DELETING...

A man who put his own life on the line to save an injured comrade. A man who would kill and maim and torture to ensure that state control was maintained. How could they be one and the same?

Deleting material from the computer was the easy part.

• • • • •

Ellen was the last of the group to be injected with the smell-pattern nanobots. Anton seemed to take a malicious pleasure in sticking the needle into her vein. For her, he made sure it hurt. Then he began to lecture them all in a very superior fashion. Ellen ground her teeth as she listened, but she said nothing. She set her expression to blank.

"The bots will take several hours to overcome your own normal smell. Possibly as little as two, but it could be up to six. I'm rigging up a tester." He gestured towards a collection of electronics on his station. It looked like a pile of rubbish. "It'll be ready soon and then I'll be able to gauge how the bots are working in each of you. We need to be sure everyone's normal smell has completely gone before anyone goes outside."

Chrys frowned. "If my bots are working in two hours, why can't I go out?"

"Your own smell would be gone, Chrys, but you might have a trace of someone else's on your skin or your clothes." Anton held up a hand when she started to protest. "Yes, I know it's unlikely, given the material we use for our clothing. Everything should be absorbed and neutralised but, honestly, do you want to take the chance?"

"No one will take the chance," Jedda said flatly. "Until everyone's had Anton's all-clear, no one goes out. Understood?"

Silence. Followed by nods.

"Good work, Anton." Jedda smiled at him. "Your piece of string got shorter."

Anton grinned.

"And when you've got a spare moment—" Anton's grin turned to a pantomime grimace of pain "—there's some snooping I need you to do. If you're up to hacking into the central information systems?"

"Of course I am. And if it's about that pack leader you shot, I can tell you now."

Jedda's eyes widened. Then she nodded for him to continue.

"In case you're wondering, I did it while the nanobots were brewing. It didn't cost me any time on the project." It was a challenge, but no one took him up on it. "The woman's name is Pell. She is the leader of the number one pack in London. Her smell implant was experimental, a one-off, developed on spec by the London labs. It's not their area of expertise – probably just got lucky – and they haven't been able to repeat it. Jedda's shot caught the skin on the side of the woman's neck so it didn't have the full force of a killshot. Huge damage to her throat and vocal chords, though. *And* to her nasal passages. She's been in a coma since she was shot."

Chrys nodded. "So even if she did smell out the fact that you and Ellen were behind the curtain, she couldn't have told anyone?"

"Correct. On that front, we're safe. Until she wakes up and finds a way of communicating." Anton shrugged. "If she ever does."

Ellen was finding Anton hard to read. Was he sorry for the Pell woman? Or did he see her as just another piece of disposable enemy liveware?

There was an uncomfortable silence. Eventually, Chrys spoke. "I've had an idea. I wanted to try it out on you all. Particularly you, Ellen."

Ellen raised her eyebrows but said nothing.

"It's about the curtain. You and Anton didn't want to risk letting K's people probe the devices, but what if we let them find just one of them? They'd take it back to their labs to try to reverse-engineer it, wouldn't they? What if we rigged it so that it exploded when they took it apart? We might get lucky and take out their lab."

"And if we were really devious, we could rig it so that the curtain effect didn't work properly anyway," Anton put in quickly. "So if they managed to deactivate the bomb, they wouldn't have anything of value. Chrys, it's a great idea. For a non-tech."

Chrys's rather serious expression cracked into a grin.

"What's your take on the idea, Ellen?" Jedda asked quietly. "It's your device."

"There's the germ of a plan there. But we need to think it through. The device has to do something that K will be desperate to probe. Not the invisible curtain – he mustn't even suspect that exists – but something else he doesn't already have. Not too basic, or his goons might decide it's just a booby-trap and blow it up on the spot."

"Hmm." Jedda pulled her hair over her ear. "You're right. We can't afford to use the invisible curtain. It's much too precious."

"Give me an hour or so," Ellen said. "I think I can engineer a device that will have K salivating when he sees it. I'll need a workbench. And tools." She turned to stare straight at Jedda, in a full-on challenge. "And bomb-making materials."

Jedda did not hesitate. "Chrys, make sure Ellen has everything she needs." She smiled mildly down at Ellen. She had stopped fiddling with her hair.

Ellen groaned inwardly. *I'm not going to like this. That was much too easy.*

"Thanks for offering to do this, Ellen," Jedda said, still smiling. "Chrys is an expert with bombs. She'll be there to help you. With the explosives, and anything else you need. I'm sure you can do with another pair of hands."

THIRTEEN

ANTON WAS HOVERING AT Ellen's back, watching her every move. She hated the feeling of being second-guessed, especially by him. *Especially* when he was making the very obvious point that he had finished constructing his new kit, and she had not.

In the end, her temper snapped. "Do you have something to contribute, Anton? Or are you just in apprentice mode?" Childish point-scoring, but satisfying.

Visibly goaded, Anton came round the workstation to face Ellen. Chrys, who had finished working on the explosives and was trying to look busy, gave him her chair. "I'll get some coffee. Want some?" No takers, so she wandered off. Clearly Anton was to be Ellen's baby-sitter, in place of Chrys. Ellen managed not to grind her teeth.

He sat down, rested both elbows on the table and cupped his chin in his hands. The picture of relaxation. Except that the tops of his ears were still tinged with red. Poor Anton – Ellen almost felt sorry for him – the man whose ears gave him away.

He stared at the innards of the unfinished device. Chrys had integrated her booby-trap into the device's separate external shell. Until the shell was attached and activated, the device was safe. "So... apart from Chrys's explosives, what does it do?"

Ellen narrowed her eyes at him. She couldn't see any ulterior motive behind the question so she said, "It's a comms killer. It creates a dead zone for about a hundred metres in all directions."

"Can't see K salivating over that."

She smiled rather enigmatically. "Oh, you will."

This time, Anton ground his teeth. "What are you not telling me?"

"I'm sure you'll be able to find that out for yourself," Ellen said sweetly. "You being a tech wizard..."

More teeth grinding, but for only a second. He reached out and snatched up her device, turning it round in his hands, and peering into it. "That's different," he burst out. Had he worked it out already? He sounded both intrigued and admiring.

Only grudging admiration, Ellen was sure. He'd have hidden it if he could.

He picked up Ellen's magnifying lens and examined her device more carefully. "You've allowed a lot of flexibility. Why?"

"Because I don't run the comms here. *You* do. You decide how far to go in this."

He nodded. "True." He put down the lens and used one of Ellen's delicate instruments to tweak several of the settings in the device. "That's all we'll need. Mustn't give too much away."

"You don't have faith in Chrys's explosives, then?"

Ears colouring again. "Of course I do," he bit back. "But no one knows how good K's labs are at detecting them. Or deactivating them. We hope for the best, but prepare for the worst."

A wise precautionary approach. Just the same as Ellen's.

She did not nod.

• • • • •

The two men retraced their steps from the labs to the director's office before they risked saying anything more.

K was the first to speak. "Can you give me an indication of how long the research might take, Dr Feliks?" He sat down, uninvited, in the visitor's chair.

"No, K, I can't. We might get lucky and have a solution in twelve months. Or we might continue to work for years, with still no solution in sight. I'm sorry." Dr Feliks shrugged unhappily, avoiding K's keen gaze.

K sat silent while he considered his diminishing options. It was a huge risk but it had to be tried. Otherwise the state would eventually collapse. Into chaos.

Dr Feliks was picking nervously at his white lab coat. "It might help if I had more staff. And money." He spoke in a rush, as if he had been steeling himself.

"You will have all the physical resources you need, Doctor. Bring any requisitions to me personally, and I will deal with them. Staffing is a more sensitive issue, as you appreciate. The object of your research is top secret, for the reasons we discussed. The more people you use, the more likely there is to be a leak. Don't you agree?" K was doing his best to humour the man. Dr Feliks was the best bioscientist in the London province, a world expert on the manipulation of human genes. If anyone could find the solution K sought, it was likely to be Dr Feliks.

The lab director had started to sweat so much that K began to question his own judgement. Was Feliks likely to buckle under the strain of keeping such a huge secret? He was clearly feeling very insecure. Not a good frame of mind for leading a programme of ground-breaking research. The man needed to be reassured, to have his ego stroked. It was a case for the carrot, not the stick.

"Dr Feliks, you are the only man in Europe with the knowledge and experience to lead this research. If you succeed, you will be showered with honours, I can guarantee that. But we both know how politically sensitive the issue is. The Council has banned any public mention of it. In fact, I can tell you – this is for your ears only and must go no further – they don't even discuss it among themselves. If the purpose of your project became known, the Council would be... Well, let's just say that Council members would lose face." They both knew that Council members would hate that.

The scientist said nothing but his dark skin now had a greyish tinge. Bad. K did not want the man to be frightened. He went on, quickly, "That is why your research is to be top secret until it has delivered results. Then the Council will announce, with a huge fanfare, that the fertility problem has been solved and that Dr Feliks is a scientific hero. Until then, nothing is to be said. Even to Council members. Walls have ears, Dr Feliks, even Council walls. The worst outcome of all would be public knowledge of your research project, followed by failure to find the solution. I'm sure you'll see the Council's wisdom in that?"

Dr Feliks nodded and stared down at his tightly clasped hands. "Better than you imagine. I know they are thinking that there may be *no* solution." He looked up and tried to smile. "As a scientist, K, I am not prepared to give up hope for the continuation of the human race. There *must* be a solution. After all, the Blues are still fertile—"

"Only a few of them," K said sharply. "And surely that's because they were immune to the Y-bug?"

"There's been no research, but we suspect a link, yes. To be honest, we don't begin to understand it." Dr Feliks shrugged again.

"And we're not likely to find the answer, either," K said, "since the Blues are a dying breed, in spite of their marginally better fertility. We all know it's just a matter of time." The Y-bug had no effect on Blues, but neither did the cleansing nanobots which now removed diseased or damaged cells from Not-Blues, promising them many decades of extra life in strong, fit, young bodies. Cancer and the other killers of earlier centuries would no longer have any effect on Not-Blues, and so the vastly expensive hospital facilities for treating disease had been scrapped. But the Blues were still vulnerable. They aged, they suffered and, with no medical help, they died. In ever increasing numbers. In the Council's view, it was a thoroughly desirable outcome.

"The Council will not permit you to study the fertility of Blues, Doctor, even if you could find scientists prepared to touch them." K scrutinised the lab director's face and decided the man needed more grounds for hope. "I'm sure you will find another way into this problem. And I must say that I do admire your dedication to your vital work on this. I also appreciate that it would be easier if you had more staff and I will do my best to help." He smiled encouragingly at the scientist. "Look, if you can make do with your current numbers for a month or so, I may be able to fix something. Do you think you can sell our cover story to your existing team?"

"I'm sure I can, K." Dr Feliks sounded more confident at last.

"Excellent. If your team swallows it and you all succeed in keeping everything under wraps, it may be possible to give you some more researchers. Carefully chosen. I'll look into it. We can discuss it when you give me your first report."

"Shall I send it to your office?"

K shook his head. "Don't *send* it anywhere. As we discussed, you will be keeping all data inside a closed system here, with no external access. Nothing written or recorded is to go outside your lab. External access means records can be hacked into." He thought for a moment. "Best if we meet by chance, somewhere public. You can give me an oral progress report. And I'll update you on security and staffing issues. Agreed?" He waited for Feliks's nod and then held out his hand to seal their bargain.

Dr Feliks flushed as they shook hands. As if the Controller of the province and a mere lab director were equals. Gratifying, for the lab director.

"About our meeting," K added, turning for the door. "You'll receive a formal invitation to a state function. Soon. Accept it."

"I— Oh, yes. I see."

"Goodbye, Dr Feliks. And thank you. If you pull this off, the state and the Council will be very grateful to you."

K strode down the corridor to the reception area where he had left his case with the doorwoman. So far, so good. But it was not yet very far at all.

If the Council discovered what Dr Feliks was working on –

supposedly in their name – the London province would soon be short of a lab director.

And probably a Controller as well.

• • • • •

The Jays were all together for Jedda's pre-mission briefing. Chrys was holding the finished device. She would activate her booby-trap on site. She was proud of it. She was pretty sure K's techs would not be able to bypass it.

"Ellen and I will go out to set it up," Jedda said.

Chrys opened her mouth to protest, then shut it again. Jedda must have a good reason for putting herself in the firing line. She always did.

"Anton will man the comms, as usual. Chrys, you're in charge of bunker defences. Now the rain's eased off, the hound packs will be out again. They won't be able to smell us out—" she flashed a smile at Anton "—but they might get lucky. If they started random building searches, for example, they might end up here."

Chance. The one thing they could never insure against.

"Viewscreen. Street map of London." Jedda touched a finger to a spot very close to London Central's main labs. "That's our target. Viewscreen, zoom in."

Right by the lion's den? It was an audacious choice. On the other hand, it was a very good choice when the aim was to catch the state's swivelling eye. K would be worried about an unknown device so close to his main research centre. His techs would want to bring it inside, to examine it in the safety of their bomb-proof facility.

Chrys was pretty sure that their facility would not be bomb-proof enough.

"What about comms for Ellen?" Chrys asked. The Jays all used Anton's amazing two-way comms devices, tiny implants embedded behind the ear. Would Jedda allow Ellen to have one? That could be risky, given the woman's tech skills. She might be able to manipulate it to pick up things she wasn't meant to hear.

Anton held out a hand before Jedda could answer. "I've done a standard earwig for her." The tiny device on his palm was designed to fit deep inside the ear. As a receiver, it was fine, though not very flexible. Its send capabilities were limited.

Jedda turned to Ellen. "Anton will fit it for you," she said quickly, not giving the woman any choice. "Call sign – alpha two."

Not giving the woman any chance to tamper with it, either, Chrys noted, admiringly. And once it was installed, Ellen wouldn't be able to remove it without alerting Anton, here at HQ. Yes, very neat indeed.

"Any questions? No? Good. Chrys, brief Ellen on how to activate your device. Then we'll get going. I want K to see this device on his doorstep before the light fails."

•••••

Linden pushed his plate away. He had hardly touched his food. His gut was churning, but his problem was not hunger.

It was day five. Of seven. And he was no nearer capturing the Jay and his women. His only consolation was that the rain had stopped at last. So the pack's smell sense would work again. Though without Pell's expertise—

RED ALERT!

As Linden swung round in his chair to look at the screeching viewscreen, K's unmistakable features appeared on his wrist receiver.

K did not give Linden a chance to speak. "Two of the Jay women are approaching the main lab complex. They're in the restricted zone. And they're openly carrying a hemispherical object. Computers predict it's a bomb."

Linden was already on his feet. He had the co-ordinates. He ran for the door.

"Remember, I want them alive!"

K's warning was superfluous. Linden knew perfectly well what he was tasked to do. The problem was – how? The women's tactics made no sense. They must know they would be detected long before they could reach their target.

He stumbled as the obvious truth hit him. They must *want* to be detected. It was some kind of trap. It must be. How had K missed that?

He picked himself up and ran faster. His pack, the remains of Pell's pack with a couple of reinforcements, would be waiting at the barrack gate. It would be six against two. Good odds.

But it had been six against two before. Weight of numbers would not cut it with the Jays. Linden's hounds had to be smarter this time.

He did not slow down when he reached the pack, merely signalled to them to follow. With weapons in default mode. The hounds tucked in behind him in single file. Delta was in the lead now. The woman at the rear was new.

The barracks had been deliberately sited close to the labs, to protect K's precious facility. So the pack did not have far to go. At first, they could not see the women. There were too many alleys and buildings in the way. But one more corner and—

Linden made out two figures down at the end of the narrow street, less than ten metres from the main wall of the lab complex. One was standing guard. One was kneeling down. Was she setting up a bomb?

"Contact! Two rebels. Distance about a hundred and fifty metres. Look to be planting a device."

K's response was loud in Linden's ear as he ran. "I'm inside the lab. I've got them on screen. It's the Greenland woman. Plus one of the two from the Franz building. Make sure you—" The comms link went dead.

"K? Do you read me?"

Nothing.

Linden veered off towards the shelter of a building and slid to a halt. The pack was still in single file behind him, trying to minimise the target they were offering. They were all vulnerable – definitely within range of enemy killshots. And they could not fire back in any real sense. Crippleshots would be pretty ineffective at this range.

He tried the link again. Still nothing. "Anyone got comms?" They all shook their heads. How could that be happening?

"Delta, send someone back to the barracks for standby comms kit. At the double. And she's to tell the duty officer to send another pack round the far side of the labs to cut off the enemy's retreat. Stress that it's weapons in default mode."

The woman from the back of the line set off like a greyhound.

"OK. Back up. I want to have at least a hundred and fifty metres between us and the enemy." The whole pack moved steadily backwards, keeping in the lee of the buildings until they reached the shelter of a solid protruding wall. Once behind it, Linden called a halt. The pack all dropped to one knee, weapons at the ready, faces turned up to him for orders. They seemed to be trusting him to make this work.

Linden's comms crackled, then resolved into K's voice. Much higher pitched than normal. "...happening? Linden? Report!"

"Comms went down. All of them. I've pulled back while we wait for new kit."

"New kit won't make any difference. We've lost all comms within a hundred metres of those women. No sound. No visuals. Everything blocked. I've had to move to the far side of the lab where voice comms still works. Are they still there?"

Linden risked a quick look round the end of the wall. A split second later, a shot whizzed past, exactly where his head had been. "They're still there," he reported grimly. And their leader was a dangerously good shot.

"Then you'll have to go in on visual. We need to know why those women are blocking comms at the lab. The device must be some kind of comms killer, not a bomb. Bring it in, if you can. We need to know how it works. And get the women, too. Especially the Greenland one."

Bring it in IF YOU CAN. Thanks for the vote of confidence, K.

Tactics. He needed to split his pack. But how, with no comms?

First things first. "Those women have set up a device to block all our comms. Before we can take them, we need to find out exactly where the dead zone starts. I want a volunteer to go back down there—" he gestured in the direction of the enemy "—and signal the second her comms fail."

"I'll go." It was Delta.

Linden nodded. She was keen. And reliable. "Right, Delta. We'll all give you covering fire. Killshots, but aimed well short of the enemy. Just enough to make sure they keep their heads down. We'll go back to default mode when we go in. Understood?" The pack members nodded. Then, as Delta moved to the corner of the wall, Linden said, "Hug the walls as much as you can. Signal the moment you lose comms. Then get back here. On the double."

Delta flashed him a grin and slithered round the end of the wall into the open.

• • • • •

"Explosives activated," Ellen reported. Jedda was standing on guard, weapons drawn, barely a metre away. The hounds had retreated when they lost their comms, but were obviously regrouping. They would attack again soon. And there would be others, too, as soon as the lab managed to get a message out of the dead zone.

"Good. Control, any sign of more opposition yet?"

Ellen heard Jedda's spoken question but she did not get Anton's answer. Was her earwig too primitive to work within the range of the comms killer? Was Anton setting her up? She didn't even have a weapon to defend herself with.

Ellen began to scan the area. The narrow streets were all empty, apart from the one with the pack of hounds. The lab seemed to consist of nothing but blank walls. Nowhere for an enemy to lurk.

Oh yes, there was.

"Right, we're done," Jedda barked. "Follow me." She started to run for one of the side alleys without waiting for Ellen to respond.

Ellen was staring up at a spot near the top of the wall, a long way over to the left. Part of the stonework seemed to have slid back, leaving a space big enough for a sniper. Trust the state to have thought of that!

And the sniper was there, targeting his weapon. On Ellen.

The sight of him hit her like a punch in the gut. She had never seen him before – not in the flesh – but her body recognised him instantly and screamed a warning against the powerful pull he exerted. This man was a soul-mate like no other, but a soul-mate who would devour her. It was going to be very bad. And now the duel had begun, the outcome was inevitable – death.

She tried to move, but she was rooted to the spot, transfixed by the sniper with the long slim barrel trained on her. The commentary in her head reminded her that it was an antique rifle. None of Anton's electronic wizardry could save her from that.

Especially when the man wielding the rifle was K himself.

FOURTEEN

GREENLAND WOMAN. HE GAZED at her and knew, in that instant, that this was his woman.

His. Only his.

But there could be no consummation for them. She was much too dangerous. This woman could be the death of him.

So Greenland woman had to die here. For K to survive.

The laser's red sighting spot rested on her heart like a lover's hand. Pity she could not feel its touch, for it would be her last. There was no alternative, not for either of them. His finger began to stroke the trigger towards her destruction.

She continued to stare. Transfixed. Waiting. A willing sacrifice?

He lowered the rifle to gaze at her again.

She had seen him. But she did not move. She knew what was to come. So she had accepted that this was fate; for both of them.

He hugged the rifle butt deeper into his shoulder and sighted on the woman once more. At this range, it would be a certain kill.

Unless she had concealed body armour?

His rational brain reasserted itself then, delivering the solution. The red spot brushed over her body in a final, deadly caress. Across her breast, her throat. No certainty there. All too well covered. Up then, to her unprotected face. Her chin. Her lips. He allowed himself a moment to trace the outline of her mouth and rest the red spot on the corner. "Our first and last kiss," he murmured, though only the cold rifle could hear.

Then higher. Deadlier. The red spot hovered.

Finally, it settled, like an Indian blessing, on the frown between her staring eyes.

• • • • •

"Move, you idiot!" Anton yelled. Ellen did not react.

Of course she didn't. She couldn't hear. Anton quickly changed the settings.

"Move, you idiot!" he yelled again, even louder.

Ellen's gaze was still fixed on the lab. Anton could not see what she was staring at. His camera angle showed only a blank wall.

"Alpha two!" he screamed. This time, she started and moved, but only a fraction. "Move your fu—"

A loud bang cut off Anton's words.

Ellen gave a single cry and fell backwards. She had been hit. But how? No modern weapon made a noise like that. The sound was still echoing round the square.

"Alpha two! Report!"

Nothing.

Anton checked her vital signs. Injured. Not dead. "Alpha two. Move yourself! Get out of there!"

A groan of pain. Nothing else. The figure shuddered but did not rise.

Anton gauged the distance between Ellen's collapsed body and the device. Near enough to be absolutely sure. His finger hovered and—

No. Better to wait until the hounds arrived to arrest her. She would die more easily if she took some of the enemy with her. Even Ellen deserved that little victory.

Anton checked on the hounds. The pack had regrouped just beyond the edge of the dead zone. They were getting ready to mount an attack. "Go on then," he urged, as if they could hear him. "All in a nice tight bunch. I want you all."

"Control, alpha one." Jedda's voice over the comms link. Sharp, edged with concern. "What's happening? Where's alpha two?"

"Still in the square. Injured. Not moving. The hounds are closing in. I'll blow the device when they reach her. They won't take her alive."

"I'm going back. Diversion. Now!"

Jedda was putting her life on the line to rescue Ellen who wasn't even a proper Jay. Jedda demanded a diversion. Huh. Anton had no diversions to offer. Except…

He swallowed hard. Ellen would have to die alone after all. He reached out.

A sharp hiss of indrawn breath at his back. Strong fingers grabbed his hand and crushed it until he yelped in pain.

"No!" It was Chrys. "Jedda leads. Jedda decides. Not you."

• • • • •

Linden finished briefing his hounds. "And we can manage without comms. Standard hand signals. Voice commands only when absolutely necessary. Questions?"

The four women shook their heads.

"Excellent. Let's—"

"Linden!" Delta was still a little out in front. She pointed. "The other one's coming back. She's going to try to retrieve the device. Or rescue her comrade."

Struck, Linden straightened. Yes, the taller of the two Jays was sprinting across the square. Straight into his firing line. He knew she had guts, but this was crazy.

Never mind what her motives were. Exhilaration surged as the adrenalin pumped even faster. He was going to capture K's quarry and deliver them both, bang on time. A triumph to savour. He'd be able to look K in the eye, and laugh.

"Forward. On the double. We'll get the device first, so they can't destroy it. Then the women. With one injured, they won't get away this time."

· · · · ·

Jedda dropped to one knee beside Ellen. Her face was screwed up against the pain. A shoulder wound. Nasty. There was blood, but it was all being sucked up by her warrior jacket. Jedda grabbed Ellen's good arm and hauled her to her feet. "Come on!" she urged. "The hounds are coming."

She glanced round to check on their progress. Almost within range. Jedda zapped off a quick burst. One of the hounds fell. All the others kept on coming.

Another burst. This time, the hounds leapt for the shelter of the nearest wall. "Put your arm round my shoulder." Ellen, more alert now, obeyed. Jedda supported her as best she could, but was struggling to keep her weapon arm free. "Can you run?"

Ellen's teeth ground audibly. "Yes. Let's go." It sounded like an order.

Jedda gave a snort of laughter and fired a long burst. "Keeps them honest."

The women zigzagged across the square. Halfway to their goal, Ellen pulled free, clamping her good hand to her injured shoulder. "Nothing wrong with my legs," she gasped.

"Then get yourself into cover. Go! I'll hold off the hounds."

Ellen ran across the square, stumbling only a little.

Jedda quickly scanned the lab wall. Nothing. The hounds were four against one. Not good odds. Jedda sprinted for cover, ducking and weaving, firing volley after volley to keep the hounds at bay.

When she reached Ellen, she risked looking back.

Her breath caught. It was the man Linden again, K's reckless hero! He was emerging from the cover of the buildings, followed by his three hounds. Was he coming for the Jays? Or for the device in the square?

Jedda glanced over her shoulder at Ellen. She had slapped a field dressing over her wound. It would stop the pain as well as the blood. "Get back to HQ," Jedda ordered. "I'll deal with the hounds."

"No. I can fight now. Give me a weapon."

Jedda did not hesitate. "Here. Shoot to kill. Let's improve the odds."

Ellen grunted and muttered under her breath.

Jedda thought she heard the name "K", but this was no time for explanations. It didn't matter if Ellen was going soft in the head, as long as she could shoot straight.

The hounds were advancing on a broad front, towards the comms killer on the ground. They were all dinking and darting around. A clear shot was impossible.

Jedda reassessed her options. "They're going to scoop up the device and then come for us. So they're expecting reinforcements to cut off our escape route. Time we left. You first. I'll follow. Control, guide us in. Take us round the hound packs."

Ellen was no fool. With a brief nod, she was off down the alley like a hare. The dressing must be working well. She didn't stumble at all.

"Alpha one, new pack approaching from the north." Anton's voice. "And another mustering inside the lab. They'll be out soon for the comms killer. And for you, too, if you don't get out of there."

They would carry the device into the lab. Into a nice confined space. With luck, lots of K's thugs would be there when it went off.

Linden clearly wasn't waiting for the lab reinforcements. Of course, he didn't know anything about them. He had no comms. He was in the process of stowing his weapon to leave both hands free to pick up the comms killer. So he was going to deliver it himself. And he was well out in front now, making a beautifully clear target.

Jedda took a deep breath and held it. Coolly, she relaxed her muscles as she had been taught. Then she sighted, and fired.

Seconds later, Jedda had disappeared from the square, without once looking back to see if her shot had gone home. There was no need. She knew.

• • • • •

"Comms restored, K. But we can't raise Linden or any of his pack."

"You must have visuals?"

"Square is full of black smoke. Impossible to make out who's there or what's happening." The officer was avoiding K's eye.

For once, K gave the underling a few seconds to suggest what should be done next. Nothing. How predictable.

"Infrared?" he barked. "Heat sources?"

"We tried that. Lots of small fires. Impossible to tell whether it's people, or bodies, behind them. Once the fires have died down, we might be able to—"

"Check the infrared again. And get a squad ready to go out. I'll lead them."

There was an audible intake of breath from all those within earshot. No, they had not expected him to do that. Gossip said K was a string-puller who protected his own skin. Time they learned that gossip could be dead wrong.

K glanced across at the innocent-looking briefcase that contained his dismantled sniper rifle. No good for hand-to-hand combat, sadly. "I need a standard weapon."

The officer rushed to offer him hers and almost dropped it in the process.

K took it without a word of thanks and checked it automatically. Fully charged. Set on default. Per standard operating procedure. He clicked through the safety programming and reset it to kill. If the watchers noticed, they did not dare to comment.

"Assemble the squad by the door to the square. No one moves until I get there. Weapons on default." People rushed to obey. In seconds, he stood alone.

Only one weapon will be on kill. Mine. If there are decisions to be made about who lives and who dies, I will make them. And this time, reason will rule.

He picked up his gun case and strode out to the stairs.

• • • • •

The explosion had blown Linden off his feet and crunched his head on the solid paving. He felt as if he had been hit by enormous hammers. Cautiously, he pushed himself into a sitting position.

He groaned. At least, he thought he groaned. He could not hear. Were his eardrums burst? He hoped not, taking comfort from the loud, painful ringing in his head. Surely if his hearing was ruined, he would not even hear that?

He put his hands over both ears and tried to concentrate on his sense of sight. Not much use either, because the whole square was full of black smoke. He could not see the lab wall. He could not make out any of the hounds either.

"Delta!" He called her name, though he did not hear it. No response. Not surprising. She had been close behind him. Her hearing would be shot, too. If she was still alive. He started to crawl forward on hands and knees, feeling for bodies. The Jays' device had detonated so there was nothing left to be afraid of. He hoped.

His questing hand found a human leg. A hound. He felt upwards to her head and felt for a pulse in the throat. Nothing. This hound was dead. *Please, not Delta!*

He gulped a lungful of smoke-filled air and tried to get his whirling senses back on an even keel. He had to look out for his hounds. Some must have survived, surely?

As he continued to crawl around, the smoke began to clear. Someone from the lab was using a suction device to get rid of it. Linden could hear nothing, but he could see at last. He looked around, fearful of how many bodies he might find.

All the hounds were lying on the ground, but two of them were moving a little. So, two injured, one dead. Plus one dead back in the alley. And Linden himself injured too. Not a good tally. The Jays had won again.

A pair of black boots appeared out of the diminishing smoke. Linden's gaze travelled up the length of a very tall body. K. Yes, of course. K had said he was in the lab. He would come out to check the damage, now that the danger was past. Trust K to ensure that his own body was never in the firing line.

Linden dragged himself to his feet as best he could. K did not offer him a helping hand, of course. K never helped anyone but himself. That subversive thought came as a shock. He had never liked his boss – K was not the kind of man anyone could *like* – but Linden had never caught himself indulging in outright disloyalty before. What had happened to him? Was the loss of the hounds getting to him?

K spoke briefly. Linden shook his head and pointed to his ears. Then he made the universal gesture of helplessness. K turned away and started giving orders to the squad at his back. Within minutes, Linden and the injured hounds had been helped inside. The dead hound was left where she had fallen. The squad was too busy collecting up all the pieces of debris littering the square. It seemed K wanted it all. No doubt to task some poor benighted scientist with piecing the bomb back together.

•••••

After several hours of medical attention, Linden could hear again, more or less, although his ears were still ringing. His injuries were mostly bruising and lacerations. The dead hound had just been unlucky. A piece of shrapnel from the bomb had sliced through her eye into her brain, but at least it had been quick. Delta said as much when Linden visited her, in the sickbay. He hadn't been able to stop worrying about her and the other hounds. As an apprentice hardman, Linden was a pretty poor specimen.

And I'm not ashamed of that! he found himself thinking.

K walked in at that very moment and gave Linden a searching look. Could he see, or smell, treachery?

"I gather you can hear again now?"

Linden tried to reply but his throat was too raw. All that smoke he had swallowed. He nodded instead.

"Those two women escaped again," K said harshly. "What the hell were you doing to let them get away?"

"I was getting the device you wanted first," Linden managed to croak. Then a thought struck him. Something Delta had told him. "It was you who shot the Greenland woman, wasn't it? You should have killed her. You could have." Attack was the best form of defence. His grandfather had taught him that.

A reaction flashed through K's eyes but was instantly masked, long before Linden could pin it down. "I could have. But I didn't," K retorted. When Linden did not reply, K frowned down at him and said slowly, as if lecturing a particularly stupid child, "We can't get information from a corpse, Linden. I told you I wanted her alive."

That was true, but somehow Linden was not convinced. Suspicion prickled across his skin. K had wounded the woman. When it was clear she was being rescued, he could have shot her dead but he hadn't even tried. Why? The woman was a threat and would remain so. What did she have, or know, that was so precious?

They were not questions that could be voiced.

"But at least you've got her DNA." Linden was on safer ground with that.

K shook his head. "The techs combed the site for debris and blood spatter. There was plenty of debris – that device was engineered to send shrapnel in all directions – but any blood spatter had been vaporised. That was probably deliberate."

"What about—?"

"If you're thinking about the shrapnel in the dead hound, don't bother. I made sure the techs didn't miss that. Nothing there either."

Yes, he would. K didn't care about the foot-soldiers who died for the state. But Linden did care, even though he should not. "Her death was a waste," he said, "and—"

"Her death was a freak," K declared. "In normal circumstances, that device wouldn't have done much damage out there. It was some kind of trap, but why? Why did they take such risks? They could both have been killed, or captured. For what?"

Linden bent his head and let K continue to talk. Yes, they could have been killed. Should have been, especially when the taller one came back to save her friend. She had guts, the tall one, risking her life for an injured comrade. He found himself admiring her resolution, even though she had beaten him twice. It should have rankled. To Linden's surprise, it did not. She was a more than worthy adversary.

But she was only a woman! Women weren't—

He had never thought of any female as an equal before. And this one wasn't just an equal. Two victories over him made her—

Linden felt an almost overwhelming urge to laugh.

A sudden chilling insight killed it stone dead. *She had me in her sights. She could have killed me. But she shot the bomb instead. Why?*

K was still rapping out a staccato recital of facts. "Those women must have been wearing combat armour of some kind. That would have limited the impact of my shot and contained all the bleeding as well. We've recovered every fragment that wasn't totally obliterated, but it's all fairly basic, just a simple bomb. What really matters is what the comms killer inside was. We don't have any of it. And we're not going to be able to recreate it with no debris. We—"

He stopped so abruptly that Linden looked up into his face. Too many puzzles. And his brain hurt too much to cope with them right now.

K had put a hand to his chin. "Yes. That would make sense," he said, nodding thoughtfully. "Yes. Clever. Very clever."

"Sorry, K. I don't follow you."

K turned his gaze back to Linden with a smile that did not reach his eyes. Then he left without another word.

FIFTEEN

CHRYS DROPPED THE BULLET into the container Anton was holding out and went back to cleaning Ellen's wound. Anton watched in silence. The delicate work took several minutes. For an assassin, Chrys was an amazingly dedicated medic. Anton had long ago given up trying to reconcile the contradictions in her character.

"Nasty," Chrys muttered at last, straightening her back with a sigh. A moment later, she was bending to her patient again and gently drawing the edges of the torn flesh together. She applied wound glue, followed by the special bandage that would ensure rapid healing without infection. Ellen was young and strong; she would mend quickly.

Anton set the bullet aside. Now Chrys was finished, he didn't have to keep quiet. "You should have let me blow the bomb. You've lumbered us with an invalid, on top of everything else. And you don't have time to be a nursemaid. Especially to *her*."

Chrys spun round to confront Anton. She looked threatening. When she took a step forward, closing the space between them, Anton found himself backing off.

"I'm the medic here," she snapped. "You're the assistant. Aftercare is *your* job."

Unfortunately, she was right. But he really, really didn't want to be saddled with nursemaiding a woman he detested.

Chrys was waiting for a reply. Still looking menacing. So Anton grunted. She would probably think he was agreeing.

"Get her back to her cell. Keep her warm. Check her every hour."

"You forgot to tell me to lock her in." He smiled a little smugly.

Chrys ignored the smile. "You need reminding?" she asked acidly.

"How long am I stuck with doing this?" He felt he had to keep arguing. "I do have other duties, you know. More important ones."

"She'll be fighting fit in a few days. Can't you cope that long?"

He muttered under his breath. Let her take that any way she liked.

Chrys began to make for the door. "Any trouble, call me at once," she threw over her shoulder. She was having the last word, making sure he knew who was boss.

His shoulders slumped. For this, he knew better than to mess with Chrys.

As soon as she had cleaned her hands, Chrys went to bring Jedda up to speed. She was in the control room, checking external sensors. She listened to Chrys in silence, nodding once or twice. "Well done. I was worried that it might be much more difficult than a normal wound. What on earth possessed them to use an antique gun?"

"Not *them*, Jedda. *Him*. K. Ellen said so, just before I put her under."

"K shot her? *Himself*?" Jedda let out a whoosh of breath. "But surely he never gets anywhere near combat? Ellen must be mistaken."

Chrys shook her head. "Don't think so. Anton said K came out into the square after you'd gone. So he *was* in the lab."

"In the—? *Shit*!" The word hissed out through Jedda's clenched teeth.

"Yeah." Chrys grimaced. "Total waste of a perfectly good bomb. We might have got K, instead of just a couple of hounds. Why on earth did it go off out in the square?" She didn't understand. One of Anton's tricks? But she'd have noticed, wouldn't she?

Actually, no. Anton could fool anyone.

• • • • •

Linden went back to work as soon as he was released from the sickbay. What had K meant by that last, cryptic remark? It sounded as if he had fathomed what the Jay women were up to. Typical of K not to share the insight with anyone else.

Attack is the best form of defence.

Linden decided to beard the lion in his den.

"Oh, you're back," K said, without lifting his eyes from his screen.

Linden did not wait for K to enquire after his health. For that, he'd wait all day. "I'm back on duty. And fully fit again. I imagine you want to be reassured of that?"

K seemed to be concentrating on his screen of information.

"Any more news on the terrorists? Did the techs put the bomb back together?"

K looked up, frowning. "I told you in the sickbay. We found nothing of value."

"But you know what the bomb was for." He waited, wondering if K would be prepared to answer him. Unlike most people, K was not intimidated by silence.

K shut off his screen and sat back, leaning his chin on steepled fingers. "So you haven't managed to work it out for yourself?" There was a distinct sneer in his tone.

Linden marshalled his thoughts and began to tick off the points on his fingers. "The two Jay women placed a device in the square, by our main labs. It was both a sophisticated comms killer and a crude bomb. Before they could escape, the Greenland woman was shot." He narrowed his eyes at K. "Wounded. By you. Deliberately, you said, because you wanted her alive. Sadly, your plan was thwarted because the other one came back to rescue her. The women made it to a safe distance, and detonated the bomb. It killed one of my hounds. And injured the rest of us."

"And the purpose of the device was…?"

"To lure us in and kill us. Obviously."

K raised an eyebrow. "The bomb killed one hound. Totally by chance."

And Linden saw what K had realised hours before. That bomb should not have gone off in the square at all. It was designed for enclosed spaces, where the blast and shrapnel would do maximum damage. He had underestimated the Jay's ingenuity. Again. The device was no simple booby-trap to blow up a few unwary hounds. It was—

"It was a Trojan horse."

"Bravo, Linden. You got there. Finally."

'But it doesn't explain what actually happened," Linden protested stubbornly. "What was the point of setting the bomb off in the square? The women must have known they had a fair chance of escaping anyway. Why not let us carry their device into the lab? Why not give their Trojan horse a chance to blow up our best techs?"

K smiled into the middle distance. "Why not indeed?" he said softly.

· · · · ·

"You sabotaged my comms. Don't deny it, Anton. You were hoping I would be killed. And you bloody nearly succeeded." Ellen's accusing finger was rock steady, in spite of her fury. She didn't even try to control that. Sometimes it was good for people to see what she was capable of. "And you detonated Chrys's explosives out in the square, even though you knew they would be next to useless there."

Anton started to shout back, but she cut him off with a fierce gesture. "Yes, OK, if you want to be pedantic. The bomb did kill one of the hounds, but what good is that? Chrys and I created that booby trap to kill people who *mattered*. You wasted all our efforts. And risked our lives into the bargain."

"It wasn't me who exploded that bomb," Anton snapped, as soon as Ellen drew breath. "You probably didn't set it properly. You—"

"*I* set it off," Jedda put in quietly.

Stunned silence. Jedda signalled to Chrys to take Ellen back to her cell. If there was going to be a row over this, Jedda didn't want Ellen as a spectator. She must continue to believe the Jays were all united.

The silence held until Chrys returned. By then, Anton was staring at the floor. Jedda had not moved a fraction. Eventually, Chrys said, "*You* did it, Jedda? Why?"

Jedda shrugged. "Needed a diversion. Anton couldn't provide one. And there were more hound packs closing in. I needed to get Ellen away safely."

Anton snorted. "You could have killed her instead. *That* would have been a diversion. And the device could still have blown up the lab."

Chrys glared at him and began to protest, but Jedda got in first. "Enough," she spat. "I told you what I did, and why. Anton, your feud with Ellen is getting out of hand. It's warping your judgement. You know I can't afford that." She did not complete her threat. Not in front of Chrys. In any case, Anton's expression told Jedda that he knew exactly what she had been going to say. *Shape up or ship out.*

Too right.

"Back to work, guys," Jedda said evenly, after a long pause. "Let's find out what K is doing. We need to know whether our smell bots are fooling his hounds. Let's hope they're all off on a wild goose chase. Maybe a wild smell chase?"

It was a lame joke but the others dutifully tried to raise a laugh.

"And if you have a moment, Anton," Jedda added airily, "find out what happened to the survivors in the square. There were three of them, I think. It could be useful to know how bad their injuries were."

Anton looked up in surprise, but Jedda refused to meet his eye.

"We might need to do it again, one of these days, so we need to find out how well it worked," she said matter-of-factly. "Let me know when you have something."

• • • • •

Lying on her back on her bunk, Ellen kept her face blank. The cameras must not be allowed to detect how angry she was. And how impotent she felt. Anton was clearly trying to get her killed, and neither of the others gave a toss about it. OK, he hadn't detonated the bomb, but he had screwed up her comms. He hadn't denied it.

Well, Ellen wasn't about to overlook that kind of treachery. She would get Anton in the end, somehow. But it would be difficult as long as Jedda and Chrys were protecting him. She would need something really clever...

She let her thoughts drift, hoping for inspiration. She had nothing to do but think, as long as they kept her locked in this freezing cell. Stupid of them, when her skills could be so useful. But of course they didn't trust her. And they were right not to.

Probably.

She puzzled for a bit over Jedda. The woman had risked her own life to rescue Ellen from the square. It was certainly logical to ensure that Ellen was not taken alive. But Ellen didn't warrant a suicide rescue mission. The logical solution would have been for Jedda to kill her. Jedda was a first class shot. So why hadn't she done it?

Impossible to know. Ellen needed to spend much more time with Jedda, observing, testing, gathering information. She needed to find a way...

Damn it all to hell!

Her diversionary tactics were not working. As soon as she lost focus even a little, her brain took her back to the square. To that moment when time stopped – when she saw K. When she knew she was going to die.

Feeling increasingly trapped by forces she couldn't handle, Ellen tried all her tricks to fend off the invading images. Useless. Even self-hypnosis couldn't make them fade. K. Always K. With that gun. He might as well have been a bronze statue implanted in her brain. Solid, impenetrable, good for hundreds of years. She wasn't going to be able to push him away.

Think about Jedda. Think about the bomb! Think about anything but K!

No use. K's brazen image was still there, holding her on the end of his rifle sight, like a specimen on a pin. Holding her life in his hands.

He was going to kill me. He should have killed me. But he didn't. Was it deliberate? Must have been. Mustn't it?

Part of her brain tried to argue. Perhaps K wasn't a very good shot? Perhaps her involuntary movement had disturbed his aim? Perhaps he wasn't ruthless enough?

Absurd! He was probably the most ruthless man in Europe. *And* the most devious. It would be the death of her if she took him on directly. Waste of time trying to fathom his motives, for the man wasn't capable of feelings. He wasn't Grant. He wasn't anything like Grant. It didn't matter what she'd felt – what she'd *thought* she felt when she saw him there, in the flesh, his gaze fixed on her. Her body had reacted but her body had been wrong. Dead wrong.

If you go there, Ellen, you sign your own death warrant. To stay alive, you have to resist him. And didn't you just decide that life might be worth living after all?

She had to cling to that. And she had to remember to fight dirty. Always. Against everyone. Especially against K. If she wanted to survive, she would have to be as ruthless, as devious, as he was. He was good. So she had to be better. She told herself it was a new challenge. To her technical expertise. To her self-control.

In the past, she had always risen to a challenge. She had never failed one yet.

·····

The shots were coming faster. Opposition growing. New sources. He threw himself to the ground, rolled and fired a sharp volley. Another roll. Another volley.

Three down? Not enough. Enemy still firing. At least two pockets of resistance left. Must keep moving.

He was sweating hard now. No time to wipe it out of his eyes. He had to move, minimise the target he made, keep the opposition off balance.

Another roll. Another long volley. Then back on his feet and running forward in a low crouch, firing a spread of shots. He must keep the enemy's heads down until he could reach cover. He needed a new angle of fire.

The enemy was regrouping. He heard the crack of shots. Much too close. He ducked lower, weaving as he ran. Finally he made it to his goal.

Breathe. Control. These shots matter. This is the end.

He made himself wait until he was sure. Single shots. Carefully sighted. Then a final long burst to clear the last pocket. Silence. It was over.

Was it?

He got to his feet and wiped his face with his left hand, keeping his weapon at the ready. Still nothing. It really was over. He had won.

"Computer. End program." His voice came out in a croaking gasp. His lungs were burning as he struggled for breath. His heart was still racing. Not good enough. Not nearly good enough. He leaned back against the blank wall and tried to relax his screaming muscles. "Computer. Assessment."

KILL RATE: 100 PERCENT. PERFORMANCE ASSESSMENT: 82 PERCENT. DETAILED PERFORMANCE DATA—

"Computer. End assessment." K didn't need to be told that his performance was still off. Reactions too slow. Too many shots wide of target, too many times when he had only just avoided being shot himself. He had killed all the enemy. Eventually. But that was not good enough. It had to be right first time. One shot, one kill.

Wounding should never be an option. Death was always the answer.

Today, with Greenland woman, he had failed. He had wounded where he should have killed. And he was not at all sure why.

No point in brooding over it. If it was a mistake, he would just have to live with it. Until it could be remedied.

K forced himself to stretch his aching limbs and then began to go through his post-exercise routine. Clean, reload and stow his weapons. Strip off his combat kit. Stand under a cold shower. Swim the equivalent of thirty lengths in his private training pool.

When he had finished that, he would indulge himself with some target shooting with his sniper rifle. It was such a pleasure to use, smooth and lethal in the hand. He would keep practising until he was putting ten successive shots in the centre of the bull. He had to be absolutely sure he would never miss his target again.

SIXTEEN

IT WAS DAY SIX.

Linden was alone in his private apartment on the top floor of the Marujn mansion. If only he were on duty. He needed to do something, because time was running out. He could imagine what K would say, in less than forty-eight hours, if Linden had not delivered on that rash promise. Being superior was K's default attitude, followed by rubbing it in when others failed to come up to his exacting standards.

Could K himself have done any better?

Linden was not going to underestimate his boss again. He had assumed that K was a string-puller behind the scenes. He was certainly that, but only a dedicated marksman would use an antique rifle. Did that make K a warrior? Or just a man who liked a bit of target practice? Preferably on sitting ducks like the Greenland woman.

At least K hadn't trained his rifle sights on the taller one. She didn't deserve to be shot down in cold blood.

Where the hell did THAT come from? I'm supposed to be bringing her in. By tomorrow! If— No, when I do, she'll be wishing that someone had shot her dead.

He shivered. Was he going soft? He could hear his grandfather's voice, accusing him. How many times had the old tyrant said it? Linden must learn to go for the jugular, every time. Cold calculation was the only way.

Linden began to pace up and down. The polished oak floor was so well cushioned that his boots made hardly any sound. He called for classical music to help him sort out his thoughts, something mathematical, precise, rhythmic, something that would prevent another lapse into emotional weakness. He must remain taut, and alert. He was dedicated to his task, wasn't he? Of course he was. Absolutely dedicated.

The luxury mansion's sound systems had everything, so the

computer started trying to narrow down his choice. *ORCHESTRAL? CHAMBER MUSIC? SOLO—?*

Linden swore at it. "Computer. Solo music. Any instrument. Scarlatti."

SCARLATTI, ALESSANDRO, SCARLATTI, DOM—?

"Domenico!" he yelled, exasperated. "Scarlatti, Domenico. Anything. Play!"

Staccato notes from a vintage piano filled the room. A sonata. Played with exactly the clipped precision Linden needed, every note clear but curtailed. Every emotion swallowed by cold, mathematical beauty. He continued to pace, now in time with the music. It soothed him. His breathing was slowing and his senses had stopped jangling. Exactly the kind of mood a man needed in order to plan a meticulous, and ultimately successful, operation against the enemy.

• • • • •

"I've got the info you wanted, Jedda." Anton swung his chair round to Jedda.

Jedda blanked her features and turned her head slowly. "Sorry, Anton. What?"

He shrugged his shoulders. "If you don't want to know about those hounds, that's fine by me. I can bin this stuff and get on with something more important."

"What? Er…no. Sorry, I'd forgotten I asked for it," she lied, hoping she sounded convincing. "But if you've gone to the trouble of digging it out, you'd better tell me what you've discovered."

"Nothing terribly useful about the pack. It was originally six strong – the leader and five hounds. One of them was detailed off to return to the barracks after the comms failed." He grinned. "They didn't have a clue what was happening. Shame, eh?"

Jedda frowned at him. "Let's get on with your report, shall we?"

"OK. OK. So there were five in the alley. You went back to rescue Ellen. That was when they advanced. You shot one. She died instantly. Good shooting, I'd say."

"You're not telling me anything I don't already know, Anton." Jedda forced herself to breathe deeply. She must not lose her cool. Not over this.

"And then there were four." Anton grinned again. He was winding her up.

This time she did not react at all.

Anton's grin faltered and faded. "All four came out into the square, though they didn't leave cover until it looked pretty safe.

You and Ellen were a good hundred metres away by then. Still, the guy in the lead can't be *that* bright. He'd seen how well you can shoot. He should have known they were vulnerable out in the square."

True. Jedda could have dropped them all, in seconds. Instead, she had…

"If you'd detonated the bomb a few seconds later, you'd have done a lot more damage. It killed one of the women, but I reckon that was a fluke."

"What about the others, Anton? Any of them dead? Wounded?"

"Nope." He sounded disappointed. "Too far from the bomb. The blast blew them off their feet and deafened them, but that was it, apart from cuts and bruises. They can all hear again now, more's the pity. K's medics have passed them fit for duty."

Jedda nodded slowly. "Pity. Good work though, Anton. We'll know next time to let them get closer first." There was a mischievous look in Anton's eye that said there was more to come. She waited a beat. Nothing. Jedda's patience was wearing thin. "Anything else?" she demanded. "Do you know who the man was? There's something odd about him. First time I've ever seen a man leading one of K's goon squads."

"That's the most interesting part of it." He smiled smugly and waited.

"Come on, Anton. Give. I'm not in the mood to play games today."

"Spoilsport. OK. His name is Linden and – get this – he's K's number two."

Jedda tried to look both surprised and impressed.

"Wait. There's more. Linden has connections. In spades. His grandfather is one of the Old Ones."

"He can't be," Jedda protested vehemently, knowing it would make Anton even more determined to win the argument. "A man like that wouldn't be out with a pack of hounds. He might get himself killed."

"Absolutely right, Jedda, but it doesn't change the facts. I'm not wrong about this, you know." He was so keen to prove his point that he hadn't noticed anything odd about Jedda's interest in Linden. Anton's ego was making him careless.

She shook her head, as if in confusion. "It makes no sense. But if you're right, Anton, there must be an explanation. Let's look at it again." At that moment, the door opened and Chrys came in. "Come and join us, Chrys. You need to hear this, too."

All three gathered round Anton's workstation. Jedda set out the background for Chrys who simply nodded, her face expressionless. "So we have a warrior, a male, whose grandfather – according to Anton – is on the Council," Jedda finished. She glared at Anton who swallowed whatever he had been going to say. "Let's assume, for a moment, that it's all true. Do we have a name for the old man, Anton? Background?"

"Baron Jago Marujn. Not much background yet. Keeps a low profile. Keeps his systems pretty well protected, too." Anton was looking quite jaunty again. The crafty gleam in his eye suggested the Baron's secrets would not stay hidden for long.

"Does the Baron have other relatives apart from Linden? Any females?"

"No females. Just the one grandson. And Linden's parents are both dead."

"The Baron has only one heir – and a male heir too – and he lets him risk his life on the streets? Makes no sense to me. What do you think, Chrys?"

The air hissed through Chrys's clenched teeth. "Most Council members would sacrifice anything, and anyone, for a male heir. We all know the lengths they've been going to." The corner of her mouth twisted in disgust. Those old men had tried everything, from science to magic, even virgins as young as ten. "So if they ever managed to get themselves a son, or a grandson, he wouldn't be put in harm's way. Not ever." She shook her head. "Logic says Linden can't be the Baron's grandson."

"I tell you he is! He—"

"Cool it, Anton. Actually, I believe you." Jedda cut off Chrys's protest with a quick gesture. "You've never been wrong before on this sort of research. So there must be another explanation. Maybe there's something odd about Linden?"

"Or the Baron," Anton put in.

"We need to find out what it is," Jedda continued, ignoring him. "Anton, get on to it. The Baron may have decided Linden is disposable for some reason. Deficient genes, maybe? Maybe the Baron would rather have no heir than this one."

"Only if he were pretty sure he could get himself another. Or if he had one already," Chrys said darkly. "Are you absolutely sure, Anton, that there isn't another heir hidden somewhere behind the systems you haven't managed to penetrate?"

"I'm…uh…well… Actually, I can't be a hundred percent on that." Anton's ears had that familiar reddish tinge. "But I will. Soon."

"OK. Then it's priority one until we find out what's really happening with this man," Jedda said crisply. "We've never been this close to the Council before."

Anton turned back to his screen but Chrys just stood there, staring at Jedda with narrowed eyes. At last she said, "We've never been close to the Council. And we're not close to them now. What's your angle, Jedda?"

Jedda sighed out a long breath. She smiled. Confidently, she hoped. "I think Linden may be vulnerable. In fact, I'm sure of it. So I'm going to try to turn him."

• • • • •

They had argued back and forth for over an hour, but Jedda was adamant. "Linden is not like all the others. He's not amoral, for one thing. K treats hounds like disposable machines; Linden looks after his. Come on, guys, we've seen that with our own eyes. Remember the backup hideout? Linden used all his forces to get wounded hounds to safety. If he'd left the injured women where they fell, he'd have been able to attack us. We'd have been outnumbered. We could all have been killed."

"Could be just self-preservation," Chrys said. "If he leaves his hounds to die, they won't put themselves at risk when he's in a tight corner. You scratch my back…" Chrys shook her head. "If K were leading hound packs, he might do the same."

Jedda snorted in disbelief. "Not K. He'd be leading from the rear, so he could shoot down anyone who didn't obey his orders."

Chrys shrugged. She rarely argued, especially with her leader.

Anton had been surprisingly quiet for a while. Finally, he broke the strained silence. "I agree that there have been signs Linden's not a dyed-in-the-wool K-type thug. But only tiny hints, Jedda. If you try to turn him, you'll be putting yourself in danger. And the rest of us, too. What if he took you prisoner? What if he pretended to be turned, but was actually still working for K? We could lose everything we've worked for. The other groups would never forgive us." His eyes widened as he spoke. "Not that any of us would be around to ask for forgiveness," he added acidly.

Jedda swallowed. "I've thought of all that." Her voice was so soft it was almost inaudible. "I think there could be a way."

Disbelief was written across Anton's mobile features, but he said nothing. Chrys's face was still expressionless but her lithe warrior's body looked unusually tense. So she didn't like Jedda's proposal either.

"It has to be a one-shot deal," Jedda began earnestly. "I need to talk to Linden. Alone. No hounds. No backup from here. I'll make him the proposal. He'll have to agree, or not, on the spot. He won't have time to consult anyone or to plan any clever tricks. Anton will ensure he has no comms, so no earwigging from K or anyone else. I'll be totally in control." She looked for signs that they might be wavering. Nothing. "It's worth a try. We could get so much inside knowledge if we could bring him over."

"Too risky." Anton was dead serious for once.

"I only need fifteen minutes. Ten would probably do. If I can't turn him in that time, I *will* kill him. He'll never be able to tell K what we were prepared to do."

Silence. It felt as if the whole room was humming with tension.

"You're set on this, aren't you, Jedda?"

Jedda nodded. "It's my neck, Chrys."

"Ours, too," Anton put in. "If it goes wrong…"

"It won't," Jedda retorted. "I've told you. I'll give him a straight choice, to join us, or not. If he refuses, I'll kill him there and then. Don't you believe I will?"

Chrys raised a placating hand. "No one's doubting your word. But Linden's a warrior too." She paused, making her point. "What if you try to kill him and fail?"

"I've thought of that, too," Jedda replied immediately. She had known this moment would come. She straightened her back and gazed directly at Chrys. "I'll be wearing a heavy-duty suicide vest. If Linden gets the better of me, you're not to allow him to take me alive. That's an order. Understood?"

Chrys swallowed and dropped her gaze. Anton turned his head away.

"Understood?" Jedda repeated harshly. "It will be your finger on the button, Anton. Chrys gives the order. You carry it out. Understood?"

Jedda glared at them both until, eventually, they agreed. A nod was not enough. She made them say it, promise it, out loud.

"Good," she said, in her normal voice. As if she was giving routine orders.

She rolled her shoulders to ease the tension in her neck and back. Then she smiled. It meant they were about to get down to business.

"Now, we need to plan how we're going to do this. Chrys, fetch Ellen from her cell, would you? She's full of ideas. If we dangle a good enough carrot in front of her nose, she'll probably be prepared to help. We're going to want something really devious to entice Linden away from his protection detail. I've got to get him alone. And in a place of *my* choosing."

• • • • •

The message came through on Linden's personal comms line. From Delta. Who was not on duty, either. Linden puzzled over it for all of five seconds. She wanted to meet him urgently. And in private. She gave no reason.

Now, why?

Linden did not have to cudgel his brains to work it out. Delta must have information. And she was not prepared to report it to K. What could it be?

Only one way to find out. He replied in guarded language, agreeing to meet her at the place she had suggested. He knew from her cryptic hints that she meant the Franz building, though she had not named it. Anyone intercepting the message would probably fail to work it out. At least, he hoped so.

It took him no more than ten minutes to put on his combat kit and check his weapons. He considered leaving a message for his grandfather and then decided against. Delta was a trusted colleague. There was no danger in going alone to meet her. Once they had talked, he would alert K, or his grandfather, if there was something they needed to know. For now, he would trust to Delta's instinct. She was asking him not to betray her confidence. She deserved that much from him.

And at least her message gives me something to do! So far, I've come up with precisely nothing. Maybe Delta will provide the answer? If she doesn't, I'm sunk.

He ground his teeth. He had only one full day left.

It took him nearly an hour to reach the rendezvous. It was almost dark. And the rain was beating down again. The place was deserted. No sign of Delta, or anyone else. Honest Londoners tended to bolt their doors after dark. Being out on the streets was dangerous; too many people disappeared without trace. Most of the city's once vibrant nightlife had fizzled and died long ago.

Linden sensed danger all around. The high walls loomed ominously and the pelting rain had not managed to wash away the pervasive smells of filth and decay. Rats and other vermin would be emerging soon. Some of the vermin might be human.

He loped across to the main entrance, hoping to find shelter from the weather.

"Linden!" Delta was signalling frantically from a hidden alcove by the disused door. Her words came tumbling out before he was close enough to catch them. "…and I picked up a scent trail. One of the Jay women. She's inside the building."

"Just one? Which one? Is she alone?"

Delta nodded eagerly. "Only one scent pattern I recognised. There's something odd about it, but I think it might be the Greenland woman."

"But surely you can tell which—?"

She shook her head. "Can't be absolutely sure. It's obscured by older scents, people I don't recognise. I don't have Pell's skill, remember. And a big part of the woman's scent signature is missing. It could be someone else – maybe one of the other two? – wearing the Greenland woman's clothes. Definitely a woman, though."

No point in pursuing it. One lone Jay woman was a good quarry, whichever one it was. But could he trust Delta's ability to scent in the rain? "Are you absolutely sure there's only one? What if there are more, but the rain has washed away the traces?"

She shook her head vehemently. "I caught it before the rain started. I'm sure."

"But you didn't report back to K," Linden said softly.

"I'm not on duty. Neither are you. We all know what you said to K about capturing these women. And the timescale." She ignored Linden's gasp of surprise. "If I'd told K, he'd have ensured you had no chance. He'd have made sure you looked like…" She let the words tail off. She was avoiding his eyes.

"I'd have looked like a fool, and a failure," he finished brutally. "So you decided to give me a chance. Brave of you, Delta. Thanks. I owe you." He did not add what they both knew: by failing to obey standing orders, Delta was risking her own skin.

She had done enough, he decided. He had powerful allies, but she did not. "Do you have any idea where the woman has gone? Upper floors? Basement?"

"Not from here. But when we go in, I should be able to follow her scent. The building leaks, but not enough to wash away all traces."

She was right. He still needed her, for a bit longer. "OK. We'll go in together. Far enough so you can tell me to go up, or down.

Then you go back to barracks, Delta."

"But you need me to—"

"I can do one-on-one without backup." He sounded harsher than he intended. "You sniff out the general direction and you're done. That's an order. Understood?"

She gave him a long, narrow-eyed stare. It was impossible to read what she was thinking. In the end, she had no choice, though. Linden was still London Central's number two. "Back to barracks. Understood."

"And you say nothing to anyone. You haven't seen me since we went off duty."

This time, she simply nodded.

It was the best Linden could do to keep her safe. "Right then. Let's go."

SEVENTEEN

"YES!" ANTON HISSED TRIUMPHANTLY. His nose was so close to his screen that he was almost touching it. "He's sent his hound back out, just as Jedda said he would."

Chrys put a hand on Anton's shoulder and pulled him back. At last, Ellen could see. The screen showed the exterior of the Franz building. Linden's hound had just emerged. She hesitated for a few seconds, gazing back at the building as if making up her mind. Then her head dropped and she trotted off into the murk.

"What was it Jedda called him? *Chivalrous?* I'd never have guessed it about one of K's cronies..." Anton shook his head.

"Never mind her. What's happening *inside*?" Ellen reached impatiently across Anton to get at his controls, but he batted her hand away and took charge himself.

A faint infrared image appeared. They could make out a deserted corridor where several passages joined. Ellen strained her ears, but could hear only the sound of water dripping onto the Franz building's rubble-strewn floors. At least Anton's sensors did not pick up the smells of mould, and worse. Here in the bunker, they had a safe and solid refuge, by comparison with Jedda's choice for her confrontation with death.

Anton broke the silence. "This is where Jedda finished laying Ellen's old scent trail. It's a good spot. Even the hound wouldn't know which way to go from here."

"The hound's long gone. It's Linden we need to see," Ellen insisted.

Anton sat back and rolled his shoulders with slow relish. "Oh ye of little faith... He hasn't got this far yet. He's in the dark, remember, without a hound's nose. She'll have given him a general direction, but he'll have to check every passage he comes to. So much for chivalry, eh? If he'd used the hound, he'd have been here ages—"

"There!" Chrys pointed. At the far edge of the screen, a shadow was moving slowly forward. "Computer – magnify!" Chrys ordered. Within seconds she was reporting to Jedda via the comms link. "Linden. Alone. Reaching the end of the scent trail now. No lights. Infrared goggles. Two weapons visible, possibly more in reserve. Standard body armour and helmet. Vulnerabilities: lower jaw and throat; lower legs."

Ellen had to admit that Chrys was good. Not a word wasted. Jedda didn't need to be told that Linden's standard body armour might not protect him at really close range. But would Jedda get close enough? Still, if she needed to disable Linden, she now knew exactly how to do it.

"Show us Jedda."

Obedient to Chrys's order, Anton split the screen. The right half tracked Linden's progress through the darkness. The left half showed the basement where Ellen had been caught by the Jays. Half-hidden by a crumbling buttress, Jedda stood facing the direction from which Linden would come. She looked amazingly relaxed, Ellen thought, considering that she might not come out of this alive.

But the odds are definitely in her favour. She's wearing my armoured bodysuit, for starters.

That thought made Ellen's stomach churn. If Jedda was taken alive, Ellen's armour would be captured too, and that would give K a huge advantage against the Jays. Against Ellen, too. It was true that Jedda had rigged her explosive vest to destroy herself and the armour, but would Chrys and Anton have the guts to blow it?

Surreptitiously, Ellen edged even closer to Anton's controls. She would just about be able to reach the detonator, though she would probably have to fight off both Chrys and Anton to get to it. She would do it, though.

Jedda had to win here. Or die failing.

• • • • •

Now which way?

It was worse than Piccadilly Circus. Delta might have been able to follow the scent trail, but Linden hadn't a clue. For a second or two, he regretted sending Delta back to barracks. She could have been very useful.

No. This is my fight. If Delta got the scent right, there's just one woman in here. So it will be one on one. And I'll have my chance to deliver on that stupid boast to K.

Methodically, he began his search with the first passageway on his right. Nothing. He tried the second and the third. Still nothing. He was losing valuable time. What if there was another way out? What if the Greenland woman got away before he could capture her? He still had three more passages to explore.

Chances are, she'll be in the very last one I choose. If she's still here at all.

He raced down the fourth passageway, realising far too late that he was making too much noise. If she heard him coming... But no one heard him. There was no one there. He sprinted back to Piccadilly Circus, breathing hard.

Four down, two to go.

He hesitated, wondering which to choose. And then he heard it. A tiny sound, like the scuffing of a boot on gravel. Linden grinned into the darkness. Maybe Fate was helping him after all.

He started cautiously down the passage towards the sound. If he was lucky – and he reckoned he was due some luck – it really would be the Greenland woman. For some reason, K was especially keen to get his hands on that one. And Linden would enjoy delivering her to K. She'd fooled far too many of London Central's systems.

Concentrate! You don't know what's up ahead.

He slowed even more. All his senses were on full alert, even his sense of smell. It detected a slight freshening in the air – he must be about to reach an open area. That's where she'd be. The real battle would start any second.

He crept forward. Two careful paces. Two more. His hand tightened round his main weapon, safely on default. The spare in his left hand was on max, but he had no intention of using it. Not unless it came to a straight choice between her life and his.

It wouldn't come to that. A male warrior had to be odds-on to win here.

Zing! A shot slammed into the wall. Much too close for comfort. Linden dived for the shelter of the opposite wall.

Where was she? He risked a quick glance round the end of the wall. Another shot. Close, but not that close.

Now he could guess where she was. She shouldn't have fired off those loose shots. In fact, what she'd done was stupid. Those women had never been stupid before. Why now? Some kind of trap? Were there others hiding, waiting to take him from behind?

He checked again. No shot this time, but he saw part of her outline ducking back into cover. Only one infrared signature, though. The woman *was* alone.

She was at least fifty metres away, across an open space, with no cover he could use. There was only that crumbling pillar. And she was already behind it. It would be suicide for him to attack her from here. Far too much open ground between them.

If she wants a fight, let her come to me. And if her shooting is that bad, I'll be able to drop her long before she can do me any damage.

He reached an arm round the wall and fired a couple of shots in the vague direction of her pillar. Keep her honest. Keep her head down.

No reaction. No return fire. No movement.

But he could tell she was still there. She hadn't tried to escape. Did that mean there was no other way out? Odds improving, then.

"Looks like a stand-off, doesn't it?" he yelled into the darkness.

Silence.

"Drop your weapons and come out into the open. I won't shoot." Worth a try.

Silence.

She was trying to force him to make the first move. Well, she'd get her wish. "OK then. Since you won't play ball, I'll send for reinforcements." He'd wanted to take her alone, but he wasn't foolhardy enough to get himself killed doing it. A dead hero was a stupid hero. "Control. Message." His made sure his voice was loud enough for her to hear. Give her one last chance to surrender to him before much nastier opposition arrived.

Silence.

Too much silence.

"Control. Urgent message. Come in. Over."

Still silence.

"Backup isn't part of the deal, Linden. This is one on one. Just you and me."

The words hit him like a blow to the gut. She knew his name. She *knew* he had no comms. *So she'd arranged it? How the hell…?* It was a trap. It must be!

"No, it's not a trap. There's no one behind you. You can escape if you want to." The disembodied voice was calm, almost melodious.

This can't be happening! K's Greenland woman is reading my mind.

"But if you run, you'll never know whether you could have taken me down, will you? Are you Linden the warrior? Or Linden the coward?"

She's deliberately goading me.

Silence once more. Tense, thick, menacing silence, billowing out like thunder clouds to fill the dark space between them. She was waiting for him to do something that would give her the advantage. Well, Linden wasn't about to oblige.

He began to assess his options. And her motives.

She's very sure she's going to win. Now why?

If she really was on her own – and the infrared seemed to confirm that – then she was either in a better tactical position than he was, or she was a better shot. Or both. Her shooting hadn't been good so far, though that could have been a blind to lure him out. Reports he'd seen said that all three women were first class shots. He had reason to believe it. He'd been on the receiving end of some of the leader's deadly fire.

If he stayed where he was, it would be stalemate. He had to take her on, or turn tail and leg it to safety. She probably wouldn't follow. She'd probably laugh at him instead. His pride would be hurt, but nothing else. And, after all, who would know?

I would know. And she would know. And she'd find a way of taunting me. It's what the Jays always do when they have an edge. I can't risk giving them that.

He was going to have to bow to her terms. Or appear to.

"I'm not going anywhere until I know what this is about," he said loudly, with just the right mixture of arrogance and contempt in his voice. "So what are you after?"

"You."

She couldn't have missed his sharp intake of breath. As if he'd been stung. It took him a moment to collect his wits. Then, "That's bullshit and you know it. If you're hoping I'll be ransomed, forget it. K doesn't do deals. He'd rather kill me himself."

"K doesn't do deals because K doesn't put any value on human life. Not Pell's, not Delta's, not any of your team. Not even you. In the end, you're all disposable."

Linden's gut began to churn. How did she know about Pell and Delta? Their names were not public. How did she know so much about how K thought?

"And *you* are just as bad, Linden. You don't care how many die for you, either."

"No! That's not true, I—" He broke off, but it was too late. She'd goaded him and she'd won. His own stupid tongue had betrayed him.

When you lose one round, come out punching in the next.

Linden didn't stop to think. He ducked his head into his chest and charged out into the darkness like a bull, firing as he went. An Olympian burst of speed took him to the crumbling pillar in seconds. She didn't have time to fire a single shot.

Made it! Yes!

He caught his breath and pushed his weapon round the edge of the pillar. Aim impossible, of course, but what did it matter? "Drop your weapons."

Silence again. Damn the woman!

"Drop your weapons and come out. Or I *will* shoot."

No response.

A threat is a threat. Linden shot.

Nothing. No groan of pain, no collapsing body.

"I'm over here, Linden."

His head jerked round. Her dark silhouette was crouching directly opposite him, about ten metres away. Her weapon was pointing at his throat. His own weapon was still clamped against the side of the pillar. Useless. That only left the spare, the one set on kill...

He hesitated.

And in that instant, she shot the spare weapon clean out of his gloved hand.

The weapon clattered across the floor and was gone. No point in trying to find it. He had to take cover or her next shot could be the end of him. He scrambled round the pillar, tucking his stinging left hand into his armpit. It wasn't broken – it must have been a very lucky shot – but it hurt like blazes, in spite of the armoured glove.

"Now we're even. Care to come out and face me?" She still sounded amazingly calm. And in control.

Renegade control was not acceptable. Nor female control. So he would—

"I have one weapon. You have one weapon. As I said, we're even now. Don't you *do* fair fights, Linden?"

Damn her! She thinks I'm just like K!

He did not stop to answer her insults. He dropped his left arm back to his side, raised his weapon and walked out into the open.

And saw.

It's her! The leader! Not the Greenland woman after all.

She was standing now, waiting for him. He knew her instantly, in spite of the shapeless clothes and the protective helmet. It was her posture as much as anything else, the warrior's carriage – alert, focused, ready to spring. Yet her shoulders were relaxed and her head was slightly tilted, like a coquettish courtesan assessing a mark.

She's good at this. And she knows it, too.

No time to wonder how she'd got away from the pillar. Time for an attack. "I'll ask you again," he snapped. "What do you want?" He kept his weapon trained on her heart. She'd be wearing some kind of armour under those clothes. Bound to. So his crippleshot shouldn't do too much damage, even at this close range. Good.

She straightened a fraction. "And I'll *tell* you again. You. I want you."

He had to laugh. "I can't imagine it's my magnificent body you're lusting after. So what exactly do you want me for?"

She laughed back at him. For all of one second. "I want you to join the Jays."

What? Bloody hell! This woman is out of her mind.

She didn't give him a chance to say a word. "You're too good a man to want what K wants. You're too good a man to do what K does." She splayed the fingers of her free hand in a gesture of frustration, then tightened them into a fist. "Don't you know yourself at all? You care about your hounds. You help them bury their dead. You even defend them against K. I saw you put your own life on the line to save other people. Because you think they matter." She was shaking her head at him. "Don't you realise that's what *we're* fighting for, too?

"People *do* matter, Linden. More than systems, more than order, more than control. But K and your precious Council don't believe that. As far as they're concerned, people are disposable objects, to be used to maintain the Council's control. Over everything. Life, death, friendship, trust… Over everything that really matters. You know it's true, Linden. So join us, and help us to destroy this rotten system."

She was breathing hard, leaning towards him, willing him to believe. She was utterly magnificent. In that moment, he began to—

No! She's wrong. She has to be wrong.

He shot her in the heart.

EIGHTEEN

K RESISTED THE TEMPTATION to pace. Or to check for cameras. If the Baron's spies were watching, they must see a man who was totally at ease in the elegant surroundings of the Marujn mansion.

Adopting a nonchalant pose, K leaned against the wall and slowly surveyed the room. It was sparsely but expensively furnished. The cream leather upholstery on the sofas was a rare luxury in the modern, hand-to-mouth world. A very old Persian rug covered most of the floor. On it was a low table made of exotic wood, polished to a mirror finish. The ornaments – one heavy antique sculpture and an abstract painting on the wall opposite the window – were probably unique. It was a soulless room, intimidating in its opulence, a place where supplicants would be left, worrying and wondering, before being admitted to the presence of Baron Marujn, leading member of the Council of the Old Ones.

K would not be a supplicant. Not here. Not anywhere. He had never allowed himself to be intimidated by wealth and luxury. But power? That was what really mattered. Power and control. K himself had both now and used them ruthlessly. Baron Marujn had power, too, but his was the kind of power that manipulated from a distance. It was impossible to know how many strings the man could pull.

K shut off that train of thought. It was not useful. Marujn must have weaknesses. K needed to find them.

He sauntered across to the window. Two storeys below was a carefully tended garden, with an unseasonably lush green lawn and manicured evergreens, contrasting with the stark outlines of leafless trees. Even in winter, it would be a very pleasant place to take the air. K could imagine the Baron doing his "wise father of the world" act down there, drawing on the beauties of nature to help him make the decisions that would save the planet from chaos. All for the benefit of others, of course.

Some Council members probably did believe that was their role, and might even act from altruistic motives. But Marujn was not one of them. K was certain of that.

He had no proof, though. Not yet.

A slight change of air pressure as a door opened soundlessly. He did not turn.

"K?" It was a woman's voice.

He turned then and raised his eyebrows at her. Another unremarkable female, wearing some kind of uniform. One of Marujn's many servants, he supposed.

She shrank a little under his hard gaze but her low voice remained under control. "Baron Marujn will see you now. If you would be so good as to follow me?"

She led the way, soft-footed, along a bare, windowless corridor. The only sound was the click of K's boots on the smooth oak floor. At the far end, she knocked briefly on a door and immediately flung it open. Then she almost flattened herself against the wood to make way for K. He strolled through as if she were invisible.

Behind him, the door closed silently.

Marujn, immaculately dressed as usual, was sitting behind a massive wooden desk with his back to a picture window. With the light streaming in, it would be difficult to get a fix on his expression. Clever.

Without even glancing up from his screen, Marujn gestured to one of the low chairs in front of the desk. "Take a seat, K. I'll be with you in a moment."

K recognised one of the oldest tricks in the book. And as for the low chairs…? The nanobots might perhaps be able to offer Jago Marujn years and years of healthy life, but they could not fix his height. Almost everyone Marujn met was taller than he was – even the women. Here, in his private lair, he had put his own chair on some kind of pedestal, so that he could make visitors sit where he, the mighty Marujn, could look down on them. No doubt it made him feel superior.

Another man might have smiled at Marujn's petty manoeuvrings, but K knew better. He still thought he was more than a match for the Baron, but K hadn't kept his power by underestimating potential enemies. Marujn was a dangerous enemy for anyone. Even for K. Keeping his face impassive, K calmly took the seat indicated and stretched his long legs out in front of him. He leaned back, fixed his gaze on nothing at all and waited, motionless, for Marujn's next move.

It was a long time coming.

And it was not of Marujn's making.

"I have someone with me." Marujn's soft voice broke the silence. It betrayed a tiny thread of irritation as he responded to some kind of incoming message.

K glanced across, looking for signs of an earpiece. Nothing was visible. No surprise there. Marujn was rich enough to command the latest devices.

K returned his gaze to his feet, trying to appear totally uninterested in Marujn's conversation.

Marujn was obviously listening to his caller. He was frowning and stroking his neatly trimmed grey beard. At length he said, "Five billion. At that level. No higher."

Another pause to listen.

"Yes, but get shot of them within a month. Use any of the normal methods. If you need to do anything…um… unusual, consult me first."

Marujn stopped to listen again. Then a vehement, "No!" He took a moment to swallow and regain control of his voice, before continuing. "No, this line only."

Very interesting information. Marujn didn't want to be contacted on any external comms link. Here, in his mansion, he thought his comms were totally secure. Here, he was prepared to do his plotting, even in front of someone like K. Such arrogance could make him vulnerable. The man had chosen his words carefully, but K was not fooled. It was some kind of money-making scam. And Marujn believed he was untouchable.

Information like that might give K an edge one day. He resolved to investigate further, as soon as he could, even though he would have to do all the work himself. No one else could possibly be trusted to probe the Baron's secrets.

No one else would dare.

The Baron would be finished in a moment, and he would wonder how much K had understood. K allowed his otherwise blank expression to register the tiny touch of irritation of a man kept waiting while his boss conducts mindlessly boring business.

Marujn cut the link and looked down at K. "My apologies," he said smoothly. "A burden of being on the Council. One must always be available to give advice." He smiled the smile of the weary ruler who sacrifices everything for his people.

"Quite so," K responded, with an equally false smile. He held the

Baron's gaze – not challenging, just waiting, as if for instructions.

Marujn lifted a hand to smooth his thick hair. It was already very neat and needed no smoothing, but it was part of the man's vanity to preen, to draw attention to his good points. He clearly enjoyed playing the distinguished elder statesman.

"Thank you for coming so promptly," the Baron began, as if K had had a choice. "I understand there was an incident outside the main lab yesterday. And that you *happened* to be there at the time. Perhaps you would update me?" The tone was silky but the threat was clear. He had the ultimate power here, and he wanted K to feel it.

Questions raced through K's mind. And warning bells. Was Marujn concerned about his grandson? Did he know about K's business with Dr Feliks at the lab? How did he know K had been there?

K felt his throat tighten nervously. He managed to resist the urge to swallow.

Focus!

K forced himself to think rationally. Marujn might simply have had a report from Linden. But what if he had his own sources in the labs? Bugs? Not a risk that K could afford to take. Especially since he'd made that deal with Dr Feliks.

"There was an attack, as you say, Baron. As it happened, I was inside at the time, doing a spot check on security. There had been some suggestions of slackness."

"They had not been reported to me."

K let himself be seen to relax. "Routine matters, Baron. A Yellow-1 alert. You will recall that the Council receives alerts only if they are at Amber-4 or above." He shrugged nonchalantly. "So many of the low-level alerts prove to be false alarms."

"But this one was not."

"On the contrary. The alert inside the lab *was* another false alarm," K said immediately. Confidently. "The terrorist attack was outside. *Attempted* terrorist attack, rather. It was foiled. And partly by the excellent work of your grandson, I should add."

"There were casualties."

"Your grandson received minor injuries. He is fully recovered. One hound was killed by enemy fire. Another died in the blast, but that was a freak accident."

"And the terrorists? You have them in the cells, of course?"

This could be a trap.

The Baron knew about the attack. So he must know none of the terrorists had been caught. Did he also know that K had shot one? Dangerous ground if he did. And K must stop Marujn from asking about the Jays. That could be even more dangerous.

Right now, I need a diversion. Linden. Yes. The precious flesh-and-blood heir.

"It was unfortunate that your grandson was unable to arrest the terrorists. Their bomb seems to have detonated prematurely. Your grandson acted perfectly properly in the circumstances – and with a great deal of courage, I should add – so no blame attaches to him." Verdict and sentence in one. K smiled thinly. "In my opinion."

The Baron dismissed that with a contemptuous wave of the hand. "In *my* opinion, Linden should not be doing menial fighting tasks. He is your number two, is he not? *You* do not go out with hound packs. Why should he?"

Careful! Keep the focus on Linden.

"We are very short of resources, Baron. Your grandson volunteered to lead the hound pack after the previous pack leader was incapacitated."

"And whose fault was that?" Marujn snapped.

He's looking for ammunition to use against me.

"I assumed that your grandson briefed you on that? He *was* there."

"You are implying that the casualties were Linden's fault."

They were, but we both know I can't say so to your face.
Or can I?

Struck by his insight, K took a precious second to search for signs of concern, or warmth, in the Baron's expression. Difficult to tell, against the light, but the Baron's jaw seemed to be clenched hard, the dapper little beard sticking out even more than usual. And another thing. Most men would rejoice in having a male heir, but this one did not even mention it. Why did Marujn never refer to Linden as his "grandson"?

Time to find out. In spite of the risks. Knowledge is power.

"Your grandson showed remarkable personal courage in that action," K said calmly, deliberately using the word the Baron seemed to be avoiding. "Although he had no experience of leading hound packs, he took over without thought for his own safety and brought all his pack out, including the injured. No doubt you are proud to have such a warrior in the family." K stared into the Baron's face, for half a second. Then K smiled a little obsequiously.

It was what the Baron would expect.

The Baron smoothed his hair again. Did he even know he was doing it?

Another potential edge.

"Young men like to think of themselves as warriors. I am gratified to hear that you rate Linden's skills so highly." Marujn didn't sound gratified at all. He sounded peevish. "However, he is working with you in order to learn how to run a province, K, not how to shoot renegades. Any fool can do that."

"I will reassign your grandson at the first opportunity, Baron," K replied, without missing a beat. "As soon as I have the resources to replace the dead and injured hounds. You will sanction the extra spending, I assume?"

The Baron leant forward and jabbed a finger in K's direction. "First, you will have to convince me that it is necessary. I am hearing suggestions of profligate spending in this province. Such excess would be unacceptable. For *any* Controller. So… what is the truth behind these rumours?"

"Malice. Pure malice," K replied immediately. It was only a rumour. He was safe. For now. "You may send in the auditors whenever you like. Though it would be a waste of precious Council resources, I can assure you. There is no profligacy in my province. I make it my business to run a very tight ship." *And to ensure that the things I want to keep hidden can never be uncovered by any of your blundering auditors.*

"Very well." Marujn relaxed a fraction, then returned to the charge. "Money is very tight everywhere. Not just in America. I cannot sanction an increase. Not for hounds."

K resisted the temptation to gaze at the luxury around them before replying. That would be a crude tactic. Unwise, too. Instead, he said, "We would get better value from existing hound packs if their smell implants were upgraded. We did have one hound with a local experimental upgrade, but she was put out of action, unfortunately." He shook his head sadly at such waste. "That was the raid when your grandson took command," he added, hoping for a revealing reaction from the older man.

There was none. "Impossible to sanction that either, K. Enhanced implants are unproven. Warsaw hasn't even started testing yet. And there are too many demands on the Council's resources as it is. Only projects with the highest return can be approved."

Like the billions you just approved via that link call?

That cynical thought forced its way into K's mind. He pushed it aside, instantly. He dare not lose focus here. Or allow the Baron to suspect what he was thinking.

"I understand, sir." It was not a form of address K used often, but it had the expected effect. Baron Marujn leant back into the shadow and preened again. Then his puffy eyelids blinked once, slowly, like a lizard's. K realised, startled, that Marujn still had the weak, soft-focus eyes of a very old man. They looked like cheap transplants in his smooth, youngish-looking face. But they were almost certainly real, even if nothing else was.

"I do need to press you about the extra hounds, I'm afraid," K went on. "I can cut the numbers to the bone and I'll lengthen their tours of duty, of course, but I won't be able to take Linden off front-line duty unless I have more foot soldiers."

K was on safer ground now. He might even risk haggling.

The bargaining began in earnest. It quickly became clear that the Baron prided himself on his negotiating skills, so K started high and let himself be beaten down to almost nothing. What mattered was to leave the Baron with the feeling that he had won. Even when he had actually been conned into giving K pretty much all he needed.

Satisfied at last, the Baron sat back in his chair and smiled, savouring victory.

Time to leave. And to give him something else to think about, so that he'll forget any questions about the lab.

"Thank you, Baron." K rose quickly and turned to face the desk. He towered over Marujn, who frowned angrily in response. "I will move your grandson from operational duties as soon as I can. I understand that his reassignment is a priority."

The Baron's frown eased a bit.

K tried to look apologetic. "Your grandson's training is going well, but he needs to spend time on resource allocation. It is not a topic he relishes. He prefers action."

The frown was back, and deeper. The Baron did not like what he was hearing.

"I...er... I wonder if you could have a word with him? About the need to consider the resource implications of his operational decisions?"

Marujn's eyes narrowed and his mouth tightened into an angry line. He really did not like being told what to do, even politely. And he was clearly not going to reply.

Job done.

K straightened so that he was almost standing to attention. The Baron would like that. "If you have no other orders for me, sir, I'll get back to Central."

Marujn nodded and waved K to the door without another word.

K marched out, closing the door silently behind him. Keeping his breathing under careful control, he strode back along the windowless corridor. The uniformed female had not reappeared, but that meant nothing. There would still be watchers. So it was important to look like a man who took orders, a man who knew his place.

With luck, the Baron would never discover how he'd been manipulated. And if he did find out…

K refused to think about how dangerous an enemy the Baron could become.

What's done is done. I had no choice.

He had most of the extra hounds he needed. For now, nothing else mattered. The Council might not agree, but maintaining fighting resources was vital.

If K was going to sort out the Jay and his band, he would need every single warrior he could get.

• • • • •

His shot should have dropped her. It *should* have.

But she was still standing.

Linden was *not* seeing things. His weapon had *not* malfunctioned. His crippler had hit her in the heart. She had rocked back a fraction. She had made a low noise somewhere between a grunt and a sigh. But apart from that, nothing.

She was not invincible. She couldn't be. No one was.

So what kind of clever trick was protecting her?

"Not very chivalrous, Linden." She shook her head as she spoke. Sadly, as if disappointed.

What the hell…?

Instantly, Linden was lashed by guilt. He couldn't stop himself. She'd used his mother's exact words. Even her tone of voice. He'd rather she'd shot him.

Faced with this lone woman, he had breached his precious code.

Why? Why now? Why for *this* one?

He admired her. Was that why? Or was he afraid she might beat him? He had started out so sure he would win against any of the Jay women. Now he had doubts.

Especially against this one. This one was a class act.

147

This one was clever, too. She hadn't moved and she hadn't said another word. She clearly knew she was getting to him. But *how* did she know?

Maybe she was reading his mind after all. That could be how she'd escaped from behind the pillar. Had she known he was going to make that mad rush, even before he'd begun? Had she known he was going to shoot her, too?

He shrugged aside the seductive tug of admiration. She had some kind of clever deflector so she wasn't being that brave. She'd known his shot would not harm her.

But she couldn't have been absolutely sure my weapon was still on default. And no deflector could have stopped a killshot. Yet she simply stood there, making herself a target, while she tried to talk me into joining them. Joining her.

The blood pounding up the side of his neck, echoing like a drumbeat inside his skull. He shook his head but it would not clear. "You really expect your enemy to be chivalrous?" he said at last, trying to sound scornful. He wasn't making a great job of it.

"No. I really expect my enemy to use every dirty trick in the book." She stared back at him, waiting for her venom to take effect.

It came as a perverse relief. She couldn't read his mind after all. Or she would have known.

"But I do expect *you* to be chivalrous."

His relief evaporated. This woman was—

"You are not my enemy, Linden. You believe in fighting for what is right. Just as the Jays do." She drew herself up a little straighter and put her free hand to her throat. "Is it right to fight to keep K and his grasping bosses in power? Is it right to gun down unarmed women? If it is, then do it now!" With a jerk of her fingers, she undid her helmet and threw it aside. Her weapon followed. Apart from her goggles, her head was totally unprotected, fragile as porcelain. At this range, it was impossible to miss.

It was impossible to shoot.

He let his weapon hand drop to his side. Then he stood motionless, waiting. It was all he could do.

That was when she smiled. Hesitantly at first, but then it broadened until it lit up her whole face. Even in the dark, even through infrared, she was radiant. He saw then that she had won.

But so had he.

He raised his hand, palm up, and offered her his weapon. It sealed their strange bargain. She accepted it, with a little nod.

Neither of them spoke another word.

There was no need. They knew.

• • • • •

Ellen let out the breath she hadn't noticed she was holding. "I don't believe it," she whispered, gazing at the screen. Jedda and Linden were standing motionless, smiling at each other.

At the same moment, Anton relaxed back into his chair and threw his arms wide. "Wow," he said, puffing his cheeks and blowing out hard. "Well done, Jedda."

Even Chrys was relieved. She gave a nervous little snort of laughter.

Ellen's relief didn't last. OK, Jedda had done it. She had turned Linden when she could have killed him. Should have killed him. But her methods were insane. And how had she known Linden wouldn't shoot her? It had looked as if she were reading Linden's mind, as if she could manipulate him into doing exactly what she wanted.

Ellen had been so sure she had a monopoly on that. She was already vulnerable enough here with these three maniacs and their hidden devices. If Jedda could out-psych her as well...

A knot of fear formed in her gut. She closed her eyes and forced it to dissolve. At least she could still do that.

When she opened her eyes, the other two were staring at her. She shrugged. "So Jedda delivered after all. I'll admit she was good. Very good. Satisfied?" She glowered at them both. The challenge was clear.

For once, even Anton didn't respond. "I'm going to make some coffee, real coffee, to celebrate," he grinned, pushing his chair back with a screech. He glanced at Chrys, who shook her head. He didn't bother to ask if Ellen wanted any. No surprise there. Then he almost danced out to the corridor. Under his breath he was singing.

Self-important little creep!

Now there would be four of them. They'd all be jubilant that Linden had joined the light. They might even try for more defections, more people to undermine K. More ways of ensuring the triumph of good over evil.

Only it wasn't that simple. Never had been. Never could be.

Ellen felt that knot of fear beginning to return. This time, she couldn't will it away, no matter how hard she concentrated.

She must be losing her grip.

Life would never be simple while K was in charge.

NINETEEN

"LINDEN."

Jedda reached out to catch his arm as he got to the foot of the stairs. "You... We..." She swallowed hard. She was the leader. She was used to giving orders. So why couldn't she get the words out now?

He spun around to face her. It was a warrior's lithe movement, but his eyes were not warrior's eyes any more. His gaze caressed her face. "What's the matter, Jedda?" His voice was a caress, too. In the few minutes since he'd learned her name, he'd used it over and over, exploring the sound as though it were something precious.

Jedda fixed her eyes on his vulnerable throat and forced herself to sound much more rational than she felt. "Linden, you know I trust you. But my comrades won't. Why should they? You'll have to prove you're not a spy. And, until you do, I can't let you into our secrets. I'm going to take you back to our bunker but – sorry – I can't let you see where I'm taking you."

Linden responded with a half-smile and a nod.

He understood. Of course he did. Why had she thought otherwise?

Jedda dug into her pocket for the pressure syringe.

He glanced at it and grinned briefly. "Yup, that'll do it. I won't be much of a threat to anyone once you've shoved that trank into me. But you do realise you'll have to more or less carry me afterwards?" He looked her up and down assessingly. "I know you're strong, but I'm no lightweight."

Jedda stroked the syringe with her thumb. Then she looked him over. Slowly. And *very* appreciatively. Why not? They were safe enough here for a moment's self-indulgence. And, however much she wished it, they might not be alone again for a very long time. "Hmm. Nice muscles," she quipped, grinning back at him. "Rather too many for one woman to manage, though."

"So, what will you—?"

"Control. Assistance. Standard tart trap. Plus one."

"Wilco." Chrys's voice in Jedda's ear. "Rendezvous?"

"Ground level," Jedda said aloud. "Franz."

"Wilco. Ten minutes, max. Security?"

"In progress. Out." Jedda didn't need a reminder from Chrys. She'd been about to do the security stuff. Problem was that it would involve a body search. Even thinking about that was...um... unsettling.

Linden raised his eyebrows at her. His grin had gone but he still looked relaxed. "Standard tart trap? Care to explain?"

"You'll see soon enough." Jedda shrugged her shoulders, trying to look as relaxed as he did. "It won't be too good for your image, though."

Stop farting about, Jedda! You've got less than ten minutes and loads to do.

Not for the first time, her stomach lurched. "I need to search you for comms devices and bugs. You know the drill." She looked expectantly at him, waiting for him to raise his arms and spread his legs.

He did neither.

"You said you trusted me."

She nodded. "I do."

"Then let me do it." Within seconds, he produced two comms devices from his clothing. Then an earwig. He disabled them with a wry smile. "Here. That's the lot. And you'd stopped them working anyway. Going to let me in on how you did that?"

Jedda ignored his question. Her warrior's instincts were warning her that it was a diversion. Those same instincts had saved her many times. "I still need to search you for bugs." She dug out her sweeper.

"There aren't any."

Shit, shit, shit! Why did he have to say that? He knows I have to do this.

Jedda weighed the sweeper in her hand and waited.

"Funny kind of trust," Linden said at last. With a shrug, he raised his arms.

There were no bugs. Of course there weren't. She rather expected Linden to say "I told you so," but he said nothing at all. His jaw was tightly clenched. Maybe he was stopping himself from saying something he might regret later?

"We'll go up to ground level. I'll give you the trank there. I don't fancy hauling you up all those stairs by myself." It wasn't a very good joke and it didn't produce a reaction from Linden.

"Fine. You want to lead the way?"

"No." Instinct again. "No, you go first. I'll follow."

This time he did react, with another shake of his head. "Point taken. But it's still a funny kind of trust," he said again. Without giving her a chance to answer, he set off up the stairs, taking them two or three at a time.

OK. You're fit. I already knew that. And you're pissed off at me. I knew that too. But it doesn't change what I have to do. If YOU trusted ME, you'd understand.

They got back to ground level in record time. Linden wasn't even breathing heavily. Neither, to her relief, was Jedda.

"Your *plus one* meets us here?"

"Backup will be outside. But first..." She pulled out the syringe and primed it. "Any preferences?" The standard application site was the side of the neck, but some people hated having it there. She'd give him that choice. It was all she could offer.

"I'd prefer to do it myself." He held out his hand for it.

She hesitated, but only for half a second. She was immune to this trank, so he couldn't use it as a weapon, and he had no others. Besides, she'd know immediately if he didn't give himself the full dose. Why not let him retain a little dignity? "OK then. Lean against the wall, though. You don't want to rely on me to catch you, do you?"

"I want to rely on you for a lot more than you imagine." He took the syringe, checked it with a swift glance, and applied it to the side of his throat before she could say another word. A second later, his knees were buckling.

He was nowhere near the wall.

Jedda grabbed him before he fell and managed to get her arm under his shoulders. She swore aloud. He was even heavier than she'd expected, practically a dead weight. She'd never manage him on her own.

"Backup?"

"Coming in now." A minute later, Chrys was beside her, helping to prop Linden's limp body against the wall.

"Is he clean?"

"He handed over all his weapons. And his comms kit."

"What about hidden bugs?" Chrys demanded sharply.

"I swept him. Nothing."

"OK." Chrys still sounded doubtful. No wonder. Taking K's

number two into their main bunker could be worse than madness. It could be suicidal.

"He's not a spy," Jedda said firmly.

"Doesn't matter either way. We're taking him in. He can give us a lot of useful information. Then we'll decide what to do with him." Chrys's tone was easy to read. She'd pump him dry. She'd leave him a wreck of a man and then dispose of the husk.

No, no, no, no! Jedda could never let Chrys terminate Linden. Never. Not after what had passed between them.

Her logical brain fought to regain control. It told her there was no point in arguing. Not now. "Let's get changed and get going. We need to take him back to the bunker before someone realises he's missing."

Chrys pulled out their tart kit. It took a full five minutes for the transformation. Warriors became whores via a change of dress and layers of thick make-up. Linden wasn't spared, either, though changing him took precious extra minutes.

"We should have done this before you gave him the trank," Chrys gasped, struggling to tug a rumpled jacket onto his arm.

Linden muttered something. Then he giggled. He was only just conscious.

"No. Standard procedure." Jedda was glad to be back in leader mode. "He had to be tranked before you got here. He's seen me. That's all he gets to see. He's still more or less awake, but he won't remember anything that happens from now on."

"And he doesn't have long, anyway," Chrys said firmly. She seemed determined to kill Linden. For the good of the Jays, of course.

He gave himself up to me. His life is mine. I won't allow anyone else to take it.

"OK. Let's go. Control, keep watch. We're coming in." Jedda checked that Linden was adequately supported and started for the door. He would look, for all the world, like a rich man being entertained by two prostitutes. Even the watchers would not wonder at it. Rich men did it all the time. Prostitutes were two a penny. And rich men were much too powerful to be molested by the watchers. They wouldn't dare.

• • • • •

"Linden. Come in."

Still no reply. What on earth was the man doing? He was a maverick, but even mavericks had limits. Where the devil was he?

Linden should be on duty. He wasn't. So was he off doing something he shouldn't be doing?

"Barrack comms supervisor, this is K. I get no response from Linden. Where is he?"

A pause. Then a crackling response. "We've no response from him either, sir."

"Where is he?" K said again.

"We don't know, sir. We've had no contact for several hours."

K couldn't afford to lose the Baron's grandson. Linden had been a bargaining chip in their last encounter and could be again. If he disappeared – worse, if he was killed by the Jays – the Baron would want K's hide, no matter whose fault it was.

"Computer. Check cameras. Find today's last sighting of Linden."

WORKING...

K drummed his fingers on the arm of his leather chair. There must be—

LAST SIGHTING OUTSIDE FRANZ BUILDING. WITH HOUND DELTA. NO SUBSEQUENT SIGHTINGS OR TRANSMISSIONS. The computer played a video recording. The light was low and the picture was grainy, but it was definitely Linden. He was talking to the hound. Then they both entered the Franz building. Eventually, the hound came out, alone. She looked uncertain, but after a moment, she loped off towards the barracks.

Leaving Linden inside the Franz building. Alone?

"Send the hound Delta to me. Immediately."

Find out the facts and work from there. According to the computer, Linden stayed in the Franz building. Why? Is he injured, or even dead? Or has he been spirited away somehow?

K knew that even his own computers had been fooled in the past. That knowledge was beginning to make him feel uneasy.

Delta appeared within minutes. K fancied she'd been waiting for his summons. She looked worried. And rather guilty.

It should be easy to play on her nerves, but it was important not to spook her. She was a solid, dependable hound. He needed those. No doubt she'd just done as she was told.

If there was to be blame here, it must fall on Linden, not on the woman.

"Delta. Thank you for coming so quickly."

She was standing to attention. She didn't move a fraction.

"I'm concerned about Linden," K went on, keeping his voice

friendly and non-threatening. "He's disappeared. I need you to tell me what happened."

K leant forward and smiled in a way he hoped was encouraging. "I'm aware that neither of you reported anything from that location. So you agreed to investigate first, and report later, right?"

"Linden is my pack leader, K. I was following his orders."

K resisted the urge to smile. What else had he expected her to say? "I understand that," he said soothingly, "but I need to know exactly what those orders were. You owe it to Linden – and to me – to be honest about what you both did. Otherwise, we've no chance of saving him. So what did happen?"

Delta shrank a bit in her skin. She seemed to be struggling with herself. Loyalty to Linden, pulling both ways, no doubt. "I…I found a scent at the Franz building. One of the women who'd planted the bomb by the barracks. I…er… reported it to Linden."

She should have reported it direct to Central, but K was too good an interrogator to say so now. He needed her co-operation. Retribution would come later.

"He came to the Franz building right away."

"Alone?"

Delta nodded. "Yes, alone. I was pretty sure there was only one woman in there. He was determined to be the one to take her. He wouldn't even let me help him."

"So you left him there?"

She nodded again. "He ordered me back to barracks. I…I had no choice, K."

No, she had had no choice. She had been wrong to pass the information to Linden rather than to London Central, but everything she'd done after that was by the book. Nothing to be gained by sending her to the cells. It wasn't anyone's fault that Linden was missing. Except Linden's.

Still, even K had to stick to the rules. Dereliction of duty merited penalties.

"Hound Delta." She jerked to attention. His stern tone had told her what was coming. "You are formally reprimanded for your failure to report your intelligence to central command." Her face registered shock, swiftly followed by relief. She would have been expecting much, much worse. Especially from K.

He let his tone soften a fraction. "Now, return to barracks. Get your pack together. You're to search the Franz building and report back to me within the hour." Logic told K that Linden was either lying dead in the Franz building, or hidden somewhere, a prisoner of the Jays. "I don't expect you to find Linden there, but we must be absolutely sure before we conclude he's been kidnapped."

"Sir." She clearly didn't expect to find Linden at the Franz either. But she didn't see how K was going to rescue him if he'd been kidnapped.

"I'm sure I can count on your hound pack to help mount the rescue?"

"Of course, sir. But… do you think you know where he is, who has taken him?"

"Yes," K said flatly. Whether he was right or wrong, the hounds had to believe he was infallible. "Once I have a rescue plan, I'll call out the hounds. Be sure of it."

For the first time, her shoulders relaxed. She had been strung up, but now she believed in salvation, provided by K. It had been worthwhile treating her more as a victim than a criminal. She had believed in Linden. Now she believed in K. Feelings were so very powerful. And so easily manipulated by a man who had none.

"Go now. Keep the hounds busy so they don't have time to worry about Linden. He will be alive. His kidnappers will want information from him and that takes time, especially as he's bound to resist. So we'll have a window of opportunity to rescue him. He will not be allowed to suffer at the hands of his kidnappers. You have my word on that." He kept his own face unreadable as he watched her smile with relief.

If necessary I'll kill him myself. He has too much valuable information inside that handsome head of his. Better dead than read.

"Thank you, K. And I…I'm sorry that I…" Her voice tailed off. Just as well. If she'd said anything more, she'd have put herself in the cells.

"You did your duty. Now let me do mine." He waved her towards the door.

She seemed glad to go. Probably happy to offload her guilt onto someone else.

And now what do I do? Someone has to tell Baron Marujn that his precious – or not so precious – grandson is missing. Not exactly a fun outing.

I suppose it falls to me.

Then what? That nasty, aristocratic little toad will want someone to blame. Not himself, obviously. Probably not his precious

grandson, either. Which doesn't leave many in the line of fire. Apart from me, of course. He'll enjoy blaming me.
I'd better make sure I get my retaliation in first.

• • • • •

The journey back hadn't been easy. No one had sussed them for anything other than the drunken trio they appeared to be, a rich man supported by two high-priced whores. But Linden's reaction to the trank was odd. He should have been half-limp and quiet, but able to help propel himself along. Instead, he'd been noisy, giggly, and a dead weight. Still, none of his mutterings had been intelligible to anyone they met.

Just as well. Jedda suspected some of those mutterings had been about her.

As soon as they were inside the bunker, Chrys applied another dose of trank. She didn't ask Jedda's permission. She clearly felt she didn't need to. What mattered was to put Linden under so that he could see and hear absolutely nothing.

They carried him into one of the empty cells.

"We can leave him to sleep it off."

"No," Chrys said firmly. "We strip him, we search him, and *then* we lock him up till he recovers." She was in charge of security and she knew when she was in the right. "I know you think he's one of us now, Jedda, but we can't be sure. Your instincts tell you to trust him. My instincts tell me he's more likely to be one of K's spies."

Jedda couldn't argue. Instinct wasn't enough. *Knowing* wasn't enough. Chrys was an old, valued comrade. Her doubts couldn't be lightly dismissed.

She shrugged. "OK," she said calmly. "I'm pretty sure we won't find anything, but let's search him anyway. Once we're sure, we can leave him to sleep."

The two women started pulling off Linden's clothes, first the guise of the rich playboy, then the warrior's uniform from underneath. It was difficult to do, because all his limbs were limp and heavy. Half-way through, he began to snore, loudly.

"Trust a man," Chrys said, with a wry laugh. "Just imagine sleeping with him!" She shook her head in disgust.

Jedda gulped and tried to laugh it off, but the picture forced its way into her mind and stayed there. *Sleeping with him...* That was an image she really, really didn't need. Its effects were even worse. Deep in her gut, she could feel heat uncurling. Did it show on her face? Luckily, Chrys was bent to her task which gave Jedda time to get her body back under control.

Chrys finished stripping him. "As male bodies go, that's a beaut," she said. "Keeps himself fit, obviously." She could have been assessing a prize bull.

Jedda found she couldn't speak. Looking at Linden's naked body was all she could manage. What was it he'd said? *It's not my magnificent body you're lusting after.* But it *was* magnificent. And she was...

Chrys wasn't fazed at all, of course. She got on with her job. She searched all the orifices of his body. She examined his teeth. She combed carefully through his shock of fair hair. Then, continuing methodically, she searched through all the rest of his body hair – chest, underarms, genitals. Jedda could only watch, dry-mouthed.

Chrys still hadn't finished. She ran a sweeper over every inch of skin. Apparently that wasn't enough either. She started smoothing her hands over his body, feeling for anything that might be hidden under the skin.

"Nothing on this side. Help me turn him over, Jedda."

Jedda breathed a silent sigh of relief. Gazing down at a beautiful male body was not good for any red-blooded woman's self-control.

Chrys ran the sweeper over Linden's back. Nothing. Then she started with her sensitive medic's hands. "There's something..." She straightened. "He lied to you, Jedda. There's something under his skin. Here." She pointed to a patch of skin just behind Linden's left shoulder blade. There was a tiny, almost invisible lump.

"It can't be anything. The sweeper would have found it."

"Sweepers can be fooled. Let's get it out and see." Chrys reached into her medic's kit for a scalpel and deftly made a tiny slit in the skin.

Even Jedda could see that it was not flesh underneath.

Chrys stood up and stretched out her open hand for Jedda to see what she had retrieved. The thing on her palm was the size of a grain of rice. Shiny, electronic rice.

He lied to me. He said he wasn't carrying any bugs.

"Sorry, Jedda. I admit I don't recognise this, but I'm pretty sure it's some kind of bug. And if it is, everything you've done, and everywhere you've been with him, could be known to his watchers. He's conned you. We could be under attack at any minute."

Had she sacrificed everything because of some stupid conviction that Linden was a chivalrous man? Had she sacrificed all her friends? For this?

Chrys took out her weapon. She was very calm, and icy cold. "Let me kill him. Then, even if they storm the bunker right now, they won't get their precious Linden back."

Jedda couldn't speak.

Chrys waited a beat. Then she lost it. "Jedda? Say something! They'll be on us soon. Let me do it *now*!"

Jedda stared at Chrys. Then down at Linden's naked body. Chrys was surely right. Linden had promised he was clean. Jedda had believed him. He had betrayed her. That bitter realisation settled in her stomach and started clawing its way into her gut. She wanted to throw up.

She had risked everything she believed in. And for what?

She was a complete and utter fool.

TWENTY

"WHAT'S KEEPING YOU TWO?"

From the open cell door, Ellen's voice cut through the tense atmosphere like a guillotine through a naked neck. She saw Jedda's indecision fall away. Jedda instantly stood taller and straighter, with the spark of challenge back in her eyes.

Ellen knew a moment of perverse relief. Even though she was a prisoner here. If Jedda went to pieces, the leaderless group might walk into one of K's clever traps. On the other hand, if Jedda went to pieces, perhaps Ellen would be able to escape?

Not a hope. Chrys was always too watchful. And too handy with her weapon.

Jedda ignored Ellen. And Anton hovering suspiciously at her back. "We'll deal with Linden later, Chrys. He has valuable information. If we have time to extract it, then we will. *You* will. Using any means you like." Jedda was back in leader mode, but the sting of betrayal was all too clear. "First and foremost, we need to deal with this new bug." She took it from Chrys and weighed it in her hand. "For all we know, it could be transmitting our location right now. The sweepers say it's not, but sweepers can be wrong. If it is transmitting, we need to destroy it now, this minute. If it's not, we could perhaps take it apart and find out how it works and what it's been doing."

Jedda glanced across at Linden. His face was half-buried in the pillow. "Turn him over. We don't want him to suffocate." As Chrys did so, Jedda shook out a rough blanket and threw it at Linden's body. It settled in an untidy heap across his chest and chin. From the waist down, he was still naked. "Bring all the clothes he was wearing. We need Anton to search them, thread by thread."

Chrys put out a hand to adjust the blanket.

"Leave it," Jedda spat. "Lock him up." She marched out.

Ellen and Anton had to jump out of the way or they'd have been mown down.

160

Back at Anton's workstation, Jedda dropped the tiny bug. "Is it transmitting?"

Anton sat down and checked it with his specialist kit. "No."

"Are you sure?"

"Yes. That is…"

"You don't know?"

"I've never seen anything like this before," Anton admitted. "It's either very new or very old. Look." He put a probe on it and a magnified image appeared on his screen. There was nothing to see beyond the shiny outer shell. "It's shielded," he said glumly. "I'd have to take it to bits to find out how it works."

"And because of that shield, you don't know what it will do when you break the shell?" Jedda was beginning to sound exasperated.

Anton shook his head. "I'll take precautions. It won't be able to harm anyone."

"Or transmit?"

"Probably not."

Jedda swore. "*Probably* isn't good enough, Anton. If we don't know, we can't take the risk. You'd better destroy it."

"Don't do that," Ellen put in quietly. "I know what it is." She reached across Anton's shoulder for the bug. He was so stunned that he did nothing to stop her.

She cradled the little grain in the hollow of her hand and examined it through a lens. She'd let herself sound as if she knew for certain, but the truth was that – until this very moment – she'd been only half-sure of what they were dealing with. Now, seeing the telltale mark by the seam, she was sure. Grant's Irish labs had made it. Years ago, probably when Ellen was just a trainee engineer. But she knew she wasn't mistaken. She straightened and stared down at Anton, sitting immobile in his chair. "It's a cloudburst," she said with relish.

Anton's eyes widened. Then he frowned. He hadn't a clue.

She was going to enjoy showing them how ignorant he was. "It's a cloudburst," she said again. "Don't *any* of you read tech history? It's not *that* old."

"Just tell us what it does, Ellen, and stop gloating," Jedda growled. "Since you're looking so pleased with yourself, I assume that the thing is *not* transmitting?"

Ellen gave a little snort of laughter. "No, it's not. It can't. Not here."

"So what does it do?" Chrys put in.

"It's purely a passive recording device. That's why sweepers can miss it. It records everything happening around it, including where the subject is. If it's the Mark 2 version, it also records the subject's bodily responses. Heart rate, and so on."

"Funny kind of bug that doesn't transmit, though," Chrys said thoughtfully.

Ellen turned to her. "It does, in a way. That's why it's called a cloudburst. Each device is matched to its own receiver. When the bug gets within range of its base, its receiver extracts all the data in a rapid burst and wipes the bug clean to start again."

"So it can keep going for years? What about power?" Anton asked, breaking his sullen silence at last.

Ellen shook her head. "You *really* don't know your history, Anton. This was pretty much the first useful development of thermal nanobatteries. It charges itself from the heat of the body it's in."

Anton said nothing but his ears had begun to turn that betraying red. He hated being shown up. Especially by Ellen.

Jedda had not moved. She had not spoken, either. And she'd gone very pale. "How long do you think this bug has been in place?"

Ellen looked down at it. "Years, probably. It's pretty old. There was a fad for these devices – among those who could afford them – years ago. I'd need to check exactly when. The craze didn't last long, though. Miniature recorder-transmitters soon replaced cloudbursts. Easier to use. And much cheaper too, so—"

Jedda cut her off with an impatient gesture. "Did he know it was there?" Her voice was so strained it was almost inaudible.

"No way of knowing." A thought struck Ellen. "Where did you take it from?"

"Behind the left shoulder blade," Chrys said.

"That makes it more likely he didn't know it was there, I suppose," Ellen said carefully. "It could have been injected while he was asleep. Or unconscious. Think about it. Most people can't easily reach the middle of their shoulder blades to check the skin. So he wouldn't have felt it. Probably. Doesn't *prove* anything, though."

She waited for Jedda to say something. She didn't. "You could just *ask* him," Ellen said, twisting the knife with relish.

Jedda looked as if she was about to spit in Ellen's eye. "I will. Chrys will. When she interrogates him. In the meantime, we need to know what's on that recording device. Anton? How do we do it?"

Ellen smiled, waiting for Anton to admit his ignorance. Jedda shouldn't have exposed him like that. She wasn't as much in command of herself as she was trying to make out. In normal circumstances, she would never have made such a basic mistake.

So there really was something going on between Jedda and Linden. And it had got to Jedda, in a big way.

Ellen banked her new and potentially explosive information. It might give her an edge when she finally decided to get out of this hellhole.

She waited until Anton's ears had turned the full glorious scarlet before saying, "If Anton hasn't come across cloudbursts before, he won't be able to get at its recording. Open the shell and the recording self-destructs. You can't crack it, can you, Anton?"

Anton muttered darkly. The slight shake of his head was clear enough, though.

"But I can," Ellen announced. She waited a beat. "For a price."

"Of course," Jedda said grimly. "We wouldn't expect anything else from you. But don't expect us to let you go. I'd rather destroy this thing right now."

Ellen raised an eyebrow. "Nice to know how much I'm valued."

"We value your skills, Ellen. And we'll go to any lengths to ensure you don't share them with K. That includes eliminating you."

Ellen felt an urge to laugh in Jedda's face. The woman didn't know the half of it. Sharing *anything* with K would be the end of Ellen. He wanted to own her, mind and body and soul. And what she'd felt when— No, the very thought of being with him terrified her. Surely anything was better than being in his power?

"Look. You don't trust me," she said bluntly, "in spite of the stuff I've done for you. You were prepared to trust that pampered aristocrat you just dragged in—" she ignored Jedda's gasp "—but you won't give *me* the benefit of the doubt. Will you?"

"Tell us what it is you want."

"To stop being a prisoner. Not much to ask, is it? I'm not asking you to give up on the suicide vest. You'd be a fool to go that far and we both know you're no fool."

Jedda thought for a moment. "OK. We'll stop locking you up, though the sleeping cells are not much more comfortable than the lock-up, I warn you."

Ellen laughed dutifully. And waited. They both knew it wasn't enough.

"You can have the run of the bunker." Jedda silenced Anton's spluttering protest before he could get a word out. "No weapons, though. Not unless you're on an op with me, or with Chrys. And the suicide vest stays operational."

"Even here in the bunker? So how do I take a shower?"

Jedda turned to Anton. "You tell her."

He smiled nastily. "It's carefully calibrated, Ellen. You could strip naked and nothing would happen. But get hold of a weapon, any weapon, and the system primes itself automatically, alerting us." He let his smile broaden. "Neat, don't you think?"

Smartass.

But Ellen wasn't about to let Anton guess how much he could rile her. "Fine," she said, looking directly at Jedda. "And I can get on with my own research?"

"Provided you share it. Yes."

"OK. It's a deal. Right now, I need a workstation and tools for the cloudburst."

"You can use that workstation." Jedda pointed to the station furthest from the door. Furthest from escape. "Anton will get you whatever tech stuff you need. How long's this going to take?"

"An hour or two to build the receiver. If I'm lucky, it'll talk to the bug on one of the first links I try. If I'm unlucky…" Ellen shrugged. No need to spell it out.

Jedda said nothing more. She just nodded. Then she walked out of the room and closed the main door very firmly at her back.

Whatever Jedda was going to do now, she wanted to do it alone.

• • • • •

Jedda sat in her tiny dank office and stared unseeingly at the screen. It could have been showing a herd of stampeding elephants for all the difference it made.

No one would disturb her here in her sanctuary. Chrys didn't need to be told. Ellen would be up to her elbows in tech wizardry. Anton would be watching her every move, storing away all the new tricks he saw, looking for ways to get back at her. They were like a pair of quarrelling children. They could do with a good slap, both of them.

None of that solved Jedda's problem.

Linden had sworn he wasn't carrying any bugs. But he had brought one right into the middle of the Jays' precious bunker. That vicious little device was probably still recording their every move.

What kind of range did it have? She didn't know. Ellen hadn't said. Probably not too much. Probably not through thick walls. Probably.

Had Linden known it was there? How could he possibly have missed it?

She argued back and forth with herself, round and round and round. It got her nowhere. Impossible to decide. Impossible to be sure.

Even if she asked him directly, she couldn't be sure. If he'd lied once, he could lie again. He could look into her eyes, soften his gaze, and tell her a bare-faced lie.

And if he was telling the truth, if he really didn't know, how could she accuse him of lying to her? There would be no more trust between them if she did that.

Hell's teeth. What was she to do?

Chivalry. It had got through to him before. Chivalry was the key to him.

Wasn't it?

Enough of this. You're turning into a total wimp, Jedda. What matters here is the future of the Jays. Above everything. Including your sodding hormones. Work out a plan of action and just do it! You can deal with the consequences when they happen.

Action was always good.

She pushed back her chair and strode down the corridor to the cell where they'd left Linden. She put a hand flat on the locked door.

She found herself hesitating.

He was on the other side. What would he say when he saw her?

Deal with it, Jedda. You owe it to the Jays.

She keyed in the code to disable the electronic lock and slid back the bolts. Quietly. No need to announce she was there. She opened the door even more quietly.

He hadn't moved. Nor had the blanket. He was still exposed.

He gave a little snort of a snore and turned his head on one side as she crept in and stood by his head. Trying to decide.

Then she remembered something. She eased her fingers under his left shoulder and raised his body a fraction. There was blood on the bed. And there was blood around the little wound where Chrys had extracted the bug. Normally, she would have applied wound glue. But she'd been too focused on the hidden bug.

Jedda bent down to examine the wound more closely. The bleeding had stopped. So the cut would heal by itself now. She extracted her fingers slowly and carefully and let his body sink back into the bed. Without wound glue, there would probably be a scar. But it would be too small for anyone to notice. Not unless that someone was very intimate with Linden's body, and—

Jedda jumped back from the bed as if she'd been stung. She closed her eyes and took a deep breath. It was no good. This was not solving anything.

Linden had stopped snoring when she put him down, but he had not woken up. He looked totally peaceful. And totally innocent.

He would, wouldn't he?

Jedda sighed and smoothed the blanket down his limp body, gently tucking it under his legs. She didn't want him to get cold.

Didn't want to see his naked body, more like. It was getting to her. Big time.

Let Chrys interrogate him once he'd recovered. Let Chrys find out the truth.

• • • • •

The hounds had found no sign of Linden inside the Franz building. Just as K had expected. They'd lost Linden's scent when the rain started bucketing down again. Still, the local cameras had helped a bit. K knew what he was looking for now: Linden had been smuggled out in the guise of a rich drunk with two prostitutes.

Delta had reported that the two women's scents were not in the data banks. But, in spite of that, K was certain it was some of the Jay's women again. It had to be. No one else would dare mount a kidnapping right under K's nose.

The Jay had to be caught!

K had sent out all available hounds to scour the city for any trace of Linden or the two prostitutes. He was scanning through the video records himself. So far, nothing. Some of the cameras seemed to have been hacked and disabled. Still, that was a kind of clue. If he mapped out the locations where the cameras had been disabled, he'd have some idea of where to start looking. He—

The office door crashed into the wall. The unmistakable figure of Baron Jago Marujn stomped in and planted himself in front of K's desk. "Don't get up," he said brusquely.

Predictable. Standing, Marujn could look down on K in his chair.

"I hear that Linden has been kidnapped. Why did I not hear it from you?"

K assumed a puzzled expression. "I sent a report half an hour ago, Baron, as soon as I knew myself." He would ensure that the logs showed precisely that. "If you didn't receive it, I'll need to get your systems checked. It should—"

The Baron waved a hand impatiently. He probably guessed there was no point in arguing about whether a report had actually been sent. "What are you doing to recover him? Do you know who's holding him?"

K gave him a sketchy overview of the steps he had taken. He ignored the Baron's second question. Much too risky to mention the re-emergence of the Jay and his women. Let the Baron find out once K had the Jay safely in the cells. K really did not want Marujn meddling in anti-terrorist operations. The old despot would do it, given half a chance. He would deliberately screw things up, too, if it suited his ends.

"These terrorist women. They took that Trojan Horse bomb to the labs, didn't they?"

How the hell does he know that? I must have a leak somewhere. Linden?

"As I said, Baron, Linden was drugged and kidnapped by two unknown women," K said quickly, playing for time. Linden couldn't be the leak. He'd undertaken not to tell Marujn, and Linden's code would never allow him to break a promise like that. But if not Linden, then who? "We do not have either of the women in our data banks," K continued, "so I can't tell you whether they are the ones who planted the bomb. However, I can assure you that they won't escape justice for long. All the hound packs are out searching the city." He paused. He needed to divert Marujn from the Jays, even if it meant making a real enemy of the man. "It's a pity I don't have more resources," K said calmly. "I could have used them."

The Baron's eyes narrowed. Time to move onto more conciliatory ground.

Unfortunately, the only conciliatory ground had an executioner's block sitting right in the middle of it. K had no choice, though. He laid his head squarely under the axe. "I expect to discover where Linden is being held in the next few hours."

Marujn's eyebrows rose. "You are very sure of yourself, K." When K did not answer, the Baron said, "You will mount an immediate rescue, I assume?"

"Of course." K took a deep breath. He needed to appear deeply concerned. "I am sorry, Baron, but there is a real risk that we will not bring your grandson out alive."

"You think I don't know that?" The Baron's neck was reddening angrily now. It contrasted starkly with the iron grey of the beard above it. "I'm not a fool, K. I know what terrorists are capable of. If you don't get Linden out, they'll kill him anyway. *After* they've got the information they want from him. That's not a price we can afford."

"You are right, of course. I'll get—"

"And another thing. Bring Linden to my HQ, whatever state he's in. He's not to be taken to the central medical facility. Not under any circumstances. Is that clear?"

What? Marujn must be out of his mind.

"I understand your concern for your grandson, Baron, but surely the military facilities are the best we—"

"Bring him to me, K! That's an order. I'll deal with Linden. Your job is to get him back, dead or alive. So *do* it." He turned on his heel and marched out.

Dead or alive? His only flesh and blood?

There was something very odd going on here. For his own protection, K needed to find out what it was. He couldn't really afford the time, but he closed his eyes and replayed the whole scene in his mind, from the moment the Baron had forced his way in. Every look, every gesture, every word the man had said, until...

Marujn had called the bomb a "Trojan Horse".

That's what Linden called it, too. Here, in this very office.

TWENTY-ONE

JEDDA HEARD A STEP outside her cramped cubicle. She turned as Chrys stuck her head round the open door and said, "Got a minute?"

Jedda raised a hand to wave her in, but said nothing. Right now, she couldn't be sure of controlling her voice. She'd been sitting here for what felt like ages, thinking... picturing... She hadn't been coping very well with what her imagination had conjured up. At least with Chrys here, Jedda would learn the truth of it.

Chrys slipped inside and leaned against the wall for a second or two, gazing down at Jedda in that assessing way she had. Jedda didn't move. After a moment, Chrys reached out to close the door.

Ah. This isn't going to be good.

Stark reality booted out self-indulgence. *Come on, Jedda. Get a grip. You owe it to the Jays.* With an effort, Jedda stretched a vague half-smile. "OK. Tell me."

If Chrys noticed the croaky voice, or any of the other signs of tension, she ignored them. "Nothing," she said flatly. "He won't say a word."

Worse and worse. Jedda swallowed. She had to know. "What have you tried?" Chrys was an expert at extracting information. And inflicting pain. Only when absolutely necessary, of course, but when she had to, she used her skills with scientific detachment. Jedda had never known Chrys to fail.

"I haven't. So far, I've just questioned him. No drugs. No other *encouragement*. I didn't want to do any of that without getting your say-so first. Because you and he..." Chrys raised her chin and shook her head a fraction. As if she had said more than she should. Clearly, Jedda wasn't the only one who had been knocked off-balance by Linden's arrival. In Chrys's case, though, it was surely because of her loyalty to Jedda.

Get a grip, Jedda! Now!

This time, Jedda did obey her inner voice. She focused on her role as leader, and spoke as a leader. "Did he say anything at all?

Any physical indications that he might crack eventually? Heart rate? Blood pressure? Sweating?"

Apparently reassured, Chrys launched into her report. "No physical signs at all. He has amazing control. So some of my normal methods may not work. At a guess, I'd say he's been taught by experts."

"No surprise there," Jedda said quickly, before Chrys could continue. "With his heritage, he can afford the very best. No expense spared in educating the future masters of the world, you know."

Chrys frowned a little, looking rather uncomfortable. This was not the kind of report-back session Jedda usually ran.

"Sorry," Jedda said. "Go on."

"He appears to be taking longer than normal to get over the trank, but that's the only physical sign. Otherwise, he's in first-class shape."

Jedda already knew that. Being reminded by Chrys did not help at all.

"When I questioned him, he gave me a one-sentence answer. Twice. Then he closed his eyes and deliberately ignored me. I got the message. He's an arrogant sod."

Jedda waited.

Chrys looked thoroughly disapproving. "He will talk, but only to you."

Oh.

"What did he say, exactly, Chrys?"

"Um. 'Jedda can have what she wants, but no one else gets it.' Odd choice of words. I put it down to after-effects of the trank. Why not just tell me to piss off?"

"Did you warn him what would happen next if he didn't answer you?"

"Yup. That was when I got the closed-eyes bit. No signs of fear. Total self-control. If I hadn't known better, I'd have said he was enjoying himself." Chrys nodded to herself. So she had been impressed. "If it weren't for that cloudburst bug..."

Jedda waited a beat, but Chrys had finished. There were no more facts, and Chrys wouldn't speculate in front of Jedda. OK. Time for action. "I can have what I want, can I?" Jedda stood up and kicked her chair out of the way. It crashed into the edge of the desk and fell over. "Let's see if he's a man of his word, shall we?"

Jedda threw open the door and strode off in the direction of

Linden's cell. "Bring that cloudburst thing, will you, Chrys?"

"Ellen's still working on it," Chrys protested.

"Bring it." Jedda didn't have to look over her shoulder to know that Chrys would go back to obey her order.

Reaching the door to Linden's cell, Jedda stopped. *Time to regroup. Think. What am I going to do if he refuses to tell me the truth?* She shrugged away the instant mental picture of Linden as a battered corpse. He *had* to co-operate. Otherwise, he'd be signing his own death warrant. There was nothing even Jedda could do to prevent that. When it was a matter of survival, the Jays had to come first.

She pinged the lock and went in. Linden was lying on the bunk with his eyes closed. The blanket was still tucked carefully around his naked body, as Jedda had left it. So Chrys really hadn't done anything to him.

Jedda stomped across the floor and stood threateningly over the bed, legs spread, arms crossed. No reaction. "You wanted to talk to me?"

He opened one eye, took in the situation, and closed it again. No other reaction.

"Funny kind of talk," she snapped.

"Funny kind of trust," he bit back.

Don't lose your cool here, Jedda. He's trying to get to you. And he knows just which buttons to press.

In that moment, her whole body seemed to turn into one giant button. Waiting—

Focus! You can't afford feelings here. This is life and death. His. And yours.

Jedda forced herself to laugh. Let him think she didn't care. "Trust, Linden, is a two-way street. Or had you forgotten? You're living proof that I would have been mad to trust you. We found the evidence."

That single eye opened and closed again. Maddeningly. "Evidence, eh? Roger that." It wasn't a question. More a sarcastic put-down.

"It'll be here soon. If you don't mind waiting." Jedda stepped back and leaned against the wall. She'd have liked to close her eyes, too, to shut out the sight of him, but she wasn't fool enough to do so. Linden might be naked and without weapons but he was strong and, given the element of surprise, he might be able to overpower her.

On the bed, Linden's muscular chest rose and fell in slow,

rhythmic breaths. He could have been asleep.

Jedda knew he was fully alert, fully in control of himself, waiting for her to make a mistake. She wasn't about to oblige. She could wait, too.

"Stalemate?"

Only his lips had moved. Jedda could almost have sworn that there was the thread of a laugh behind that single word. Smartass! Deliberately, she relaxed her shoulders and closed her eyes. Two could play this game of bluff and double-bluff.

She hadn't closed her ears, though. The slightest sound of movement would alert her to defend herself. They were more than two metres apart, after all.

Not far enough.

In an instant, he had seized her, trapping her arms against her sides. She hadn't heard a thing. Next moment, his whole weight was pinning her against the wall. She'd lost. She couldn't move. She could hardly breathe.

Then he kissed her, and she couldn't breathe at all.

He took his time. Exploring. Relishing. As if he were tasting some priceless exotic fruit that he might never taste again.

She should have struggled. She couldn't move, but she should have struggled.

She didn't.

But at least she didn't respond. Even though her body was screaming for her to kiss him back.

At last he broke the kiss and moved back a fraction. "Hmm. Definitely a woman of contradictions." His gaze was fixed on her lips.

Jedda clamped them tight shut.

He laughed. "Doesn't make your mouth any less kissable, you know."

Bastard!

"But as we'll probably be having company any moment, I won't attempt to prove my point." He let her go and vaulted back onto the bed, tucking the blanket back exactly where it had been and closing his eyes. Everything was the same as before.

Except for the prominent bulge under the blanket.

Jedda laughed. For real this time. No doubt her colour was high and her lips were a little swollen, but Linden wasn't immune either. His yoga-master might have taught him all sorts of bodily control, but at least one of them wasn't working. "You might want to loosen that blanket a bit before Chrys comes back."

He opened his eyes and looked at her. Just as he had when they were standing together in the Franz building. Before any of this began. Then he raised his head a fraction and glanced down his body. "Nope. Don't think I will." And lay down again.

Damn the man. He's proud of himself!

Jedda put her fingers to her mouth. It didn't feel much different. *Kissable?* She had to forget that. And her stupid, dangerous reaction to Linden. If he was a spy – and why else would he have brought a bug into their bunker? – then reducing the rebel leader to a puddle of hormonal jelly was a great way to get exactly what he needed. She had been so sure that she was more than a match for him.

Now she knew she wasn't.

She pushed the thought away. Chrys would arrive at any moment. Jedda needed to be back in charge. She rubbed her hands roughly over her face and through her hair. Better to look dishevelled than aroused. She forced her brain to focus on what would happen now. Chrys would produce the bug. Jedda would confront Linden with it. Then they'd see where the trust really lay.

Jedda leaned back against the wall again, closed her eyes – she knew for certain that Linden would stay exactly where he was this time, so she wasn't taking a risk – and practised the breathing techniques that would give her the control she needed.

It took a while, but it came. Just as the door opened.

Chrys, looking wary. She glanced round the cell. First at Linden, whose erection had subsided a bit. Then at Jedda. "He attacked you?"

"Nothing I couldn't handle," Jedda lied. She gestured towards the figure sprawled on the bed. "He's not a threat any more. As you can see."

"Yeah, right." Chrys held out her hand. The sinister little grain of rice was cradled in her palm.

Jedda took it. "Care to join the conversation, Linden? You did say you'd talk to me, didn't you? And I've got something here that I'd really, really like you to explain."

Linden stretched lazily and got to his feet, wrapping the blanket round his body like a toga. It left his legs bare from the knees down. And one shoulder.

Bloody hell! Did he HAVE to do that?

He reached out to take the bug but Jedda was too quick this time. She closed her fingers over it. If he got it, he might destroy it. And

173

Ellen hadn't finished with it yet.

"You get to see. You don't get to touch."

Linden dropped his arm. He shrugged. "I know when I'm outnumbered. OK. Let's do the seeing bit."

"Back off." Only when he'd done so did Jedda open her fingers again.

Linden bent and stared at the bug for a long time. "Haven't a clue," he said, squaring his shoulders, and looking Jedda straight in the eye. "It must have been planted. By this scary mate of yours, maybe?" He jerked a thumb in Chrys's direction.

That was going too far. Jedda gave Chrys a tiny nod.

Chrys reached a hand behind Linden's back and pinched his flesh. Linden's sharp intake of breath proved she'd got her aim just right. She followed up by showing him the bright blood on her fingers. "Your blood. Your back. Your bug."

Jedda held his gaze. "I'm waiting, Linden," she said into the silence.

His face was beginning to look strained. Was he struggling to concoct a plausible lie? There wasn't one, was there?

In the end, he just shrugged his shoulders. A spasm of pain crossed his face. That unhealed wound was small, but nasty. Chrys had made sure it hurt. "I told you. Haven't a clue. Make of that whatever you like."

· · · · ·

K himself swept his office for bugs. Clean. At least the sweeper *said* it was.

K's doubt remained; and festered. There was nothing he could do about that, or about anything else. Not until he had some clue to Linden's whereabouts. The hound packs were all out, but so far, nothing. Same with the computer searches. K was effectively a prisoner here in Central, waiting for news. It could be hours yet.

He needed exercise. Get the adrenalin pumping, to get rid of his frustrations.

He slipped through the private door and down the passage that led to his apartment. He could have a quick session in his holo suite. See if he could do better than last time. His concentration had been off then, because of—

He flatly refused to think about that. He had lost control. It wouldn't happen again.

He allowed himself fifteen minutes to prove it. And he did. Much more satisfying results this time. Back to his usual practically perfect score. Possibly because one of his holographic opponents had been made to look a lot like Linden?

Linden, the real flesh-and-blood Linden, remained a real flesh-and-blood problem. And as for that pocket Napoleon...

Marujn was much more of a threat. Marujn had the power to interfere with K's operations, perhaps even sabotage them. Linden couldn't do that, except perhaps by accident. Linden was more of a nuisance than a threat.

K swam in his private pool afterwards, though he could not afford the time for his usual quota of lengths. Much less satisfying. On the range, the mind was fully occupied with staying alive, and with eliminating every last one of the enemy. In the pool, the mind was free to wander, and to worry. Normally the mathematical rhythm of his strokes could produce an almost zen-like calm. Today it failed totally.

He kept his focus on the Linden problem. It had to be sorted. In the final analysis, it wasn't difficult. Linden had to be rescued. Or Linden had to be terminated.

Termination was easier, almost certainly. Given recent incidents, it was probably better, too. Provided Marujn would buy it.

What kind of man wants his only grandson returned, dead or alive? It makes no sense. Marujn himself makes no sense.

Even more reason to be wary of Marujn. He was dangerously unpredictable. A large part of K's success depended on his ability to predict what men would do. K had honed that skill over years, developing his own personal list of character types, from the bullying weakling to the cerebral coward. But Marujn didn't fit into any of K's neatly-defined boxes. He was as difficult to second-guess as K himself.

Less than forty minutes after he had left it, K walked slowly back along the passage to his office, still mulling over his options, still trying to decide *how* to achieve his goal. His body felt pretty relaxed, but his frustrations still lurked, nagging at him.

Before he had even touched the door handle, the smell told him who was waiting for him. And that it had nothing to do with Linden.

Tauber had made himself at home and was smoking one of his disgusting cigars, filling K's immaculate office with stinking fug. K steeled himself not to react.

Tauber jumped to his feet the moment K appeared. A stream of words poured out of him, almost every phrase accentuated by his flabby right hand waving the half-smoked cigar. "Where were you,

K? I tried to reach you but got no reply. We had an emergency. A male birth, about an hour ago. Premature. In your absence, I had to deal with it myself but, as you know, that is not a problem since I am fully versed in—"

K did not attempt to get a word in. He merely raised his eyebrows, fixed his narrowed gaze on the South American's face and looked his question. *Explain.*

Tauber stopped dead. Swallowed. "Antenatal screening malfunction. It was a Blue."

Ah. Very quietly, K pulled out his chair and sat down behind his desk. He did not take his eyes from Tauber's.

"The mother was immediately sterilised, of course."

"And the child?" The stink of the commissar's tobacco was really getting to K now, quite apart from the man's insufferable arrogance in daring to smoke here without K's express permission. K felt the mask of disapproval settling on his features. He tried, but failed, to keep looking neutral. Very annoying to lose control like that. Tauber must have noticed the change in K's expression, however, for he had stopped talking altogether. "Well? What about the child?" K repeated.

"DNA testing proved it beyond doubt. Standard procedures were followed, K." Tauber took a long, rather nervous pull on his cigar.

"So the child is dead?"

"Yes."

"Are you sure?"

That question had exactly the effect K intended. Tauber's shoulders relaxed. He thought he knew where he stood. "Oh yes. I terminated it myself."

Yes, Tauber would enjoy that. His name was thoroughly misleading; he was not a German, and he was certainly not a dove.

"The body has gone to the lab for further investigation."

That was standard procedure, too. The body would be tested to the nth degree to discover how the blue gene had managed to manifest itself in spite of all the state's precautions. The crucial fault would lie with the mother, of course. It invariably did. Either she had a recessive blue gene that the screening had somehow managed to miss, or she'd had a random mutation in her egg. The sperm was to blame too, of course, but there was nothing to be done there. Viable Y sperm was as rare as water in the Sahara. It couldn't be discarded even if it did have recessive blue in it.

Tauber would have to ensure that future breeding from that batch of sperm was only from women who had been proven to have totally pure Not-Blue genes.

In fact, Tauber should have done so this time round. He had failed in his duty there. Precious Y sperm had been wasted, not to mention all the other scarce resources involved in a live male birth.

K relaxed into his big black chair. He was trapped here, waiting for news. He might as well spend the time pointing out Tauber's many shortcomings.

Yes, he would enjoy that.

• • • • •

"I can't let you loose on him until we find out what was on that bug, Chrys. I know you don't trust him, but it is just possible he didn't know it was there. If there's any chance he might be useful to us, I don't want to waste it. But Ellen's taking for ever." She turned to shout across the room. "Ellen, how much longer?"

"I've just got the last of it. Come and see for yourself."

All three Jays crowded round Ellen's workstation. Her screen was playing some kind of recording – street noises, the muffled sound of a slow, regular heartbeat, then voices. Ellen stopped the recording. "That's Linden talking to one of the hounds. Delta. They're outside the Franz building. She's clearly the one who found the scent trail we laid and called him in. Unfortunately we don't have a recording of what she said over the comms link. The bug didn't start working till he got out into the street."

"And there's nothing from earlier?"

Ellen shook her head. "No. The bug must have been wiped clean not long before he set off."

"Not necessarily," Anton put in. "The bug might not record at all inside the mansion. Or only record during certain hours of the day. That's possible, isn't it?"

"Yes, in theory," Ellen admitted grudgingly. "But the earlier stuff is definitely not there. So the bug was read and wiped very recently. Maybe in K's office."

"I don't think so. That's—"

"Save it for later, Anton," Jedda said sharply. "Let's hear what we do have. Then you two can figure out the working parameters of this little beauty. Ellen?"

Ellen nodded and restarted the playback. It was all there: the discussions with Delta, how Linden had sent her away – Jedda noted smugly that he was just as chivalrous as she'd said – his search for the owner of the scent trail, and his confrontation with Jedda.

"OK. That's enough. We know exactly what happened from then on."

"No, we don't, Jedda," Ellen put in. "You're forgetting that we have a readout of his physical reactions, too. Not just his heartbeat. But all this as well." She pointed at the lines being traced at the bottom of her screen. "If we play it through to the end, especially the bit where he's giving himself up to you, we ought to be able to work out whether he's genuine or not. His physical control is good, but not that good. Look. See that spike?" She pointed to the screen again. "Now, if I run it back a bit and play the recording from just before that spike, we'll see what it was that got to him."

Jedda couldn't bear to look at the screen. She turned her back and left them to it. She heard the long silence of his surrender. Then she heard his voice. That caressing tone. And then hers, full of distress as she forced him to go through the body search.

Ellen stopped the playback right there. "I think we've heard enough."

Silence. No one spoke. No one moved. Were they embarrassed at hearing – and understanding – such a deeply personal encounter?

Jedda knew it was up to her. She turned back to face them. Hands on hips, frowning dangerously, she spat out the question. "Well? Is he a spy, or isn't he?"

TWENTY-TWO

"RUN IT FROM THE point where I started the skin search," Chrys said.

Obediently, Anton pulled up the video recording from Linden's cell. It showed him lying on his back, naked, with Chrys running her sensitive hands over his skin. "What do you want this for?" Anton said, with a glance back over his shoulder. "Surely *you* haven't got the hots for him as well?"

"Shut it, Anton!" Chrys snapped, losing her cool for a moment. Usually she could tolerate Anton's nasty tongue, but occasionally he caught her on the raw. She shouldn't lash out at him, though, even if he deserved it. "You wouldn't have said that if Jedda had been here. So keep it buttoned when she's not." True, even if a bit curt.

Anton tensed visibly. Did he think Chrys was calling him a coward?

Possibly. But Chrys had more important things to do than massage Anton's ego. She needed to be sure. She gestured towards the screen. "Turn him over."

"Eh?"

"We're really not on the same wavelength here, are we, Anton? Think about it. It's his back I want to see. Run it on to when I'm doing his back."

"Oh." He sounded a bit chastened. Good.

"Stop it there." The screen froze just before Chrys's fingers discovered the cloudburst bug. "Can you blow it up? I want to see that in detail." She circled an area of the screen with her forefinger.

"What are you looking for?" Anton asked. "I can't see anything."

"That's what I'm looking for."

"Eh? You're not making sense."

Chrys chuckled. "You'll see in a minute. Can you increase the contrast? And the resolution?" She continued to peer at the screen. "You're right, Anton. There's nothing. And everything." She allowed herself to smile. It was satisfying to be sure.

Anton gave her a very strange look. "Are you losing your marbles? You never used to talk in riddles."

She could tell him. She probably should tell him.

On the other hand, she could leave him trying to puzzle it out for himself. Yup. That would do it. Score one for the Warriors against the Geeks.

• • • • •

K was back in Marujn's soulless antechamber, waiting for the summons to the august presence. This time, however, the meeting was K's idea.

He had no choice. He had to tell Marujn before someone else did.

K had rashly said it would only take hours to find Linden. It had. In a way. But K was no nearer getting Linden back.

A uniformed woman delivered him to Marujn's office, just as before. Nothing else had changed either, except that Marujn could not conceal his eagerness for news. He spoke before the door had closed. "You asked to see me? I take it you've found where Linden is? So when are you going to get him out? I told you, I want him here."

No point in prevaricating. Give it to him straight.

"I am sorry to tell you, Baron, that your grandson appears to have defected. He's joined a bunch of terrorists."

Marujn looked as if he had been coshed. Eventually, after a long silence, he spluttered, "That's impossible. He can't have. You're trying to cover up the fact that you haven't been able to rescue him. I'll have your hide for this, K."

K did not say a word. He stood in front of the Baron's desk and stared him out. *Give him time to realise that it can't be a lie. That it's too easy to check. Watch him realise whose hide will be nailed to the barn door when this news reaches the rest of the Council.*

It worked. Marujn's normal healthy colour leached out of his face as he thought through the implications – for himself – of a family defection.

"You have proof?" Marujn's voice cracked on the last word.

"The terrorists announced it themselves. Cards found all over New Piccadilly."

"What? Why wasn't I told?"

"Because the message was in code. Intelligible only to London Central." He pulled out a small white card and passed it to the Baron.

It was much the same as before. Except worse, because it was Linden. *"Stop looking. We have him and he's staying. He's joined the light."* The signature, the cartoon of that damned bird, was exactly the same.

As proof of Linden's treachery, it was not exactly conclusive, and K knew it. But his gut told him it was true. It fitted with everything he'd suspected about Linden's character. Too chivalrous by half. Easily seduced by idealism.

K waited while the Baron digested the fact that the Jays had reappeared. And what they were claiming about Linden. He expected the old man to argue, to say it was a terrorist bluff, to insist that Linden must still be rescued.

Marujn's words came out through clenched teeth and with more venom than even K would have thought possible. "He's corrupted. That woman corrupted every man she touched. First my son, and now Linden. He's to be shot on sight."

"Don't you want to—?"

"And I want his body. Here. Untouched. Do I make myself clear?"

• • • • •

"You really didn't know it was there, did you?"

Linden stared up at Chrys, trying to read her. She'd simply marched into his cell and rapped out her question. Her voice was a bit different, though. She didn't sound quite like the icy inquisitor of the previous day. So what had changed her mind?

He wrapped the blanket more securely round his middle and started to get up. He hated having a warrior standing over him, especially when he was defenceless.

"Just a friendly chat, Linden. You don't need to get ready to spring."

Against Chrys, he'd have no chance. She'd kill him in a heartbeat.

"Where's Jedda? Has she changed her mind too?"

"Since you didn't know it was there," Chrys said calmly, ignoring his question, "we need to work out how it got into you. And when."

"I don't know. How many times do I have to say it? *I don't know!*"

Chrys took a deep breath and sighed it out slowly. For a moment, she reminded him of an old schoolteacher, trying to hold on to her temper while explaining the basics to a particularly thick

181

pupil. "You don't *know*, Linden, but with the application of a little brain power – and I know you do have that, somewhere in that thick skull of yours – we may be able to work it out. Between us."

"Where's Jedda?" he asked again. "Did she send you?"

"What Jedda needs, right now, is more info about that bug you brought in with you. So can we concentrate on that? Then I can report back to her."

Then maybe I'll get to see her? Is this grand inquisitor telling me I don't get to see Jedda unless I co-operate?

It seemed she was. She asked a series of questions about Linden's past, where he'd lived, where he'd been educated, when he'd first started working with K, when he'd moved into the Marujn mansion. It went on and on. By the time she got to medical stuff, he'd had enough. He couldn't attack her, so he swore at her, using the worst gutter language he knew.

She didn't turn a hair. "Better?" she said sweetly, when he ran out of breath.

He had to laugh. Jedda's grand inquisitor was a class act.

"Your regular medicals," she went on. "Have you been conscious throughout?"

"I…" Ah, he was beginning to see where she was going. "Yes, I have. For all of them."

"OK. Any emergency treatment ever? Anaesthetics?"

"Not since I was a kid. When I broke my leg not long after my mother died."

"Uh huh. That could do it." She nodded to herself, with pursed lips.

"Oh come on. That was years and years ago. You're not really saying that—"

"I'm not *saying* anything, Linden. I'm looking for possibilities. Look, someone put a bug in your back. There was no visible scar, so it wasn't recent. Either that, or someone did it recently and took great care to ensure that there was no scar. Seems unlikely, given what we know."

Know?

They might know, but he didn't. "*What* do you know? Come on. Give! It's my body we're talking about here."

"You said yourself that you'd always been conscious when dealing with medics. You'd have known if they'd been fiddling with your back."

That wasn't all of it. Her response had been too quick, too glib.

"And?" he said calmly. "I do have to sleep. We both know that. I could have been tranked and I wouldn't have known a thing. But you're not even considering that as a possibility. So why? What else do you know that you're not telling me?"

Chrys clamped her lips together. She might have changed her mind about Linden the spy, but she wasn't going to drop her inquisitor's role. She only did questions, not answers.

Linden said nothing, waiting. Why should he volunteer information if they didn't trust him enough to share?

The silence lengthened. Stalemate. No, a stand-off. Fine, he could do both.

The click of the opening door took them both by surprise.

Jedda was standing there, looking good enough to eat. There was something about her skin – had she been out in the early morning air, taking the wind and rain in her face? Her eyes were sparkling, bright as fresh raindrops. She was slightly flushed, too, and her colour deepened a fraction more as she looked at him. He didn't dare to think about how satisfying that was. Not with only a thin blanket round his middle. And not with Chrys watching, eagle-eyed. He'd embarrassed Jedda quite enough the last time. She wouldn't forgive him if he did it twice.

"Good morning," he said politely. Even Jedda couldn't object to that.

To his surprise, she ignored him and turned to Chrys. "Tell him."

Chrys's eyebrows rose. Then she shrugged. "The bug is very old technology. Hasn't been used for years. But we've managed to break it."

His pulse shifted up a gear. "So you know what it was for? And who was using it?" He ran a hand through his hair. "K, I suppose. I wouldn't put anything past him."

Jedda shook her head. Rather sadly, he thought.

K wouldn't use out-of-date technology. And how would he have got it into me?

Suddenly, old words sang through Linden's brain. *"When you have eliminated the impossible, whatever remains, however improbable, must be the truth."* Yes. There was only one possible culprit. Linden took a deep breath. It burned into his lungs with poisonous certainty and the bitter sting of betrayal. It had to be—

"I'm sorry, Linden," Jedda said softly. "It must have been your grandfather."

· · · · ·

"You've really put the wind up K, Jedda," Anton said, with obvious satisfaction. "The moment he got his hands on one of your cards, he was off to give Marujn the glad tidings. I'd love to have been a fly on the wall. Wouldn't you?"

"K's too clever to let Marujn pin the blame on him," Jedda said, with a shrug. "Pity. It would be good to have his head on the block."

"It might be Marujn's head," Chrys put in. "He may be in the Council but he has enemies. Even a Council member will have difficulty explaining why one of his family has defected to the Jays. Linden may get revenge for that bug, without lifting a finger."

Jedda noticed that Ellen said nothing. She had been listening silently, sitting apart from the main group, free now, but still not fully accepted or trusted.

Jedda knew that Marujn was beyond the Jays' reach, at least for now. "Forget Marujn. We need a decision about Linden. Are we all agreed that he's not a spy, that the bug was planted on him by Marujn?" She fixed her gaze on each of them in turn, waiting for their nod of agreement. Chrys. Then Anton. "What about you, Ellen?"

She straightened, surprised. "Do I get a vote then?"

"Yes," Jedda said simply. Without Ellen's tech skill, the Jays would never have been able to break the cloudburst's secrets. Jedda was beginning to think that Ellen was an asset the group could not afford to lose. Which meant she had to be fully won over. Somehow. "Well? What do you think?"

"The bug was planted by Marujn. I'm sure of that. Can you trust Linden? That's another question altogether. Funny thing, trust."

"Not another one," Jedda muttered, and immediately wished she hadn't. Chrys and Anton gave her very strange looks. Ellen – who was much too perceptive for comfort – looked a little smug. Unlike the others, she had listened to every word of the recordings. Her choice of words could have been deliberate. She liked rattling people.

"We'll trust him as much as we trust you, Ellen," Jedda retorted, deciding as she spoke. "Anton, fix him a set of clothes. Same deal as Ellen's." She did not bother to warn him that Ellen must not see how the destruct mechanism was concealed. "When you've done that, you need to fix his smell bots, too. Every hound in the province will be looking for Linden's scent trace."

The clothes they had put on Linden's tranked body at the Franz building had been heavily impregnated with Anton's bogus scent patterns. The Jays had even sprayed his boots. With luck, it would have confused the questing hounds.

Jedda glanced at one of the monitors. "Look. The weather gods are on our side. It's pouring again," she announced, with satisfaction.

Chrys nodded. Anton grinned. Ellen just sat.

I have to find a way of bringing her into the fold. But Linden first.

She could feel that betraying warmth again, uncoiling deep in her gut. Would she ever be able to control her reaction to him?

I'm a leader first. And then a warrior. Personal stuff – the word "lover" jumped into her mind and she pushed it away, fearful of where it might lead – *comes third.*

"Chrys, I need some of your kit. Then I want you to help Anton. I'm going to tell Linden what we've decided."

Chrys's startled expression was too easy to read. She didn't think Jedda should be alone with Linden. Not after the last time.

She may be right. But I have to find out for myself. I have to know.

She had given her orders. She didn't have to justify her decisions. With a bland smile, she strode off to collect what she needed for her one-on-one with Linden.

· · · · ·

Jedda pinged the lock on Linden's cell. "Make yourself decent, Linden," she called through the door. *No more nasty surprises. Please.* She gave him a full minute.

He was lying on the bed, staring at the ceiling, and naked to the waist. The blanket was folded thickly and lay loosely over his lower body. So there should be no betraying bulges. Was he trying to spare her? Or himself?

She nodded a greeting. "I've come to dress your wound," she said briskly, waiting for him to sit up. "We should have fixed it at the time, but we…er…"

"You had other things on your mind," he said quietly, not moving at all. "Like defending your hideout. You thought that bug would bring in K's attackers."

He *did* understand.

"How do you want me?" he went on, in precisely the same quiet voice. But his eyes, behind half-closed lids, gleamed mischief. And more.

He understands too much and too well.

Jedda dug into Chrys's medical pack and pulled out a pressure syringe. She waved it at him. "I *want* you co-operative, Linden. Do I have to use trank again?"

He flashed her a grin and sat up, exposing his naked back down to his buttocks. Then he leaned forward, clasping his arms round his bent legs and dropping his head onto his knees so that his face was turned away from her. The movement stretched the little wound in his back and it started to bleed, sluggishly.

"So the scary one does the wounding, and you do the healing?"

"What? No. No, that's not it. Chrys is the medic. I…my skills are pretty basic." She was having difficulty keeping her mind on her task. That long expanse of silky skin was demanding to be touched. No, not touched. Caressed.

"OK. So why are *you*…?" He let the question hang in the air. And it brought Jedda back to earth with a bump.

Screw him. He knows precisely why I want to do this myself. Now he's winding me up. Deliberately.

Without a word, she started cleaning the wound. She was hurting him a fair bit – and she meant to – but he did not make a sound. He did not flinch, either.

Tough cookie. Only to be expected. We both know we're playing games here. But what's the prize for the winner? And do I want the winner to be him, or me?

She didn't know the answers, so she worked on, waiting for Linden's next move.

And waiting. And waiting.

Linden was so focused on deciding what to do that he barely noticed the rough handling. He didn't care about it, anyway. What he cared about was the fact that Jedda had come to do it herself, when she could have sent the medic. So had she forgiven him for attacking her? And embarrassing her in front of the inquisitor?

He didn't regret any of it. That kiss had been worth it. And he would really, really like another. Plus everything that came after. That mental image was an invitation to lust, and his body responded like a stallion scenting a mare in heat.

Bin the sexy thoughts, Linden! You can't afford a cock for a compass. It's still odds-on that this mob will kill you. Lust won't keep you alive. Brains just might.

He had to find a way of convincing Jedda that he did trust her, that she could trust him, and that he really did want to join the Jays. For her. And for all the things that he'd believed in, long ago, before his grandfather had persuaded him to become a warrior for the state, against the forces of chaos. *Damn him!* The old man had been so clever, knowing exactly what to say to convince an adolescent who had lost all the other anchors in his world. He'd even brought Linden into his London home, as if it were a mark of affection. But the old man only did betrayal. All he wanted was a portable spy, someone who could carry a bug into K's secret lair, and the barracks, and the labs—

A feather caressed Linden's back.

His heart stopped. And raced out of control.

It wasn't a feather. It was the back of Jedda's hand, stroking so lightly that her skin barely touched his. It felt like a brand. His skin was burning. Throbbing with something like pain.

He grabbed wildly and pulled her down on top of him in a tangle of bodies and blankets. This time, she did respond.

It started as a clumsy, desperate kiss. But soon she settled into his embrace and they started to explore each other, with long delicious kisses that were getting more passionate by the second. And more urgent.

He knew where this was going, in spite of the cameras in the cell. He didn't care. If Jedda wanted this – and her eager mouth told him that she did – then so did he.

He struggled with his one free hand to pull the blanket out and throw it on the floor. Better. Now he could pull her close against his naked body. "You're wearing too many clothes," he groaned, halfway through planting a line of tiny kisses along her luscious lower lip. He put his fingers to the fastenings of her combat jacket. The rip closure gave way when he tugged.

There were more layers underneath. But thinner. Now he could caress the swell of her breasts. She was on her left side, with his arm between her body and the bunk. Her left breast was resting tantalisingly on his biceps – warm, and heavy, and inviting. But her right breast was more accessible to his free hand. He let his fingers wander down from her throat until they brushed her nipple through the fabric. Just once. Then, with two fingertips, he started to trace a path round and round her breast, a couple of centimetres away from her nipple. He refused to let the path get any closer.

She groaned into his mouth.

Yes, two could tantalise. And two could yield. He allowed his wandering touch to trek nearer, until, at last, he was caressing her nipple. It was swollen, waiting.

He needed to see her breast. To kiss her glowing skin.

He reached for the neck of her shirt. Not long now.

"No."

He didn't hear the word. He *felt* it like a scalpel through his flesh. His world crashed around him.

He couldn't speak. He thought he might explode. He pulled sharply away from her and leaned back against the wall, trying to ignore the demands of his body. He closed his eyes, but it was no help. He wanted her, more than any woman he'd ever known, and she was rejecting him.

She hadn't moved. Her face had gone white, but there was still a flush of arousal on her throat. Her hair was all over the place. For the first time, he saw that she had a long white scar beside her ear. His brain wanted to know how she'd got it, how she had survived. His baser instincts wanted to kiss his way from her hairline to the end of the scar, and then to start nibbling the lobe of her ear. Followed by all the rest of her.

She put a hand to her face, touching her skin as though uncertain of what she would find. Linden thought he saw a tiny tremor in her fingers.

"I'm sorry, Linden. We can't."

He clamped his lips together. He wanted to know why she had led him on, but he was too proud to say it. She knew he wanted her. He was naked, for fuck's sake, so it was blatantly obvious. He started to slide down the bunk, to reach for the blanket.

She stopped him with a hand on his arm. "I'm sorry, Linden." Her voice was barely a thread. "I do want you. But it's impossible."

It made no sense. He turned back and just stared. She did want him. She did.

"Why?" No sound came out. He cleared his choking throat and tried again. "Why, Jedda?"

"Because of the Jays. We're warriors here. A team. Each of us relying on all the others. Feelings...sex... Oh, they make life impossible for everyone. If you're going to become one of the Jays for real, we have to stick to the rules. And that means no emotional entanglements. And especially no sex."

"You know what, Jedda? Your precious Jay's rules stink. And when I finally get to meet this guy who makes up stupid rules and hides behind warrior women, I'm going to tell him exactly what I think of the way he runs this outfit. Why the hell is a woman like you loyal to a leader who treats you like dirt?"

"I'm not. He's been dead for years. *I'm* the leader of the Jays. I make the life or death decisions here. And *my* warriors carry them out."

Linden felt like an amateur boxer who'd done ten rounds with the heavyweight champion of the world. Winded didn't begin to describe it.

And then she took a deep breath. And some primitive part of his brain was still riveted on her body, watching how her breasts rose and strained against her clothing.

"Linden, if you join us, you stick to the Jays' stinking rules. They're *my* rules."

TWENTY-THREE

ELLEN WAS PRETTY EXHAUSTED when she got back from the workout in the holo suite. It had been barely half an hour, but Chrys certainly knew how to make a woman sweat. Of course it had been done to keep Ellen out of the way while Anton created the destruct-suit for Linden. Ellen knew that; Chrys knew that; both of them pretended that it was routine exercise, something all warriors needed to do.

Chrys was applying Jedda's rule three: courtesy at all times.

Fair enough. Chrys is tough and dangerous, but she plays by the rules. Do I?

Ellen was not at all sure. Part of her wanted to. But that would mean giving up the wriggle room that she might need to use to get away.

I'll decide when I have to. Not before.

Ellen stopped in the doorway, looking round central control. Jedda was back at her usual station. She'd lost the glow she'd had when she came back from planting the New Piccadilly cards. In fact, she looked a bit off-colour, suddenly. Ellen didn't waste energy on that puzzle. She had recognised, early on, that Jedda kept her troubles to herself. Probably because she'd been taught that it was what a leader had to do.

Eventually it will be the end of her. She'll break down completely, or explode.

It was not Ellen's problem. She put it out of her mind.

Chrys, looking much fresher than Ellen felt, was checking the various monitors. Anton was working on the smell-bots for Linden.

"So where's Linden?" Ellen said casually.

Jedda didn't raise her head from her screen. It was Chrys who answered. "He's still in his cell. Anton's just given him his clothes. He'll be here in a few minutes."

Lucky Linden, to be accepted so quickly. What did he have that Ellen didn't?

The answer was so obvious, and so crude, that Ellen was startled into laughter.

Jedda raised her head. "What's so funny, Ellen?" She sounded more than cross.

Ellen shrugged and started across to her workstation. "I was thinking about poor Anton," she lied glibly. "He's going to have his finger on two destruct buttons at once. How will he ever cope?"

Anton glanced up as she passed and gave her a look that was pure venom.

Ellen responded with the politest of smiles. Very satisfying. But it was time to get down to business. "I've almost finished working through the stuff from the cloudburst bug. I should be able to guess where the receiver is and how it's been used. Question for you, Jedda. Do you want my report before or after Linden appears?"

Jedda frowned a bit and started fiddling with her hair. She still looked distinctly pale. Eventually, she said, "After. I think we all need to see how he reacts."

Ellen would have done it twice – both before, and after, with the second report carefully staged to sound like a first revelation. But all she said was, "OK. You're the boss. I'll be done in less than ten minutes."

She got a surprise. "Thanks, Ellen," Jedda said. "We're really grateful. We couldn't have got this far without you. You're a real asset to the team."

For a second, Ellen glowed inwardly. Then she damped it down viciously. *She's buttering you up. To use you. You would have done the same in her place. You're still alone, Ellen. And your only chance of surviving is to stay that way.*

• • • • •

"Sit over there, Linden." Jedda pointed to a chair between Anton and Ellen. "Ellen's going to tell us the history of that neat little parasite you were carrying. Ellen?"

Ellen swung her chair round. From her station in the corner, she could watch them all and gauge their reactions. Particularly Linden's. She glanced back at her screen to remind herself of the main points she wanted to make, and launched into her report. "I'll make it brief. The bug in Linden's back was an old cloudburst. It's a passive recorder, for sound and for the physical responses of the body it's in. It cannot transmit so most security systems don't pick it up." Linden opened his mouth to ask a question but she flung up a hand. "I'll do questions at the end," she said sharply. "If you listen carefully, you may actually find you don't have any."

"Ooh! Nasty." That was Anton, of course.

Jedda glared at him and he subsided.

"The active part of the system is the receiver. Every time the bug passes within range of it, the receiver downloads all the cloudburst data and wipes the bug clean."

"So the receiver has to be—"

Ellen didn't give Linden a chance to finish. She just spoke over him. "So the bug is always recording, *unless* it's been programmed for time or place. In the early versions, it was common to save storage space by having the recorder turned off when the carrier was sleeping, for instance. Your bug, Linden, could have been programmed not to record at all when you were at home. With your grandfather."

This time, Linden grimaced, without saying a word.

He doesn't like that one bit. Even though it would be totally in character for Marujn to ensure there was never any record of anything that might incriminate him.

"In fact, this little beauty is a later model." Ellen opened her fist and tossed the bug into the air, catching it neatly. "No problem of storage capacity. Actually, this one was always on. The receiver was obviously at the entrance to the Marujn mansion. People were only ever allowed to use one, weren't they? For security reasons?"

Linden nodded glumly.

Ellen smiled. She'd been sure she'd guessed right. "So every time you went in, the receiver downloaded the recording from that day. And when you went out again, it got the recording of everything you'd done at home. Nothing done inside the mansion ever went outside. Neat, isn't it?" She paused for effect. "Questions?"

Linden seemed to have shrunk. "So the old bastard knows everything."

Jedda shook her head. "No. No, he doesn't, Linden. He—"

Ellen interrupted again. This was her work and she was going to milk it. "*We* have the recording of everything that happened after you left home last night. The last thing Marujn got was the recording of you at home. Including Delta's call. Only you can tell us how much that matters."

"It doesn't," he said quickly, and much more decisively. "Delta asked for an urgent meeting. No specifics. She didn't even name the place. She's a clever woman."

"Be grateful," Ellen said. It was time Linden began to see

females as equals. Then she saw how he glanced at Jedda before looking quickly away. Very revealing.

Maybe he's already found a reason to change his mind about females.

• • • • •

K's fingers were drumming again. As if they had a will of their own.

He dealt with it by getting up and starting to pace up and down his office. Suddenly, he was beset by problems. No, puzzles. Riddles. First Linden's defection. Correction: apparent defection. K still did not know whether Linden was merely a prisoner somewhere. Though Marujn had seemed totally, and instantly, convinced that Linden had gone over to the enemy. Not much family feeling there, just pure hatred, where any normal man would have shown concern. So Linden was not loved. Or valued. *Except as a dead body to be delivered like a parcel.*

The second riddle was Marujn himself. Nothing he did seemed to make any sense. And that was dangerous.

If you don't understand how a man thinks, you can't predict what he will do. If you don't understand what a man wants, you can't find a way to control him.

K was going to have to make a serious study of Baron Marujn. But first, he had to deal with the immediate problem of Linden. Marujn wanted Linden shot on sight and delivered back to him. So K had to take Linden alive, to find out why his dead body was so precious to the old man. And to do it without arousing Marujn's suspicions.

Not easy. If Marujn discovers I've deliberately flouted his orders, he'll be out to get me. Can I afford to take that risk? It could be terminal.

That spineless thought stopped him in his tracks. Since when had he let personal risk stop him from doing what had to be done? Never yet. And not now.

Once he had fathomed the secret of Linden, K would decide what to do with him. If he really had defected, he'd be executed, though the bloodsuckers would have him first, to drain any useful information. He would have picked up intelligence about the Jay and his women somewhere along the way, even if he didn't realise how much he knew. He would have to be bled. Which made it sheer madness to shoot him on sight.

Marujn was not mad. Not in any normal sense. There must be something more.

K continued to pace. And to pick through the scanty evidence he had.

The solution shattered his thoughts like a shard of ice cleaving a skull. He shivered with the intensity of it. Linden himself was Marujn's spying device! K's control centre was not bugged, he was certain. So the bug must have come in with Linden – *in* Linden – and be undetectable even by K's state-of-the-art security screening. It would probably be biological rather than electronic. Perhaps…?

For the moment, it didn't matter how Marujn had done it. K could resolve that later, as well as discovering which scientists were working for Marujn on the side. They would have to be disposed of, especially if they were working in Dr Feliks's labs. Marujn must *not* find out what Feliks was doing. That was vital.

But the clock was ticking fastest on Linden. That had to be K's priority. Marujn wanted the body so he could remove the evidence before the autopsy robots found it.

K had to get there first.

• • • • •

Linden was so angry he thought he might explode. The Greenland woman's analysis had to be right. Her logic was impeccable. Everything his grandfather had done – over years and years since he'd taken in his orphaned grandson – everything he had promised was a total sham. He had said he wanted to further Linden's career, to prepare him to sit on the Council one day. Utter crap! The old man simply wanted to use Linden to get information to shore up his own position. As a long-term strategy, it was utterly brilliant, utterly ruthless, and the ultimate betrayal.

Shooting is much too good for the old bastard! If I ever get the chance to kill him, I will make it long, and slow, and excruciatingly painful.

"Linden?" Jedda was not quite managing to conceal her concern. Could she tell what he was feeling? Possibly. She seemed to be pretty good at reading his mind.

"Sorry," he said gruffly, trying not to look at her. If it was a choice between feeding his anger or feeding his lust, he preferred anger. He might manage to take his anger out on someone, some time. But lust was totally off limits. Jedda had said so. And Jedda was the bloody boss round here.

"I've discussed things with the others," Jedda said, "and we're agreed you can join the Jays. If you're prepared to abide by our rules."

He threw her a dagger look which she ignored, though she coloured a little.

"I should explain what they are. New recruits have to prove themselves unless they're transferring from an allied group which vouches for them. You're not. Neither is Ellen. So both of you are wearing clothes that can kill you, if you give us reason to believe you're a traitor."

Shit! Linden glanced down at the combat jacket and trousers he had put on without a thought. A bomb? The moment he was alone, he'd do a systematic search—

"Don't bother, Linden," Ellen said sardonically. "I've tried. You won't find it."

Oh.

Everything he knew about the Greenland woman – no, he must start thinking of her as *Ellen* – told him she was more tech-savvy than he was. That's why K was desperate to get hold of her, wasn't it? If she hadn't found the kill-kit, how would he?

"And you can't avoid it by taking your clothes off," Jedda added in an odd voice.

She's thinking about how we were. Back there. Just hours ago. He swallowed hard. Now he was thinking about it, too. Naked bodies. Skin on skin. Really, really not good. This time, he swore out loud. Let the others think it was because they had him cornered. Jedda would know the truth of it.

He hoped it was making her feel as frustrated as he did.

"And when you—" Jedda broke off and got up. She had clearly changed her mind about whatever it was she'd been going to say. "Anton will brief you about the detail of how you shower and so on. Right now, what I need to know is – do you still want to join us? It means giving up everything. There's no luxury here. You'll be a fugitive. Hunted. K will want your guts, never mind what your grandfather will want."

She didn't say that I don't have a choice. But I don't. I can't go back to where I was. I know too much. I join Jedda's band or I don't leave here alive.

Funnily enough, that thought did not bother him. Even though he'd abandoned Delta and her pack, a team of women he trusted and valued, even though he could never go back to them, he had no regrets. He had committed himself to Jedda down in that basement. She had now made it clear that she was off limits, but he wasn't about to change his mind. Deep in his gut, he had decided. This was

195

where he belonged.

At least here, I might have a chance to recover my self-respect. And get Marujn.

That made him smile. He'd give his right arm to meet Marujn in a dark alley.

"I will join you," Linden said firmly, not taking his eyes off Jedda. "And I accept your terms. *All* of them."

• • • • •

Linden was glad the briefing was over. Jedda and Ellen had gone off together without saying why. Chrys was busy with her monitors, probably checking the external sensors. It was totally quiet apart from the muted hum of the various machines.

Linden had pulled a chair alongside Anton's station and was mulling over what the geek had told him about living with a killsuit. He was a clever bugger, no doubt about it. The women were pretty switched on, too. Chrys was downright scary, partly because she said so little. She just watched, mostly, but you felt she was sizing you up for a knife, or a garrotte. Ellen was scary, too, in her own way. Technically brilliant, he suspected, and with a tongue that cut like a razor. She didn't like being a rookie Jay – actually he wasn't convinced she wanted to be a Jay at all – and she made sure that everyone knew it. Anton distrusted her. It seemed to be mutual.

What kind of a team was Jedda running here? They seemed to be at each other's throats. Where on earth was the trust?

Don't go there, Linden. Stick to anger.

"I'd give a lot to know what my gra— what old Marujn is doing now," he said casually. "Shitting himself, I fervently hope."

I will never think of him as my grandfather again. Never.

"Well…" Anton looked at Linden with narrowed eyes. "Guys together, I guess. Yup, I might be able to help you with that."

"Really?" Linden asked eagerly.

Anton sat back in his chair. He had a smug look on his face. Without a word, he started inputting commands so fast that Linden could not keep up. "There you go." Anton waved a careless hand at the screen.

"You're a sodding genius, Anton," Linden said, amazed. There, on the screen, was the inside of the Marujn Mansion, the place that had the best security in the whole province. Linden suspected that K had tried, and failed, to penetrate it. Yet this renegade geek with the tatty ponytail had somehow got through every one of the state-of-the-art safeguards that Marujn had installed. Bloody brilliant.

"Could you get into my apartment? There's…er… something I want to see." Something he'd have brought away with him, if he'd known he was never going back.

Anton's fingers were already working. "I haven't actually been into your apartment before—"

Linden was relieved to hear it. He didn't want to think of any more people spying on him. That old bastard was already one too many.

"—but I don't imagine it'll be any more difficult than the rest of the place. Yup. Got it. Oh!" Movement on the screen had caught his eye.

"That's—" Linden began.

Anton didn't need telling. "Chrys! Come and look. Marujn is prowling around Linden's quarters." In seconds, all three of them were gazing intently at the screen.

"What the blazes is that old pervert doing there? He never visits me. I have to go to him. He's—"

Chrys raised a hand for silence. "Just watch!"

Marujn was walking slowly round the room, picking up odd things to check them and putting them down again. It looked random, but Linden was sure it was nothing of the sort. When Marujn reached the antique bookcase, he reached out.

No! Leave it alone, you fucking bastard!

Marujn picked up the old-fashioned photograph frame and held it at arm's length, as if it were diseased. Calmly and deliberately, he spat on it.

Linden choked.

A second later, Marujn hurled the picture to the floor. The frame shattered. He smiled and bent down to retrieve the print between finger and thumb, fastidiously shaking it to get rid of any clinging fragments of frame. He tore the picture into tiny pieces and let them flutter to the floor.

Linden turned away. He felt sick.

"What was *that* all about?" Anton asked, shocked.

Linden shook his head and closed his eyes. The room was spinning. With an effort, he turned back to Anton. "That was the only thing of hers I ever found, in all the years I searched. A single printed photograph. Of my father and my mother. On their wedding day."

TWENTY-FOUR

JEDDA WALKED BACK INTO main control just in time to hear Linden's strangled words. A photograph? She had no idea what he was talking about, but his anguish was all too clear. She could feel it starting to grip her own gut, as if their two bodies were one.

Even though they never have been.

In an instant of grim self-knowledge, she saw that she would have sacrificed anything to end his pain. Most of all, she wanted to—

Bloody hell! Five minutes groping with Linden and my brain's turned to jelly. What is it with me? I used to be able to think! I'm the leader. I have to be able to plan.

The truth was, she couldn't. As a strategist, right now she was pretty much useless. If she couldn't plan, she couldn't lead. If she couldn't lead, she was nothing.

It was her own fault. Though he'd been the one to kiss her that first time, the second time was her doing. He would probably have behaved if she had not caressed his naked back. From then on, it was all her own fault. Now she was thinking about it, about *him*, even though the Jays needed a strong leader more than ever. The hunt would be on, with a vengeance. K would be desperate to get hold of Linden before he betrayed the secrets of London Central. Marujn simply wanted the cloudburst back.

Chrys looked up and caught Jedda's eye. No need for words. Chrys moved silently across the room and murmured in Jedda's ear, bringing her up to speed.

Jedda froze in horror. Linden's only living relative had betrayed him; and then he had wrenched out what was left of Linden's heart and ground it into the dirt.

• • • • •

Chrys couldn't immediately read Jedda's reaction. Puzzling. The two women were usually on the same wavelength, in spite of their differences of outlook.

198

Chrys soon began to *feel* how disturbed Jedda was. Jedda had always been able to deal with casual sexual attraction, so she must be struggling with something that went really deep. She hadn't been firing on all cylinders since the first time she'd fought Linden, but this major loss of focus was new, and dangerous. Right now, the Jays needed to go on the offensive, to strike at the core of K's empire while he was still off-balance after the loss of his number two. A successful op could weld Linden and Ellen into the team as well, making everyone stronger.

Without a leader, it couldn't happen.

Jedda would soon be herself again, surely? She was too strong, and too dedicated, to abandon everything she and her parents had fought for over so many years. She just needed time to come to terms with the way she was feeling about Linden.

Until she did, someone else was going to have to take the initiative.

Chrys would have to do it. Who else was there?

Leading was not her strength. It did not come naturally. She would do it to protect Jedda from her inner demons – and from Linden – until she was ready to take the reins again. Chrys had to do it, even if Jedda saw it as a bid to supplant her.

Chrys refused to think about what that might do to their relationship. It was a risk she had to take. For the future of the Jays.

She took Jedda out into the corridor where no one else would hear. "Look, Jedda, we've got K on the back foot. He'll be totally focused on getting to Linden before Marujn does, and before we've got any information out of him. Will you let me mount an offensive, somewhere under K's radar? That might throw him completely. It would be another chance to test Ellen's loyalty, too."

Jedda took a deep breath. "Good idea. Mmm, yes. A very good idea."

"I'd like to start preparing an alternate bunker, too. We can't really use the one where the hounds sniffed us out. We need a fallback location, just in case." K was not likely to find their main hideout – it was very well hidden, largely thanks to Anton – but it would be stupid and short-sighted to bank on that. K was throwing all his resources into the search for Linden. One lucky break and it could be curtains for the Jays. So they had to set up another bolthole, complete with Anton's wizardry.

Jedda brightened. "You're right, Chrys. Thanks. Should have thought of those myself. To be honest, we need the spare bunker right now, but we daren't delay the op. K will get his act together very quickly. If we delay, we might miss our chance."

"We could split our forces. There are five of us now. Team of two and team of three? Anton plus one for the new bunker. The rest for the op. What do you think?"

Jedda nodded. "Terrific. And your idea, so your choice. Which team do you want to lead?"

Chrys couldn't help smiling. "If it's OK by you, I'd really like to lead the op."

Jedda grinned. "Now, there's a surprise!" She was sounding much more like her normal self again. Perhaps she was relieved that Linden would be in Chrys's team? "Right, tell me what you've got in mind."

• • • • •

Everyone had been assigned their roles and sent off to prepare.

Chrys was the first back to control. Anton had never left. All his kit was there.

"Got a minute, Anton?"

He looked up and said sharply, "Not really. Got to finish packing all this stuff."

"I need your help," Chrys said simply. That got his attention, double-quick. She rarely asked anyone for help. "About the self-destruct buttons. For Ellen and Linden."

"Ah."

"You can't be monitoring them both while you're off with Jedda setting up the new bunker. I know that. You know that. Problem is that Ellen and Linden might twig it too. I don't think either of them will actually try to abscond, but I'd rather not let them think they can get away scot-free."

"You never did believe in taking unnecessary chances, did you?" He grinned and dug into a box beside his desk, producing a small remote control. "Take this. I'll tell 'em both that I've passed the switch to you. That if they step out of line, or make a move to escape, you'll terminate them on the spot."

"And can I?"

"Nope. Doesn't work." He shrugged. "It would take me hours to make a portable switch from scratch. Don't have the time right now. Jedda needs me to do all this." He gestured to the bags of kit strewn around the floor and the part-assembled stuff on his desk.

"Not a problem. I'm sure they'll believe you. Especially Ellen. She's convinced you wouldn't pass up a chance to finish her off."

"Darn tootin', I wouldn't."

Chrys shook her head sadly and tucked the fake switch into her combat jacket. "I suspect the two of you are going to have to make peace, one of these days. It'll need to be like hedgehogs mating, though – very, very carefully."

Anton snorted with laughter.

"And while we're on the subject of making peace… That photograph of Linden's, the one Marujn destroyed. Any chance you could replicate it? It might put Linden back on a more even keel." That might help Jedda get back to normal, too.

"Don't have access to photographic materials. They're scarce as hen's teeth these days," Anton said with a quick shake of the head. "But I suppose I might be able to create a digital replica of the photo. I could—" He stopped. "Is Jedda OK with this?"

"She's a bit preoccupied, so I'm taking care of the tactical stuff." Almost true.

"Oh. OK then. No promises, though, since all I'll have to work with is a few seconds' side-on view of the original. It might not be doable at all."

"If anyone can do it…" Chrys grinned at him. "You're a star, Anton. But keep it under your wig till it's done, eh?"

He pulled a gurning face at her. He was very proud of his long hair. "The normal phrase is 'keep it under your hat', you know."

Chrys made for the door. "I do actually know that," she said over her shoulder. "But you're not wearing one. So…"

Anton laughed and threw a screwdriver at her.

It missed. But only because she ducked.

• • • • •

K got up to ensure his office door was firmly closed behind Delta. He wanted to be undisturbed to think. Delta's report had been efficient, clear, and totally negative: the hound packs had sniffed out no trace of Linden anywhere, nor was there anything to be found where those nasty little white cards had been dropped. K was beginning to think that the smell implants, developed at such a cost in scientific resources, were not the breakthrough he had hoped. Fine for run-of-the-mill targets, but not for the Jays. For nearly two days now, the hounds had not picked up any of the scents associated with the Jay women. K did not believe for a moment that those women had stopped leaving their lair. They'd been able to strew their cartoon cards round half the city, after all! So they must have found a way of disguising their scents.

That meant the Jay had a tech who was very, very good.

Greenland woman? That would not surprise him in the least. What little he knew about her was truly impressive and this extra wrinkle proved she was exactly the kind of asset his province needed. He told himself he was glad that he had failed to kill her at the labs. Luck must have been on his side that day.

A vague shadow of doubt clawed at the door of his consciousness, but he refused to let it in. He would not think about her like *that*. What mattered was finding a new way of dealing with this band of terrorists, one that did not rely on the hounds' smell implants. He needed to regain control. He needed to lure the Jay into a trap. But how?

K paced up and down his office, seizing and discarding ideas. All unworkable. The Jay was much too clever to let his warriors be suckered into any of those. K had to find something really subtle, preferably including an element of double-bluff. At the moment, his rational brain was not coming up with the goods.

He allowed himself one single foul expletive – which was less satisfying than he had expected – and moved on. He would leave the problem with his subconscious and work on practical issues. The solution would come to him in the end. It usually did.

He had personally checked out the disabled cameras and sensors, looking for patterns that might lead to the Jays' hideout. At first, he'd thought there was a clear trail, but then he found several other trails, all equally clear. It could have been any of them, or none of them, so K's potential lead was a non-starter. The Jay definitely had outstanding tech support; K had no one who was even half as good. Tauber claimed to have tech skills but he tended to think on predictable lines. Useless, because the Jays were so devious. They would only be outthought by a tech who was full of off-the-wall ideas. Definitely not Tauber. Not anyone else in London Central either, K decided dispassionately. He knew his own limitations. He was good on the tech side, and on some aspects he could be very inventive, but he was no tech genius. The Greenland woman, on the other hand, might well be.

What's more, the Jays only reappeared after she arrived. So maybe she's the only tech they have? If I could capture her, would the Jay be unable to operate?

He stopped dead.

If I had killed her when I had the chance, would I have prevented all this?

He made himself start pacing again, with a measured, calming tread. He had to focus on concrete plans. He had given up trying to fathom why Linden had gone over to the enemy. What did it matter anyway? Right now, K needed a new number two. There was no chance of getting Linden back, not when Marujn had decreed that his grandson was to be shot on sight. Even if K got to Linden first and brought him in for interrogation, Marujn would get his wish sooner or later – Linden was a dead man.

K reviewed the potential candidates. Not many of them and all female, apart from Tauber. The South American commissar had disgusting personal habits – not only those foul cigars he was always smoking – but that was not why K was wary of appointing him. Unlike Linden, Tauber had no integrity. He was an arse-licker, out for himself, first and always. He would throw K to the wolves without a moment's thought. If Tauber became K's second-in-command, K would have to watch his back all the time. And waste precious hours checking on what Tauber was up to.

The Council would want K to appoint a man. But perhaps there was a way round that? If K could get the President to rubber-stamp the appointment of a female, the Council would have to accept the *fait accompli*. They could hardly do anything else, given how they proclaimed that they never interfered in operational matters, which were solely for the Controller and the President of each province.

K allowed himself to smile. He would enjoy thwarting the Council. *Especially* Marujn. It would be so subtly done that they would not be able to accuse him of anything improper, however much they might suspect.

Satisfied, he sat down at his desk to start reviewing the confidential files on the potential female candidates. All solid, dependable, committed officers of the state, but none of them stood out for courage, or integrity.

Delta has both of those!

K threw himself back in his chair and stared at the ceiling. *Delta?* A recently promoted leader of a hound pack?

Why not? K made a mental checklist of pros and cons and compared it with Linden. Delta came out better than expected. She had all the same warrior skills that Linden had brought to the job. She was inexperienced on the tech and strategic aspects, but Linden had been, too. In fact, he still was. He always wanted to be *doing* things, rather than thinking, or planning. And on resource control, Linden was a waste of space. Delta was more tractable. She would probably be willing to learn.

But she had given her loyalty to Linden, and women's loyalty was so often tied up with feelings, rather than logic. A man would give you loyalty out of pure self-interest. Many could simply be bought. K was pretty sure that didn't apply to Delta. His softened reprimand had earned her gratitude, maybe even a spark of admiration, but loyalty? It would be very risky to appoint a deputy – a woman, too – who was less than totally loyal to K and to everything he needed to do.

If it was to be Delta, he would have to wait for her to prove where her loyalties lay. If she abandoned Linden – as she ought to, since he was a proven traitor – K would be able to appoint her without any qualms.

Yes, that was a very acceptable plan.

In the meantime, K himself would have to fulfil both roles.

He brightened at that thought. Linden, as Director of Enforcement, had had a monopoly on tactical operations. He'd been able to go out and fight if he chose. It was a long time since K had been involved in combat, and the prospect was...

Actually, the prospect was exciting. Especially coming face to face with the Greenland woman. Someone had to take her down and that someone ought to be—

She had to be his.

· · · · ·

Ellen listened to the final briefings without saying a word. It was all routine. Besides, she was more interested in watching Jedda's body language, and Linden's. They were trying so hard not to look at each other and yet the electricity was sparking between them all the time. They were both desperate to touch, but they didn't dare. Was Ellen the only one who could see what was going on?

On reflection, Ellen was pretty sure that Chrys had noticed and was doing everything she could to keep male and female apart. Any kind of op – even scuttling through the underground tunnels to set up a backup command centre – could be compromised by lovers worrying more about each other than the main objective. That was one of the reasons why Grant had never allowed Ellen to join his renegade group.

But I was never like a bitch on heat!

Jedda and Chrys had finished giving their orders when Anton put his oar in. "A word to the wise," he said, tapping the side of his nose. "Just in case you two—" he nodded to Ellen and Linden "—

think you've got a chance to escape. You haven't. Your killsuits are still operational. Chrys has the portable detonator." He smiled smugly.

Ellen saw deep shock on Linden's face. Perhaps he hadn't really believed that his precious Jedda would do that to him? Gullible *as well as* love-sick?

Ellen made sure that her own face was showing no reaction at all. Her mind was working at top speed though. Chrys had the detonator. That figured. Anton would be away from central control for quite a while, so he wouldn't be able to keep watch. He'd been forced to delegate his favourite task. He'd hate that. But if Ellen could kill Chrys and take all her clothes before Anton got his finger back on the button, Ellen might be able to get away.

While I'm killing Chrys, and stripping us both naked, Linden is going to stand back and watch, is he? Yeah, right. Never mind all those hound packs that are out searching for us all over London. And where the hell would I go if I got away with it? I'd have Chrys's clothes and Chrys's weapons, but that's all I'd have.

As a plan, it was pretty ropey. She would have to do much better than that.

Especially if I want to keep out of K's clutches.

She ignored the sudden tiny shiver. She put it down to disgust at her own weakness, and made herself focus on the task ahead. She checked her kit one last time and followed Chrys out of the bunker. It would be good to be in action again and to have a chance to show Linden what she could do. Ellen reckoned she was a match for him as a warrior, and streets ahead of him on the tech side. If the Jays had to choose between the two of them, it would be no contest.

Wouldn't it?

TWENTY-FIVE

K SURVEYED THE STREETS as his official car glided silently along, driven by the automatic systems he had so carefully specified. Evening in early December. Predictably dark and depressing. Turning cold enough to chill bone. He was surprised to see how many ordinary people were still out, apparently curious to watch the VIPs arriving at the reception. Normally, the vast majority of law-abiding citizens were back at home by nightfall, with their doors firmly locked against strangers. People caught on camera after dark were almost invariably very rich, or criminal.

Why were so many Londoners still out, and standing, staring, instead of scurrying back to relative warmth and safety? Did they imagine this presidential shindig was a show put on for them, in preparation for the Dark Days festival? If so, they were wrong. The timing was pure coincidence, nothing to do with the annual celebrations that the state ran, from late December into January. For some, the winter festival still had religious significance, but for most, it was an excuse to eat and drink at the state's expense and to party through the longest nights of the year, idly watching the spectacles that were laid on to keep them entertained and out of trouble.

Bread and circuses. It had been the Roman recipe for keeping the population in check. More than two thousand years later, it still worked, though the food ration was rather mean, nowadays, and the alcohol was doctored to keep drinkers docile.

The Roman crowd would have been largely men, of course; women were kept in the background then. Not any more. Almost everyone K could see was female. There was just the odd old man, and even fewer precious children. Every single one of the crowd was huddled in layers of drab grey clothing, to keep out the penetrating cold. Their shapeless bodies were as indistinguishable as mounded bushes in a shrubbery, after a heavy fall of snow. They barely moved, though their dark eyes tried to peer into every car that passed, coveting the wealth, feeding their sullen resentment. With more males, there might have been a risk of violence. As it was, the elite were safe enough.

But not from terrorist gangs like the Jays.

At least the rain had stopped. In the colder, drier air, the hounds should be able to pick up scents easily. Greenland woman might have been able to disguise the scents of her existing comrades, but Linden had been with them barely a day. There must be a chance that the hounds could still sniff him out.

K's car slowed a fraction for the automatic security check at the iron gates to the President's palace and then sped up the long drive into the gravelled courtyard. No hostile eyes here – ordinary citizens were never allowed past the gates – just the blank stares of soldiers, in parade uniforms, organised more for display than for defence.

K's car swung round and stopped so that its sliding door was precisely opposite the centre of the stairs to the main entrance. Straightening his uniform cuffs, K stepped out, and the soldiers on either side of the bottom step came smartly to attention. K acknowledged their salute with a slight nod, before walking swiftly up to the open doorway and into the glittering hallway beyond. Such a contrast with the dilapidated city beyond the President's gates. It was as well that the common people never got to see the opulence behind the high security walls.

K was not late, but the high-ceilinged reception room was already full, and buzzing. He glanced around, as if he were simply mildly interested in who might happen to be present. No sign of Dr Feliks. Woe betide the man if he had failed to come. K's instructions had been explicit.

"K?" It was a uniformed flunkey. When he nodded, she said, "His Excellency Baron Marujn has asked if you would join him. Will you follow me, please?"

That was the last thing K wanted, but he had no choice, so he strolled across the floor to the dais at the end. The President had not yet made his entrance, but various Council members were already there, seated on ornate red velvet and gilt chairs that had been crafted in an age when backsides were broader and corpulence a sign of status. The chair made Marujn's short, slender figure look almost like a child's.

"Ah, K, just the man I've been wanting to see."

Marujn was all smiles and bonhomie. K's antennae twitched a warning.

"It's not the Council's responsibility, of course, but we've been thinking about the Dark Days festivities. It's been a difficult year, for everyone, and so the Council has decided... That is, some Council members would like to make a personal donation to the celebrations. Another firework display, more generous rations, that sort of thing."

And you'll want to ensure that the source of this astonishing largesse is trumpeted at every opportunity, won't you? To stress how public-spirited you all are, and to make the state look mean by comparison.

K did not allow his reaction to show. Instead, he said simply, "Commissar Tauber is in charge of the arrangements this year. I will pass on your message and get him to contact the Council secretariat first thing in the morning."

"Excellent. But there are one or two specifics that you, as Controller, will need to be aware of." Marujn stood up and put a hand on K's shoulder to steer him to the end of the dais where they were less likely to be overheard. "Have you any news?" he hissed.

K did not pretend to misunderstand. "As yet, there is no trace of him." Best not to mention Linden's name. "All available resources have been deployed."

The old tyrant's puffy eyes narrowed and focused on K's face. "With the orders I gave you?" It was a naked challenge.

"Your orders were explicit. The leaders have all been fully briefed." With K's orders to bring Linden in alive, rather than the Baron's to shoot on sight. "We should have a result soon," K added, hoping to divert Marujn's attention. But the man looked far from satisfied. K needed to try something else.

"Have you managed to square your colleagues about the...er...problem, sir?"

Marujn flushed deep red. If they had been alone, he would have exploded with rage, K was sure. But here, even the Baron did not dare. His fellow Council members would notice, and they might enquire about the cause.

"My dealings with the Council are a matter for me alone, K." His voice was lower than normal. And distinctly strained.

"As you say, sir." K bowed slightly. "Then, if you will—"

A fanfare sounded. The President.

For once, K was truly grateful for that nonentity's arrival. Marujn had no choice but to return to his allotted place. K could seek the relative safety of the throng of guests, to listen to the speeches, and to find the elusive Dr Feliks.

K spotted his man as the President was coming to the end of his welcome to the trio of foreign visitors for whom the reception was being held. By the time the guests of honour had finished replying, K was standing right behind Dr Feliks.

K resisted the temptation to speak before the scientist knew he was there. The man might jump out of his skin and attract far too much attention. So K waited until the buzz of general conversation had begun again and took a step forward to bring himself into his quarry's eyeline. "Good evening, Dr Feliks," he said politely. "How fortuitous that we should meet here. There are one or two business matters that I've been meaning to raise with you but – you know how things are – there never seem to be enough hours in the day." He shrugged nonchalantly. Then, just as Marujn had done to him, K drew Dr Feliks aside for a private word.

It was only then that K realised his plan was flawed. In a crowded reception, it was impossible to avoid eavesdroppers, never mind the ever-present cameras and listening devices. Frustrated, and annoyed at his own lack of foresight, K forced himself to ask questions about the labs' normal business. Dr Feliks, initially rather nervous, soon relaxed enough to sound pretty normal to anyone listening. He even began to talk with animation about the benefits of greater capital investment at his labs.

K stopped him in mid-flow with a quick gesture. "I'm so sorry, Doctor, but I'm afraid I have to leave." He nodded towards the empty dais. The President had left, so the guests were not obliged to stay any longer. "Urgent state business. But your equipment budget is urgent, too, I know. Perhaps I could give you a lift home and you could fill me in on the way?" He chuckled. "Kill two birds with one stone, eh?"

Dr Feliks's eyes widened for a fraction of a second. The man was no fool. He smiled back, though he did not seem relieved. Maybe the thought of giving his report to K was even more daunting than being among the bigwigs at a state reception? "That is very kind of you, K," he began. "I—" Before the man could say anything more, K steered him towards the exit.

By the time they reached the courtyard, K's black limo had responded to his call button and was waiting for them. It pulled away as soon as the two men were safely inside, and started back the way it had come. Dr Feliks had perched himself on the edge of his seat as if he were uncomfortable in such an prestigious vehicle,

K noted, even though it was not particularly luxurious by Council standards. K had chosen a relatively small size and a spartan interior. He hated ostentation and he hated waste. Apart from the state-of-the-art security that he considered essential, the only indulgence he had allowed himself was optional manual control.

"Where shall I drop you, Doctor? I'm afraid I don't know where you live."

"I'd like to go back to the lab, actually. There's some work I'd like to finish."

"Of course. Make yourself comfortable and enjoy the ride." K gave the car its new destination and sat back, encouraging his guest to do the same. "Now, if you'd be so good," he began courteously, "I'd like to hear your report."

Dr Feliks glanced nervously round the interior of the car. "Is it safe? I mean—"

The limo might be spartan, but it had been built to K's exact specification. The systems and internal surveillance worked only on voice command, and only from K himself. It was one of the few locations where he could be absolutely sure that his secret activities could not be spied on. "It's perfectly safe." K nodded reassuringly to his passenger. "For both of us," he added, with a conspiratorial smile.

Some of the tension seemed to leave Dr Feliks's shoulders, though he did not return the smile. "Very well," he said curtly, and launched into his report. He had made progress in scoping the work, he said, but it had not yet begun in earnest and so there was nothing concrete to report. K could not expect anything more, considering that he had only commissioned the research a few days earlier.

K nodded encouragingly.

"If you are able to give me the extra resources I need, it may be possible to complete the first stage by next summer. With luck and a following wind."

K smiled dutifully at the man's weak attempt to keep the discussion light.

"But if we come up against unforeseen difficulties – or if we are deliberately obstructed – it could take considerably longer. Years possibly."

"Yes, you said so when we spoke before," K said evenly. He must not let his exasperation show. He needed the man's undivided support. "As I said then, I am acutely aware of how important and difficult this work is. That is why I chose you to lead it. I know I dare not hope for early results or hints of a breakthrough. Even a scientist as eminent as yourself cannot be expected to make that sort of progress." He sighed, possibly a little too theatrically, but the eminent scientist did not seem to notice.

"Well, on that score I may be able to surprise you," Dr Feliks said quickly.

K congratulated himself silently. It was an old trick, but nine times out of ten it worked, especially when the barb was directed at a man's professional pride.

"I've been doing a survey of the published research – though there isn't much – and I've spotted strange inconsistencies. I wasn't planning to tell you until I was sure what they meant. It's always possible they mean nothing at all. On the other hand…"

Result! "I am not in your league where the science is concerned, Dr Feliks, but I will always be more than happy to act as a sounding board. And we both know that I am the only person you *can* talk to about this, given that it must remain top secret. So please do go ahead. Take as much time as you need. My other business will wait."

• • • • •

Chrys led the way around the square, past the rows of parked limousines. Some of them even had human "drivers", though that was merely a status symbol these days. Modern vehicles had been automated for years, and very few people knew how to drive, but some of the elite insisted on a human minion to stand by the door and carry their parcels.

The Jays were wearing normal outdoor clothes over their combat kit. It helped them to blend in with London's have-nots, and the loose hoods, pulled low over their eyes, made it difficult for the state's face-recognition systems to identify them. Even so, the team would be lucky to get much further without being stopped. Only those who dripped wealth and privilege were welcomed into the huge Marujn emporium.

No one tried to stop Chrys until she reached the main entrance. There, the security guard flung an arm across Chrys's path. "No entry here for the likes of y—" The woman was crumpling to the ground before she could finish speaking. She would not die – it was not part of the Jays' code to kill poor workers unless it was unavoidable – but she would be out for hours and sore for a great deal longer.

Chrys looked round for other guards. There were none. The

managers of this grand store were either complacent, or the financial crisis had led to cost cutting. Quite a lot of ordinary civilians were hanging around, too, which was unusual so late in the day, especially in winter. Were they desperate enough to be trying for hand-outs? She doubted there would be any. Not from this lot. Besides, they might soon be a little bit short…

She stepped through the beam that worked the black glass doors. No one from the underclass was permitted to see into the treasure trove beyond, but the one-way glass permitted customers to check that all was safe before they emerged. As the doors slid open, Chrys saw what lay inside. She had been told what to expect – she'd even seen the interior via one of Anton's clever hacks – but the real thing was almost overwhelming. No shortages here. Lights everywhere, reflecting off the mirrored walls and the glass display cases full of jewellery that filled one side of the huge hall; the other side, hardly less extravagant, was piled high with exotic foodstuffs in packaging that sparkled almost enough to rival the diamonds. The rich were being tempted with gifts for the festive season and they would be vying to outdo one another in extravagance.

By the door, a woman in ankle-length furs turned to assess the newcomers. The beautiful folds at the back of her coat fanned out as she moved, like a ballerina's gauze skirt. "Get the hell out of here, scum!" There was nothing beautiful about her voice.

Chrys threw back her hood with one hand and felled the woman with the other. Her huge fur hat came off and rolled across the thick gold carpet. It came to rest against a sales assistant's foot.

No one moved to pick it up.

Chrys had not drawn a weapon. She knew that both Ellen and Linden, at her back, were covering the customers and the staff. Nevertheless, it did no harm to make the point. She pulled out her own weapon and weighed it in her hand.

No one moved. No one spoke. Everyone was staring, wide-eyed and terrified, at the three warriors by the entrance.

Chrys gestured to the sales assistant. "You. Yes, you. Bring that hat and put it down here." She tapped the carpet in front of her with the toe of her boot. "Upside down," she added, as the assistant rushed to obey. "I need a bucket."

There was a sharp intake of breath from someone. Then a squeak of alarm, quickly muffled.

Chrys let her gaze roam slowly through the crowd, pausing every now and then to focus on a particularly wealthy-looking patron.

None of them dared meet her eyes. Good. "All the ready money you are carrying. In the bucket. Now." Cash might be a dodgy asset these days, but it would have to do. Chrys pointed her weapon at a richly dressed woman who looked to be on the point of collapse. "We'll start with you." No reaction. Chrys took half a step towards her victim. "Move it!"

The woman was panicked into action and scuttled forward, bent almost double. She scrabbled about in her bag and finally pulled out a wodge of banknotes which she dropped into the hat. Chrys saw tears pouring down the woman's cheeks.

That's probably a first.

One by one, the other customers made their "donations". At least a third of them were carrying no cash at all, so the Jays relieved them of other valuables. "In lieu of cash," Chrys announced harshly as the first gold watch dropped into the hat.

Linden and Ellen, hoods thrown back, were gradually herding the customers into a corner alongside the sales staff. Soon they had all been fleeced. Time for stage two.

"Right," Chrys began. "Get—"

"But you're Linden!" cried the tear-stained woman from the front of the herd. She sounded outraged. "Baron Marujn's—"

"Baron Marujn's *nothing*!" Linden spat through clenched teeth. "And you can tell him so when you see him."

A distraction. Dangerous. Chrys spotted a suspicious movement among the staff while all other eyes were turned to Linden. To a hidden alarm button? Why did it always have to be the underlings who put their lives on the line?

"Get the rest, you two," she ordered. "I'll take care of our guests."

Ellen and Linden ran to scoop up the jewellery from the display cabinets and throw it into the soft pouches they had brought with them. Precious metals and stones held value better than cash. They could be bartered for essential supplies. Eventually.

"Enough. Time to go," Chrys shouted after a few more minutes. Ellen and Linden had not finished, but Chrys's gut was warning her that they had been here too long already. "You lot. Down on the floor. On your bellies." The hostages dropped like stones. "Hands clasped behind your backs. Keep them there. Now roll over."

It would have been better to cuff them but there wasn't time. It was the best she could do. They wouldn't be able to get their hands free quickly enough to be a threat.

Chrys grabbed the hat and raced for the door, with the others only a pace behind.

"Contact! Hounds!" Chrys's warning came a second before the team reached the doors. Everyone stopped dead, just short of the sensor beam. The doors stayed closed.

Only seconds to regroup. The hounds were pushing bystanders aside, clearing a path to the door. They'd be in range soon.

Chrys's orders came instantly. "OK. Split up. You go right, Linden. Ellen, left, with me. Ditch the haul if you have to. Make sure you save yourselves."

Chrys stepped through the beam. The doors began to slide apart. The advancing hounds would see exactly what they were up against.

• • • • •

Linden had already tucked the pouch of jewels inside his jacket. He ducked through the doors as soon as there was space. He sprinted right, along the blank wall, keeping his eyes fixed on the opposition.

Six of them. Stopping for precious seconds to break into teams of three. Good odds for Chrys. Dreadful for him. They really *did* want him.

I wanted a chance to prove myself to Jedda. Now I've got it. If I survive.

At least he had two weapons to improve the odds a little. The hounds were advancing in single file. Slowly. Making a smaller target.

Almost in range now. He dropped to one knee and picked off the hound in the front with a carefully aimed shot. She fell, clutching her leg.

One down and—

The next one in the group was Delta!

Hound three moved out alongside Delta. The two women dodged round their injured comrade and started to pound forward. Then they split up. Delta was coming for Linden. Her mate was running to cut off his escape route.

Linden froze. He would be a sitting duck. A woman he had trusted was shaping up to shoot him.

TWENTY-SIX

DELTA SKIDDED TO A halt. She took aim at Linden's unprotected head. Impossible to miss from this close. He was a dead man.

For Linden, time slowed to a crawl.

He would not run. He would not buckle. He would meet death as a warrior, open-eyed and straight-backed. Jedda would mourn with pride.

He raised his chin another notch. He looked Delta straight in the eye. And waited calmly for the end.

It did not come.

No movement. No shot. Nothing at all. Delta had him in her crosshairs and she was refusing to take the kill.

His gut lurched. His blood started fizzing again. Maybe be wasn't going to die here after all? If he—

"Linden!" Chrys, from the far side of the doorway. "Get going! We'll cover you!" In the same instant, Ellen started firing at the hound on Linden's far right.

Linden leapt to his feet and started to run, firing cripplers as he went. None directly at Delta, but enough to slow the pursuit and keep the shrieking civilians back.

For her part, Chrys took on all three of her opposing hounds so that Ellen could cover Linden's escape. Chrys's three were brave, but poor shots. Chrys dropped one of them without really trying. The other two kept coming forward.

She risked a glance sideways. "No!" she yelled, in sudden horror. Ellen was trying a long-range shot at one of Linden's hounds. Impossible with a ducking, weaving target. And the hound was much too close to the crowd. Civilians would get hurt.

Chrys reached out and knocked Ellen's arm up. "Leave it. Help me with these two," she gasped. "Linden'll be OK now."

Ellen obeyed without a word.

Chrys needed just those few seconds' respite. She grounded her weapon. With two hands, she seized the fur hat and flung it into the air. High over the heads of the hounds and the terrified crowd. "The Jay's back!" she yelled. "Happy holidays!"

And then it was raining money.

• • • • •

Anton pushed Jedda through the door to the main bunker and scrambled in after her with the rest of the kit. By the time he'd secured the door, she was leaning drunkenly against the wall. Her legs were starting to collapse under her.

He managed to get an arm under her shoulders before she hit the floor. "You need to lie down. And I need to get Chrys back here. She'll know what to do."

Jedda muttered something, but he couldn't make it out.

"OK. Let's go!" He half-carried, half-dragged her to the nearest cubicle and pushed her onto the bed. No time to make her comfortable. He undid the tourniquet on her arm, waited, counting rapidly until sufficient time had passed, and tightened it again. Then he stuffed pillows under it, so it was higher than her heart. He needed Chrys. He didn't have the skills to deal with this.

He raced back to his station in the main area and fired up his computer. "Come on, come *on*." Why was it taking so long?

At last! Now, where were they?

Chrys's comms implant produced a fix, and the computer pulled up a hacked image – Chrys and Ellen, weapons drawn, standing shoulder to shoulder in the square outside the target building. They should have been gone long before this. Trouble.

And Linden. Where was Linden?

Anton's fingers worked automatically to access another of the official cameras. He needed to see the whole area. He mustn't distract Chrys with voice comms until he knew what she was up against. Neither Chrys nor Ellen was actually firing right now, but that might mean anything.

Then he saw. Unbelievable. There were dozens of ordinary civilians milling around the area in front of the Marujn building, all screaming and shouting. They seemed to be fighting. There were bodies on the ground. People were scrambling over them. Anton was pretty sure he had caught sight of at least a couple of uniforms in the melee, but they disappeared again, hidden by the struggling mob.

Anton made a quick assessment of the forces in the surrounding area. "Bravo one from Control. I'm back. And I need *you* back here." He gave her concise instructions – route to take, what opposition she might meet. Chrys acknowledged. She touched Ellen's shoulder and they were off, like a couple of greyhounds.

It took Anton longer to find Linden. But he was alive, and still free.

For a second, Anton wondered if Linden was trying to escape from the Jays. Then he saw the hounds in pursuit. Two of them, and not gaining on Linden, but still…

Anton wasted precious seconds changing to the frequency for Linden's basic earwig. Great for security. The pits when it came to flexibility.

At last! "Bravo two. I've got you on camera. I'll guide you in."

"Roger," Linden gasped.

"Keep going, faster if you can. You're losing them."

"Thanks a bunch."

Linden couldn't be all that desperate if he could still say that. Anton grinned and checked his maps. If Linden really got a move on, he should be able to lose his pursuers *and* join up with Chrys and Ellen. That would make it much easier for Anton to bring them all in safely. And if the hounds did manage to keep him in sight, Chrys and Ellen would deal with them. Could make for an interesting firefight.

Then Anton remembered. He started issuing urgent instructions, to Chrys, and to Linden. If Linden didn't make the rendezvous, he'd be on his own. Anton would not allow Chrys to wait for Linden, or anyone. He needed her here to help Jedda.

Anton had his finger back on the destruct button. If Linden looked likely to fall into enemy hands, Anton would not hesitate.

• • • • •

Anton risked leaving his station to meet Chrys and Ellen at the outer door. Linden was missing. He had not made it to the rendezvous in time. Anton would have to go back and guide him in. Or terminate him.

But Jedda came first.

"Chrys! Jedda's injured. Snake bite."

Chrys paled. An instant later, she was back in control. "Where is she? How long ago? What kind of snake?"

Anton gave her all the information he had, which was not much. He was not sure about the species. Not native, he did know that.

"Didn't you bring it back with you?" That was Ellen, sounding outraged.

"It was all I could do to get Jedda back. And the kit."

"Enough!" Chrys rapped out. "Anton, get back to your station. Your priority is to bring Linden in. When you've got a moment, use the database to identify your snake. Ellen, you help him. Come and tell me the moment he's found anything." Chrys raced off to collect her medical kit, without waiting for either of them to reply.

• • • • •

"It could have been that one." Anton pointed at one of the snake images on the screen. He sounded very unsure.

To Ellen, it felt surreal. First Jedda let herself be bitten by a snake – in December, of all impossible things – then Anton failed to kill it and bring it back. And now, faced with images and videos of snakes, he couldn't quite remember what it looked like. He'd picked out two possibles, both foreign imports, both with venomous bites. One of them was painful but short-lived; the other was absolutely deadly.

The environment had changed so much as the planet warmed. Many animal species had died out. Others – including some escaped from zoos during the Water Wars – had thrived. It was possible to find all sorts of exotic creatures in very unexpected places. Like that underground hotspot on the way to the backup bunker.

The snake was only defending itself. Maybe, since it was winter, its venom would be less concentrated than when it was more active?

Anton was still staring at the screen. "Make up your mind," Ellen growled. Chrys would be waiting. The clock was ticking.

"I…I'm not sure. It could have been either of them."

Ellen knew then that she was wasting precious time. "Concentrate on getting Linden back. Even you can do that." Ignoring his blustering protest, she downloaded the details of both snakes to a mobile screen, snatched it up and raced off to find Chrys, hoping desperately that she would not be too late.

Chrys was calmly tending Jedda's wound. Jedda was clearly in pain, but she was coping with it. And still conscious. Surely a good sign?

Chrys straightened. "What have you got?"

Ellen explained quickly and passed over the screen.

"Hmm." Chrys glanced assessingly at Jedda. "The symptoms look more like this one." She pointed at the less dangerous of the snakes. "The blood bots should deal with that, given time. But I'll do a test, just in case."

Methodically, she prepared her kit and took a blood sample. "Take this to Anton. He's to test for these chemical signatures." She tapped a fingernail on the list below the image of the deadly snake.

Ellen took the blood and the mobile. The last thing she heard was Chrys's reassuring voice: "OK, Jedda, I'm going to give you a booster for your blood bots. I'm going to put you out for a bit while they get to work. After that, you'll be clean."

Chrys sounded so calm and confident. But then, she always was.

• • • • •

Anton was too busy to do the blood test. It was taking every scrap of his concentration to keep Linden from being captured by the chasing hounds.

"Tell *me* what to do," Ellen said, grabbing the phial. "Chrys needs this *now*."

Anton shook his head, but her urgency must have got through to him. A few moments later, between hurried messages to Linden, Anton barked out basic instructions for Ellen. It probably took her much longer than it would have taken Anton. But after what seemed like hours of careful work, the results came through. Ellen whooped with relief. "It wasn't the killer!"

Anton nodded without raising his eyes from his screen. So Linden was still nowhere near safe. After such a long chase, he must be getting really tired.

Ellen rushed down the corridor to deliver the news to Chrys and Jedda. She found them in Jedda's cubicle. Chrys was trying to persuade Jedda to sleep for a bit. Jedda, still fully dressed, was resisting. Ellen's good news did not help there. Jedda kept resisting, but eventually, and reluctantly, she agreed to rest for a couple of hours.

"Good. We'll leave you then," Chrys said. She shepherded Ellen out.

Ellen waited until they were out of earshot before she told Chrys that Linden was still not safe. Together, the two women ran back to see what was happening. It looked like good news, at last. Anton was leaning back, rolling his cramped shoulders to get the blood flowing. His face no longer looked so tense. His eyes were closed.

"Anton? What's happening?"

He opened his eyes but, apart from that, he did not move. He looked exhausted. "He's safe. I took him into the northern tunnels and he managed to lose them. He should be here soon. Ten minutes, tops."

In fact, Linden arrived back at the bunker in less than eight minutes. Ellen let him in. In spite of everything, he was barely panting. Impressive. He must be really fit. She led the way back to control where Anton and Chrys were waiting.

Anton looked as if he was waiting to be thanked. Ellen had to admit that, this time, the geek deserved it. She waited, too.

Linden looked at each of them and settled on Chrys. "Where's Jedda?"

"In bed, I hope. Recovering."

"Wha...?"

"She was bitten by a snake."

"Poisonous?" His voice was a croak. His face had gone sheet white.

"You mean *venomous*?" Chrys corrected scathingly. "Yes, but not life-threatening, though for a while we thought it was. Her blood's clean now. She's pretty shaken up, but she'll be fine after a night's sleep."

He started for the door without another word.

"Better if you leave her to—"

"No!" He threw open the heavy door to the corridor and stormed out. The door hit the wall with such force that the whole room shook.

"I think he's just sent us a message," Chrys murmured, crossing to close the door quietly. That old enigmatic smile was curling the corner of her mouth when she turned back to Ellen and Anton. "Possibly best if we leave them both to it for a while."

Ellen knew better than to react, but Anton snorted in disgust.

"You had a point to make, Anton?" Chrys asked silkily.

He shook his head, avoiding both women's eyes.

"Right. Perhaps you and Ellen would make a start on completing the comms links between here and the new bunker? If you wouldn't mind?"

• • • • •

Linden stopped outside Jedda's cubicle. There was only emergency light in the corridor. Barely enough to see by. The door was closed. Maybe Jedda was asleep?

He put an ear to the door. Nothing.

He ought to leave her to rest. He owed her that much. She had had a horrible – terrifying – near-death ordeal.

He couldn't. He had to know. He had to see her.

He tapped softly. If she was asleep, she wouldn't hear. Then he would go away.

The door opened a crack. A gasp. "Linden!" She opened the door wider and stood with her back against it to make room for him. For a split second, he thought he'd seen joy in her face. No, wrong, she was looking embarrassed.

"You OK, Jedda?" How totally lame that sounded.

She nodded. "Yes, I guess. Chrys fixed me up. She says I'll be fine." She looked anything but fine. Something was very, very wrong.

"What is it?" he asked gently. "Tell me."

She took a deep breath and started to speak so fast she was almost gabbling. "I've always had a thing about snakes. Ever since I was a kid. Can't help it. Believe me, I've tried everything. If I see a snake – or even something that *might* be a snake – I freeze. Nothing works. My brain goes into shutdown." She shivered convulsively. "And it's so *stupid*! Most of the snakes here can't do me any real harm. Most of them aren't nearly as dangerous as the ones in really hot climates. But knowing that doesn't help." Her shoulders slumped and she closed her eyes. She was a picture of dejection. "It was my own fault I was bitten. I feel a fool. And *utterly useless*."

Linden did not try to argue. He simply took two steps forward and pulled her into his arms. It felt good. And right. "What about *me*?" he murmured softly into her hair. "I nearly got myself killed tonight. By rights, I should be dead. If it hadn't been for Delta's— Actually, I don't know what it was, but something stopped her. I wish—" He swallowed hard. "Hell, I can't even say what I wish. I— Oh, sod it!" The scent of Jedda's hair was getting to him. His fine prepared speech had shattered into incoherence. Along with what little composure he had left.

He had just seen death. So had Jedda. Mere words didn't begin to cut it.

Next time, they might not be so lucky. This might be their only chance of being together. He eased her away from the door and shut it firmly. They needed each other. It had to be now. And she had to be willing.

"Jedda?" he said, a little hesitantly. He stroked her cheek with the very tips of his fingers. Was she blushing?

She lifted her head to look up into his face. There was desperation and longing in her eyes. They probably mirrored his own. "Yes." It was a hoarse whisper, and more arousing than he could ever have imagined. "Yes, I want you, too. *Now*."

Without another word, she pulled his mouth down to hers and began to kiss him as if it were their last hour together on earth.

"You asked to see me?" K's voice was as cold and hard as he could make it.

Delta drew herself up a fraction straighter and continued to stare at a point on the wall, somewhere above K's head. "Yes, sir. In spite of..." She swallowed hard.

She had been demoted. Rightly so. She had had Linden in her sights and she had let him escape. If there hadn't been such a shortage of hounds, she would have been kicked out of the ranks altogether. After a lengthy spell in jail.

K himself had had a narrow escape. He had so nearly appointed her as his new deputy. Only his logical appraisal of her character had led him to wait those few vital hours. He had been absolutely right to want proof of where her loyalties lay. Bloody women! Why could they not control their feelings like normal people? Like men did?

Delta began again, with slightly more self-control. "The commissar dismissed my report, sir. He said I was mistaken, that my implant was off. Or that I'd been misled by my own emotions, and my own stupidity, when I..." Her throat was reddening. She was clearly ashamed to admit that she had failed to do her duty.

Too late for that now! K leant his chin on his steepled fingers, keeping his eyes fixed on her face. He said nothing, though his mind was in overdrive. *The commissar?* Yes, if there was any stupidity going, Tauber was bound to have a share in it.

"The point is, sir, that I *know* what I smelt. It *wasn't* Linden's scent. There was no trace of that, even though I was only yards away from him. That terrorist band has found a way of disguising its scents."

"Or changing them altogether," K said quietly.

Delta's eyes widened. She probably thought it was impossible, whereas K knew it would be foolhardy to underestimate what the Jay – and his Greenland woman – could do.

K never did anything foolhardy.

"You were right to come to me with this, hound Delta. It *is* important. I will deal with it." He sat back in his chair. "And I will ensure that your good work on this is reflected in your record. The commissar will be informed."

She did not move a muscle, but her eyes were shining. With gratitude?

"Have you anything else to report?"

"No, sir."

"Very well. You may go." He ignored her smart salute. He had much more important issues to deal with.

First priority was to capture Linden. Second was the appointment of a deputy.

TWENTY-SEVEN

AFTERWARDS, JEDDA AND LINDEN lay on the bed in a tangle of hot, sweaty limbs. Jedda could not bring herself to pull away, even for cooling air. That skin-to-skin connection was vital; it proved it was all real.

Besides, she was so exhausted she could barely move. Linden must be the same. Their driving passion was spent – gloriously and joyously – and now their exertions were bound to start catching up with them. Jedda's bitten arm was still a little red and swollen, but, apart from that, and plain fatigue, there was nothing physically wrong with her. In her head, though, there was a great deal that was far from sorted.

Admitting to her snake phobia had opened the floodgates for Jedda. She had never been able to share thoughts and memories before, or fears. Somehow, lying here with Linden in the near-darkness made it easier to tell.

"My mother was afraid of snakes, too," she said, after a long silence. "Though that was the only thing she *was* afraid of. She was the bravest woman I've ever known."

Another long silence, broken only by slow, relaxed breathing. Jedda made herself focus on the good times, when her family had been together, happy and laughing. Those rare and precious times when they hadn't had to fight.

Very softly, Linden said, "How did she die?"

Jedda screwed up her eyes against the memory. She did not want to revisit those images. Even in the dark.

"Jedda? Can't you tell me?"

Maybe he had a right to know. "My parents were freedom fighters," she began, a little hesitantly. "Their parents, too. It's the only life I've ever known, really. It started in the Water Wars, with all that horrific culling. When the Council and their goons started scooping up all the wealth that was left – so that ordinary people had to beg and scavenge to find enough to eat – someone had to fight them. So my grandparents fought. And then my parents." She swallowed. "And now me."

Linden did not speak. He put a gentle hand on her upper arm and began to stroke her skin. Slowly. Hypnotically. It was very reassuring.

"My grandparents all died quite young. Natural causes, mostly. We had no bloodstream bots back then, of course, and no real medical care either. Basically, the sick or wounded got better by themselves or they died."

"Your parents, too?"

"No." She tripped on the word. "My parents died saving me. And Rebecca. My little sister." She tried to swallow the huge lump that was suddenly trying to choke her. "We had left the main group. The soldiers found where we were hiding. We were running. But my sister was too small to run fast and carrying her was slowing me down. So my father took on the soldiers, the whole squad of them, while the three of us kept running. And then… Then, when they had finally overpowered him and were catching up on us again, my mother did the same. She made me promise to save my sister. To run and not to look back.

"But I did. I did." She shuddered. The tears were filling her eyes. If there had been more light, she wouldn't have been able to see anything but dazzle.

"But you did get away. And your sister?"

"We…we jumped into the river. It was spring. The river was high and very fast. It saved us— Saved *me*. But the force of the water was so strong…" She could hear the tears in her own voice now, but she could not stop. "It pulled her hand out of mine and swept her away. I tried to grab her, but she went under. And I couldn't find her again. I tried so hard. I *did*. But she was gone. Drowned. My little sister drowned. It was my job to protect her and I failed. I promised I would save her."

"How old were you, Jedda?"

"Thirteen."

Linden pulled her even closer and began to stroke her hair with those same long soothing motions. "Hush, my darling. It's not your fault." He ran a callused thumb along her tightly closed eyelids. "Don't cry. It wasn't your fault. And you have done so much to avenge their deaths. They would be proud of you. *All* of them. You've become a fine leader, Jedda. They taught you well, your parents."

Another long silence. Then Jedda whispered, "I wanted to bury them, but their bodies were mutilated and thrown into a lime pit. I didn't have anything to weep over."

Linden's stroking stopped abruptly. "Neither did I," he said bleakly.

She was shocked into awareness. "You? An aristocrat?"

"Even aristocrats have accidents. My parents' plane crashed in mid-ocean. Nothing to salvage. No bodies. Nothing at all." His voice had turned hard, and cold, and bitter, like the Siberian wind in winter.

Jedda sensed the deep hurt he must have hidden away for years. For a split second, a vague memory stirred in her brain. Surely, something wasn't quite right here?

"I was sixteen," Linden went on. He was seeing his past, as Jedda had done. He had started to tell. He needed to finish it. "*Sixteen*. A kid. And an only child. There was just me, and my *kindly* old grandfather. Now, *there's* a joyful prospect for any orphaned boy, don't you think?" The hurt and the bitterness was even deeper.

Jedda could not bear it. She reached out and drew his head down to her naked breast, stroking his hair as gently as he had done for her. They were a pair, the two of them. They belonged together. She dropped a kiss on the top of his head.

"Now *that*," he said sharply, "is the kind of kiss my mother used to give me. I admire you in so many ways, Jedda, but I do *not* want you to be my mother." He lifted his head and laughed softly, deep in his throat. She could feel the vibration rippling through her body, as if they were still fully joined. Then the ripple became a deep shiver of excitement and anticipation. Her own passion was rising to welcome his.

There was no need for words. He began to kiss her, slowly and thoroughly, in a way that banished all her tortured memories and took her and made her complete. He brought her, at the last, to a place she had never even dared to dream of – a haven of dappled sunlight on fresh green leaves. And freedom.

• • • • •

The corridor lights were back on when Jedda finally woke. It must be morning.

What time was it? She had no idea. Beside her, Linden was still sleeping peacefully, his long legs spread over far more than his fair share of the narrow bed. One arm was still under Jedda's shoulders.

Poor Linden. He would have no feeling in it at all. His other arm lay loosely – possessively – across her middle.

Very carefully, she lifted his arm away and slid out of the bed. Her bare feet on the cold floor pulled her up short. It was freezing. Of course it was. This was not the sunlit idyll she had been dreaming about. She was still in the Jays' underground bunker, still fighting for that distant freedom, still—

She was still the leader and she had broken the most sacred of her own rules. It did not matter what had gone before. It did not matter that it had felt like the end of the world. She had broken the leader's cardinal rule. How could she continue after this?

She turned and stared at Linden's limp body with fresh eyes. In the harsh light streaming through from the corridor, the discarded clothing and crumpled sheets all looked rather sordid. She closed her eyes. The image remained. Accusing her.

I— We— Oh hell! And after I'd told him my history and wept all over him! I will never be able to look him in the face again.

That was not even the half of it.

Chrys and Anton know exactly what I have done. How can I stay as leader now?

She grabbed her clothes from the floor and bundled them together with shaking hands. Clutching the pile against her naked stomach like armour, she hauled open the door and ran for the sanctuary of the shower.

• • • • •

Anton had stayed in the control centre all night. He was tired, sure, but that had mostly worn off once he was sure that Jedda was OK. Besides, he knew the others were too whacked to stand watch. So he had taken over without being asked.

He'd admitted to himself that it was not all altruism. There was something very private that he wanted to do, and a solo night watch had seemed to be the chance he needed, while everyone else was sleeping like the proverbial logs.

He had been working for hours. Getting nowhere. It was a good job that he could rely on not being disturbed, because it was taking far longer than he'd expected to get through the security barriers. Someone had gone to a great deal of trouble, and expense, to keep their secrets secret. The security levels had been upped by several notches since Anton's earlier discovery of the hidden location. Did they suspect they were being spied on? On the basis of one single chance intrusion? Unlikely, but it couldn't be discounted. He'd have

227

to be even more careful this time to make sure he left no traces. That was if he could get in at all. Anton gritted his teeth and continued to work doggedly, cudgelling his brain for new approaches to try.

Then, at last, he was winning, but it was still slow. Too slow? He checked the time. Nearly morning. One of the others would probably be about soon. If he didn't make a breakthrough in the next twenty minutes, he'd have to give up.

And then he saw it. Yes! He was in at last.

He held his breath as the screen resolved to take account of semi-darkness. He hadn't expected that. He'd had only seconds that first time, but he remembered it all. Vividly. The picture was poor this time, but the room looked the same as before.

No, it wasn't! That extra shadow... There was someone in the room with her.

Anton tried desperately to make the picture clearer. No good. He would have to make do with what he had. Still, he hadn't lost the signal this time, and he even seemed to have some sound. He realised that he really, really wanted to hear her voice. He'd been imagining it as low, breathy, sexy – to go with the fabulous body he had half-glimpsed before. If he could only hear her voice, it might finally make her real.

He couldn't improve the picture but he could turn up the sound.

Nothing. Anton was almost sure he could hear breathing, though. She *was* real.

He was stunned to see that this time her body was naked, sprawled motionless across the huge bed with her eyes closed. He gazed at her hungrily. His ideal woman. She had been perfect before – he knew he hadn't imagined that – but she was not perfect now. Her long red hair was loose but not the glorious glossy mane he remembered. It was a mess. Her pale redhead's skin didn't have the glow of health he'd seen before, either. Maybe a trick of the light? Anton looked harder. And saw things he didn't want to see. The sheets – dark-coloured satin or silk, judging from their dull sheen – were in a heap at the bottom of the bed. One of them looked to have been ripped.

A manicured hand reached forward and threw one of the sheets over the woman's lower legs. "Cover yourself." A man's voice, hard and grating, from the camera's blind spot.

Anton gulped. Sounded like a nasty piece of work.

For a moment, the woman did not react. Then she turned her head lazily on the pillow and reached one slim hand for the sheet.

She pulled it up, but only to her waist, leaving her beautiful breasts bare. She still had not opened her eyes. Did she want to avoid looking at the man in the shadows?

"I said—!"

"I'm hot, OK?" she protested. It was a low, breathy voice, though there was a thread of petulance in it, too.

"Do as you're told," the man snapped angrily.

This time she obeyed. Much too quickly.

She's afraid of him.

"Think of that as a hopeful sign," the woman murmured.

Now she's trying to placate him.

"Really? I hadn't heard of that one. But let's hope you're right. Tell me as soon as you know." The unseen man's voice was higher, and tighter than before. Whatever it was that he wanted to know, it clearly mattered a lot to him.

A door opened. Lights came on. Masses of them. For a split second, the surveillance camera was blinded. Then it readjusted.

A statuesque blonde, dressed in something long and filmy, sauntered into the room, hips swaying. "Sonja, do you have—?" She stopped dead. "Oh. Sorry. Didn't know it was Sonja's time… I… Sorry, sir." She backed out hurriedly.

The door closed but the lights stayed on. Anton could see the whole huge room now. Much clearer than the first time, when he'd had barely a glimpse before the signal failed. Yes, those sheets were definitely satin. Everything else seemed to be equally luxurious, from the thick pile carpet and the antique furniture to the abstract paintings on the walls. An open bottle of champagne sat with two tall glasses on the table beside the bed. One of them looked untouched. The bubbles were still rising.

Anton felt hollow. His gorgeous gal – his Sonja – was some nasty rich man's plaything. By the looks of things, playtime had only just finished.

That thought made Anton want to throw up.

Curiosity soon got the upper hand. He peered closer to the screen. Who *was* that dark shadow with the voice that rasped like a blunt file?

"Well, well, well. Adding a spot of stalking to your other achievements, are you, Anton? Must say I hadn't figured you for a voyeur."

Ellen! The bloody woman had crept up on him!

"Don't," she said curtly, reaching out to grab his wrist before he could blank the screen. "I'd like to see who it is you're spying on." She stared at the screen for several seconds, taking it all in. "So who's the redhead? Must be someone pretty rich. That's a very classy pad she's got."

"I don't know who she is. I was hoping to find out when you interrupted me."

"Oh? OK then, go ahead. Let's see if you're any good at detective work."

"Look, Ellen, the others will be here soon. I don't want— I mean, no one else needs to know about this, do they? It was a…a practical joke I was planning. I can assure you that it's definitely not relevant to anything we do."

"It? You mean the woman? Or the fact that you're a Peeping Tom?" Ellen said nastily. She was enjoying getting one over on him at last. She decided to twist the knife in the wound. "So, what's it worth to you?"

"You really are a bitch!"

"Yup, that's me. My silence can be bought. I suggest you start bidding."

Anton's jaw dropped and he rocked back in his chair. At the same moment, the door from the corridor began to open. Anton looked too dazed to move. Ellen cut the video feed herself. She'd found some leverage over Anton. No point in sharing it.

It was Jedda. She looked dreadful.

"Morning, Jedda," Ellen said breezily. It sounded all wrong, as she meant it to. She wasn't one of their group and she wanted them to know it. She'd allowed herself to get much too close to them during yesterday's crisis. That was a mistake she couldn't afford. Not when they still wanted to kill her. "Feeling better?"

Jedda muttered something. Possibly a greeting. She was avoiding their eyes.

Anton jumped up and went over to Jedda. He put a hand on her good arm. "You sure you're OK?" He sounded worried. He really did care about her. Weird.

Jedda waved a dismissive hand and sat down at her workstation without a word.

"I'll get you some coffee. That'll do the trick." Anton started for the door.

"Wait, Anton." Jedda lifted her chin and turned towards him.

Ellen sensed that Jedda was having to force herself to show her normal steely determination. But she was starting to make it work.

Yup, Jedda was good. A snake bite plus a night of hot sex should put anyone off their game, but not Jedda. Give her a few minutes more and she would be back on top form.

"I need some information. Before Linden appears. You remember when you did that research on Marujn?" Jedda waited for Anton's puzzled nod before continuing, "You said that the records of Linden's parents were sealed?" Another nod from Anton, not puzzled this time, but eager. "I want to know exactly how they died."

• • • • •

K had worked all night, with only an hour's break for a workout and a swim. In spite of that, he had made no progress in his bid to capture Linden. There was no longer any doubt about his defection, though. The bastard had been a willing member of the terrorist gang that raided the Marujn store. One of the hostages reported that he'd almost spat in her face when she mentioned the Baron's name.

The Baron had not been told about that. He was already furious enough that one of his stores had been targeted. Terrorists in his precious, invulnerable empire! K expected another summons to the *presence* as soon as it was fully light. The Baron would have slept with his wrath and they would rise together, hungry for a victim. K would need to be very careful. Or very lucky.

The computer beeped. It would be Marujn. K set his expression to neutral.

"On screen."

It was the President.

"I'm hearing disturbing reports about these terrorists, K," the man began. No preliminaries, no greeting. Very unusual. The President prided himself on his gracious manners. "And I'm even more disturbed that I didn't hear them from you."

Ah, that explains it. Someone has been whispering in his ear. Someone with enough clout to make him worry about his own future.

"We're on the back foot against these people. That has to change. Immediately. First and foremost, you need to capture Linden. His loss is a PR disaster."

Trust a politician to put PR first!

"Linden will be dealt with, sir," K said reassuringly, before launching into a list of military measures that he knew would bamboozle the President. The man had very limited experience of anything except political manoeuvring.

"I'm pleased to hear that you have things in hand, K," the President said, once K had finished, "but plans need forces to execute them. I know you're short-handed, especially after the loss of Linden. I understand that Tauber is a good man."

Do you really? Who told you that, I wonder?

"I'm willing to approve his appointment as your deputy. You need a good man."

Yes, I do. And Tauber is not it.

The pass was sold. K nodded for the camera and lied quickly, "Your timing is immaculate, sir. I was intending to ask you to approve Tauber's appointment this morning. On probation, of course, but I'm sure he'll soon prove himself."

Prove himself to be a waste of space.

The President seemed satisfied. For now. He smiled a farewell and cut the link.

K flung himself out of his chair the moment the screen went blank. He began to pace the floor like a demon, in order to stop himself from punching the wall. He was going to be stuck with Tauber! The man was incompetent, self-serving, unreliable...

K stopped in his tracks. He had missed something. Something obvious.

Tauber was almost certainly being planted on K. By Marujn.

TWENTY-EIGHT

"YOU UNDERSTAND, I HOPE, that this is not yet a permanent appointment?" K fixed his bland gaze on Tauber's face and waited for the man to nod. "There will be the standard probationary period of six months, and then a decision will be made about your future."

And I have already decided what that decision will be. You will be demoted again, even if I have to manufacture the evidence to make it happen.

Tauber frowned. "May I ask how that decision will be made? And by whom?"

K decided that it would do no harm to stroke Tauber's ego a little. He might be Marujn's spy, but he was also stupid. It should be easy enough to persuade him that K had no suspicions, and no antipathy, either. "Well, the final decision is mine, as head of the administration of the province. I do normally consult the President, but that's just for form's sake. He's never interfered in my staffing decisions, so I don't expect any objections from that quarter. I imagine it will all go very smoothly. I wouldn't worry about it, if I were you, Tauber. Just get on with the job. I'm sure you'll do very well."

K could see the tension melting out of Tauber's body. The man thought he'd been handed a free pass. Good. It might make him a little less dangerous. Six months of Tauber was a nuisance, but manageable, provided K was watchful. It would give K time to check out potential candidates from other provinces – in absolute secrecy – and to select a new deputy for when Tauber's probation was up. It could have been worse.

"So, now you're Director of Enforcement, Tauber. Congratulations." K did not offer to shake hands. That would be going too far. Equally, K did not remind Tauber that he was only *acting* Director. That would be a tactical error. "Your first priority, obviously, is Linden and that band of terrorists he's defected to. I realise it's asking a lot when you've only had the job for five

233

minutes, but perhaps you'd share your ideas for catching them? You're a seasoned professional. I know you'll have made plans."

The man had, of course, and they were all worthless. Tauber proposed to go down all the predictable avenues that K had already examined and discarded – bring in possible informers from the underclass and *persuade* them to act as spies; round up anyone and everyone with a question mark on their record and beat information out of them; work the hound packs round the clock until they produced a real lead.

"I'm impressed, Tauber," K said when the man had finished laying out his plans for coercion and brutality. "You've obviously given a lot of thought to this. So I'd better let you go and get on with your work. No time to be lost, eh?"

Tauber started. Perhaps he had not expected to be dismissed so quickly? He recovered and rose from his seat. His cigar had burnt down. He needed somewhere to stub it out. He looked anxiously around K's pristine office for an ashtray.

"I'm afraid I'll have to ask you to take that away with you, Tauber," K said in the kindest of voices. "I don't *normally* allow people to smoke in my office, you see."

Tauber paled, but recovered. "I beg your pardon, K. It won't happen again."

"What? Oh, well, thank you for that. We all have our foibles, don't we?"

Tauber's eyes widened, but he merely nodded and left.

K immediately ordered the computer to change the air. He could not think surrounded by Tauber's nicotine fug.

Actually, there wasn't much thinking to do. Tauber's brute force would not work, not unless he was amazingly lucky. The underclass would suffer, but that was a price the state was always willing to pay. Still, Tauber's operations would keep him busy and that had to be good. K would be able use the time to work on more subtle plans. The Jay and his band – including Linden – would not be caught by Tauber's tactics. It needed low cunning.

K set himself to second-guess what the Jay might do next.

• • • • •

Jedda felt as if her whole body had been doused in freezing water by the time Anton finished recounting the tale of Linden's family. But she was still the leader – for the moment, at least – and she had to respond as a leader. "Thanks, Anton. Great work getting all this information so quickly. No one else could have done half as well."

Anton grinned and almost bowed. "At your service, ma'am." Then, perhaps because Jedda could not bring herself to smile back, he added, "Though I'm really sorry that what I found was so terrible. For Linden, I mean. Are you going to tell him?"

Jedda knew she couldn't. He had to be told the truth, but not by her. "You do it, Anton. You know what you found. If Linden has questions, I won't be able to answer them. I only know what you told me." Trying to keep her tone light and unemotional, she said, "You're the organ grinder and I'm the monkey here."

Anton laughed briefly. "OK. But you'll be there when I tell him?"

"Yes." It was not something she could duck. "I'll ask Chrys to bring him down, and to keep Ellen out of the way. There's no need for either of them to be in on this. Linden will want to keep it private." Actually, she did not know that for sure, but it was what her gut was telling her. Thus far, she had always been able to read what was in Linden's mind.

He was going to hate this. Anyone would. Afterwards, he was going to find out what Jedda had decided to do. And that would almost certainly make him hate *her*.

• • • • •

The first thing Linden saw in the control centre was Anton, sitting at his station, looking extremely uncomfortable. The second thing he saw was the nod of dismissal that Jedda gave to Chrys. Something was up. It wasn't going to be good. Still, it couldn't be about his relationship with Jedda. She would never involve Anton in that.

He took the seat that Jedda indicated, and waited. He was surprised to see that she stepped back into the shadows so that he couldn't see her properly any more. Was that deliberate? Was she too embarrassed to face him? He'd woken up just in time to see her running away from him, like a villain escaping from the scene of the crime.

She probably does see it as a crime. Breaking her stinking rules! Guilty as charged, m'lud.

"Linden, I've been doing some checking on your past," Anton began in a low voice. It sounded so unlike him that Linden's attention was caught. Anton had fixed his gaze on his screen, too, as if he couldn't bring himself to look at Linden. "There's no way to make this easy, so I'll make it brief. Your parents died in a plane crash."

"I know that," Linden said acidly.

"Their plane was sabotaged. It happened over the deepest part of the ocean and all the evidence was lost. That was intentional, too. I'm sorry, Linden."

The wave of grief that engulfed him was quickly replaced by raw, searing fury. Followed by the gut-wrenching realisation that, deep down, he had always suspected there was something fake about the story his grandfather had told him. Only one part had rung vaguely true – the old bastard's bitterness over the loss of his only son.

Linden swallowed hard and forced his emotions back below the surface. He must not appear weak. Jedda was watching. "I don't understand, Anton. How can you be sure when all the evidence was lost? You did say that, didn't you?"

"Yes. But your g— But Marujn kicked up a stink when he found out your father was on the plane too. He started digging around to find out how it happened. He—"

"You mean the crash?" Linden said quickly. "Or the fact that my father was on the plane?" It was the only question that mattered. He thought he knew the answer.

Anton seemed to shrink. "I...I found a hint that your father's principal assistant – his minder, I assume – was shot not long after. The assistant certainly disappeared. The formal enquiry into the crash got nowhere. It blamed a catastrophic failure, or pilot error, or a combination. Without the wreckage or the black box, it couldn't reach a definite conclusion. The case records were sealed. At Marujn's insistence."

"No doubt he said it was too painful to allow the whole world to rake over his grief," Linden spat back, remembering how the old hypocrite had behaved at the time.

"Um. Er...yeah, that's about the size of it," Anton said.

Silence. They were both waiting for Linden to do something. How could he? What he wanted to do was shout abuse and break things. And take Marujn by the throat and slowly throttle him, till his tongue turned blue and his eyeballs popped out.

Fat chance of that.

Linden took a deep breath and turned to stare at Jedda. This was for her. "Anton's pussyfooting around it, but you both know, don't you? Marujn did it to kill my mother, to get her out of the way so that he could find a new, more compliant breeder for his precious son. But his nasty little plan rebounded on him. My father wasn't supposed to be on that flight. Somehow, he escaped from his minders and went with her. And so they both died."

Linden stood up slowly. Jedda had not said a word. She had not even moved. He still could not see her face.

There was only one more thing for Linden to say, and he could leave. "Marujn was saddled with me, the sixteen-year-old offspring of a tainted mother. Poor old bastard! What a disappointment I must be to him." He straightened his shoulders and turned for the door. He wanted to be alone – more than anything, right now – but he would not run.

"Linden, I…" It was not Jedda who spoke; it was Anton.

Linden half-turned, hoping his face did not betray his pain.

Anton was holding something out to him. "It's for you. A digital replica of the photograph that Marujn destroyed," he said simply.

Linden forced himself to maintain his composure. He focused on Anton just long enough to take the picture and give a brief nod of thanks. Words were impossible. He marched out of the room with all the fiends of hell clawing at his soul.

•••••

Checking the records, K was satisfied to see that Tauber was behaving precisely as he had predicted. A great deal of heat was being concentrated on the search for the terrorists, but it was producing zero light. The man was spreading his limited resources far too thinly, too. If one of his hard-pressed teams struck lucky, they would not have the numbers to outfight the Jay's warrior women. Tauber had failed to set aside an emergency reserve; he had no backup to send in to any battle.

If Tauber had ever received proper military training during his time in South America, he appeared to have forgotten it completely.

K, on the other hand, had not. He knew the importance of honing his fighting skills with regular practice. He also knew the importance of being able to outthink and outflank the enemy, tactically and strategically. So far, the Jay had attacked a variety of apparently unrelated targets. The only one that really made sense was the Marujn Emporium, because that had won them cash that they could distribute to the people. Predictably, none of the street vermin had been rash enough to be caught with the rings and other jewellery that the Jays had taken in lieu of cash. Almost all of those pieces had been recovered by the store's security guards, once the scrum was over. The anonymous cash was a different story, though. That had all disappeared.

So the old stories would be circulating again, about how the Jay was a modern-day Robin Hood, stealing from the rich to give to the poor.

A clever fiction. They didn't throw the diamonds up in the air, did they? Worth a small fortune, and the Jay has kept that bit of the haul for himself. Some Robin Hood!

The Dark Days festival would be starting soon. The people would be expecting more hard cash from the Jay. In the old days, he had sometimes managed to dole out more than the state itself. That was the way to make a real impact.

So what will the Jay do now? Will he be after more cash?

The answers seemed too obvious. The Jay was never obvious. K must be missing something. He began again and combed through every scrap of information.

Eventually he allowed himself the luxury of one fleeting and very satisfied smile. "Computer, send a message to Dr Feliks at the lab. I need some specialised equipment and I believe he may be able to provide it. Tell him I am already on my way to his office."

K did not stop to consider whether his insights might be wrong. He knew he was gambling. Most gamblers could expect to lose their shirts, but this gamble was definitely worth the risk. If K was right, he would close his fist round them all.

He might even come face to face with Greenland woman again. That was a meeting he would relish. And that was one battle he was definitely not going to lose.

• • • • •

"Chrys? Could we have a word in private?" Linden gestured towards his sleeping cubicle, inviting her in.

She looked surprised, but she did as he asked, with a simple nod. She was such an impressive woman. Never a word wasted. As usual, it was impossible to read what she was thinking from her expression. Still, her loyalty to Jedda was absolute. So she was bound to agree to Linden's proposal. He'd thought it all through. Gone round it for hours. There was no other way. It was the best – and the only – solution.

Linden closed the door and turned to face her. He didn't know how to begin.

Chrys, of course, would not be the first to speak. She was inscrutable, waiting.

Floundering, Linden grabbed the photograph from the bunk and said, "If I'd had any doubts about your team's motives – and I can assure you I don't – this would have dispelled them. I really owe

238

Anton for thinking of this."

Was that a tiny frown? Maybe Chrys was not inscrutable after all. Maybe she could get as impatient as anyone else.

"But that's not what I wanted to talk to you about," Linden hurried on. He'd promised himself he would not even think about his parents until he had sorted the really pressing problem. "It's about…um…it's about Jedda. And me. I'm a…a liability to her. To all of you. Because of me, she broke—"

He stopped short. Chrys was really frowning now.

Linden replayed what he had just said. Idiot! He had implied it was Jedda's fault. It wasn't. Hadn't he spent hours trying to deal with his own guilt over what he'd done? He took a deep breath and began again. "Jedda is feeling guilty about what happened between us, but it's not her fault, it's mine. We broke her rules. That is, I…"

"I get the picture. You had sex with Jedda. Did you get me in here just to tell me that?" Chrys crossed her arms and glared at him.

"No. No, I need you to help me get away from here."

"Nope," Chrys said. "Having sex with the leader doesn't get you a free pass."

"Oh, for fuck's sake…! Look, Chrys, you know better than I do how much Jedda means to this group. As long as I'm here, I'll be a distraction. She'll keep feeling guilty – though it wasn't her fault – and she'll lose her focus. That will endanger all of you. I can't let that happen, and neither can you." Was he getting anywhere?

"Go on. I'm listening."

"The group needs Jedda here. To lead. So the distraction has to be eliminated."

Chrys gave a snort of laughter. He had clearly surprised her with that.

"Sorry, not your kind of elimination. I hope."

This time she did not react at all. Her face could have been carved from stone.

"My proposal is simple. I'm a good warrior and I can be useful in the fight. But not *here*. If you can get me transferred to another group, in another province, I can do my bit there. And make it up to Jedda. It's the only solution. Don't you see?"

"I see."

He waited, but she didn't say anything more. It was like drawing teeth! "If you see, you know why I need you to get me into another group. Yesterday, if possible."

No, not yesterday. In spite of all the problems he had caused by taking Jedda to bed, he couldn't ever wish it hadn't happened. It had been life changing.

Chrys let out a long breath. "No deal, Linden. I won't go behind Jedda's back. She's the boss here. I can get you to another group, sure, but *only* if she OKs it first."

"But you can't—"

"No, *you* can't. You don't make the rules. She's the leader. She gets to decide."

He had been trying to spare her everything. Guilt. Embarrassment. Pain? He had failed. There was nothing more he could say.

Chrys broke the silence. "It *is* the right thing to do, Linden. I'll ask her to approve a transfer." She started for the door.

He stopped her with a hand on her arm. "No. Don't. I'm not that much of a coward. I'll tell her— I'll *ask* her myself."

• • • • •

"Jedda?"

She turned. Linden was standing in the doorway of her tiny office, where she had retreated to be alone to think. To plan how to deal with Linden. Now he was here, in the flesh. She wasn't ready for that yet.

He made to close the door. "No," she snapped. "Leave it open."

He raised an eyebrow but did as she instructed. He remained standing by the door, looking down at her. She swung her chair half-round towards the screen. She did not want to be looking directly at him.

"I need to talk to you, Jedda. About...about what happens now."

Jedda heard him out without allowing any reaction to show. By the time he had finished, she had made up her mind. She knew exactly how she was going to handle things. What a relief! At least some of her old leadership skills hadn't deserted her.

She was not going to push her luck, though. She spoke without turning to face him. "The answer is no. I can't OK a transfer until you've proved yourself. Besides, none of the other groups would have you, as things stand. They'd say you were a spy."

"Oh."

It sounded as if he hadn't thought of that. Which suggested he hadn't thought very much at all. He just wanted to get away from Jedda and so he'd come out with the first idea that had popped into his head. To get what *he* wanted.

What else did I expect? He's a rich aristocrat, used to getting everything he wants. When has he ever had to put the needs of other people before his own desires?

The anger helped. She could face him now. She had recovered her old strength.

She swung her chair round and rose to her feet. He was still looking down on her, but not by much. It did not intimidate her. Not one bit.

"You'll remain with the Jays for now. A fighting member. Under new rules."

He tensed. His eyes narrowed. With hostility?

"From now on, you and I will not be alone together. Someone else will always be able to see. No more closed doors." Quite deliberately, she took a step towards him, forcing him to retreat. "Understood?"

TWENTY-NINE

THE SECURITY FORCES WERE making their presence felt, especially in the wealthier parts of the city, K noted. There were little squads of troops outside all the main haunts of the wealthy and powerful, presumably ready to prevent the Jay's raiding party from taking hostages again. Tauber, predictably, was re-fighting the last war, rather than preparing for the next one. The man needed to learn to think. Could he not see that the Jay was much too clever to pull the same trick twice in a row?

K's drive back from the lab was taking longer than expected, largely because he had been stopped so many times at Tauber's checkpoints. Another waste of resources, since there were hardly any civilians on the streets. The bush telegraph had been at work, and in double-quick time. London's underclass could almost smell a crackdown coming, and they all knew that their best tactic was to keep their heads down.

Here was another one!

K glanced at the box beside him. Its many official markings and seals had intimidated the various searchers so much that he had not had to open it for inspection. Would this time be any different? Not that it would matter, except for the time wasted. The contents of the box had been made to look totally innocuous.

K's car slowed automatically in response to the soldier's raised hand. He lowered the window and prepared to sit stoically through yet another search.

"Oh, beg pardon, sir. Didn't recognise you in this unmarked vehicle. Please carry on." The woman snapped to attention, ready to salute when K's car moved off.

"Wait," K instructed. "Soldier! A word."

The woman turned very pale, but obeyed instantly. "Sir?"

"Why did you not search this vehicle?"

"Wha—? Um...because...because it was you, sir. The Controller."

242

"If you have been instructed to search all vehicles, you will search them. All of them. *No* exceptions. Not me, not the President, no one. Do you understand?"

"Yessir."

K demanded the woman's name and number. "Be sure this dereliction of duty will go on your record, soldier. That is all. Drive on."

"Wait, sir!" The woman stuck her arm across in front of the car. "Sorry, sir, but your orders... I have to search your vehicle. Would you step out, please, sir?"

K swallowed a smile and started to get out of the car. One lesson learned, by one soldier. If only it were always that easy.

• • • • •

Ellen and Chrys had been called in to control to join the planning group for the next op. There was a very definite atmosphere. Ellen could feel it, and she was sure that all the others must, too, even without her highly tuned senses. Jedda was back in charge, no doubt of that, and Linden's body language screamed resentment. It looked as if he and Jedda had had a set-to and he had lost.

What did he expect? She's the leader. She's not going to come over all meek and cuddly just because she went to bed with him.

Ellen managed not to shake her head in disbelief. She told herself sternly that greater self-control was vital from now on. Most important of all, she had to guard against developing any empathy with these people. She had let her emotions win yesterday, when Jedda was injured, and it must not happen again. Besides, the Jays had barely noticed that she had helped to save Jedda. They certainly did not trust her, and she would be a fool to trust them. Over the years, she had learned the hard way that the only person she could trust was herself. Her primary goal had to be escape, in one piece and, preferably, with all her own kit plus as much of Anton's as she could steal.

Yes, that would be immensely satisfying. If she could pull it off.

"Gather round. Tomorrow night's target is the New Thames Barrier. We're going to blow it up."

Jedda's sharp tones brought Ellen back to earth with a jolt. Given the number of patrols on the streets, this op could be seriously dicey. It was probably odds-on that at least some of the team would not come back alive.

"The barrier will have to be rebuilt, in order to protect the vital assets in the city. Unless the state is prepared to invest in weather warping on a grand scale, of course."

"Don't think their technology is up to it," Anton put in. "We're not talking local weather events here. We're talking about controlling major forces – tides, the jet stream, that sort of thing."

"Good. Thanks for that, Anton. So, if we can blow the barrier and do real damage, pretty much all the state's construction resources will have to be devoted to rebuilding it. That will give us an opportunity to attack their underbelly while their attention is on the barrier." Jedda waited a beat. No one spoke. "Map, please, Anton."

They gathered round the viewscreen while Jedda outlined her plan of attack. She pointed out the weaknesses by the anchor points where the explosives would be laid. It would take a team of two. The other pair would mount a diversion nearby, to draw off the security forces. Anton would remain back at base, as normal.

"Wouldn't it be more effective to blow it up from the inside?"

Jedda turned to Linden. She did not smile. Ellen found she was not surprised. They were not exactly bosom buddies at the moment, those two.

"In theory, yes," Jedda said carefully, "but I don't see how we could make it work in practice. We'd be picked up by the internal cameras before we could get far enough into the structure to set the charges. Even if we did manage to lay them, the watchers would know exactly where they were. In the time it took us to get out again, the bomb squad could get in and defuse our devices."

"There aren't any cameras," Linden said flatly.

"You're kidding." Anton sounded amazed.

Linden grinned at Anton. "Nope. I've been inside. I know it for a fact. You're forgetting that the New Thames Barrier was built, at the gallop, by Marujn Construction, a much-admired organisation that is a byword for quality."

Anton snorted with laughter.

"Quite," Linden said. "I suspect that almost everything about it is sub-standard, including the lack of cameras. None of the inspectors dared to say so. The barrier passed its tests with flying colours. And Marujn Construction made a very tidy profit, which gave its proprietor a great deal of satisfaction. That being the case, it would give me great pleasure to blow up the bastard proprietor's favourite London landmark."

"Are you volunteering?" Anton asked quickly.

"No one is volunteering," Jedda said flatly. "It's not courage we need here, or a desire for revenge. First, we need expertise to build the explosive devices. That's you, Chrys. Second, we need technical know-how to lay Chrys's explosives where they will do the most damage. I can't send Anton, so that has to be your department, Ellen."

Silence.

Ellen didn't waste a second on the risks she was taking on. She was more interested in trying to read their faces. Chrys was inscrutable, as usual. Jedda's colour was up a bit, but she wasn't fiddling with her hair, for once. In other words, she was absolutely determined this op was going to be done her way. And Linden? He was staring at the floor, his jaw working. The tension was coming off him in waves.

In Jedda's place, Ellen wouldn't allow Linden to have any part in the op. He was much too wound up. He could easily do something stupid and get them all killed.

Then again, Jedda had said there would be two teams of two. One warrior couldn't create a diversion. It would take two to tackle the barrier – one to guard the entrance and one to lay the charges. In other words, a minimum of four. Linden was in.

At least Linden the Liability would not be part of Ellen's team. She would have either Jedda or Chrys watching her every move, ready to call on Anton to press the button on that sodding killsuit she still had to wear. She almost laughed.

"Right, we've got less than twenty-four hours to prepare," Jedda said calmly, as if they were packing for a holiday instead of a suicide mission. "I want everyone well rested and well fed before we go in. Specific tasks. Chrys, you'll put together the explosives. Lots of small, flexible devices. There must be a fair chance that Ellen will have to squeeze them into pretty tight spaces. Anton, I want you to recce the area all around the barrier. Inside as well as outside. Work out what routine the patrols are using, where the surveillance kit is. Usual stuff. You know the info we need."

Anton nodded, looking serious.

"Once you've done that, you can give Chrys a hand."

Anton grinned like a schoolboy. He probably thought of bombs as toys.

"Ellen, without cameras, you're going to be flying blind once you're inside. Anton won't be able to help you much. You'll have voice comms, but nothing else. I'm counting on your expertise to make this happen. I take it you're OK with that?"

What am I supposed to say here? "Gee, it's wonderful to be chosen as point man – thanks so much for the vote of confidence, Jedda."

She refused to give Jedda the kind of response she wanted. Ellen didn't do grovelling. Or fawning. Instead, poker-faced, she asked, "Who's my wingman?"

"I am," Jedda said immediately. "Chrys and Linden will be the decoy team."

"Fine by me," Ellen said, relieved. She could cope with Jedda. Probably. But she was not at all sure she could cope with having Chrys in her blind spot.

"Linden, I want you to sit down with Ellen and give her all the data you've got about the inside of the barrier. Entrances, exits, points where the structure—"

"OK. OK. I get the picture." Linden's sharp interruption was not helpful. Was he deliberately trying to undermine Jedda's position as leader?

Jedda scowled at him.

He had the grace to look a little sheepish. "Sorry. Grannies and eggs. I'm not trying to teach you how to do your job, Jedda, but you shouldn't—" He stopped. Took a breath. "But I hope you will also appreciate that I do know how to do mine. I guarantee that Ellen will have all the data she needs. I'll even draw her a map."

Ellen was tempted to clap. Diplomatic *and* forceful at the same time. Linden was turning into less of a liability than she had feared.

"A map would be extremely useful, Linden. Perhaps you'd make a start on that?" Jedda was being so polite it hurt. She turned to Ellen. "Can you come into my office first? As we'll be working together, there are a few things we need to get straight and I don't want our discussion to disturb anyone else's work." She gestured to Ellen to go ahead, but the briefing wasn't quite over. "Anyone got any more questions? No? OK. Everyone know what they're doing for the next few hours?"

The others nodded, even Linden. As a leader, Jedda knew her stuff.

"Great," Jedda said, smiling broadly at each of them in turn. "Thanks, guys. If you'll forgive the pun, I think this is going to be a blast."

• • • • •

Ellen was even more professional than Jedda had expected, so the one-to-one briefing did not take very long at all. Ellen listened, she considered, and she asked short, sharp questions when anything was unclear. Even though she wasn't a full member of the Jays yet, she was totally committed to making this op a success. Or at least, she *seemed* to be committed.

Until Ellen had taken Jedda's test, and passed or failed it, it would be impossible to be sure where her loyalties lay. She was certainly using every available opportunity to snipe at team members, especially Anton, but that might be only a defence mechanism to hide her own fears. She still had a potential death sentence hanging over her, after all. The killsuit would remain operational 24/7 until Jedda was absolutely sure Ellen would not try to escape. On the other hand, there had been encouraging signs. Yesterday, for example, according to Chrys's report. Which reminded Jedda...

"One last thing, Ellen. Chrys told me what you did yesterday, how much you helped. I want to thank you."

For a split second, Ellen looked surprised. Then she muttered something unintelligible.

"It goes to prove what an asset you are to us," Jedda went on, hoping to find a way through Ellen's tough shell. "And it's the kind of support that we always give each other. If you'd been the one with the injury, everyone would have rallied round to save you. Of course, you already know that. We did get you out after you were shot in the square." Jedda did not mention the obvious truth, that Ellen had only been in the square in the first place because Jedda had forced her to go there.

Ellen raised her chin and cocked her head on one side. She had a very calculating look in her eye. "Where are we going with this?" Her tone was not hostile, but it was not friendly either.

"I guess I'm trying to persuade you that you would be better off here with us, as part of our team, rather than out there on your own. In spite of all your skills." She paused. Ellen was trying very hard not to react, but Jedda thought there might have been the tiniest hint of softening in her expression. Progress? Maybe.

Jedda touched Ellen gently on the arm. "Think about it, hmm? It can be good to sleep sound while someone else stands watch."

• • • • •

It was fully dark, and the blessed rain was falling steadily by the time the Jays reached the Barrier area. They had come in separate pairs, by different routes, in order to avoid drawing attention to themselves in the almost empty streets. Anton had guided them round the checkpoints and warned them about oncoming mobile patrols. The rain was a help there. The mobile patrols – tired and bored after long hours on duty with no enemy engagements to break the monotony – were losing their edge. Anton reported that some of them were huddled in the lee of buildings, trying to keep dry, when they should have been marching down the streets, intimidating anyone they met.

"New info." Ellen thought she detected glee in Anton's voice, but it was difficult to be sure via the earwig. She would hear better if she had a comms implant, like Jedda and Chrys, but only fully paid-up members of the Jays were trusted with such precious kit. Anton had assured Ellen and Linden that the earwigs and the implants were on the same frequency this time, so all four of them would be able to hear Anton's calls. Ellen was not sure she believed it. In any case, he could easily switch frequencies on the fly.

She could hear him for now and his news was good. "The regular patrol at the Barrier has been on duty for a double shift today. They're waiting to be relieved, but the reliefs have been delayed. The patrol is getting a bit mutinous. They've stopped doing proper rounds and they're all sitting together in the patrol house, moaning."

"How long till the reliefs get here?" That was Jedda, focused as ever.

"Haven't left barracks yet. At least twenty minutes. Maybe thirty."

Jedda faced her team. She was smiling grimly. "Stroke of luck for us. No need for a diversion until we see a patrol. Chrys, Linden, keep watch for opposition movement. You know what to do as soon as you see any. Alert me if you have time. Otherwise, just get on with it. Rendezvous back at the bunker. Control?"

"Roger that."

"Separate team frequencies now. Message relay via Control."

"Wilco. New frequencies. Three, two, one, mark."

Ellen reckoned Jedda was being over-cautious. Why separate the frequencies before the teams went into action? Anton could fix that in a nanosecond, couldn't he?

Wrong! Action couldn't wait. Action was right now.

Jedda raised a hand to Chrys. Without a word, Chrys darted off, followed by Linden. Jedda did not waste a second watching them. She was right on top of the job, focused on her own task. She nodded towards the concealed entrance Ellen was to use.

My turn now!

Ellen glanced round one last time. Chrys and Linden had almost disappeared into the murk. She could see how watchful they both were. Watching for the enemy. Watching each other's backs.

No one would be watching Ellen's back once she was deep inside.

She tightened the straps securing the backpack of explosives and did one last quick check – armour, weapons, headset, comms, torches. All OK. She raised a thumb to Jedda, who nodded in response and mouthed the order. *OK, go!*

Ellen dropped to her knees and crawled through the tiny entrance that would lead her into the bowels of the New Thames Barrier.

Her whole world turned pitch black.

The first thing that hit her was the smell. Damp, decay, rot. So foul that Ellen almost gagged. She forced herself to breathe through her mouth and to keep crawling down the metal tunnel. It seemed to be getting narrower and narrower. But it should open out soon. She should be able to stand upright. She really needed that.

Please let it be soon!

The weight of the backpack was crushing when she was on all fours. But she had to go on. Even though movement was almost impossible in the increasingly cramped space.

At least I won't have that problem on the way out.

The slim beam of her torch hit darkness. Bigger darkness. That must be the main tunnel, up ahead. She crawled faster. Her backpack was scraping along the tunnel roof as she forced it through.

Yes!

She got to her feet cautiously, feeling her way up the metal wall with her gloved hands. A second to straighten her back and roll her shoulders. She stood still, listening.

Nothing.

Nothing *human*. Dripping water. The low hum of motors and pumps. Nothing else. Nothing she hadn't expected.

She glanced at the headset display. She had memorised the layout, using Linden's rough map, but it was good to be reminded. A hundred and twenty paces down this tunnel, then left into a feeder loop. From there, she'd be able to reach the target location where she would plant the first set of bombs.

"Control. Point Whisky reached. Going for Point X-ray now."

Silence. Not even a crackle.

"Control. Do you read?"

Absolutely nothing.

So much for Anton's sodding comms. Now I'm definitely on my own.

THIRTY

ELLEN SPRINTED LIGHT-FOOTED ALONG the tunnel to the feeder loop. It was another very narrow passage, but probably designed as an occasional access route. For thin people.

So this time she would not have to crawl. But she would have to take off her backpack and carry it. She shivered. There was no sign of anyone else in the complex, but still… It was so much safer to keep both hands free.

She tried the comms link again. Nothing. She was going in alone, totally blind.

Taking a deep breath – and refusing to let the stench get to her – she fixed the torch to her jacket. She shifted the backpack to her left hand and drew her weapon with her right. Set on kill. There would be no live witnesses.

Quicker and kinder that way. The bombs would kill them anyway.

Weapon first, she squeezed into the feeder loop. It was not just dark and narrow, it was lumpy, as if the walls had not been properly finished when it was built. Just the sort of corner-cutting a Marujn company would do. Ellen didn't bother trying to check the walls with her torch. She couldn't afford the time. She kept the beam of her torch pointing straight forward. That was the way she needed to go. The sooner she planted these bombs – and the second set – the sooner she could get out of this stinking hole.

Like the first tunnel, this one got narrower. Almost as if it were alive and crowding in on her, determined to crush her. She forced that subversive thought away.

Focus!

At one point, she had to turn sideways to edge her way between the lumpy walls. She could feel the hard-edged bulges digging into her, back and front. Her whole torso was going to be beautifully bruised after this.

She checked the headset plan. There was no other feeder tunnel for this target, on this level. To get out, she would have to use this passage again. More bruises.

That bloody snake Marujn and his profits.

The going was easier after the first fifty metres. For some reason, the walls were better finished, too. After another twenty metres, the feeder loop widened a lot and she was able to up her pace. And then she was there.

She dumped her backpack and did a quick assessment, letting her torch play across the huge joints and stays. She was spoilt for choice. There were at least four obvious places to plant explosives. Without really trying!

It was going to be easy. And the devastation would be brutal.

She stowed her weapon and dug out her bomb-making kit. She would need several charges, carefully placed and timed, first to weaken and then to destroy the main part of the structure at this end.

She tackled the biggest bombs first. Two sets of six charges each. She attached them carefully at the lowest joint on the main supporting struts, less than a metre above the floor. She checked detonators and anti-tamper devices. Good, done. These bombs would be timed for zero hour. But she would not set the timers till she had finished everything else. She started on the smaller bombs next. They were to fracture the upper structure so that it would collapse completely when the main bombs went off. She did quick mental calculations and measured carefully. She had to get these right.

She decided on four smaller charges, placed individually, twelve centimetres from the Y-joints supporting the external parts of the barrier. Working rapidly, she finished the four devices and set the charges for zero minus twenty seconds. Then she set the timers for her main charges. The twenty second gap was too short for anyone to interfere with the bombs that mattered.

Once they had all gone off, only the bottom of the supports would be left, sticking up like bleeding stumps in a mangled jaw. If she could ensure that her second bomb site blew at the same time, a huge section should collapse into the river.

Up yours, Marujn!

Her clock was ticking. She still had to plant the second set of bombs at the next site and get herself to safety. Yup, she could do that. Grinning, she did one last check with the torch. Perfect. Even if a guard checked the area, she would probably not spot the bombs. Chrys had done a first-class job when she put those together.

Now for trial by lump-wall!

The smell seemed to be getting worse. If she had had a free hand, she'd have been holding her nose when she got to the narrowest part of the feeder loop. As it was, she just kept breathing through her mouth. She promised herself the prize of good fresh air, and rain on her skin. *After* she had completed the rest of her mission.

Quicker progress this time. Not surprising. She had only half the load to lug.

Back at the main tunnel, she straightened gratefully and swung the backpack up to her shoulders. As she bent to get her right arm through the straps, the torch beam shone onto her midriff.

Ellen went very cold. And very still.

She dropped her backpack by the wall and raced for the entrance tunnel.

• • • • •

Jedda was getting anxious. "Control. Progress report, alpha two."

"Nothing to report. No message." Anton sounded worried, too.

"Team bravo?"

"Team bravo at target. Dug in. No enemy sighted."

Jedda breathed out. Chrys and Linden were safe and holding a good position. They could probably defend it for as long as Jedda needed.

But how long would that be? Why hadn't Ellen reported in? Surely she couldn't be trying to escape from inside the barrier? It would be suicidal in a killsuit.

Jedda scanned the area again for opposition. Nothing. The mutinous patrol must still be moaning to each other about how hard-worked they all were.

They should try being a freedom fighter.

"I've got her." Anton, and panicky. "She's coming out. Something's wrong."

Jedda reached the tunnel entrance as Ellen started crawling out. Jedda couldn't quite stifle an exclamation of disgust. "You stink," she groaned.

Ellen stood up and Jedda saw.

"What the hell happened?"

"Booby traps. Dye and stink, mixed." She ripped open her jacket and checked the inner layers of clothing. "It goes right through. It's fouled every stitch I've got on."

Jedda's mind was whirling. An all-pervading stink. For the

hounds, of course. It would be impossible for Ellen to escape them in those clothes. She could lead the enemy right to the door of the bunker. But the dye? Why couldn't Ellen's combat clothes neutralise it?

"OK, stink for the hounds. What's the dye for? Why can't the fabric absorb it?" she asked quickly. If she understood the enemy's plans, she could counter them.

"Not sure," Ellen replied. "Hidden sensors? Maybe inside the Barrier? Whatever it is, it'll be clever. Not Marujn's doing. This is K."

"Right. We abort the op now and get you out of here. Control, tell—"

"No!" Ellen shook her head vehemently. "I've only done half the job. I came out to warn you that our comms don't work inside. And that I've been turned into a moving beacon. You and the team have to stay away from me or we'll all be taken."

Jedda couldn't argue with the logic of that.

Ellen shoved her watch right under Jedda's nose. "Look. There's still time. I'm going back in to do the rest of it."

"You're crazy," Jedda snapped. "If you're right about the dye, they'll see you coming. You'll never get to the target site. It's suicide."

Ellen shook her head. "I'm going to finish what I started."

Jedda made up her mind in half a second. She grabbed Ellen's sleeve and dragged her into the shelter of the building, out of the rain. "Strip." In the same moment, she started pulling off her own clothes. "Control, alpha one. We're changing clothes. Do not operate destruct. I say again, do not operate destruct. Acknowledge."

A pause. "Control. Wilco."

The two women completed the swap in record time. Jedda gave Ellen a quick once-over. "You'll do. No dye. Your smell's subsiding. Your smell-bots will take over now. You'll probably be clear by the time you get through the entrance tunnel. Unless that's where the booby traps are?"

"No. In the feeder loop walls. I won't get caught again. But how will you—?"

"Forget about me. You're good to go. So go. Check in as soon as you get comms. The rest of the plan stays as agreed."

Ellen threw Jedda a very strange look. Jedda ignored it. Ellen thought Jedda was committing suicide. So what? What other option was there?

Ellen didn't stop to argue the toss. She disappeared back into her tunnel.

Watching, Jedda told herself she had done the right thing. Ellen was a warrior. For Ellen, the mission came first. But Jedda hadn't the slightest idea what she was going to do to save the rest of the mission. Or her team. Or herself.

Now I'm the moving beacon. Out here where every hound in London will smell me from streets away. And every camera will see me as bright as a neon sign.

• • • • •

"Relief patrol leaving barracks now," Anton reported tightly. He was fuming. He had used every trick he knew to check inside the barrier and he'd found no sensors. So he'd assumed – perfectly reasonably – that Linden was right about the cameras. But now bloody Ellen was telling everyone that Anton had failed.

Although he had lost contact with her again, he knew he still had the upper hand. She might think the change of clothes would save her from the killsuit, but she was wrong. Jedda's was a suicide suit, too. All the Jays' combat kit was. A quick death by choice was always better than a slow death by enemy torture.

If Ellen did try to escape the Jays, Anton would make sure he got his opportunity to terminate her. With extreme prejudice.

"Patch me in to team bravo." Jedda broke into Anton's grim thoughts with a crisp order. "Bravo, diversion attack in five. Let's get that idle patrol out here. I want to deal with them before the relief arrives." She waited a beat for Chrys's acknowledgement. Then she started counting down over the new comms link.

• • • • •

Without the bulky backpack, Ellen reached the main tunnel in record time. She ignored the smell. She knew how to avoid getting any more of it on her clothing.

Her backpack was just where she had dropped it. She grabbed it and raced for the next site. Every second counted. She was sure there must be sensors that Anton's systems hadn't found. If the sensors only reacted to K's fancy dye, she had an outside chance of completing the mission. If they reacted to heat, or movement…

This is between you and me, K. From here on, this is personal.

The son of a bitch had already shot her once. She owed him for that. All this latest stuff was K's doing, too. She knew it. Deep in her gut. She *knew*.

She had a double score to settle with Mr Too Clever By Half.

She was going to destroy K's precious barrier, even if she blew herself up in the process.

• • • • •

Anton was starting to worry that Jedda might never trust him again. She might fire him. Unless he could prove himself with something spectacular. Right now.

"Control, how long before relief patrol contact?" Jedda's voice, sounding strained. Anton could hear firing in the background. His screen showed shadows moving through the rain. The mutinous patrol were taking on Chrys and Linden.

Anton checked quickly. "Eighteen minutes. Less if they move at the double. Don't count on more than twelve."

"Roger. Out."

Yes! He knew how to redeem himself. The timing was going to be even tighter than Ellen's bombs.

• • • • •

Linden and Chrys were well dug in. A solid pillar for each of them, plus a low wall in between. A blank wall at their backs. They picked off the first few patrol members easily. But the rest kept coming. Lots of them. With much greater care.

"Odds not good," Linden gasped, between shots. "We need alpha here."

"No. Not wearing that beacon kit. She's no chance of getting across the open ground." Chrys took careful aim and downed another of the advancing enemy. "Better where she is. We'll get them in the crossfire."

"But she's got no one at her back. They'll kill her."

"They'll kill us all if we don't concentrate. Shut up and keep shooting!"

He didn't care about his own life. But he did care about Jedda's. He risked a quick look and let off three more rapid shots. Wow! Three more kills. It seemed he was on fire. "I'm going to bring her in. Cover me!"

"No! Stay here!"

Too late. He was already out in the open, and running.

• • • • •

Ellen was much faster at the second site. No calculations or measurements needed. Just quick-fingered methodical work and it was done. She dumped her backpack. The bombs would destroy all the evidence. She needed to be able to run.

Last of all, she set the timers. After all that time outside, she was cutting things very fine. Four minutes' delay for the small charges. Four twenty for the others.

Done!

Ellen raced for the feeder loop. Even as it narrowed, she kept on running.

She skidded to a halt just before the booby-trapped section. To be safe, she needed to crawl through at ground level. After that, she still had to make it back outside. How much time was left? She checked again. Not good.

Great choice, Ellen. Stink and live. Or crawl and die.

• • • • •

Jedda saw Linden fall. She cried out. She couldn't stop herself.

A moment later, Chrys's voice came through her implant. "Alpha one, stay back. I'll get him. Give me cover."

Jedda couldn't think for the pounding of her blood. She felt as if her head was going to explode. She couldn't move.

"Cover me!" Chrys was shouting now. And firing as she ran out.

That message did get through. Jedda started firing again. Then she dug out her spare weapon and let rip with both at once. Wide arc. Rapid fire. Aiming not great, but the effect was good. The patrol was ducking for cover, rather than firing back.

She had to do more. The relief patrol could be on them in less than five minutes. At least half the existing patrol members were still able to fight. "Control?" she gasped. "Update. How long?"

Silence. *Shit, shit, shit.*

"Control. Update!"

Silence. Then, "Relief diverted. I say again. Relief diverted." Anton's voice. Anton the miracle worker! "Get out of there, alpha."

"Roger. Out."

Chrys was helping Linden back to the pillars. Jedda set her jaw and kept on firing, faster and faster. She even managed to wing a couple. So luck was on her side?

"Team bravo back." Chrys wasn't even breathing heavily.

"Damage to bravo two?" Jedda was still firing. She hoped the noise would conceal the anxiety in her voice.

"Wait one." A pause. Too long. "Not life-threatening. Severe. Needs treatment. Soon."

Soon. A single terrifying word. A split second of white-hot fear. Then Jedda's years of training and experience slotted into place. Her tumbling mind cleared and calmed. Her pulse slowed. She knew exactly what she was going to do.

She rapped out her orders. "Team bravo to return to base. Team alpha will regroup here." To wait for Ellen. Or the explosions that told her Ellen was dead.

"Come back now!" That was Anton, sounding panicked, breaking protocol.

"No! I'm a beacon!" Jedda cried. Surely it was obvious?

"Bravo to return to base. Wilco," said Chrys's measured voice, repeating her orders in standard military fashion. "Then to return to back up team alpha. Soonest. Good luck, alpha. Out."

That last bit wasn't following orders at all. That was Chrys promising to risk her life for a friend.

Jedda screwed up her eyes to peer through the rain and the gloom. Was that Chrys she could see over there, helping Linden? He seemed to be limping. But he was supporting most of his own weight. They would make it out. They had to.

Jedda could second-guess what was in Chrys's mind. She would dump Linden back at the bunker. Then she would grab new combat kit and come back to rescue Jedda. And Ellen too, if she ever made it out.

Jedda grinned into the darkness. It might even work.

Provided team alpha could manage to stay alive until backup arrived.

• • • • •

Linden was just about managing his wounded leg. Chrys had slapped a field dressing on it while they were crouching down behind the wall, and the local anaesthetic had taken effect almost at once. The pain was more or less under control. But his blasted leg wasn't. It didn't seem to want to work properly. So far, they were only half-way home, and his leg was getting more and more floppy. And numb.

He stopped for a second to catch his breath. He swore through gritted teeth.

Chrys put an arm round his waist. The extra support was wonderful, but it couldn't last. If he had to put his weight on Chrys, they would never get back in time.

"It'll mend. Can't do anything till I get you back to base." She straightened and withdrew her arm. She looked steely. "We need to move. Can you walk? Run?"

"Yes," he gasped. "Run." He had no choice. Chrys was heading back to base for spare clothes for Jedda. If Linden couldn't keep up, she would abandon him. And she couldn't afford to leave him alive.

In her place, he would do the same.

He ran through the pain. When his leg started to wobble under him, he used two hands to force it back straight. They avoided all the patrols. Anton was doing his stuff there, clearly trying to make up for his failure to detect the sensors inside the barrier or to make his comms work inside. Given half a chance, Linden would thump him for his mistakes. It was the least he deserved. Useless idiot!

A flash of pain shot up into Linden's hip. He forced himself to keep running.

I deserved that. Anton's not the only idiot here. Another smug idiot announced that there were no cameras inside the barrier.

Then the pain was not in his leg any more. His whole body was one giant ache.

If Jedda dies, it will be my doing. I gave her a bum steer. And I insisted on those stupid heroics. To save her? Utter crap! All I've done is leave her to the mercy of K's thugs with no backup at all.

Guilt was spurring him on. At last, he had finally conquered the pain and his leg was beginning to respond better to the desperate signals that his brain was sending out.

"Not far now," Chrys muttered. "Keep going, Linden. You can make it."

"Yeah." That was all the breath he could spare.

No matter what Chrys does now, I am definitely leaving. I'm nothing but a liability for Jedda. I have to go. Before I become the death of her.

• • • • •

Ellen tried to avoid the obvious bulges in the narrow passage. But some of them still caught her. Her choice was no choice. She didn't have time to drop to a crawl. She had to get out before the bombs went off. At least into the main passage.

She would worry about dealing with the stink and dye once she was safely out. If she didn't make it out soon, she would be past worrying about anything.

She squeezed through the narrowest section of the lumpy walls. The booby trap bulges really got her there, almost breaking her ribs. The stink was getting stronger again, too. But she was nearly through. The feeder loop was getting a little wider at last, so she could avoid the booby traps. She could see the main passage. Once there, she could sprint. She would even have a bit of protection from the blast.

She risked a time check. Just over two minutes.

She had made it. She could breathe again.

She drew her second weapon and sprinted down the dark passage to the exit. With a weapon in each hand, she shouldn't be taken by surprise. Even if they could see her via their fancy sensors. If they came at her, she would fight and die here. And—

"Argh! Uh!"

All the breath was knocked from her body as she tripped and fell her length. Her right hand hit the deck and she lost her grip. Her weapon skittered away across the tiles. But she still had the one in her left hand. She could fight left-handed if she had to. She clenched her fist on it and started to get up. She could still get out in time.

A booted foot came down hard on her left hand. A fraction of a second later, a large splayed hand pushed into the middle of her back, pinning her to the ground.

"Not yet, I think." The voice was deep and very harsh. A man's voice. Another hand prised the weapon out of her useless fingers.

"Now you can get up. Slowly." The heavy boot was removed. And the hand from her back.

She had no weapons, but she could still run. She started to ease herself up on to her haunches. Pain shot up her left arm. Had he broken her hand?

Doesn't matter. I've got a spare! And two good legs.

"Don't try anything," the voice said quietly. "You'll be cut down."

Ellen knew what was waiting for her if they took her alive. "Control. Press destruct. Now!" She screwed her eyes shut, waiting.

Silence. Nothing.

No comms. Still no sodding comms.

Then she remembered that she was wearing the wrong suit anyway. This one was Jedda's. This one couldn't kill. They were going to take her alive.

She did the only thing she could. She started to run. Into the dark.

"Lights!" the voice yelled.

Instantly, great batteries of lights came on. Ellen was blinded. She stumbled. She couldn't see where she was going. She couldn't see a thing. Long fingers grabbed her injured hand and jerked her to a halt. She gave a sharp scream of pain.

"Did that hurt?" The voice sounded amused. And quietly terrifying.

It was a moment of revelation for Ellen. A weird calm descended on her. The terror melted away. She knew exactly what she was going to see. She narrowed her eyes against the glare and turned, ignoring the glistening trip wire and forcing herself to focus on her nemesis. It was K. Of course it was.

He thought he had won.

Inside Ellen's head, a clock began counting down. Tick, tick, tick. A few seconds more. That was all it needed. K's precious barrier would be blown sky high. It might not kill him. It might not kill her. But at least she would have the immense pleasure of seeing the horror on his face when he realised what she had done. She would hold that in her mind, whatever came next. Whatever he did to her now.

Tick, tick, tick.

THIRTY-ONE

IT WAS THE LONGEST TWENTY seconds of Ellen's life. She was staring at K. He was staring back at her. Neither of them moved a muscle.

An explosion. Small. Distant.

Must be site two. What happened at site one? Did I get the timing wrong?

He should have looked shocked. He didn't. "You look puzzled, Greenland lady." His eyes narrowed, assessing her. His lips thinned into a smile.

K's cold-blooded smile made Ellen think of a predator cat, the kind that would amuse itself with injured prey before finally devouring it. She was definitely the prey. She clenched her good fist and waited. Less than twenty seconds for the main bomb at site two. At least she'd got that one right. Then he would feel it.

"Don't bother to count."

What?

"It's not going to happen. The bomb squad have disabled your other devices."

"That's not poss—!" She clamped her mouth shut. No point in arguing with a man like K. The truth would be obvious soon enough. In about five seconds, actually.

Five seconds passed. Ten. No more explosions.

"Convinced now?" he asked sweetly.

Smug bastard!

She could not afford to waste time thinking about how K had disabled her devices so quickly. She had to focus on getting away from him. It was still one on one. He appeared to have no backup. And he was a fixer not a warrior. If she could just—

"Don't even think about it," he snarled. No smile now.

Is he reading my mind?

He was still holding her weapon. His eyes were hard. He reached for her.

Is he—?

The question evaporated as the pressure syringe was jammed against her neck. Ellen's world turned black.

• • • • •

Jedda's two-handed firing was keeping the remains of the patrol pinned down. The goons had retreated together, like amateurs, and were huddled behind the corner of the barrier, with their backs to the river and no scope for crossfire or pincer movements. No scope for escape, either. Until help arrived for them, Jedda should be able to hold them. One warrior against at least five, maybe six. Incredible, but it was happening.

It couldn't last, Jedda knew. Reinforcements would arrive soon and she'd have to make a run for it before they spotted her. But she desperately wanted to hang on for a few seconds more, in case Ellen managed to escape before her bombs blew. So Jedda kept firing, listening for the sound of explosions. And she kept checking for Ellen.

Then she heard it. Definitely an explosion. Muffled and rather distant.

Surely it should be louder than that?

The patrol members had heard it too. She could see unruly movement among the group cowering behind the barrier. They would wonder what was happening and what they should do. If they had failed to leave anyone on guard inside, they would all be in deep trouble when the inquiries began. So they might be panicking. Good.

Jedda fired another couple of quick volleys. The patrol ducked back into cover again. She nodded to herself. *Keep 'em honest. Keep 'em scared.* But where was Ellen? There was still time – just – for her to get out before the real bombs went off.

Somewhere in her head, Jedda was counting down. And puzzling. The first explosion hadn't sounded loud enough. But everything depended on the size of the charges that Ellen had laid. Preliminary charges could be quite small. Jedda told herself not to assume failure. The main explosions would be any second now – bigger, louder, and truly devastating. They would come. Ellen had definitely laid all the charges at site one, even if she had failed at site two.

Jedda checked the time. She felt her body tense in anticipation. She had to keep firing. She couldn't risk covering her ears with her hands.

Five, four, three, two...
She ducked down and closed her eyes, firing all the while. Aiming didn't matter.
...one, zero.
Nothing. *Nothing at all.* No explosion. No Ellen, either.
They had failed. The bombs must have been defused. Somehow. And Ellen?
She's dead. Or as good as. I'm the leader. I've got to think about the living.
She hauled in a ragged breath. "Control from alpha one. Do you read?"
"Go ahead, alpha one." Anton. Always reliable, always there.
"Operation failed. Retreating to location Lima. Bravo to rendezvous soonest."
"Location Lima. Roger." Anton sounded grim. "How many, alpha?"
"One." The admission was like a blow to Jedda's gut. She hated losing people. It was always her fault.
"One. Roger. Bravo not yet available. Alternative rendezvous after Lima?"
Clearly, Chrys had not made it back to the bunker yet. She'd have to settle Linden, and then come out again with the supplies for Jedda. It could take a while. Jedda might have to hang around for five or ten minutes at the rendezvous. Location Lima gave her the best chance, but it was impossible to guarantee that anywhere would be safe for that long. What if a patrol just happened to come round the corner? She needed a second escape route. One that would never occur to K's brainwashed minions.
"Location Lima first. If compromised, location Foxtrot."
"Foxtrot?" Anton sounded shocked. Then, "Foxtrot. Roger."
Location Foxtrot was right on the river. It was December, and it was dark, but if Jedda was cornered there, she would be going for a swim.

• • • • •

K carried his limp and stinking parcel through the corridors of his Central HQ. She was heavier than she looked. Lots of lean muscle, of course. He could feel some of that through the rough blanket he had wrapped her in. All in all, quite a warrior.
K was going to have to congratulate Dr Feliks as soon as he got a chance. The man's clever concoctions had done everything he promised, and more.

More? Too right. My vehicle will have to be fumigated to get rid of the good doctor's special stink.

By the time K reached his office, his arms were beginning to feel the strain, but he squatted down and lowered his burden gently to the floor. Then he found himself wondering why he had done such an extraordinary thing.

Standard operating procedure. No point in giving her bruises when she isn't conscious to feel them.

That wasn't all of it. He wasn't thinking clearly. Probably because he was still fizzing with adrenalin. He'd been away from action for such a long time, and he hadn't realised how much he'd missed it. The holo suite couldn't compete with the real thing.

"Need to get out more!" he said to the blank wall. And laughed.

"Sorry, what?"

K leapt to his feet and whirled round to see who had spoken. It was Tauber, standing in the doorway, with a slack jaw and a puzzled expression on his face. For once, there was no accompanying cigar.

Tauber's expression quickly changed to revulsion once he began to breathe the air of K's office. He gagged. Then he swore. He did it in Spanish, but the message was universal. "What the hell's in that stinking bundle?" he choked out eventually, flapping a hand towards the heap on the floor. The other hand was trying to cover his face.

K drew himself up even taller and looked down his nose at his very temporary deputy. "That stinking bundle," he said softly, reaching out to prod the blanket with his boot, "is the Jay woman who just tried to blow up the New Thames Barrier. Or hadn't you noticed the explosion there?"

"Yes, of course I did. I put the emergency procedure into action at once. I've sent reinforcements to the perimeter. And the major incident bomb squad to assess the damage." His initial nervousness was lessening noticeably. So he thought he was covering his back pretty well. "The on-site patrol's report said the explosion was small."

"Did it? Interesting. And where was the on-site patrol at the time?"

"I'm not sure." The man was sounding worried again. Good.

K knew the answers. But he would not reassure Tauber. Let him sweat. K said smoothly, "No doubt your inquiry will tell us. The President and the Council will expect to be briefed urgently. I take it I can expect your full report on my desk in the morning?" He turned away without waiting for an answer. It was a gesture of dismissal.

Tauber failed to take the hint. He cleared his throat rather too loudly. "I'll take the Jay woman off your hands now, K."

K spun on his heel. He stood stock still, letting his gaze drift pointedly over Tauber's rumpled clothing. He allowed his disapproval to show for a couple of seconds. Then he blanked his expression and said quietly, "I think not, Tauber."

Tauber was visibly shocked. "But...but I'm the Director of Enforcement. It's my job to organise interrogations."

K nodded slowly. "You're the Director of Enforcement *and* External Operations," he began musingly, as if he were thinking aloud. "But you had no forces at the barrier to prevent this attack, and you did not capture this woman. You will concede that you didn't catch her, I take it? Or play any part in catching her?" He smiled sadly and switched to officialese. With luck, Tauber would be frightened stiff by it. "In an evaluation of your first period in charge of external operations, that would seem to be – very unfortunately – rather below the standard required."

Tauber's face was beginning to look as crumpled as his uniform.

"That being so," K continued in the same detached, official-sounding voice, "the President might be concerned to learn that I had delegated the interrogation of such a valuable prisoner to someone who was...er...still learning the ropes." K refused to indulge in a nastier rebuke, even though quite a few had suggested themselves. There was no value in antagonising the man now. Fear was enough. When the eventual showdown came, the rebukes would be lacerating, and the dismissal would be final. Until then, K could wait.

"I...er...I see what you mean, but—"

K stopped him with a gesture. Then he decided to appear to unbend a little. "Your priority is your report, Tauber. You won't have time to do an interrogation as well. And you wouldn't want to delegate it, would you? Not for *this* prisoner."

"No. No, of course not."

"We are agreed then. You will proceed with the inquiry and the report. I will relieve you of the burden of interrogating this prisoner. Actually, I think you're getting the better end of the bargain. You get to escape the stink."

Tauber laughed dutifully but he looked beaten. He left without a word.

K watched through the open doorway for a long time. He would have to manage Tauber more carefully in future. The man was stupid, but even he would notice if K was openly mocking him. It might be satisfying, but it was not good tactics.

He locked the door and turned back to the bundle on the floor. A much worthier opponent. His tactics with her would have to be better than good. He would have to remain dispassionate throughout. Dispassionate, calculating, distant. And cold.

He pulled on a fresh pair of surgical gloves. Then he bent and seized the edge of the blanket with both hands. Took a breath and held it. With a stout pull and an upward flick, he propelled her out of the blanket and across the floor.

Cleopatra was delivered to Caesar in a rolled-up carpet. Just like this.

Not at all like this. Cleopatra had been bent on seduction. Greenland woman was bent on destroying everything K was trying to defend – order, security, the stability of the state. Greenland woman was poison. She had to be neutralised.

He prepared carefully. He cleared the space all round her unconscious body. There was nothing within reach that she could use to attack him. He checked the weapon he had taken from her. After a moment's reflection, he clicked it from kill back to default. It was important that there should be no deaths here. Not by accident. Satisfied, he applied the syringe of trank antidote to the side of her neck and leaned back against his desk to wait. A minute – perhaps ninety seconds – should do it.

It took longer. A full two minutes. Either that, or she was faking it, pretending to be out for the count in order to gather her wits. He wouldn't put that past her. He wouldn't put anything past her.

Her eyes opened. For a moment they seemed glazed. Then she screwed them up against the light.

"Dazzled again?" he said lightly. "That's twice in one night."

He saw the exact moment when she realised what had happened to her. It was as if her whole being had been blurred and had suddenly come into focus. She became taut, alert, ready to seize an opening. She was good. No doubt about it.

But K was good, too. This was no longer a contest of equals.

"Stand up." He barked the words like a military order.

She looked across at him, registered the weapon in his hand, and got slowly to her feet. She did not shiver or avoid his gaze. She raised her chin just enough to make her point. She was not beaten. The expression in her eyes was pure, venomous hate.

No more than he had expected.

"Excellent. You appear to be back on top form." He straightened and aimed the weapon at her heart. Her own weapon. "Now strip."

· · · · ·

Jedda had been hanging around at rendezvous Lima for much too long. Another few seconds and she would have to give up, and go to Foxtrot. She shivered at the thought. She really did *not* want to have to swim for it.

Had Chrys and Linden made it back safely? If Chrys had had to choose between saving Linden and saving Jedda...

Jedda gulped. She had to concentrate on her own mission now. To be the leader of the Jays. That meant putting Linden out of her mind. Completely.

Anton should have contacted her again by now. It seemed ages since she'd spoken to him. "Control. Update." She heard impatience in her own voice. Bad. A leader should not let her team see her weaknesses.

She waited. Silence.

Have I lost comms here at Lima? If I have, I'd better get going. For all I know, there's a patrol coming round the corner and Anton has no way of warning me.

She was standing in the shadows, weapons in hand, in a carefully chosen spot with good sight lines in all directions. If the enemy came at her, she would see them before they saw her. But she knew that, once she moved out of cover, she would lose that slight advantage. Her back would be unprotected again.

Anton, where the hell are you? Come on, comms genius. Make it work!

"Alpha one from Control. Come in." Instantly, as if he had heard her!

Jedda found she was smiling into the murk. Anton was a genius, after all. "Control, alpha one. Comms intermittent. Update."

"Bravo one on way to Lima. Bravo two safe. Maintain position, alpha one."

Linden was safe! And Chrys was coming back to rescue Jedda. The best possible news. "How long?"

"Five minutes, max."

Probably too long. With the state's forces on high alert, any lurking woman would be suspect. The mixture of dye and smell on Jedda's clothing wasn't helping. Any working sensors would see her and the hounds would sniff her out easily, even at pretty long range. They must be following her trail by now. "Control, suggest meet half-way. Lima feels unsafe."

"Maintain position, alpha one," Anton said again. "Bravo one's instruction."

Shit. Chrys must have decided there was no safe meeting point nearer the bunker. Jedda pictured the street map in her mind's eye. Yup, Chrys was right. Shadows weren't enough. There had to be a place – like Lima – where Jedda could strip and put on new clothes without being spotted. Besides, the dye and the stink must not get too near the bunker. Keep the enemy looking in all the wrong places.

Jedda had to comply with Chrys's order. She owed it to her team. "Maintain position. Wilco. Update on alpha two?" She was pretty sure that Ellen was lost, but she had to be sure. Ironic that Ellen had finally proved she could be trusted.

"Negative on alpha two. Only one explosion."

Jedda's gut clenched. That one small explosion would not have killed Ellen. If she had escaped, Anton would have spotted her by now. So she could not have escaped. If she had been taken alive, K would soon extract all the information she had. The Jays would be betrayed – eventually – however much Ellen tried to resist.

Jedda did not try to dodge the issue and she did not hesitate. "Control from alpha one. Terminate alpha two. I say again, terminate alpha two."

"Terminate alpha two. Wilco. As soon as comms established."

Jedda swallowed hard. She knew she could rely on Anton. But how long would it take? The Jays were in jeopardy as long as Ellen was alive. "Make that order priority one, Control." She hated doing it, but she had no choice.

"Priority one. Wilco."

Ellen would want it. She would be grateful.

Jedda forced herself to put Ellen out of her mind and to focus on her own immediate problems. "Control, update on enemy movements."

"Major activity at Barrier. Including bomb squad. Existing checkpoints reinforced. Hound patrols awaiting instructions."

That made no sense. The hounds should have been on Jedda's trail the moment they reached the Barrier and got that incredible scent. "Control, clarify position on hound patrols."

"Called back to barracks for briefing. Awaiting instructions." Anton was failing to conceal the sudden glee in his voice.

Absolute genius! However he's done it, he deserves a medal.

"Surveillance systems down in Barrier sector," Anton went on, in a more neutral voice. "Adjacent sectors intermittent."

A medal and bar! I bet that, as soon as they fix one sector, he's crippling a different one. They won't have a clue what's going on, for a while at least. Maybe just long enough for Chrys to make it here to Lima?

Movement. In her peripheral vision. Was it Chrys? Or was it the enemy?

"Control, I have movement. East of me. One hundred metres."

"Alpha one." Chrys's wonderful voice in Jedda's ear, even before Anton had time to respond. "Have you in sight, alpha one. Coming to join you now."

This part of the plan was going to come good. In a few minutes, Jedda would dump Ellen's stinking clothes somewhere they could be safely detonated. Meanwhile, Jedda would be on her way back to the bunker, with Chrys guarding her back.

Which would give Anton space to find a way of establishing comms to Ellen. And executing Jedda's priority one order.

THIRTY-TWO

THIS CAN'T BE HAPPENING. It's not possible. I must be in some kind of nightmare.

"I said *strip*. So do it. Or I'll do it for you."

It was all real. K had captured her. He had turned Ellen's well-laid plan into a humiliating failure. Now, heaping humiliation upon humiliation, he was going to force her to strip naked while he watched. Getting off on it, no doubt. She felt unclean.

She raised her chin another notch. "No."

"No?" He had the gall to laugh. He moved her weapon a fraction so that it was aimed directly between her eyes.

"No," she said, even more firmly. "I will not provide a floor show for a sadist like you. If you want to kill me for it, go ahead. You're going to kill me anyway. Go on. Do it now. Get it over with." She stared at him, waiting. If she had to face her own private firing squad, she would do it with her eyes open and no blindfold.

"You are either very brave, or very stupid," K said silkily. "Or perhaps both?"

Ellen said nothing. She could not begin to fathom the workings of this man's mind. Deep down, she knew she was scared to try.

"You know exactly why you have to strip. Your clothing has to be searched for hidden weapons, for comms devices, for suicide pills. The state has a particular aversion to those. Prisoners are not permitted to die at a time of their own choosing."

If he was intending to scare her witless, he was well on the road to succeeding. But she would not – *not* – let him see it. She kept staring. And she kept silent.

He shook his head. "Stubborn as well as stupid. Very well." Without taking his eyes from her face, he reached behind him and retrieved something from the desk.

Ellen saw that it was another pressure syringe. Another drug. That was the one thing she could not fight. She felt her muscles tense. What would it do to her this time?

271

"Don't imagine, woman, that I am naïve enough to try to strip you while you are conscious. I know the kind of fighting skills you have. But I'm a generous man. I will give you a choice. You strip yourself, here and now, while I watch. Or I knock you out and do it myself. You have five seconds. Choose."

When Ellen had first arrived at the bunker, Chrys had stripped her and methodically searched every orifice of her body. Was K going to do that, too? Or had he already done that search, back at the Barrier? That was too much. She shuddered.

"Now that does surprise me," K said. "I didn't expect fear. Not from you."

"You didn't get it! That wasn't fear, it was revulsion. At you and all you do."

He smiled then. The predator's cruel smile. His voice, when he spoke, was not cruel; it was sweet reason, laced with irony. "Your revulsion is probably because of those stinking clothes you are wearing. Which is why it makes perfect sense to take them off."

Why did he have to make it sound so reasonable? There was nothing even vaguely reasonable about being K's prisoner, waiting to be tortured, waiting for him to allow her to die. If only she hadn't changed clothes with Jedda. If she hadn't done that, she could have relied on Anton to finish her. He would have made the comms link work, somehow. He would. And she would have been grateful.

"Your time is up. You have refused to make a choice. So I—" he jammed the syringe against her neck with the speed of a striking snake "—shall have to make it for you. Sweet dreams, Greenland lady."

He couldn't actually be saying those final words. She must be imagining them. They were unreal, some kind of hallucination from the trank as she was drifting down into unconsciousness. In a moment, she was going to collapse on to the floor. Would she fall on her injured hand? She needed to…

• • • • •

K removed each piece of clothing in turn and examined it meticulously. He concentrated on looking for comms devices. He had removed and destroyed the woman's earwig back at the Barrier, when he'd tranked her that first time. But the earwig seemed incredibly primitive, not the kind of advanced technology that the Jay usually used. There would be other devices, better hidden. It was his job to find them, to stop them from capturing and betraying valuable state secrets.

It was proving to be a filthy and tiresome business. By the time he had examined the first two layers of her clothing – finding nothing – he smelled almost as disgusting as she did. He had Dr Feliks's magic dye on his gloved hands and much of his own clothing. It was alien stuff but, without it, K would not have been able to follow her movements inside the Barrier. Without the dye, and the portable sensors K had installed, he would not have been able to second-guess her. And win.

He had enjoyed their contest, and he had enjoyed doing the tech side himself, too, which had surprised him. He'd had no choice, of course. Now that Linden was gone, there was absolutely no one K could rely on, even for a standard op. And this op had been anything but standard. Delicate, and distinctly dicey, based purely on K's hunch about what the Jay would do next.

If the Jay had attacked some other landmark instead of the Barrier, it could have been Tauber occupying this office, with me as his downtrodden deputy. Or worse.

What mattered was that he had won. He intended to go on winning.

He sat back on his heels and stretched his back. He'd been working for more than twenty minutes already and there were still several layers to go. It would take him at least an hour to finish. Perhaps more. A waste of valuable interrogation time.

And, now I come to think of it, it's not really necessary at all.

He ripped off the rest of her clothing and threw it across the office to join the heap of things he had already examined. One of Tauber's minions could do the rest of the checking. Later. In the meantime...

In the meantime, he had a naked and unconscious woman lying awkwardly on his floor, and an office that stank to high heaven and was becoming totally unbearable. Along with his own body.

It was a mistake to bring her here. What was I thinking?

He was not sure he had been thinking at all. Or not with his brain. He prided himself on his ability to outthink opponents. With her, he had failed. On all counts.

He was going to remedy that, right now.

The solution was obvious, provided he kept his cool and followed all the necessary steps. It had distinct advantages for him, too, as an interrogator. For this suspect... No. For this *proven terrorist*, he needed to work where he could not be observed. His office did not qualify.

First things first. Back at the Barrier, he had examined her mouth, her ears, and her hair. Before he moved her out of his shielded office, he had to examine the other orifices in her body. He had to be absolutely certain she was clean of comms devices.

He wiped his filthy gloves on his jacket and carefully stripped them off. He must not get any dye on his fingers or on her bare skin. It was important to keep her free of it, and of the smell, when he moved her out of the office. He really did not want to contaminate anywhere else. Satisfied, he pulled on fresh gloves, rolled her onto her back, then spread and bent her legs. He gazed down at her for a long slow breath. She ought to look inviting, open to him like that. His body ought to be reacting. It was not.

She looks vulnerable. At least she's not awake to know what I'm doing to her.

The intimate searches were over quickly enough. He found nothing at all. Clearly, any devices she was carrying were hidden in that heap of stinking rags in the corner. He glanced across at them. He would have them removed in the morning. Then he would have his office fumigated and cleaned from top to bottom. For now...

He slipped off his own stained and stinking outer clothing and threw it into the corner with hers. The gloves followed. He slid his bare arms under her shoulders and her knees, to take her weight. Her skin was much softer than he expected. She was limp, and floppy, as helpless as a child. He felt—

I don't DO feelings! That's women stuff. And look where it's got them!

This was business. He rose, with his naked prisoner in his arms, and marched out into the sensor-free corridor that led to his private apartment.

· · · · ·

It was the scent of wood smoke that got through to her. Applewood.

Ellen was drifting in and out of a dream. It was as elusive as the wisps of sweet applewood smoke, twining themselves round her memories and inviting her to reach out to embrace them. She saw an image of Grant, smiling at her, holding out a hand for hers. She felt her body responding to him, softening with love and longing. She saw that he was speaking to her, but she could not make out his words. Yet she could taste the forbidden foods they had shared.

The taste on her tongue turned bitter and the apparition melted into dripping shards, like wax in a flame. Everything vanished. Every part of the dream.

Except the scent of applewood.

She lay absolutely still, on her back, eyes closed, totally focused on her sense of smell. Yes, the scent was still there. How could that be? Where was she?

She struggled to remember, but her mind was refusing to function. With an effort, she forced herself to concentrate on things beyond that beguiling scent. Was there more? She was lying on something soft, silky, cushioned – a couch or a bed. What could she hear? Did she dare to open her eyes?

She could hear running water. Splashing. A waterfall? No. She could not feel the tingle of fresh air on her skin. She was indoors, somewhere with water. And a fire burning applewood logs. She listened for the crackle of dry wood yielding to flame, but it was not there. Not a real fire, then? Another illusion?

Her head was beginning to ache. She wanted to cough. Her nose wrinkled and twitched. She desperately needed to scratch it. But she didn't dare move. Then she realised her wrists were bound together with plastic handcuffs.

Apart from the handcuffs, she was totally naked.

Reality struck like a slap in the face. She remembered everything. The pain in her left hand returned. For a second, it paralysed her. She was breathless. She opened her lips just enough to suck in a silent gulp of air. She felt as if she were surfacing from drowning.

I am K's prisoner. I don't know where I am. I do know he is going to kill me.

She could still hear the sound of water splashing. Maybe K? Gingerly, she opened her eyes a crack. Was she alone? She must not let him suspect that she was recovering from his trank. If he had expected her to be conscious this soon, he would have been waiting and watching, like a spider eyeing a doomed moth. So maybe he had misjudged things?

It took her a while, but eventually she made out something of her surroundings. She thought she might be lying on a bed but, without raising her head and risking drawing attention to herself, she could not be sure. Some things she could make out just by swivelling her eyes. It was a large room, sparely but luxuriously furnished, with a fake log fire burning in one corner and low hidden lighting that threw no shadows. One dark wall was curtained, possibly concealing a window behind. In the corner opposite the fire, a door stood half open, with bright light beyond. Beside the door was a

275

simple wooden chair, with a pile of neatly folded clothes on top and a dark jacket hanging on the back. On the far side of the door there was a bathroom, she supposed, for that was where the water was still running.

She had an advantage, even if only for a few seconds. Even though her hands were bound. There must be another door, another way out of here. And her legs were free. Perhaps the door was behind her? She tensed her stomach muscles to spring up and fight her way to freedom.

• • • • •

"Anton. Any progress?" Jedda was trying not to sound as anxious as she felt. Her team at the bunker was just about OK, even Linden, whose leg wound was already responding to Chrys's expert care, but they would all be as good as dead once Ellen betrayed them. They all knew that it wasn't a matter of *if* but *when* Ellen gave up the information she carried. It would have been the same for any of them.

Jedda had already decided that she could only allow Anton a few minutes more. After that, she would give up on terminating Ellen and make everyone focus on moving their operation to the alternate bunker. At least Ellen could not betray the fallback location. She had no idea where it was.

"K took her to his HQ in London Central," Anton said without raising his eyes from his screen. His fingers were still working, too. "It's heavily shielded. I've never managed to get through the inner defences there."

Jedda wanted to scream, "Try harder!" She swallowed her frustration. Screaming at Anton would achieve precisely nothing.

"I'm trying everything I can think of, Jedda. I do know that every second counts."

Jedda sighed in sympathy and kept her eyes on his screen.

"Yes, no, *yes*! I'm in." His initial excitement vanished the moment he hit the button. "It's done."

THIRTY-THREE

AN EXPLOSION ROCKED THE room. The walls trembled.

The acrid smell of a different kind of fire hit Ellen's nostrils. The running water stopped. "Hell and damnation!" K's voice, Ellen realised. So the explosion was not his doing. But it was nearby. Probably within this complex. Whose doing was it? Were the Jays mounting a rescue bid? No, not possible. That would be suicidal.

Her head was spinning, but she had to decide what to do. K would come back at any second, she was certain. Best to lie motionless. Pretend to be still unconscious. He might ignore her. Maybe if he went to find the source of the explosion, she could still—

He appeared in the bathroom door. His hair was wet and slicked back. He had a white towel wrapped around his loins. Nothing else. He stared down at her motionless body as if he were staring down the sight of his sniper rifle. It was back to the square, all over again. Again, Ellen felt that dull punch to the gut. Again, she could not move. She ought to close her eyes, to shut him out, but she could not. She needed that tiny crack of vision. To see. To judge.

To wonder.

He was not at all what she had imagined. Even his body was not. Apart from his pale skin, her image of him had been wrong, wrong, wrong. It made everything so much worse. She saw him clearly in that instant. He was strong, lean, muscular. This was a man who prided himself on keeping his body honed and ready for any challenge.

What kind of challenge could Ellen offer him now?

Her pulse was beginning to race at the very sight of him. She tried to damp down her responses, but they would not be controlled. Even her skin was starting to heat. She had known it would be like this. Feared it. Her final – utter – humiliation.

She knew him now. She understood what kind of man he was. Self-reliant. Brilliantly imaginative. Ruthlessly focused. A dangerously compelling man.

No. No! NO! Just plain dangerous.

• • • • •

Anton swung round to look Jedda full in the face and said again, soberly, "It's done. She's dead. A blessed release, probably."

Jedda shared his instant, overwhelming relief. Release for Ellen. And deliverance for the rest of the Jays. Except... She swallowed hard as her rational thought processes kicked in once more. Very quietly, she said, "Anton, I'm sorry, but we have to be sure. It's well over an hour since Ellen was taken. It's possible that she wasn't wearing the suit when... It's possible she's still alive. If she is, we'll all need to get out of here."

Anton didn't try to argue. He nodded and said, "OK. I'll do my best to get video. If I'm lucky, the explosion will have disrupted the shield. How long have I got?"

• • • • •

"Computer. Report on explosion."

Ellen could hear the suppressed rage in K's clipped tones. Not being in control. This man had to be in control. Always.

She shivered.

He seemed not to notice. In fact, he was ignoring her. "Computer! Activate on my voice command! Report on explosion!" He was almost shouting.

The computer's unflappable voice responded this time. *EXPLOSION AND FIRE IN LONDON CENTRAL. LOCATION: CONTROLLER'S MAIN OFFICE. AUTOMATIC SPRINKLER SYSTEMS TRIGGERED. FIRE EXTINGUISHED AFTER ONE MINUTE TWENTY-THREE SECONDS.*

"Computer. Damage report."

ONE WALL DAMAGED. DEMOLITION AND RECONSTRUCTION REQUIRED. ONE WALL CRACKED BUT REPAIRABLE. CONTENTS OF OFFICE DAMAGED BEYOND REPAIR.

In the silence that followed, Ellen fancied she could hear him grinding his teeth. Her spirits lifted a tiny fraction. Perhaps he was not invincible after all?

"Computer. Cause of explosion?"

EXPLOSIVE DEVICE IN CLOTHING PILED AGAINST DEMOLISHED WALL. DEVICE DETONATED BY REMOTE CONTROL. SOURCE UNTRACEABLE.

In clothing? *Her clothing?* But she'd changed clothes with Jedda. There couldn't have been a bomb. It was only in Ellen's own clothing that—

Oh what a fool she was! Of course there'd been another bomb. Jedda had been testing Ellen, to see whether she'd try to escape once she thought she was free of the killsuit. Jedda was much too astute to risk losing Ellen. So she'd given Ellen another killsuit to replace the original. Ellen's choice was precisely the one Jedda had offered that first time: join the Jays, or die.

It was a stupid, ridiculous joke! Any normal person would laugh. At the very moment when Ellen was putting her life on the line to plant their precious bombs, the Jays were making sure they could kill her. And Anton couldn't even do that properly! If he had pressed his sodding button when she was back in K's office, when she still had her clothes on... She would have died then, and been grateful for her deliverance.

She drew in a long, surreptitious breath. Time to take stock. For the Jays, she was already written off. For K, she was not even a hostage, not a human being at all, a mere pawn to be used and discarded. He was angry that his office had been destroyed. He was angry at his loss of control. He was even angrier that the Jays had got the better of him. He would blame her for all of that. No doubt he would have his revenge for it, on her defenceless body. There was absolutely nothing she could do to stop him.

She was a prisoner, abandoned by everyone, and humiliated beyond bearing. Once he realised how she was reacting to him – the compulsion that she could not fight, that he was much too keen-eyed not to see – she would be humiliated even more. Her only consolation was that it could not last long. She would die soon.

Probably not soon enough.

He thought he had won? She *knew* he had won. On every single count.

Ellen sank into black despair.

•••••

"Computer. Instruct Tauber that the whole explosion site is out of bounds. As of now, no one enters without my express permission. Then shut down all surveillance and non-essential functions in this apartment. Re-activate only on my voice command."

MESSAGE DELIVERED. DEACTIVATING...

K stared down at Greenland woman's unconscious body. He would not wake her up until he was sure they could not be watched. The Jay's tech skills must be even better than K had imagined if he had managed to penetrate K's ultra-shielded office to set off that hidden bomb. That danger was over and K would deal with it later.

For now, he must focus on stopping the Jay from penetrating here, to K's private domain. Shutting down all the systems should do it. K was determined that this coming encounter would be one on one, just himself and the woman.

The Jay would not be permitted to see or hear his precious Greenland woman while K was extracting every last ounce of the information she held.

A memory stirred, clawing its way to the surface.

She had a name. It was... Yes, Helen. Helen Birch.

He could call her that. To her face. She would be rattled to learn that he knew her name. It would be good to keep her unsettled, wondering what else he knew.

But first...

He reached the pile of clothes in two strides and dragged on underwear and trousers. His fingers reached automatically for a shirt.

No. That last stinking shirt was enough of a penance for one day. I want to feel the air on my skin, now that I'm clean again. It's warm enough in here to manage without a shirt. Or boots. After all, I'm not going anywhere. No one in this province would dare to interrupt me after that order.

He padded across the room to study her motionless body more closely. The polished wooden floor was smooth and pleasantly warm under his feet. He took the syringe of antidote from the drawer in the bedside table and reached for her.

What am I thinking of, letting her come round here, in my bedroom? Fair enough to dump her here while she was unconscious and I was so desperate to get clean again, but for an interrogation?

He swore softly. He kept losing his sense of perspective whenever this damned woman was around. Even when she was out for the count. He needed to take her somewhere else, somewhere that—

Greenland woman was no longer breathing!

• • • • •

"I've got video, Jedda," Anton called out. Jedda started across the room just as he said, "No, it's gone again. Sorry."

"Keep trying, Anton. We haven't got long." Jedda was doing her best not to hover over him. She forced herself to sit at her own station and not to stare at Anton.

He went on working doggedly. He clearly expected to be given space by the rest of the team. Fair enough. He was the tech genius among them. None of them could do the things that he could do with comms.

Apart from Ellen. She was – had been? – a tech genius in her own way, too. If Jedda could have got her back, somehow, it would have made the team much stronger. But if Ellen wasn't dead already, she soon would be. It was Jedda's fault.

It was Jedda's fault that Linden had been wounded, too. Not for his mad heroics – those had been all his own idea – but for imagining that just four Jays could get away with attacking and destroying the Barrier. It had gone wrong, because K had outthought them, and booby-trapped the place. And because Ellen had insisted on going back in.

That was my fault, too. I really got it wrong there. I'm the leader, I said we should abort the mission, but I let myself be persuaded. Against my better judgement.

Or did I? Maybe I let Ellen go back in because I knew it was my one real chance to test her loyalty. Was that it? An ego trip for me? Did I do it because I wanted to prove to the team that my judgement of Ellen was right?

She ran her fingers through her messy hair and dropped her head into her hands. She was afraid that it had been an ego trip. And that she alone was responsible for everything that had gone wrong. What kind of leader did that make her?

I didn't even get Linden right. I assumed he was desperate to get away from me once he'd...once we'd been together. I was angry at him and it clouded my judgement. But he was prepared to put his life on the line to try to save me at the Barrier. I heard him say it. So he does have...um...feelings for me. And I don't know what to do about him. He wanted to leave, to save me, and I stopped him. What do I say to him now?

"Jedda. Come and look. I think… Yes, I'm in this time."

Jedda raced across to Anton's workstation, forgetting everything but the urgent need to *know*. His video signal was poor, and grainy, but it was good enough to show a scene of devastation. Walls were cracked and crumbling, pieces of furniture were littered all over the floor, and there was fire and water damage everywhere.

"There's no sign that anyone was alive in there when the bomb went off," Anton said carefully, avoiding Jedda's eye.

"Is it possible there was a body and it's been removed?" Jedda's last hope.

"I…" Anton peered at the screen, trying to adjust the picture. It became marginally clearer. "If there had been a body, we would see a space where it had lain. There would probably be signs that rescuers had been in. There's nothing like that. I'd say nobody has been in that room since the bomb went off." He shook his head sadly. "We failed Ellen. *I* failed her. I'm sorry about that. Really sorry."

Jedda closed her eyes and took in a long deep breath. Those blessed, blasted years of training kicked in all over again. "We don't have time to mourn her, Anton. I want us out of here in the next twenty minutes. All four of us, carrying all the kit we need to get the fallback bunker up and running. Understood?"

"Understood," he said quietly and began work without another word.

She forced herself to stop and smile at him. She owed him more than barked commands. "Thanks, Anton. You're a star. If you get started on the tech and comms kit, I'll go and brief the others. Between us, we can make this work."

• • • • •

The solution was obvious. Why else had she spent so many hours, so many years, mastering the skills of hypnosis and mind control? She would not let this man set the limit on her life. It was hers alone, and she, Ellen, would decide when it would end.

She had decided it was now. She had decided... She had decided... Decision: death. Decision: death. Decision... Death... Death... Death...

Her body was shutting down as she repeated the words, over and over. And at last she was free. She was floating, out of her body, no longer part of it. She was surrounded by a soft, strange light – peaceful, embracing, sweetly seductive. She saw her breathing sink shallower and shallower and shallower, until it was barely a suspicion of a sigh. She saw her heartbeat slow and slow and slow, until at last it was sliding into silence. She was soaring... Floating higher... Floating away...

"No! You can't die on me!"

Mmm? No-o-o-o. Let me be. Shhh. I'm floating... I'm floating away...

"Helen. Helen! I won't let you die on me!" K wasn't thinking. He was panicking. She mustn't die. She must *not*! In desperation, he tried to pull her to him, to shake her, to force her to breathe. The bloody cuffs were in the way, holding her arms in front of her body. He wasted precious seconds finding his knife to cut her loose.

It didn't work. She was like a floppy doll. She was gone.

No, no, NO! I won't let you leave me!

He dropped her back onto the bed and touched his fingers to the side of her neck. She wasn't gone. There was still the tiniest tremor of a heartbeat. He could save her!

The antidote. He'd dropped the syringe. Where the devil had it got to? He needed to get rid of the trank. She'd had some kind of reaction to it. Must have. Something was killing her. It had to be the trank. He'd used it too often. Too quickly. It was his fault. *He* was killing her.

He couldn't find the antidote and he didn't have time to search. She was nearly gone. He didn't have time…

Her heart was beating. Just. But he had to make her breathe.

He pinched her nose and covered her mouth with his. He blew his own breath into her, gently, steadily, willing her to respond. To come back to him.

Once. Pause. Check if she's breathing. Again. Pause. Check if she's breathing. Again. Pause. Again. Come back to me, Helen. I won't let you leave me. Again. Pause. Again.

• • • • •

No-o-o. No-o-o-o. Oh, no-o-o-o-o.

It was too late. He had broken the spell. Her cocoon of control was gone. He had brought her back to earth, simply by putting his mouth on hers.

It felt beautiful.

Her body had been soaring, floating away. Now it was melting. She could feel his bare skin on hers, the touch of his fingers on her face, the weight of his shoulder on her breast as he leant across to kiss her mouth.

They called it the kiss of life. It was. She was alive again.

And she wanted to be kissed. For real. By this man. Only by him.

She wanted to put her arms round him, to pull him closer, but something warned her it was impossible. From somewhere distant, she remembered that her arms were bound. No. Not so. How strange. Her wrists were free. How had that happened?

Maybe she was still floating? Maybe she was still in her trance? In her trance, her body was her own. In her trance, her body was free. And shimmering.

She took his gentle breath and blew it back into his mouth, willing him towards desire. She raised her free hand to stroke his naked back, slowly, hypnotically, showing him the way. She felt the shock that quivered through him and stroked it away. His breathing slowed again. His fingers left her face and touched her shoulder, then down, light as a whisper, to her breast. His mouth remained on hers, but tasting now, and tantalising – no longer desperate, no longer panicked. He was trying to tempt her, seeking her response. She gave it. Willingly.

K's body was on fire. He had brought her back. Saved her. She was alive!

He wanted her.

And she wanted him.

Kissing wasn't enough. Her mouth was delicious, but it wasn't enough. He was kneading her breast, feeling it swell into his hungry hand, but it wasn't enough. They had to be together. It had to be now.

He took his hand from her skin, just long enough to rid himself of his clothes. Was that a moan of disappointment? Because he had left her?

He settled himself on top of her, skin to skin. He put his hands to her face. He kissed her, long and deep and slow. She sighed into his mouth and began to stroke his back, all over again, soothing him, seducing him with every long, teasing touch. Just as he thought he was going to explode, she moved further beneath him, pushing her hips down into the bed and opening even wider. It had to be now.

He thrust into her and she rose to meet him with a glad cry.

Then, they were moving together, fast, hard, urgent, both grasping for release. More! Harder! *Now!* It was…

It was over, and he had no words. He let his body sink on to the bed beside her and closed his eyes on the wonder of it.

• • • • •

"Wakey, wakey, sleepy head."

Wha—?

"I said 'Wake up'. Are you deaf?"

Something prodded his ribs hard. He opened his eyes. Slowly. Expecting to be dazzled by the light. But she was standing over him, blocking out most of what light there was. It was hard to see her face. But she was—

She was fully dressed. In state uniform. His uniform! With a knife in her hand. Where the hell had she got a knife from?

From where you left it, you idiot. On the table by the bed. After you'd been stupid enough to cut off her cuffs. And before you—

He stopped thinking. He launched himself at her. He had to get the knife.

She was too quick for him. She danced back, out of reach. She laughed. Then she made a pass with the knife. At the level of his balls. Close enough for him to feel it swish through the air.

"You should have killed me while I was out," he spat. "You won't get away. I'm stronger and heavier than you are." He feinted to the left, then lunged right, hoping to catch her.

She had read his moves. His hands grabbed nothing but thin air. She laughed again. "*You* forget I've got the knife, K. And I'm going to use it on you. While you're awake to feel it. Good, eh?" She swished the knife again. Same level. A lot closer.

The next one would draw blood. Or worse. He needed to do something.

"You tease me into fucking you and then you want to cut off my dick? You're selfish, Helen Birch. You've had what *you* want, so no one gets any after you, right?"

"My name is Ellen. *Ellen! Got it?* And what makes you think you're such a great performer in the sack? Maybe I'll cut off your dick because it's fucking useless."

K laughed in her face. *Fucking – yes. Useless – no. Oh no. Not for either of them.* He was going to overpower her, and then he was going to fuck her again. And she was going to enjoy it. Again.

Neither of them spoke another word. They circled one another, looking for openings. She didn't make any more passes with the knife. Close enough to do damage was close enough for him to grab her arm. She was too canny to risk that.

He tried to back her towards the fire. No good. She was still reading him. Then they were circling again, and every time she knew exactly what he was trying to do. The bloody woman seemed to be a mind reader! OK, let her read his mind. Let her *feel* what he was planning for her. Let her be afraid.

He stared into her eyes, willing her to know fear, to know that he would win.

She stared back, deep and calm and unwavering.

He couldn't move. Couldn't think. Then the moment shattered as the knife sliced through the top of his bare thigh. He cried out and fell. He was bleeding.

"I missed. Dear, dear."

He wasn't playing any more of her games. If he rolled over, he could just about reach the hidden ledge under the fire. He had a weapon there, primed and ready. If he—

She marched across to the bed and tore off the top cover, bundling it up in her arms. "You're bleeding all over your beautiful floor. Can't have that. Take—"

He rolled and reached. Grasped the weapon. Rolled back to face her.

She threw the cover over him.

By the time he'd wrestled himself free of it, his weapon was pointing at empty space. Greenland woman had vanished.

THIRTY-FOUR

ELLEN TOOK OFF AS fast as her too-big boots would let her. She had stuffed the toes with bits of K's clothing, but it was still hard going. She had very little time. And only a knife as a weapon. As soon as K got over the shock of his wound, he would call for a security lock-down. She had to find a way out first. Otherwise she was dead meat.

She did not want to die. Not any more. She was alive again. And buzzing.

There must be a back way out of K's lair. His office – nah! what was left of his office! – was bound to have permanent surveillance. He wouldn't always go out that way. Some of the time, he would want to be able to sneak out, unseen. So where…?

She forced herself to take precious seconds to think it through. Not here among the offices on ground level. Too many people coming and going. Down in the basement? She clattered down the stairs and found herself in what was clearly K's private pool and training area. *You don't stint yourself, do you, sunshine?* There was a state-of-the-art holo suite. And a self-contained computer system.

"Thank you, K," Ellen said aloud. "Exactly what I need." It took her hardly any time to bypass K's security and override the computer's voice-recognition settings. As she expected, it had been programmed to obey only K. Now it would obey the very next voice it heard. Hers. "Computer, store and obey my voice print."

VOICE PRINT STORED. READY.

"Computer, indicate K's private exit from this building." The display flashed up. The first door she needed was at the back of the pool, at the top of a small flight of stairs. "Computer, unlock doors in and out of private exit. Once the doors have been reclosed, lock them and remove all record of my movements."

UNLOCKING…

Ellen grinned and started running. For freedom.

• • • • •

It took K longer than he expected to sort out the mess. His leg wound was deep but the edges came together well enough. The knife hadn't severed anything vital.

Vital? It certainly could have. With me standing there as if I'd taken root, she could easily have cut off my balls.

Then the real question came to him. *Why didn't she?*

He had no answer for that. He told himself he could not waste time worrying about hypothetical questions, especially questions about a woman he could never understand. She was totally unpredictable. But she had certainly turned him on. More than any woman he had ever known. The sex had been mind-blowing.

He refused to think about that. He busied himself with putting a self-healing bandage on his leg and pulling on fresh underwear and trousers. He should have called for medical attention, he knew, but that would have led to far too many complications. The last thing he wanted was for anyone to know he had taken a female prisoner to his private rooms – handcuffed – and that she had got the better of him.

Never mind all the other things she had done.

He could not fathom some of those. She had been dying of too much trank, not breathing, hardly any pulse. He had given her mouth-to-mouth. She had come back to life and instantly started seducing him. How come? Had the dying been an act?

No, she had definitely stopped breathing. No one could fake that. She had used seduction to catch him off-guard so that she could escape. It was logical enough.

Actually, it wasn't logical at all. Could anyone think that quickly? One moment nearly dead, the next with a fully worked-out seduction and escape plan? It made no sense.

He would never understand women.

He shrugged and set about removing the blood stain from the floor. Luckily the high polish on the floorboards had prevented the blood from soaking in, so the cleaner sucked it off easily. There were only a few drops of blood on the bedcover. Easy enough to explain away. Still, it would be safer to have the robots burn it. No one would question that, since it was well known that K required his rooms to be immaculate. And it would get rid of the last piece of evidence.

Satisfied, he got up and went across to the bed, limping slightly as he tried not to put too much weight on his injured leg. He ought to take a shot of pain-killers.

He ought to do a great many things, but he was not going to do any of them.

He would not reactivate the computers until he was absolutely sure the cameras would see nothing out of the ordinary. So he had to stop limping, for a start. He would not alert the hounds to Ellen's escape until he had given her time to get clean away. And he would ensure Tauber was not allowed to play any part in what came next. This was a personal battle. After what had gone on between K and Ellen, it had to be. He would relish winning it, in the end. However long it took, he *would* win.

He had been so sure he would get the better of her tonight, even when she was armed and he was not. He'd been wrong. She had certainly cut him down to size!

He gave a snort of laughter at that, and instantly wondered why he was reacting in such an odd way. He should be applying cold logic, as he always did when it came to dealing with an enemy of the state. He ought to be totally focused on recapturing her, putting every available soldier on her trail. He ought to have reactivated the computers and sealed the whole of London Central so that she was trapped and available for his vengeance. No – for his justice.

Maybe that was it – justice? She was a lone warrior. Would it be justice to set all the hounds of hell on one lone woman? Besides, if he had to use an army to capture her, she would accuse him of being too weak and cowardly to take her on himself.

And she would be right.

It was well after midnight. He would take no action until the morning. In any case, he needed a few uninterrupted hours to work out how to explain his prisoner's disappearance and to ensure that the evidence on the ground backed up his story. Tauber – probably with Marujn lurking behind him – would be on the lookout for any lever he could use to undermine K, so K had to make sure there wasn't one. Everyone would assume that K had deliberately let her go. She was a powerless prisoner. How else could she have got away? They would never imagine that she had fought him, and won. So… why had he let a valuable prisoner go free?

The answer came to him so quickly that he laughed aloud. The simplest solutions were always the best. Feeling smugly satisfied, he lay down on his bed and went to sleep.

• • • • •

Getting out of K's lair had been the easy bit.

At first, she hadn't been sure where to go, even though she was free, at last. No more killsuits, no more cuffs. She could escape them all, if she wanted to, couldn't she?

Nope. Not a chance. She had no weapons, no kit, and nothing she could sell. Hell's teeth, she didn't even have a pair of proper boots. She couldn't go back to K – that would be suicide – so she would have to go back to the Jays. At least for a while.

Ellen decided to keep moving and trust to luck. She knew she would have no chance if she met a patrol. The knife stuck down the side of her boot was useless against real weapons. Her left hand wasn't broken, but it still hurt too much for fighting.

With no one to watch her back, she had to go very cautiously. Even in the middle of the night, there were people in the streets. Perhaps because it was not raining, for once. She found herself wishing she had Anton's voice in her ear, telling her where the sensors were, giving her a route around them. Maybe he did have his uses, after all?

She soon realised that wearing the state's uniform was no way of blending with the crowd. Ordinary people took one look at her unrelieved black and kept well away. They knew better than to tangle with state officials, even one who looked rather the worse for wear, in a uniform that was much too long for her.

She should have stolen a hat, though. For the cameras. It would have covered her hair and shadowed her eyes. But at least K did not go in for the sort of gaudy uniforms favoured by the generals. His had no gold braid, no medal ribbons, and the insignia of rank were so small and dark that it would be impossible to make them out from any distance. K clearly did not do ostentation. If the cameras did pick her up, it would not be because they had recognised K's uniform. To a casual observer, she looked like any common state employee.

Ellen was about half-way to the Jays' bunker when she felt the hairs rising on the back of her neck. She kept moving steadily, but with all her senses pricked. She had learned, over the years, to trust her antennae. When she finally dared to risk a quick glance around, the street was deserted. Not a patrol, then.

My instincts aren't wrong. Someone is following me.

It took her more than half an hour to lose her pursuer. She never saw who it was, but she did know when she was safe again. She could *feel* it. A quick sigh of relief and she was off again, much faster now. She needed to get to the bunker. On her own, she was becoming the proverbial sitting duck.

Jedda was right after all. It would be good to be able to sleep sound.

Ellen stayed on high alert. The nearer she got to the bunker, the more careful she had to be. She must not – *not* – betray its location. She must not endanger the others. If she lost them, she would be done for. And truly alone.

• • • • •

Linden knew he was not pulling his weight. All the others were carrying huge packs of kit and making trip after trip. He had been exhausted after only one. It was Chrys who had come to his rescue, in her role as chief medic, telling him to remain at the new location to sort out the initial defences. The Jays were relying on him, she said, to protect the bunker until the others could bring over the rest of the kit they needed. And they were all too busy to carry him through the tunnels if his leg gave out. He had to admit that last bit was true. If he collapsed out there, he would be a real liability.

Jedda had not said anything, but she had not countermanded Chrys's order either. Linden had fancied there was the faintest shadow of concern in Jedda's eyes on the one occasion when she did actually look at him.

She shouldn't be worrying about me. She needs to concentrate on getting all the kit out before K's goons arrive. Damn Ellen! Why did she have to get caught?

That was unfair. Ellen had been spearheading the op, while Linden had been a spare part. He wasn't even that now, with a leg that refused to work properly.

Linden pegged away at the tasks he had been given. He stacked kit. He set up detectors and loaded and charged weapons. He linked the external sensors to the screen in the central area. Fairly rudimentary – he didn't have Anton's skills – but it was a start. The problem was that the work didn't really occupy his mind. His sodding brain refused to stop thinking!

He had no right to feel sorry for himself. Everything was his own fault. He should be grateful to Chrys – he *was* grateful to Chrys – for rescuing him at the Barrier. He owed it to her, and to Jedda, to do the right thing by the Jays.

That meant leaving. As soon as he was able.

"Coming in now." Jedda's voice over the comms link. Would this be their last trip? The danger was rising with every minute the team spent in the old bunker. It was bound to be raided soon. Linden's gut clenched at the thought of the risks Jedda was running.

He wanted her safe.

"Phew," Anton groaned, carefully setting down the kit he was carrying and letting his heavy backpack drop, "Glad that's over. I feel as if my arms have stretched down to my ankles after carrying all this stuff." He looked at Linden and grinned.

Linden recognised the camaraderie and tried to grin back. Where was Jedda?

Chrys came in next, equally heavily laden. Without a word, she started putting some order into the kit that was littered around. Anton shrugged and went to retrieve the computer and comms equipment she had brought.

Jedda, at last! Linden was horrified to see that she seemed to be carrying even more than either of the others. She looked whacked. He covered the space between them in two painful strides and took the weight of her huge backpack. The straps lifted a fraction as he did so. They had cut deep into her shoulders.

"Thanks," she said. "This lot weighs a ton." She had two packs in each hand. She let the right-hand pair drop, but the left-hand ones were obviously more delicate; she put those down very carefully. That gave Linden the chance, finally, to lift the bulky pack off her back. "That's better," she sighed gratefully, starting to ease some feeling back into her shoulders. She closed her eyes for a moment, letting her facial muscles relax. Linden realised she was utterly exhausted. When had she last slept?

A second later she was back in leader mode. "Well done, guys. We've brought out everything that matters and Chrys has destroyed everything that doesn't. You, too, Linden. I didn't think you'd be able to complete the first sensor circle in the time, but you have. Impressive, don't you think, Anton?"

Anton was sitting head down, working away at the control systems Linden had set up. He did not raise his head, but gave a grunt that could have been agreement.

Jedda laughed. "OK, Anton. I can take a hint. *Stop talking and get to work.*" She looked round their new control room, clearly taking stock of what was there, which tasks had to be done urgently, how much could wait till later. She gave her orders, quietly but crisply, allocating the urgent work. Linden realised that his tasks were chosen so that he would not have to do much walking while Jedda's own list was longer, and tougher, than anyone else's. Linden said nothing. It would undermine her authority if he argued with her decisions, but he made up his mind to finish his own list in double-quick time. If he could manage that, she could not object when he offered his help.

"Any questions?" she finished, as usual. "Right. Let's get started. Once the full security system is up and running, I promise I'll make coffee for everyone." She closed her eyes and licked her lips theatrically. "Caffeine, what a wonder thou art." She beamed round at them all and set to work with a will.

• • • • •

By the time Linden came down the corridor to offer his help, Jedda had reached the last thing on her list: setting up the key systems in her new office. The coffee had definitely been a good idea, giving her the extra kick of energy she needed to work faster. She would soon be done but she was more than happy to accept Linden's help.

The office was marginally bigger than her previous one, but still pretty tiny, so she made Linden sit down to do the main work, while she fetched and carried. She told herself she was doing it that way because of his bad leg, but a nagging little voice said differently – if she was the only one moving about, they were much less likely to touch, even by chance. Deep down, she worried that she might not cope with that. Until she could get her head together, she'd be best to keep her distance. He had to be just a team member.

Bless him, he seemed to understand. He made no move to invade her private space. He seemed to be totally focused on the task in hand.

They worked together, in companionable silence, for another ten minutes, until it was done. Jedda stretched her aching back and smiled at him. "Thanks, Linden. Again. Good of you to help. You should have been lying down, resting that leg and—"

He stood up. Deliberately, she supposed, so that he could frown down at her. "Oh, so you're the medic now, are you? Chrys might have something to say about that."

He had surprised her into laughter. She sensed that he would always be able to make her laugh, no matter how difficult things were, even when – like now – she was so exhausted she wanted to sink to the floor and sleep.

"Jedda, we need to talk."

Uh-oh. From laughing to deadly serious in one short sentence. She glanced over her shoulder. They were alone. "Yes, but not now." Not when she was too tired to think straight.

"But we—"

"Later, Linden," she said, as firmly as she could. She read instant disappointment in his face and was tempted to stroke it away. Instead, she said, "Later, I promise you, we will take all the time you want."

He parted his lips a tiny fraction. The tip of his tongue licked out as his avid gaze settled on her mouth.

Jedda knew she had to resist, but right now she wasn't sure she had the strength. As if on cue, a treacherous warmth began to uncurl in her belly.

She must not soften. She must not. She was still the leader. Still the leader.

"Later," she managed to repeat, very hoarsely. Then she made herself walk away.

• • • • •

Ellen had made it to the bunker. At last! Now she could get inside and—

No, now she was totally screwed. The bunker was deserted. The Jays had gone. And they seemed to have taken almost everything with them.

Exhaustion flooded Ellen's body. Every single muscle ached.

Inside her head, she was screaming with frustration. *This can't be happening!*

Of course it was happening. What had she expected the Jays to do? Sit on their hands, on the off-chance Ellen might escape? They were all wise to the freedom-fighting game. They would have expected Ellen to betray their location. So they had decamped to another hideout. And Ellen hadn't the slightest idea where it was.

She took a long deep breath and slowly sighed it out. Now what?

Her brain was too tired to make a coherent plan, but the next step was obvious. She forced her weary limbs into motion and did a quick tour. As far as she could tell in the half-light, her first impressions had been bang on. Everything that could be of use to an enemy was gone. They had taken all Ellen's tech kit, too. *Damn them all!*

Swearing helped, even though what was left of her rational mind knew perfectly well that they'd had to take her kit. Much too valuable to let K get it. Anton was probably poring over the loot right now, still trying to fathom Ellen's tech secrets.

I bet you anything you like, Anton, that you won't be able to do it without me.

That single ridiculous thought made her feel so much better. The only way she was going to collect on that imaginary bet was to link up with the Jays again. She wasn't sure how, but she was definitely going to try.

She peered round again, more carefully this time. The Jays had taken all the important kit and components, but they had left some basic stuff that Ellen could use. She was a tech, wasn't she? It was her meat and drink. If she could put a comms device together, she should be able to contact Anton. She knew enough about how he worked.

Within a few minutes, she'd piled up a heap of useful bits. Now she needed some tools and—

A noise. She froze. Someone had stepped on a piece of debris and cracked it.

For all of half a second, Ellen was overjoyed. One of the Jays had come back!

The joy drained away as fast as it had arrived. It wouldn't be a Jay. There was absolutely no reason for any of them to come back here. And apart from the Jays, every single human being in London was her enemy.

Ellen drew her knife, put her back against the wall, and waited for her new enemy to make a move.

It took a long, long time.

Was that footsteps she was hearing? Impossible to be sure. She couldn't even tell yet whether she was facing one person, or more than one. She peered into the gloom. Where she had seen shadows a few minutes before, she now saw potential assassins. She could feel her pulse racing.

One of the shadows definitely moved!

Ellen tensed even more. She felt the slick of sweat on her palm. She tightened her hold on the knife. She could not afford to lose her grip on the only weapon she had.

She screwed up her eyes and tried to see what was there. The shadow was moving again. It was very odd. It didn't have the stance of a warrior. It was upright and – yes! – it was stretching out its hands. Both of them. Palms up and open.

Open?

Enough of this! "What do you want?" Ellen barked. "Who the hell are you?"

The figure took a step out of the deep shadow. Ellen registered a grey shape and a grey hood, pulled low. The face stayed hidden. Was it a man or a woman?

Ellen moved forward, knife at the ready. "Who are you?" she

said again. Her pulse was slowing. She would be back in control soon.

The shape raised its head a fraction. "Call me Blue7," it said.

THIRTY-FIVE

BLUE7 WAS VERY ANXIOUS to get away.

"We need to go," she said. "They'll be flooding the city with hound packs. They could catch us if we don't get a move on."

"I have to…" Ellen gestured urgently at the heap of components she had started to assemble. "And I need tools as well." So far, she hadn't seen any.

"Here." Blue7 shoved a small bag into Ellen's hand. "Pack up the bits you need. Only essentials. Don't bother about tools. We can provide those."

This woman called herself "Blue7". *Was* she a Blue? *A real Blue?* And was Ellen mad enough to go with her, given all the scary stuff she knew about Blues? Stupid question. Of course she would go; if she stayed, she would soon be dead.

"Come on, come on," Blue7 urged.

Ellen stuffed the last handful of components into the bag and tucked it into her tunic. "OK, done. Now what?"

"Now, we leave, of course. Here." From somewhere in her grey shroud, Blue7 produced a weapon and pushed it into Ellen's hand. "It doesn't work," she said, as Ellen started to check its settings. "We can't load it. But it looks the part."

"You've lost me. Why do I—?"

"We're going out together. You're going to play the part of the arresting officer. I'm the prisoner you've just caught and you're taking me to the cells. If we meet a patrol, you say whatever you need to say to get us away and you keep moving. OK?"

It was a good plan. Ellen smoothed back her hair and straightened her uniform. It should pass muster in the dark. Pity about the boots and the missing hat. But if she had to, she could use her mind control skills on any hounds that tried to interfere.

Ellen forced herself to smile at Blue7 and weighed the useless weapon in her good hand. "OK, prisoner. You first. Me behind, with the weapon. Pity I don't have any handcuffs."

Blue7 retrieved something from the floor. A long thin piece of white string. "Loop it round my wrists. They won't see that it's not handcuffs."

Blue7 was proving to be one seriously inventive lady. That didn't fit the received wisdom at all. Blues were supposed to be subhuman.

Ellen looped and knotted the string. Blue7 could probably snap it easily, but it looked remarkably like handcuffs in the gloom. "One last thing. Where are we going?"

"You'll see. Just follow me."

• • • • •

Tauber was staring open-mouthed at the devastation of K's office.

"Not a pretty sight, eh, Tauber? The prisoner's clothing was booby-trapped. At least the combination of explosion and fire got rid of the smell." K shrugged as if exploding offices were commonplace. "Where's your report on the Barrier incident?"

"I sent it to your computer half an hour ago." Tauber frowned anxiously. "Didn't you get it?"

"Not yet. But the systems here have been...um... a little disrupted. No doubt I can access it from the system in my apartment." He turned to leave. A couple of seconds later, he turned back, as if he had thought of something else. "Perhaps you would like to join me? There are some issues we should probably discuss, in private."

"Of course," Tauber said, looking surprised. "But what about the woman? Did she die in the explosion?"

Tauber was not very bright. Any half-decent investigator could tell at a glance that no one had died in K's office. There was no blood, no body parts, no trace of anything human. But K could not afford to taunt the man with his failings. K must appear to take Tauber into his confidence, like a valued colleague. It would be an interesting charade. It might even be amusing.

K beckoned Tauber into the corridor to his apartment, saying, "No, she wasn't in here when it went off. I had taken the precaution of stripping her and moving her elsewhere. Standard procedure, as you know, Tauber." K put all his authority into his words, so that Tauber would not dare to question him. Stripping *was* standard procedure, in any case, for precisely the reasons that K had barked at Ellen. Moving a prisoner to the interrogator's private rooms, on the other hand...

Tauber opened his mouth, but K stopped him with a gesture. "These are matters for the Controller and his deputy only. Totally confidential." He strode off along the corridor. It hurt like hell, but he would *not* limp. Tauber followed K to the apartment and into the room K was using as a temporary office. Making sure Tauber heard every word, K shut down all the surveillance systems. "As I said, for your ears only."

Tauber, looking extremely flattered, took the seat that K indicated.

"I let her go," K said quietly and sat down behind his desk.

"What? But that's— No, you can't have."

"Ah, but I did. For very good reason. I've turned her. We now have a double agent right in the middle of the worst terrorist organisation we've ever had to deal with." K smiled conspiratorially at Tauber. "With your experience, you will understand the importance of this. And the importance of keeping it top secret."

"I…uh…I… Yes, of course. And I appreciate the confidence, K. May I…may I ask one or two questions? To get the full picture, you understand. I wouldn't want to jeopardise the operation by saying something out of place. Out of ignorance."

K nodded his understanding and said, "Quite right. Go ahead."

"How did you do it? Turn her, I mean. What did you use?"

K smiled again. "I can see you are an old hand at this, so I'll fill you in as much as I can. She arrived from Greenland where I happen to have back-channel contacts. She has…er… vulnerabilities there and I used them to put pressure on her. She saw the wisdom of what I was offering. Quite quickly, actually."

"Vulnerabilities? You mean family?"

K shook his head sadly. "That's one bit of information I'm not at liberty to share, Tauber. Conditions laid down by my Greenland informant. You understand, I'm sure."

When Tauber agreed, a little reluctantly, K went on quickly, "The Birch woman hasn't been in London long enough to become a trusted part of the Jay's group. All she gave us was the location of their headquarters. That's useless now, of course, because they'll be gone. They'll have decamped as soon as they realised we'd captured their bomber. In other words, we got nothing of any value from her. So I'm sure you'll agree that it made sense to turn her and send her back to them. In the long run, we'll get much better information. We may be able to roll up the whole gang eventually."

Tauber nodded thoughtfully. "What kind of bug did you give her? Do you want me to—"

"She's not bugged at all. Pity, I agree, but it was too risky. The

Jay's tech skills are far too good. He'd have found any bug we used, even an internal one."

"So how do I contact her?"

"You don't. I'll be her handler. No one will have direct dealings with her except me. That's the arrangement."

"But—"

"But I do need your help with the cover story. The fact that the woman is a double agent will be known only to you, me, and the President. So we need a plausible line for the outside world. Including the Council. Unfortunately, too many soldiers saw me bringing her back to HQ after the Barrier incident. We can't pretend she was never here. So what do we tell them? About why she's no longer in custody?"

"Hmm. No one would believe it if we said you'd been overpowered by a lone woman. You'd handcuffed her, too, I presume?"

"Tauber, you're a genius! That's exactly what we— What *you* will tell them." He laughed harshly. "I think my shoulders are broad enough to bear it. Let's see… Yes. The story will be this. The prisoner, stripped, handcuffed, and unconscious, was being moved out of my office to be interrogated, when the concealed explosives in her discarded clothing were detonated by— Ah. We'll say by a timing device, eh? We don't want it known that our comms were penetrated." He waited for Tauber's nod before he continued. "We'll say that the prisoner had some inbuilt resistance to the trank and that she came round much too early, while I was distracted by the explosion. She took her chance and knocked me out. Then she escaped."

"But you clearly haven't had a blow to the head."

K made a face and smoothed the back of his hair over his imaginary scalp wound. "I'll spend a few quiet days here in my rooms. Alone. Rest and recuperation." Yes, recuperation would be good.

"What about the handcuffs?"

"Ah, good point. Drop the handcuffs. She was wrapped in a blanket, and no one saw them anyway. We'll say I was going to handcuff her before I brought her round from the trank. Since it didn't get that far, she was never handcuffed in the first place. Well, what do you think?"

"Ye-es," Tauber said slowly. "But, to be honest, K…"

"Go on." *Here comes the crunch. Will he buy it? More important*

– will he believe it enough to sell it to Marujn?

"To be honest, it doesn't sit with your reputation. Everyone knows you don't make mistakes like that. They won't believe you were stu— They won't believe you let yourself be overpowered by a lone woman."

"They will if you tell it right, Tauber," K said firmly, "and I know you can. Drop a hint in a few carefully chosen ears. Pick the ones who'd really like to see me taken down a peg, the ones I've had disciplined. Not only will they believe your story, they'll grab it and run with it. By the time they're finished, the world will probably be saying that the woman seduced me as well as bashing me on the head."

Tauber gave a gasp of laughter. "No one would believe that, no matter how much they hated you."

"No? Perhaps you're right." K rose and started to pace. As if he needed to think things through. Eventually he said, "I'm prepared to take the flak, even from the Council, for the sake of getting information from this agent. Everyone who really matters – you, and the President – will know the truth, and that's enough for me.

"Now, one final thing, Tauber. We mustn't give the rest of the terrorists the slightest reason to suspect this woman. I don't want any cock-ups. Any sighting of her is to be reported to me. She is not to be approached – not under any circumstances – without my express permission. You do see the importance of that?"

Tauber was much more confident now. He was probably relishing the thought of bad-mouthing K all round London Central. With the boss's permission, too. "I will do my bit, K, I assure you. Er… I have one other wrinkle to suggest. If I may?"

"Certainly. We're equals here. Both loyal servants of the state."

"I could hint that you have taken it personally. The fact that she got the better of you, I mean. That's why all sightings have to be reported to you. Because you're out for revenge. And you're determined it will be your own finger on the trigger."

"Now that, Tauber, is a master stroke. I see that I can safely leave all the Machiavelli stuff to you in future. So I'd better let you go and get on with your machinations while I…er… start recuperating."

K kept his face straight until Tauber was safely off the premises. And for a full fifteen seconds afterwards. Once he was absolutely sure Tauber was out of earshot, he allowed himself a single, quietly triumphant word. *"Yes!"*

• • • • •

They had been trudging along in silence for hours. It would be getting light soon. Though Ellen's feet felt like two enormous blisters, she didn't dare to stop and she certainly didn't dare to take those blasted boots off. Most of her skin would probably come off with them. At least her injured hand was working again. Sort of.

They had been lucky. They had met only one small patrol, which was easily avoided. The fake handcuffs had not been tested. Blue7 had been glad to be rid of them, though.

The city was far behind them. Judging by the fading stars – Ellen blessed the fact that it was not raining – they were going more or less north.

After a while, she could see the outlines of leafless trees, stark against the lightening sky. The odd conifer, too. The air smelled of wet soil with the sweet top-notes of decay. Soon, there might even be birdsong.

Ellen knew she was out of her depth. She was an urban warrior, with no experience of operating in open country. She had no idea what kind of forces the state deployed out here. Ignorance was no basis for a fighting strategy, but she hadn't a clue where to start. "Can I ask a question?" she said in her most unthreatening voice.

"If you must," Blue7 said, without turning round.

"I won't ask where we're going. I probably wouldn't recognise the name, even if you told me."

"True," said Blue7. Was that a thread of laughter she was trying to swallow?

"Are you really a Blue?" It was the one question she desperately wanted to ask.

Blue7 stopped dead and turned round. She pushed back her hood, revealing closely-cropped ash blonde hair. But her eyes were brown.

She answered the question before Ellen could ask it. "Brown contacts. I hate 'em. We all do. But we have no choice when we're with your lot. We need to blend in. We need to be safe." With that, Blue7 pulled her hood up and started off again.

Ellen had no choice but to follow.

She had been rescued by a Blue. A real, living, breathing Blue. And there were more of them. Blue7 had said as much. What exactly were they? Where was their base? Were they really as dangerous as everyone said? Getting the answer to her first question had simply unleashed loads more.

Whatever they were, why on earth had they taken such a risk to rescue Ellen?

• • • • •

Jedda woke feeling amazingly refreshed. Then she checked the time and leapt out of bed. She should have been on watch more than two hours ago!

She threw on her clothes – a shower would have to wait – and dashed out. Straight into Chrys, who smiled slyly at the sight of her.

"You let me oversleep. On purpose," Jedda said accusingly.

"It was a team decision." Trust Chrys not to name names.

"Three together is a mutiny," Jedda said darkly, trying to sound cross, and failing. "OK. I admit I was very tired. I'm grateful. Even if you *are* all mutineers."

Chrys flashed her a grin but said nothing.

"Who's on watch? Anton?"

"No. Anton stood your watch. He's asleep now. Linden is on watch."

Jedda was relieved to hear it. It meant she could talk to Chrys now, and Linden later, when he came off watch. He would have no reason to feel slighted that she had consulted Chrys first. He probably wouldn't think that anyway. It would be a childish reaction, and she was pretty sure Linden didn't do childish.

"Have you got a minute, Chrys?" Jedda gestured towards her sleeping cell. "I need to ask your advice. In private."

Chrys nodded and followed Jedda inside. "Sit down." Jedda gestured to her hastily made and rather rumpled bunk. There was nowhere else. Obediently, Chrys sat.

Jedda closed the door carefully. She turned to face Chrys. "I have to tell you that I've decided to leave. The Jays will need a new leader. I want it to be you, Chrys."

Even Chrys couldn't quite conceal her shock, but she said nothing. She just stared up at Jedda.

For once, Jedda was finding Chrys's silence unnerving. "Well? Will you do it?"

"I'm sorry, Jedda, but I don't think I can," Chrys replied quietly.

Jedda took a long slow breath. *Careful! Handle it right and you'll be able to persuade her.* "I'm sure you have reasons, Chrys. Will you tell me what they are?"

"You already know, I think. You're too good a leader not to have noticed. But, since you ask... A leader has to have strategic vision, Jedda. You have it. I don't. I can lead an op, but leading the Jays is about more than instant decisions in the field. You're a lateral thinker, too. You're always planning for all sorts of options and fallbacks, weeks, even months in advance. That comms trick to make the hound packs shoot each other at the Barrier, for instance. I would never have thought of that. And the killsuit business, to test Ellen. That was sheer brilliance. I don't have your talents, Jedda. I'm a good number two. I don't have what it takes to be number one."

That was probably the longest speech that Jedda had ever heard Chrys make. And it was bang on the money.

"If I can't find someone to take my place, I can't leave." Jedda had not prepared properly. If she had really thought it through, she would have realised that Chrys was bound to react this way. A decent leader would have worked out a strategy for persuading her, in advance. Jedda hadn't. She wasn't nearly as good a leader as Chrys thought she was. It was her own fault that she had missed her chance of making a new life. But she was still bitterly disappointed.

"There's Anton. Or maybe Linden?" Chrys took one look at the expression on Jedda's face and went on quickly, "Sorry. Bad idea. Not Linden."

"No. Not Linden. Whatever happens, Linden has to leave. I was hoping to go with him. But without someone to take my place, I can't leave. So of course I won't."

Chrys sighed. Was she sympathising with Jedda? Perhaps, but what she actually said was, "I admit I'm glad. By ourselves, Anton and I would be pushed—"

"You won't be by yourselves. I told you, didn't I, that I'd arranged for reinforcements from South America? They'll be with us soon. Two seasoned warriors – Pavel and Inez."

"Pavel? A man's name, isn't it? Russian?"

"Yes, Pavel's a man. I don't know about the Russian bit. So there will be four Jays soon. Five, including me." She had managed to stop herself from saying, "Five, if I stay." She had no choice. Her duty to the Jays had to come before her own desires. She was a warrior, and a leader, first. She had to be. It was in her bones.

Maybe once Linden is no longer here, I'll be the leader I was before.

THIRTY-SIX

THE GREY DAWN WAS long over when Blue7 stopped at the top of a small hill and nodded towards the valley below. "That's where we're going."

At first, Ellen could not see anything but trees and assorted scrub. Then a stray shaft of light bounced off water. There was a river or a stream down there, though she couldn't see any people. Blue7 pointed off to the left, quite a way above the water on the opposite bank. Screwing up her eyes, Ellen could just make out some kind of settlement, much of it hidden among the bushes. It was well camouflaged, even in winter. In spring and summer, it would melt into the leafy landscape. It looked a bit haphazard and ramshackle, though, somehow not the kind of settlement she had imagined for those "dangerous" Blues. In fact, for some reason, it reminded her of stuff she had read, years ago, about twentieth-century hippie communes. Was this the same sort of deal, all earth mothers and living close to nature? Dancing around with flowers in their hair? Was that how Blues lived?

"Come on," Blue7 said and led the way down the hill.

The going was easier than Ellen expected and they reached the bottom quite quickly. The land on either side of the river had been cleared of trees, but made to look natural. If the Blues were growing food, they weren't doing it here on the river bank, where it would be easily seen from the air.

While Blue7 kept on walking, making for the water, Ellen stopped to look round. She didn't think she was among real enemies – enemies wouldn't have gone to all this trouble to rescue her – but she wasn't ready to think of the Blues as allies. So, before she went any further, she needed to get a feel for the lie of the land. And to mark possible escape routes, too. She had seen no sentries on the way in, but that didn't mean there weren't any. Trying to look as casual as possible, she rapidly checked the hillsides sloping up from the river. Yes, she could see where she would post sentries, if she were in charge here. Definitely spots to avoid, if she was forced to make a run for it.

Blue7 was wading across the water. Even though it was winter, it only reached to about mid-calf. Bang in the middle of the river, she stopped and turned back to Ellen. "Come on," she called again, gesturing urgently. "Don't stay out in the open."

Probably good advice. Ellen waved back and started for the river. Her boots – K's finest hand-stamping boots – would have to be cut off her swollen feet anyway, so soaking the leather in the river would not matter. The boots would be useless soon.

She had nearly made it to the far side when she saw the people, moving around in the shadows among the trees. There seemed to be lots of them. And—

"Children!" she exclaimed. "You've got children here!" Ellen could not believe her eyes. She had never seen so many children gathered together in one place. She looked more closely. Strong, healthy-looking children were racing around under the trees. They seemed to be playing some kind of game, though they were not shrieking and laughing as Ellen fancied children normally did. In fact, there was very little noise at all. She tried to see exactly what was going on. "And you've got boys," she said in an awed voice.

"Yes, we have boys." Blue7, who had been waiting for Ellen on the river bank, turned away and started up the slope, clearly expecting Ellen to follow.

Ellen was transfixed by the sight of the children. The Blues were able to have children! Females *and* males. How extraordinary. Not-Blues would envy them.

How was it that Blues could have lots of children, including boys, and Not-Blues were almost all infertile? Blues were supposed to be genetically inferior, practically subhuman. At least, that was what Not-Blues were taught.

Ellen stopped gazing at the children and started assessing the adults. They were all shrouded in layers of shapeless clothing which made it difficult to tell much about them. She reckoned they were mostly females, but there seemed to be quite a few males, too, more than she would have expected in a Not-Blue community. Some of their boy children lived to reach manhood, it seemed. Lucky Blues.

A stooping figure came out of one of the shelters. It moved – no, it hobbled across to a group of younger Blues and started to speak to them. Ellen was too far away to hear what they said. That didn't matter. The bent Blue was hobbling about, having to lean on a stick for support. So she – or he – was old, or infirm. Maybe both.

Why? Surely the Blues could get hold of the nanobots that cleansed and renewed the body to keep it young and healthy? Unless the Blues had some kind of law against using them? A religious taboo, maybe?

Ellen called Blue7's name and her guide stopped.

Ellen didn't want to point, so she nodded vaguely towards the figure with the stick. "Why is that person limping?"

Blue7 smiled sadly. "You don't know much about Blues, do you? She's limping because her hip is crumbling away. Because she's old."

"But no one gets old now! The nanobots—"

"Blues get old, Ellen. And Blues die. Unlike your lot, we get infections, and cancers, and heart attacks. Our joints and muscles seize up. Without old-fashioned medicine, we die."

"I don't understand," Ellen said, confused.

"You don't, do you? And if I don't fill you in, you're bound to put your foot in it while you're here. So here's your history lesson. Before you and I were born, before the Water Wars and the cull, the state health system used to cure diseases and replace failing joints and organs. It worked well, but it was very expensive. Lots of skilled medics, and high-tech hospitals, and research. When the nanobots were developed, the moneyrakers made sure that the health system was swept away. Why keep it, when your lot would never need it? These days, state medics can deal with broken bones and battlefield injuries easily and cheaply enough. What else do your lot need?"

"Nothing." Ellen figured that was what Blue7 expected her to say, though she still didn't really understand. "Why don't you use the nanobots too? Then you would—"

"Nanobots don't work on Blues. We're different. That's why we're outcasts."

"Oh." So they *were* genetically inferior, after all.

No, I'm jumping to conclusions here. "Different" doesn't necessarily mean "inferior". And there may be a lot more to this difference than Blue7 is saying.

Ellen was so struck by Blue7's hurt expression that she could not bring herself to ask any more questions. It would be like striking at an open wound. Instead, she said, "I didn't know. I'm sorry if anything I said has—"

A tiny child – a boy – was running down the hill towards them, shouting something. Even when he reached them, Ellen still couldn't make out the word he was yelling, over and over. It sounded a bit like "quirky". It made no sense.

The boy threw his arms round Blue7's legs and said his word again. He was laughing, full of delight that she had returned. His eyes were as blue as summer skies.

Blue7 lifted him high into the air for a quick hug. "Shhh," she said into his ear. "The strangers' game, remember?" She nodded towards Ellen. "You get to play it for real this time." She winked at the child and set him down. "So what's my name?"

"Seven. Your name is Seven," he crowed triumphantly.

"But your real name is Querca," Ellen said softly, when the child had run off to rejoin the others. "Querca...quercus. You're named for the oak tree?" Ellen felt a sudden affinity with this strange woman. Ellen too had taken the name of a tree – the ash – and her latest *nom de guerre* had been "Birch". She realised, with a jolt, that she had chosen a second tree-name quite unconsciously. Did that tell her something about herself?

"For you, my name is Blue7. Or Seven, if you like. You shouldn't have heard that, but he's very young. He gets excited and forgets about names. And noise."

So the silent play was something that children were taught, from the cradle. Along with fear of strangers. And the need to stay hidden.

Ellen shivered. She couldn't fault their logic. The Blues had good reason to be afraid. Most Not-Blues would be happy to exterminate them all. Ellen felt ashamed.

To her surprise, none of the adults came to meet them. A few waved a distant greeting to Seven, but that was it. No one would approach a Not-Blue, it seemed.

On reflection, Ellen was not at all surprised.

Seven led the way to a small wood-and-thatch shelter and ushered Ellen in. It was dry and quite spacious inside, though there seemed to be only one sparsely-equipped room. There were two beds, with fabric-covered mattresses over bases of straw bales, a table of planks over more straw bales, and a few wooden stools. Bowls and plates and spoons were piled in the middle of the table, but there was no sign of any cooking pots. No sign of a hearth, either. No wonder the place was cold.

With Seven's help, Ellen managed to cut off her boots. Some of her skin peeled off with the soggy, bloody leather, but not as much as she had feared. She was surprised to see that Seven carefully gathered up all the pieces of discarded leather. Strange. When it dried, it would be hard and brittle.

"Leather is always useful. We don't make our own. Impossible to hide a tannery," Seven added. "With work, we can soften this again." She finished making her neat pile. Then she started to shake out the filthy, blood-stained material that Ellen had stuffed into the toes of K's boots. "Is that what I think it is?" She started to giggle.

Ellen bit her lip hard, but it didn't work. Unable to get any words out, she nodded. Then, totally overcome, she collapsed with laughter. As did Seven.

"Anyone I know?" Seven asked at last, still hiccupping a bit.

"Yup. Belonged to the owner of the rest of the kit I'm wearing. This was the only bit I could spare for slicing up."

"Well, even shredded underpants have their uses," Seven said with a grin, folding the abused material carefully and tucking it into the pile of leather. She reached for the bowl of salt water she had prepared before they started on the boots. "Fun time over. This next bit will probably hurt."

Seven made Ellen put her feet into the warm salt water. The pain was excruciating. No laughter now. For the first few seconds, all Ellen's focus was on preventing herself from crying out. Eventually, the pain lessened enough for her mind to start working again. Salt must also be precious here, judging by how cautiously Seven had measured it out, taking care not to spill a single grain. It made sense, Ellen realised. Everyone had to have salt, and if they did not produce it themselves, they would have to buy it, or barter for it. Or steal it.

Why were they using their precious salt on Ellen's feet? It couldn't be kindness. No one did kindness any more. So they wanted Ellen alive and *whole*. But what for?

I can't possibly ask her that. Much too aggressive. I must not appear hostile.

"Why are you called Seven?" Ellen asked instead, as soon as she could control her voice properly.

"It's the name I was given."

"Is it a status thing?"

"We don't do status, Ellen."

Seven could win a gold medal for stonewalling. Ellen tried a different tack. "That sweet little boy we met." She watched Seven smile, remembering fondly. Ellen waited a beat before firing off her question. "Does he have a number, too?"

"No!" Seven gasped. "He—" She grimaced. "You're a very clever inquisitor, Ellen. And I can see I'm going to get no peace. If I tell you what you want to know, will you stop asking questions and let me concentrate on your feet?"

Ellen laughed. "Yes. Tell me about the names. And something about how things work here. I'd really like to know." She made a rueful face. "I'm ashamed to admit that, as a child, I pictured Blues as more like animals than people. It's no excuse but, all my life, I've been taught that Blues are a genetic threat to the human race. I'm afraid that most people – most Not-Blues, I mean – believe that." Most people also believed that having sex with a Blue would somehow contaminate the Not-Blue, but Ellen could not bring herself to say so. It would be far too insulting. Ellen had already said enough to make Seven look deeply hurt. "I apologise. I shouldn't have said that. It's just… Everything I thought I knew about Blues seems to be wrong. Nothing I was taught fits what I'm seeing. I feel confused and very…um… ignorant."

"And you don't like that, do you?" Seven's expression softened as she spoke.

She lifted one of Ellen's feet out of the water, inspected it, and gently submerged it again. "Very well. Children don't have numbers, they have names, private names. If they reach adulthood, they are given number-names as well. It's a special day, a big celebration to mark their passage into the grown-up world. They become full members of the group, and they can go out into your world, if they are suitable."

"Suitable?"

"Some of us – the younger, fitter women – can pass for your lot. No one notices us as long as we wear contacts. It's not very difficult to look just as dirty and downtrodden as the rest of your miserable scavengers." Seven sighed. "We can't send out the young men, of course. Too conspicuous."

Not-Blue society had almost no young men. Apart from Linden and Anton – and K, of course, she must not forget K – Ellen did not know any. Almost all the Not-Blue men were pretty old, even if they did not look it.

"Doesn't that make the young men restless? Being cooped up here, I mean?"

"Yes."

"How do you deal with that?" Groups of restless young men, full of testosterone, probably full of aggression – it sounded like a recipe for trouble.

"We deal with it." Seven was stonewalling again.

Ellen decided not to push her luck. Instead, she said, "It's a problem that the Not-Blues – my lot, as you call us – would really like to have. Any child is precious, but a male child who is healthy enough to grow to adulthood... Most of our old fat-cat men would do almost anything to get a healthy son. *Even unto half my kingdom.*" She was not sure why the quote had popped into her head, but it seemed appropriate.

"And they do have kingdoms, don't they?" Seven's question was certainly not intended as a compliment. There was deep loathing in her voice.

"Yes. Fabulously rich kingdoms of plenty. For themselves. And, unlike you, we *don't* deal with it. But we're trying. The Jays, I mean."

"Yes, we know."

"*How* do you know? How many of you are there, mingling with the Not-Blues, doing whatever it is you do in the city-world?"

"Enough."

Ellen wanted to scream.

"There are some things about us you need to understand, Ellen," Seven said gently, putting a consoling hand on Ellen's arm. "Blues are under threat, all the time. Many of our people died, because they didn't have the right—" She stopped, swallowed, and began again. "Many of our people have died. Some of us have managed to survive out here, because we look after each other and because we keep our secrets. You're not a Blue. You can never be a Blue. So our secrets are not for you."

"I'm sorry. I didn't intend to cross the line with my questions," Ellen said humbly. She meant it, too. Blue7 seemed an admirable person. If the rest of her tribe were cut from the same cloth... "I am very grateful to you, first for rescuing me, and now for this." She gestured towards the water which had turned a slightly rusty colour.

Seven smiled. "Keep your feet there for another couple of minutes. I'll go and get some salve and dressings. And something for the pain. You'll heal quickly, I imagine. After all, you're full of your magic nanobots."

When Seven came back, there was something more pressing on Ellen's mind. "Seven, do you have...um... latrines?"

"Latrines? Oh. Oh, yes. We dig earth closets. Shall I take you?"

She started to help Ellen to get up. Then she glanced down at Ellen's bare, swollen feet and said, "On second thoughts, I'd better bring you a gazzy."

"A what?"

"A gazzy." Seven chuckled. "I think the proper word is 'chamber pot'. But we have always called them 'gazzies'. No idea why." She made for the door.

Ellen would happily call it anything they liked, as long as she got one. Soon.

• • • • •

Seven waited on Ellen all day. She gave her a painkilling tea. It was unpleasantly bitter, but it worked. Seven treated the broken skin and bandaged Ellen's feet with clean white cloth. She gave her a huge pair of plaited straw slippers to wear over the top, so that the dressings would not come into contact with the hut's dirt floor. She brought water to drink – fresh from the river, she said, and wonderful for getting rid of the taste of the tea – and then, in the early afternoon, she brought food.

Ellen's empty stomach started growling in response. "That smells wonderful," she said, from the bed, where she had been lying down, at Seven's insistence. Ellen had agreed because she had nothing else to do. Seven had taken away her bag of computer bits so that she couldn't work. "What is it?"

"Food," Seven said, in the laconic way Ellen had come to expect. "Can you make it to the table, or do I need to bring it over to the bed and spoon-feed you?"

Ellen grinned and sat up. "I think I might *just* make it." She swung her legs to the floor and stood up. "Yup." She grimaced. "It's only a few steps anyway."

While Ellen hobbled painfully across to a stool, Seven ladled the steaming food into bowls. It was some kind of stew, but it smelled like ambrosia. No amount of pain was going to prevent Ellen from getting to the table to eat it.

She polished off her first helping so quickly that she barely had a chance to taste it. But for the second bowlful – generously ladled out by Seven – she was going to take her time and really savour it. The stew was like nothing she had ever eaten. There was real meat in it, for a start. She had eaten real meat before, when she and Grant were together, but always served in dainty, artistically-presented portions with subtle sauces on the side. The Blues' stew was not subtle. It was rough and lusty, with strong, clean flavours that sang in the mouth. There were vegetables in it, and herbs too, she decided, though she wouldn't have expected many herbs to be growing at this time of year.

More questions she couldn't answer. Intrigued, she dug out a large piece of meat with her spoon and tried to work out what it was. "It's delicious, Seven, thank you. Makes me feel *so* much better. I'm wondering, though, about this meat... Not chicken, I don't think. Wrong texture. Besides, the chunks are too big. This was a big animal."

"Being inquisitor again, Ellen? OK, this time it'll do no harm to give you an answer. It's venison. Deer meat. Some of the forests have quite big wild herds now and our...um... and we've learned how to hunt them. The wild boar, too."

"Ah," Ellen said thoughtfully, "so that's how you deal with your young men." In an instant, Seven had turned bright red. Ellen bit back a smile and said nothing. Softly, softly. Always a good approach, when there was time.

Given the way Seven was running this show, Ellen had nothing else but time. She really wanted to get on with making her comms device and contacting the Jays, but what choice did she have? She couldn't make a start until Blue7 provided the tools she needed. Even if she did succeed in contacting Anton, she couldn't go back to London until she could walk properly. That would take a day or two, maybe longer. While she was waiting, she might as well learn as much as she could about Seven and her Blues.

"They used to eat venison in medieval times, didn't they?" Ellen said lightly. "And wild boar too, I believe. Served up with an apple in its mouth." She chuckled. "I can imagine you all out here, sitting at a long table under the trees, feasting on baked meats like medieval lords. Our food isn't a patch on this. Ours is almost all recycled, reprocessed, regenerated. In fact, think of just about any word beginning with 're-' and it'll describe the rubbish we're forced to eat."

"I suppose you're not that far out. We don't feast – much too dangerous to let our guard down like that – but you could say there's something a bit medieval about how we live off the land. *With* the land. The difference is that we're not hide-bound by superstition and religion, as they were. We know about medicine and hygiene, and about science and technology. Mostly, we can work out the causes of our problems. Unfortunately, we can't often get hold of the solutions we need, like drugs for diseases."

"But you have your own ways of dealing with your problems, I bet."

Seven smiled. "You're a quick learner, Ellen the Not-Blue. I'm going to have to keep a very close eye on you, I can see."

Ellen smiled back and concentrated on her bowl. No point in letting such delicious food get cold. They could talk more once the meal was over. And maybe – just maybe – Ellen would find an opening to ask why Seven had rescued her in the first place.

THIRTY-SEVEN

JEDDA WAS STRUCK BY the amount of effort Linden was putting into the work of setting up the new bunker. He should have been resting his injured leg, but he had flatly refused to leave central control. Too proud to admit he was in pain, probably. Or afraid of being accused of skiving? Jedda decided that she would never understand men. Why did they always seem to have something to prove? Where was the logic in that?

By mid-afternoon, though, she was really worrying about him. He was clearly in a lot of pain, but he would not give up. She decided to make the decision for him. "Linden, either go to your bunk and rest, or sit at that workstation and let us bring the work to you. Your choice," she finished, more sharply than she had intended.

He coloured angrily and snapped right back at her. "For God's sake, stop fussing, woman! I can take care of myself! I don't need you to mollycoddle me."

She recoiled as if he had struck her. Her leader's brain was telling her to tear him off a strip – it was rank insubordination, after all – but she could not bring herself to do it. In fact, she could not bring herself to say anything at all. Instead, she turned away and went back to her own work. Give him time to swallow his frustrations. Eventually he would come to his senses and apologise.

The hours ticked by and no apology came. Linden said nothing at all to Jedda, or to anyone else. Male pride again? Perhaps he would not apologise in front of the other two. Jedda concentrated on her work, with an occasional quiet exchange with Chrys or Anton. She could wait.

It was late evening by the time they finished. They had spent the whole day working flat out, and they were all exhausted, all over again. But it was done. Time for Jedda to say something, making sure she sounded perfectly normal. "Well done, guys. Amazing work. I didn't think it was possible to do it all in a day. So... Time for a bit of R 'n' R, eh?" She smiled round at everyone, including Linden, who did a double-take. Jedda almost laughed. What had he expected her to do? Pretend he wasn't there?

"The holo suite will need a fair bit of tweaking if you want anything fancy, Jedda," Anton said, with a wicked grin. He was still up for anything. Amazing.

Jedda chuckled and shook her head. "I was thinking of something more basic, Anton. Like food, drink, and sleep." She yawned. "Not necessarily in that order."

"I'll do the food," Chrys volunteered, getting up. "If you want anything stronger than coffee, or water, though..." She looked across at Anton who coloured slightly.

"Nothing stronger than coffee," Jedda said firmly. If Anton had ferried his precious store of alcohol across to the new bunker, she did not want to know. Not today. "Water would be better, now I come to think of it. Caffeine is the last thing we need; what we need is sleep."

"I'm not drinking the water here unless it's got something in it to hide the taste," Anton said with a grimace of disgust. "On its own, it's foul. Even worse than in the other bunker."

Linden nodded, his expression mirroring Anton's. Jedda was glad that Linden was joining in at last, even over something so trivial. Or perhaps it was not trivial to Linden? For all Jedda knew, the drinking water back at the Marujn mansion was trucked in from the purest mountain streams and filtered through silk.

Where on earth did that come from?

Her exhausted brain had conjured up an extraordinary flight of fancy. Not impossible though, given Baron Marujn's enormous wealth. Until Linden joined the Jays, he might never have tasted the water that ordinary people had to drink. Poor Linden. One more shock among so many. It reminded her again of how much he had given up in order to join the Jays.

She should not forget the sacrifices he had made. Nor why he had made them.

Chrys crossed to Linden and put a firm hand on his shoulder. "Get some rest, Linden. You've done amazingly well, but you'll probably suffer for it tomorrow." Chrys was back in medic mode, and taking the lead with Linden. He would not snap at her.

"I'll bring your food down to you, so don't fall asleep yet," Chrys added with a grin, flapping a hand in the general direction of the sleeping quarters. "And don't forget to change your dressings. I'll be checking up on you later."

Obediently, Linden hobbled off down the corridor to his bunk. Jedda followed him with worried eyes, wondering if he would make it. He looked utterly spent. He would probably be asleep before he had finished changing the dressings. She told herself that, as leader, it was her duty to see to the welfare of her team. Especially when they were injured.

She would not follow him immediately. She would focus first on clearing away the debris from the day's labours.

"Come and get it," Chrys called from the food preparation area, barely ten minutes later.

Jedda and Anton went through to join Chrys. "I'm starving," Anton said, grabbing a plate and sitting down. "I could eat the proverbial horse."

Jedda ought to be starving, too, but she was not. She reached across the table to take Linden's food tray out of Chrys's hands. Chrys did not let go. "I'll see to him, Chrys. You stay here and eat. You've done enough today."

Anton gave a snort of laughter at the sight of the two women wrestling over a tray. Then he went back to his food, without a word.

Chrys shrugged and let go. She did not try to argue, either. She probably guessed it would be a waste of time. She simply said, as Jedda started down the corridor, "Don't forget to check that he's changed his dressings."

Jedda padded quietly down to Linden's cubicle and stopped in the open doorway. He was slumped on his bunk, half-covered by a blanket, with his eyes closed. He was asleep, or nearly. The wound-cleaning kit seemed to have been used. Ducking down, she spotted the discarded dressings under the bunk, where he must have dropped them. She was glad he'd made the effort. Fresh bandages would dull the pain.

She would not wake him. Sleep would do him more good than food. She turned to leave. Too quickly. The cutlery clinked against the plate.

"Please don't bother, Chrys," he muttered, sinking even further down on the bunk. "I'm not hungry. I just need to get some sleep."

"You won't mend if you don't eat," she rapped out, in a passable imitation of Chrys's brisk medic manner. She told herself it was exactly what Chrys would have said, if she had found Linden still awake.

He jerked upright, wide awake in an instant, but confused. When he saw that it was Jedda, and registered the tray in her hands, his puzzled expression cleared and softened. Did he think she was bringing a peace offering?

It was worse than that. Only seconds later he was gazing at her with wide glowing eyes. How could he change so quickly? To *that* look? He had looked at her in the same way before, when they were about to make love. When they had wanted each other so much it drove them both crazy.

She should not have come. Flustered, she concentrated fiercely on clearing a space for the tray. She told herself she needed to get rid of the discarded dressings and to tidy up, so that she could leave him to sleep. Unfortunately, Linden's intent gaze was not helping at all. She was all fingers and thumbs. Even worse, she could feel herself blushing. She willed him to stop staring at her. Why couldn't he just eat?

"Right now, the only thing I want to taste is you." His voice was deeper than normal and edged with desire. She tried to shut it out, to get her own wayward reactions back under control, but the blasted man had not finished. "When you're all pink around the edges, you look good enough to eat, Jedda."

Jedda felt her face flame. What the hell was he trying to prove? Was this some kind of warped punishment because they'd had words earlier?

He didn't have the right. It didn't matter what they had done together. He didn't have the right. She was still the leader. And she was going to tell him they could not go on like this. This very minute. She took a deep breath and—

"Jedda, I'm sorry. I didn't mean to embarrass you. But seeing you, looking so... I'm afraid I said the first that came into my head. I simply wanted you to know how much I— No. Sorry. No excuses. It was crass. I'm old enough to know better. I really do apologise."

She couldn't look at him. "Apology accepted," she said gruffly, quickly turning to leave. She needed to get away from here.

"Don't go. You...you did promise we would talk."

She stopped dead. He was right about the promise. But did he honestly think now was a good time? Without turning back to him, she said, "I did promise. And we will talk. But not now, Linden. You need your rest and I need—" She needed to go with what her role as leader demanded. They would talk, eventually. She would tell him that he had to leave; and that she had to stay. But not now. She did not have the strength. "I need my rest, too," she finished lamely and made for the door.

"Don't go, Jedda," he repeated. "Please. I've got something to say and it's long overdue. You've already put me off once." He waited a beat for the response that did not come. His voice hardened. "Don't you have the guts to face me, Jedda? Is that it?"

Furious, and glad to be so, she spun round to tell him exactly what she thought of his nasty little slur.

"Gotcha!" he crowed triumphantly, laughing up at her.

He was doing it again! She tried to feed her anger, telling herself she had every reason to yell at him. But his laughter was so infectious that she could feel it getting to her, bubbling up inside her, trying to escape. She swallowed it down, though her lips did twitch a fraction, in spite of her efforts to keep a straight face. Bloody man! It seemed he could always find a way through her armour. "Linden, you are a—"

"I am a perfectly normal man, with perfectly normal desires," he said quickly, "and while I would happily satisfy those desires right now with the lady of my choice—" he ignored Jedda's snort of outrage "—I will settle for simply talking to her." He patted the bunk by his leg. "It would be easier if you sat down, lady of my choice. Or would you rather we talked standing up?" He started to push himself off the pillows.

"Don't you dare!" She lunged forward and pushed him back onto the bed with one strong hand against his chest. Then she gave in and sat down beside him. "OK. You win, you manipulative skunk. I'm here. And your urgent point is…?"

The amusement drained from his face, leaving it shadowed and drawn. "Jedda, I need you to understand that I have to leave. What do I have to do to persuade you?"

Why did he have to push this *now*? She was so very tired. Her brain was too soggy to think straight. "Nothing," she bit out. Seeing the shock on his face, she realised how brutal she must have sounded. "I…I mean I was wrong. You…" She took a deep breath to steady her voice. "I see that you do need to leave."

For a moment, they simply stared at each other. Linden's expression changed before Jedda's eyes as her new message sank in. First, there was relief that she was going to let him go after all. Then a confusion of reactions that her exhausted brain could not read. Regret, perhaps? Or something deeper? She couldn't tell.

She couldn't leave it there. She had to explain. She owed him that much. From somewhere deep inside, Jedda dug up her final reserves of energy. She forced herself back into leader mode. She had to focus on the one issue that really mattered – the future of the Jays. She had to make him listen to her as leader first, and lover second.

"You told me you needed to leave and I refused to let you. My reasons were… Well, some of them were good and some of them were…" She broke off. She was floundering. It was beginning to sound like a confession rather than a leader's explanation. *Focus, Jedda!* "I should have listened to you," she said, trying hard to sound more coherent. "You were right to say that you would put us all in danger if you stayed. There are too many people after you and we can't guarantee to protect you. We can't even afford to try, because it would get in the way of what we're really here to do." She was more or less back in her stride now. She had to finish it while she could. "So you do have to leave. We have to get you away from all those enemies who want your head on a plate." Stark but true.

Linden nodded, his expression bleak. "Foremost among them, His Excellency the Baron Marujn," he said in a sour voice, full of hate. "I would love to prick the old bastard's arrogant bubble, but I can't see a way to do it without risking you. Risking the Jays, I mean. I'd been hoping to send back his shitty little cloudburst bug, preferably with something inside it that he wouldn't expect, but that won't be possible now. We can't wipe it and make it safe without Ellen. So my message will never reach him."

"Message?" What on earth was he talking about?

"Yup. I wanted to spit in his eye. Make him start looking over his shoulder. 'May your balls shrivel to the size of grains of sand.' Something on those lines."

Jedda was surprised into a chuckle. "Inventive," she said appreciatively. But Linden wasn't smiling. He was deadly serious. There was something more here. "Marujn wouldn't see that as a threat, surely?"

"You would think so, wouldn't you? But you don't know the half of it. I'm almost certain he's trying to father another son. Illegally. At the time, I wrote it off as an old man's delusion, but I'm having second thoughts. If I'm right, he'll know I suspect him, and he'll be terrified I might expose him. He wants to kill me now anyway, to get the cloudburst back, but I think he might have been intending to do it all along. Once he'd got himself a satisfactory replacement,"

Linden added, with venom.

Jedda was shocked into total awareness. This put a whole new dimension on the Jays' struggle. Marujn fathering more children? Gathering even more power for a new dynasty? That would truly be a generation of vipers. The implications were horrendous. "But surely Marujn's infertile now, like everyone else?" she said, grasping desperately for the only lifeline she could see.

Linden shrugged helplessly. "Can't say for certain. He's not behaving like a man who's infertile. Not all men are, remember. There are still just those few... You know, the ones the state uses to replenish the stocks in the sperm banks?"

Jedda blew out a long breath. "Hell's teeth, it doesn't bear thinking about. Few enough children are being born. But to think that some of them might be new versions of Marujn..." She ran a despairing hand through her hair, making it even more dishevelled. The touch of her nails on her scalp reminded her that she must look a mess – exhausted, dirty, probably smelly as well.

Linden seemed to be reading her mind. And then some. His eyes widened. Oh help, it was that look again. He was not reacting to a woman who was a mess. He was reacting to her in a way that was all male, all primitive. And all wrong.

"Forget it, Linden," Jedda snapped, jumping up and taking a step back from the bunk. "We agreed, remember?"

Linden said nothing.

Jedda pretended she had not noticed the bedroom eyes. She launched into her prepared speech about how he would be smuggled to South America as soon as he was fully fit again. Two new warriors were arriving from there soon, so the Jays would have a net gain of one. Five was better than four. She began to describe the sort of extended ops that would be possible in the future.

Linden stopped paying attention, half-way through. She saw the sudden change in him, as the lust was pushed aside by something even more urgent. His eyes were gleaming with new ideas, and new hope. "The Jays can manage with four," he said flatly, the moment she stopped speaking.

No! Don't go there. It's not your decision, Linden. And you can't change mine.

She couldn't find the words to stop him. And she knew he would not listen if she tried. He was convincing himself that there could be a future for them. She knew there was none. If he was determined to ask the question she dreaded, she would have to tell him the truth.

And then he would hate her.

He spoke the fatal words, even as she tried to shut them out. "Come with me, Jedda. We can make a new life together."

She replied instantly, with the only answer she could possibly give him. "No."

The light of hope died in his face.

• • • • •

She barely heard me out. She certainly didn't take any time to think about what I was offering. She just said no. A flat, instant no. Goodbye, Linden.

He was hurting all over. He shuffled himself down the bunk, trying to find a more comfortable position. At least she had closed the door when she left, so he did not have to get up. Just at the moment, he was not sure that his legs would support his weight. He was exhausted. Yet he knew he could not sleep. That encounter with Jedda was going round and round in his brain like a recording on permanent repeat. He couldn't shut it off. He had risked everything on his last card, and he had lost. Big time.

He closed his eyes and tried desperately to make his mind go blank. It didn't work. He was in too much pain. It would crush him, if he let it.

Stop wallowing and do something!

The voice in his head sounded more like Jedda's than his own. It sobered him. Gritting his teeth, he hauled himself into a sitting position. It was agony, but he made it. A first step. He reached for the glass of water on the tray and drank it down greedily, perversely relishing the vile taste. It was what he would be drinking from now on.

So what am I going to do? Decision time.

He had burned his boats with his old life. He realised he had no real regrets about that. He could not possibly go back to the man who had masterminded the death of his mother. And his father, too. The fact that his father's murder had been an accident – collateral damage, in Marujn's cold-blooded Council jargon – made it worse, somehow. It was clear proof that Marujn would commit even the foulest crimes to get what he wanted. Right now, Marujn wanted Linden's head on a plate, as Jedda had so graphically put it. So, for the Jays' sakes – for Jedda's sake – he had to leave London.

The question is, where do I go? And do I stay with the resistance?

On reflection, he wasn't sure he had much choice. The resistance was offering him a home and a role. On his own, he would have neither.

Jedda had been brought up among the freedom fighters, learning survival skills since she was in the cradle. Linden had none. He had always lived with Marujn's wealth and the state apparatus at his back. He could fight, sure, and he had some tech ability. But he couldn't cook, or build, or forage. If the enemy didn't get him, starvation would.

OK, he would have to learn how the underclass survived on next to nothing, and how resistance warriors fought with only their brains and the weapons in their hands. He could do it. He would do whatever it took to make Jedda proud of him.

Jedda. It kept coming back to Jedda.

She was the most amazing woman he had ever met. He wanted her. Lust, desire, passion – they were just words. They didn't begin to describe the way he felt about her. He knew, deep down, that the feelings were mutual. In spite of that, she was determined to send him away. For Jedda, duty to the Jays came first, last and always.

It would all be so bloody admirable in some Shakespearean tragedy. But I don't want us to be puppets on someone else's stage. I want us to be together. For real.

Angry and frustrated, he moved without thinking. "Argh!" The dressing had caught and torn at his wound. Pain lanced through his leg. He swore aloud, shouting at the walls, using all the foulest oaths he could think of.

When he had run out of obscenities, Linden stopped, gasping for breath. Beyond his own echoing walls, there was no sound in the bunker, and no movement at all. He had been behaving like a spoiled child in a tantrum, and the Jays – with their innate good sense – were leaving him to it. He felt ashamed.

"Grow up, Linden," he said aloud, though this time he did not shout. "And get a grip." It sounded so simple. If he focused, he could make it happen, couldn't he? One step at a time. That was what it needed.

He reached for the tray. First he would eat. Then he would sleep.

THIRTY-EIGHT

ELLEN HAD SLEPT AMAZINGLY well on her straw bed under the warm rag-rug blankets. She ought to have been dreaming about devious ways of extracting information from Seven, but she'd had no dreams at all, just hour after hour of deep, refreshing sleep. She couldn't remember when she had last felt so rested. And so alive.

Oh help! Yes I can. How could I have forgotten? The last time I was buzzing like this was less than two days ago, when I'd just had sex with K and I'd... Um, yes.

Her insides lurched and started to melt, but it wasn't the same. Not quite.

Man, that's weird. It feels like a lifetime ago.

Today she would start work on the comms device – if Seven would allow it – and find out more about the Blues. Softly, softly. She would *not* think about K. Not.

"Seven, I'm sure I can make it to the latrine on my own now. I'm barely limping this morning and, since the ground is dry, my slippers will be fine for outdoors. Besides, it's not right for you to be waiting on me."

Seven smiled, but she stayed in the doorway, blocking the exit. "Ellen, if you're going out, there are things – rules – you need to understand first. You mustn't approach any of the group and you mustn't touch anyone. The adults will keep well away, but the children might forget. If one of the children comes near you, yell at them to stop and go away. You mustn't get within three yards of anyone."

"Why? Why do I have to be segregated? I'm not going to hurt anybody. Even if I wanted to, I couldn't. You took my knife away."

Seven made a face. "It's not you, Ellen. Not directly. It's me."

"You?" Ellen said, shocked.

Seven shrugged. "It's a sort of...er... quarantine. Our people are vulnerable, especially the old, and the sick. And the children. When one of us comes back from being among your lot, we live alone for three days, here in this hut, to make sure we haven't brought back any infections. It does happen. And it can be devastating for us."

"Oh." Ellen, from a world where no one bothered about infection, was starting to see a completely new side to life. "So that little boy shouldn't have come down to meet you?" she asked, before she could stop herself.

Seven looked a little guilty.

Curiosity aroused, Ellen went on, "And you shouldn't have hugged him, either?"

Looking even more guilty, Seven said, "No. But he's family. And he's very young, so his mistake was excusable."

Family? Is he Seven's son? The ages would fit, so it's possible. It seems that all sorts of strange things are possible among the Blues.

Ellen had a great deal more to learn. If only they would allow her to.

Seven was already back in her normal down-to-earth mode. "Our three days will be up the day after tomorrow – provided I don't show signs of anything nasty in the meantime – and then I will be welcomed back into the community. All being well, you will be allowed to meet a few of them."

"I understand," Ellen said, though she didn't, not really. Seven might be carrying an infection, but Ellen couldn't. Or could she? She could not be carrying any infections on the inside – the nanobots eliminated those – but what about outside, on her skin or her hair? Should she offer to bathe in the river? To be on the safe side?

"I've had a message that Blue3 wants to talk to you."

"Three?" Ellen repeated, startled.

Seven didn't reply, and Ellen found herself wondering if there was some status attached to their numbering system after all.

"Come on," Seven said, offering a supporting arm. "I'll show you the way to your latrine. I should warn you that we've got a funny name for that, too. You'll see it written over the door."

"Oh?" What on earth was coming next?

Seven grinned wickedly. "We call it 'the lepers' loo'."

• • • • •

Seven allowed Ellen to spend the day working on her comms kit. The tools were primitive, though, and it was slow going.

"This is what you might call a lash-up," Ellen said in late afternoon, groaning a bit as she straightened her aching back after hours bent over the table, "but it might work. Won't know till I test it."

Seven looked up from her own work, though her busy fingers kept on knotting the lengths of rag into makeshift fabric. "How do you do that?"

"I connect power and, if nothing melts or goes on fire, I do a trial send."

"Ah." Seven got up and came across to the table. "Power. We don't have any."

"What?"

"Well, not much. We've got a few solar-powered batteries. We use them for lights, but only when we have to. It's difficult to charge batteries at this time of year."

Ellen picked up a slender tool and glanced down at her contraption. "Do you think you could lend me one of your batteries? If I reduce the power requirements of my kit, I might be able to manage with one."

Seven did not look very confident, but she said, "I'll send a message to ask."

"Thank you," Ellen said and bent to her task. It might be a total waste of time. If she reduced the power setting, there was no guarantee that the signal would be strong enough to reach the river, far less all the way to London, and Anton.

"How long will you transmit for?"

"What?" Ellen had thought the discussion was over. She collected her thoughts. "Oh, only a second or two for the test. If it works, I'd want to transmit for longer to reach the Jays. I need to get an answer and they don't monitor 24/7. Well, the computers monitor 24/7, of course, but I need an answer from a real person."

"Ellen, I can't let you do that. Not without agreement from…from the rest of the group. It's too dangerous. Transmissions are routinely monitored – you must know that as well as we do – and the state's listening service might be able to pinpoint where they're coming from. You could betray where we are."

Ellen's shoulders sank. Seven was absolutely right. It was too dangerous. "May I do the test? On the lowest power setting, so it doesn't carry far?" she asked quietly.

"I…I think so. But not for more than one second."

Ellen nodded and said, "That seems fair. If my lash-up works, could we find another location to send from? Far enough away not to compromise your camp?"

Seven smiled. "Maybe we could. Thank you Ellen."

"What for?"

"For understanding."

• • • • •

The test had worked! Ellen was jubilant. Seven had taken the battery away again though, so Ellen could not keep transmitting, even if she wanted to.

She would not have done so. She owed these people.

She must do absolutely nothing that would jeopardise their safety. If they agreed she could do a proper send, one that Anton might actually respond to, she would take her kit to the top of one of the hills, as far away from camp as possible. That would probably confuse K's listeners a bit. Maybe just enough, provided she was quick.

Of course, it would also ensure that the underpowered signal could travel better, and further. Ellen told herself that that was *not* why she had decided to do it that way. She had made her decision in order to protect Seven and her people. Besides, she was making her own life more difficult by doing so. She was going to have to get a long way from camp before she did any kind of transmission. That meant climbing thickly forested hills. She would need fully healed feet.

Seven appeared in the doorway, back from passing the solar battery to one of the other Blues for recharging, Ellen supposed. Seven had a dark bottle in her hand. She crossed to the table and put it down carefully. She was avoiding Ellen's eye.

She's embarrassed! Now why...? Ellen said nothing. She waited.

"We should have done this yesterday, when we arrived, but with your feet..." Seven swallowed and finally raised her eyes to Ellen's. "We need to wash, all over, to get rid of any bugs on our skin, or in our hair. We have to use this as well." She nodded in the direction of the bottle. "It doesn't hurt," she finished lamely.

Ellen smiled. Problem solved. She had wanted to offer to bathe, but there had never been an opportunity to suggest it. "Do we go down to the river?"

Seven looked relieved. "I will, in a minute. But I don't think you should. Not good for your feet. I'll bring water back for you. If you're OK with that?"

"I...um...yes, I am. Though I still don't like you waiting on me, Seven."

Seven laughed. "It's what friends do. Right, I'd better get started before the sun goes down and it gets even colder." She shuddered and made for the door.

When she had gone, Ellen sat down on her stool with a thump. *What friends do? Friends?* Ellen could not remember when she had last called anyone "friend". The Blues were teaching her things she had not imagined. And she found she was grateful.

Seven came back soon enough, covered in her hooded grey shroud and carrying a bowl of water. "It's cold this time. Sorry."

"If you can bathe in the freezing river, I'm sure I can manage a bowl of cold water." Ellen got up and started to strip off. "Um...is there soap?"

"No, sorry, not for this. We use this instead." Seven reached for the bottle and poured a small amount into the water. She stirred it with her hand. For a few seconds, the water turned milky and then it cleared. "There. You get to do it in one. For me, it's a two-stage process. First the river. Then this." Seven picked up one of the eating bowls and filled it with the doctored water. "I have to wipe myself all over now." She produced some pieces of clean cloth from under her shroud and offered one to Ellen. "We don't have sponges either," she said with a grin.

Ellen bent her face to the water. It smelled pleasantly herby. If it was a disinfectant, it was not based on any of the traditional chemicals. "Mmm. What is it?"

Instantly, Seven had that wary look again. "It helps to kill germs. We make it ourselves." She did not say what it was made from. Another one of the secrets the Blues would not share?

"Fine," Ellen said, and finished removing her clothes.

Seven stripped off too, and meticulously wiped every inch of her body with her wet cloth. She scrubbed the cloth through her cropped hair as well.

Ellen, half-way through her own washing, grimaced. "My hair's going to be a bit more difficult. There's far too much of it." It was short, well above her jawline, but it was thick. Just scrubbing a cloth over it would not do.

"Don't worry. We'll wash it properly. I'll help you."

She did. She even massaged Ellen's scalp, too. It was incredible, soothing and stimulating at the same time.

"I feel...wonderful," Ellen said, stretching her whole body appreciatively. "That sanitizing stuff is miraculous." She pulled on her trousers and reached for her tunic.

Seven smiled and went on with the business of getting dressed.

"Pity I don't have anything clean to put on." Ellen brought the uniform tunic to her nose and took a deep sniff. What she smelled was not her own body odour and stale sweat, as she had expected. What she smelled was K.

Her rational mind rebelled. She must be imagining it. These clothes had been piled on his chair. They had been clean. Freshly laundered. Unworn.

Wrong. They still smelled of K. And her body still responded.

• • • • •

Today's the day. It has to be. Today I am definitely going to ask her.

Ellen stretched under her blankets and sat up quietly to look around. Still pretty dark. Seven seemed to be asleep. Today was the last day of their quarantine and tomorrow Ellen was to meet Blue3, the woman Seven had mentioned with such respect. Ellen did not want to go to that interview unprepared. So she should try to get some basic information, like why Seven had rescued her and what the Blues wanted her for.

Maybe I could try mind control on Seven?

No sooner thought than rejected. Lots of stuff did not work on Blues, so Ellen's mind control skills might not work on Seven. If she tried and failed, what would Seven do? Nothing helpful, that was certain. On balance, Ellen decided, forcing herself to be totally rational, it was not worth the risk.

The two women were easy enough together now. Why not just come out and ask? Seven would not be surprised. Even if she refused, what harm would be done? If she had to, Ellen could go into the interview unprepared and just wing it. She had done so often enough before.

Decision made, Ellen lay back down to wait for the light.

It was not long before Seven woke. Ellen heard her creeping about, obviously trying not to make any noise. "Don't worry, Seven," Ellen said into the semi-darkness. "I'm already awake." She sat up, swung her feet down and began to feel about for her straw slippers. It was too dark at floor level to see where they had gone.

"Hang on, I'm coming. You'll never find them that way."

Ellen felt the touch of Seven's hand on her leg and then the slippers were slid onto her feet. "Thank you, Seven," she said gratefully and stood up.

"How do they feel today?"

"O...K," Ellen said slowly, flexing her toes. "Actually, better than OK. No pain at all. The nanobots must be doing their stuff."

"As soon as it's properly light, we'll have a look. It's what happens when you put boots on that matters. You won't be climbing hills in straw sandals, will you?" Seven added with a chuckle.

Ellen chuckled too. "What do I do for boots? I can't wear the ones I stole."

"They would have given you the same problems all over again, anyway. I'm sure I can find you some boots that fit. We keep a supply. All sizes."

"Do you?" Ellen asked, astonished.

"Yes, but only rubber ones, I'm afraid. They're more or less indestructible. We pass them to the next generation when people grow out of them. Some of them are probably older than I am."

Ellen did laugh at that.

Seven did not join in. "You will have to be careful," she said seriously. "Rubber boots don't let your feet breathe. That could lead to more blisters. So only wear them for short periods and then take them off for a bit, to let your feet recover."

"Yes, doctor," Ellen said, equally seriously, hiding her smile. Seven was going to such lengths to care for Ellen. And the *why* was nagging away at her. Maybe now was a good time to ask, here in the gloom? When they had been laughing together? "Seven," Ellen began, "I am truly grateful to you, and your group, for your help. Do you need something from me in return? Is that why you rescued me in the first place?"

In the long silence that followed, Ellen could hear nothing but Seven's breathing. It sounded rather like a series of long sighs. Probably exasperation, Ellen thought.

"I can't answer you, Ellen," Seven said at last, in a gentler voice than Ellen had expected. "Ask Blue3 tomorrow. She will decide how much she can safely share."

Ellen knew when not to push her luck. "Thanks for the advice, Seven. I'll do that." She was trying to sound nonchalant. She was not sure that it was working.

"Good," Seven said very firmly.

Seven was telling her, very clearly, not to ask again. So she would not.

Seven crossed to the table and sat down, beckoning Ellen to join her. "I think we've got enough light over here to take your bandages off now. If your feet are healed, we could take your comms kit up into the hills and try to get through to the Jays."

"But we're in quarantine for another day, aren't we?"

"Yes and no. We can go off together, provided we keep well away from all the other Blues. Your friends will be worrying about you. The sooner you contact them, the better, don't you think?"

"Um," Ellen muttered, stunned. Her brain seemed unable to get past the word "friends". Again. The word was trying to haunt her.

• • • • •

"Report as soon as you have more reliable information, Tauber." K cut the link without giving Tauber a chance to reply. The man was annoyingly smug – probably because he had so enjoyed spreading the rumours about K's incompetence – and would soon be unbearable. He would be disposed of, the moment he stopped being useful.

The man was heading in that direction already. It was more than two full days since K had let Ellen go and there had been no sightings at all, not of Ellen, or Linden, or any of the terrorist crew. Not even a single scent trail. Yet they couldn't just vanish, surely? Was Tauber too busy spreading gossip to work his hound packs properly?

Ellen is one very resourceful woman. And a class act when it comes to disappearing. I'd put my money on her over Tauber any day.

Perversely, that thought pleased K, even though Tauber was the state's man and Ellen its sworn enemy. Unlike Tauber, Ellen had finesse. She never showed the slightest sign of giving up, or giving in. A worthy opponent. Admirable, even.

It occurred to K that Ellen was the first opponent to get the better of him in all his time in charge of this province. He had always been able to manipulate everyone, his underlings, his superiors, even Council members like Marujn. Too easily? Had he become complacent?

Meeting Ellen had shocked him out of his comfort zone, certainly. He would have to work harder – and think smarter – to outwit her.

She had managed to get out of HQ without being spotted. If the cameras had been working, it would have been different, but the explosion in K's office had blown almost all the circuits on the ground floor. K had been forced to rely on liveware for security and information, which was always a risk, especially when they were badly led. Tauber again! With a half-decent officer in charge, the guards would not have been chasing their tails at the first sign of trouble. And they would not have failed to notice an unknown woman, even one wearing a senior officer's uniform. As it was, Ellen must have just walked through the chaos and out of the main entrance. If the door guards were still at their posts, they'd probably saluted her.

She would have been cool enough to return their salute! Wearing MY uniform.

He was tempted to laugh. He had almost had her, right here in this apartment – hell! he had had her, in the crudest sense of the word – but she had got away from him, using the oldest weapon women had. Was he any better than those tail-chasing guards?

Unlike them, he could learn lessons. The first of those was never, *never* to close his eyes when Greenland woman was around. No matter what had gone before.

The computer's bleep interrupted him. Probably just as well. Bad idea to be picking over what he and Ellen had done together. Better to save his energies till he could actually *do* something, once he had her back in his hands.

The message was brief. *INCOMING TRANSMISSION FROM BARON MARUJN.*

The last thing K needed, but he could not refuse Marujn. "On screen."

The Baron's face appeared, all neatly manicured beard and watchful eyes. "K, I have been hearing disturbing rumours. Is it true that you arrested one of the terrorists and that she escaped?"

At least he has not accused me of LETTING her escape.

K kept his expression neutral. "Good morning, Baron," he began politely. The older man blinked at the implied rebuke. "Yes, a woman was arrested. And yes, she escaped." He stated it all as fact, without any hint of apology or explanation.

Marujn frowned darkly. "This is all very irregular, K. Very unsatisfactory."

K would not allow the Baron to get the upper hand. "The President has had a full report, Baron. There were unforeseen operational failings—" the Council did not permit its members to interfere in operational matters, so K could stonewall quite legitimately from here on "—but they have been dealt with. Security procedures have been upgraded. You will understand, I am sure, that I cannot go into more detail." K smiled apologetically. "Even with you, sir," he added, putting the final, satisfying obstacle in the Baron's path.

Marujn clamped his lips tightly together, clearly furious at being thwarted.

"One thing you could help me with, sir," K went on smoothly.

"As you are aware, your grandson was wounded at the New Barrier. *After* our forces foiled the terrorist attack." Good to remind the old bastard that some things had gone right on K's watch. "There has been a lot of gossip among the troops about the shoot-to-kill order on Linden. Rumours do get out of hand, I'm afraid." He shook his head sadly. "The latest version – so I'm told – is that you want your grandson dead because he is blackmailing you. I…um… may I have your permission to issue a formal denial?"

Marujn went pale. He looked haunted. No, *hunted*. He managed to nod.

So K's wild guess was not too far from the mark. Interesting. And useful. "One last thing, Baron. Does it stand, your shoot-to-kill order?" K raised his eyebrows. Let the Baron be convinced that K knew his secret. And would keep it. For a price.

Marujn cleared his throat. "Bin that order, if you must. What matters is that Linden is to be arrested and brought back to my house. Immediately and untouched."

"I understand perfectly, sir," K said silkily. He didn't. Not everything. But he certainly understood that he had to get to Linden before Marujn did.

THIRTY-NINE

"CHRYS!" ANTON WAS YELLING and waving to attract Chrys's attention. "Incoming comms. It's Ellen."

"What?" Chrys dived across the control centre to Anton's workstation. "Put her on speaker." She sucked in a deep breath. No time to fetch Jedda. "I'll deal with this."

"Control, this is alpha two. Come in." Ellen's voice all right. But where was she? Where had she been all this time?

"Alpha two, this is Control," Chrys said steadily. "Pass your message."

"Control, I need to come in. Need clothes, boots, weapons. Do you read me?" There was a clear edge of anxiety in her voice. Was she being forced to make this call?

"Clothes, boots, weapons. Roger, alpha two. Wait five."

"Negative!"

That wasn't anxiety, it was panic. Just because of an order to wait?

"Control from alpha two. Waiting not – I say again, *not* – possible." Panic subsiding a bit. "Will contact you again to fix rendezvous. Alpha two out." With that, Ellen was gone. The whole transmission had lasted only seconds.

Chrys blew out a long breath. What on earth was going on? Ellen was not dead, obviously, but where was she? How had she escaped? More to the point, whose comms kit was she using? Could it be K's? Maybe she had not escaped at all?

"Not sure I like this," Chrys muttered darkly. "She could be a prisoner, forced to send that message. It could be a trap."

Anton's busy fingers had been flying ever since Chrys had taken over the call. "Wait a minute. Got it!" He ran his hands through his hair and shook his head.

"What have you got?" Chrys snapped. Why did he always talk in riddles?

"The source of the transmission, of course," he bit back. So he

334

was just as wound up as Chrys. "It's a long way north of the city. Makes no sense. If she's K's prisoner, he'd be holding her in the city somewhere, wouldn't he?"

"Probably."

"She's nowhere near the city. And the state has no stations that far from civilisation. There's nothing out there but rewilded forest. Hundreds and hundreds of hectares of trees and scrub. But that's where she is."

"Are you sure, Anton? It was a very short transmission."

He drew himself up. "I don't make mistakes over things like that, Chrys. The transmission wasn't long enough for the state to pinpoint her location – that could have been why she cut it short, now I come to think of it – but it was long enough for me. Chances are she's hiding out somewhere, deep in the forest."

"That doesn't explain how she got hold of comms kit."

"Um. No, I suppose it doesn't. Unless she stole it, while she was escaping?"

"She'd have to be amazingly good to do both," Chrys said. "I'm going to brief Jedda. She'll decide whether we respond or not." She started for the door.

"Or not? You mean you'd be prepared to leave Ellen out there?"

Chrys turned back. "Since when do you care what happens to Ellen, Anton?" He reddened and shook his head, but Chrys was not convinced. "The survival of the Jays is what matters, Anton. Walking into an Ellen-baited trap would be one great way of ensuring we didn't." This time she kept on going, and slammed the door behind her.

• • • • •

"Thank you," Seven said quietly as Ellen pulled her rubber boots back on and started to pack up her comms kit for the long trudge back to camp.

Ellen squinted up at Seven, standing behind her. Against the light, it was difficult to read Seven's face. What had Ellen done to deserve thanks?

Her confusion must have been obvious, because Seven said, "I couldn't hear what your comrades said, but I heard how anxious you were to keep things short. I know you cut the transmission to protect us. That's worth at least a 'thank you', I'd say."

Embarrassed, Ellen tried to laugh it off. "I'm protecting myself, too, you know. If they find you, they find me as well." There was no need to say who "they" were.

Seven flashed her a grin and started off down the hill, threading her way amazingly quickly through the maze of trees and bushes. Years of practice, Ellen decided, setting off to catch up with her friend before she disappeared completely.

Friend? That word again! Am I really thinking of Seven as a friend?

She must not. Friendship needed trust and, until Ellen found out what the Blues wanted from her, she could not trust them. She *must* not trust them. Not even Seven. In a moment of piercing realisation, Ellen understood how much she wanted to. And how much it hurt that she could not.

For the rest of their trek back to camp, Ellen focused on keeping Seven in sight and avoiding the fallen logs and branches that threatened to trip her up. The last thing she needed was another injury.

She was pretty much whole again, and she had to stay whole or she would never get back to the Jays. That was where she belonged, wasn't it?

If she belonged anywhere at all.

• • • • •

Jedda's expression became increasingly grim as Chrys described Ellen's message and her own fears about it. Chrys knew her own expression was probably much the same. Their whole operation could be in danger here.

"You're right to be wary. It *could* be a trap. But until we know more, we can't really decide." Jedda sighed, pulling at her wayward hair. "We have to be ready to jump either way. She asked for clothes and weapons, so—"

"And boots," Chrys put in.

"Oh yes, boots. Odd, that. If it were a trap, would she be asking for boots?" Jedda shook her head, puzzling it out. "I mean, if she's a prisoner, being told what to say, why would they include boots? Clothes, weapons – all obvious things to ask for, to make us believe that Ellen had genuinely escaped – but why mention boots specifically? To me, that makes it sound genuine. Possibly genuine," she corrected herself quickly.

Chrys hadn't thought of that. Would she ever have thought of it, without Jedda's prompting? More proof that she had been right to refuse Jedda's offer of the leadership.

Jedda said briskly, "Right. We'll pack up the stuff she wants and be ready to go out to meet her. We'll make the final go/no-go decision when she calls in to fix a time and place. That might give us more clues, too."

Typical of Jedda. Careful preparation, making space for instant decision and action. Chrys's role was obvious. "I'll be good to go as soon as you give the word."

"No," Jedda said quietly, but very firmly. "I'm the one who decides whether we take this risk. I'll go myself."

"You can't!" Chrys exclaimed, before she could stop herself.

Jedda's eyebrows rose, but she was smiling a little wryly.

Chrys swallowed. She was a good number two. It was not her job to contradict her leader, but in this case, Jedda's decision was wrong. Taken for the best of reasons, but still wrong. Chrys was going to have to persuade Jedda to change her mind.

She took a deep breath. "You get to make the decision because you're the leader, Jedda. We all accept that. I know what you're thinking. You're worrying that this could be a trap, so you're not prepared to let anyone else go. Your decision, your responsibility, so you want it to be your life on the line."

Jedda's smile widened a little but her eyes were sad. "You know me too well."

"I know you well enough to know when you're wrong," Chrys said urgently. "If you go and you're killed, what then? What happens to the Jays?" Jedda was beginning to look stubborn. Chrys had to find another approach. "I know you wanted me to take over as leader, but getting yourself killed to achieve it seems a bit…um… extreme?"

A moment of stunned shock, and then Jedda laughed.

"The Jays need you more than me, Jedda. You know that. It's why you said you would stay, isn't it?" Before Jedda could get a word out, Chrys went on, "I know why you want to go yourself, and I know why you mustn't. I also know what the risks are and I'm happy to take them. Let *me* do my job, Jedda. Please."

Jedda grimaced and shook her head, but Chrys knew it was not a negative; it was a sign that she was thinking about giving in, though very reluctantly. "You'd better be wearing Ellen's slinky suit," Jedda said at last. Then, apparently as an afterthought, she murmured, "Provided Anton can turn it into a killsuit in time, of course."

• • • • •

Day four. Quarantine was over!

Ellen grinned up into the early morning gloom. Then, remembering, she wiggled her toes and worked her ankles in circles.

No pain when her skin rubbed against the bedcovers. As far as she could tell without a visual check, her feet were whole again. There was nothing to stop her returning to the Jays.

Provided the Blues would let her go.

She pushed that aside and began to plan. She would need to take Seven's advice about a rendezvous point that the Jays could find easily. Somewhere well outside the city would be best, probably, where there would be fewer military patrols to worry about. Somewhere Ellen could change into safely anonymous clothing. And real boots that fitted. What a blessing that would be! She flexed her feet in anticipation.

The second question was timing. The Blues seemed to be able to travel amazingly well in the dark, if Blue7's skill was typical. Did blue eyes give them better night vision? No way of knowing. However, it did mean that – provided she had Blue7 to guide her – Ellen could get to a rendezvous in the dark, if she had to. Good. She needed to make it easy for whoever was coming to meet her. Chrys, probably. Let the Jays fix the timing of the meet. Whatever time they picked, Ellen would comply. And if they imposed conditions, Ellen would go along with those, too. She had no choice. Not if she wanted to get back to the Jays.

I don't belong here with the Blues, however welcoming they are. So I have to get back to the Jays. At least for a while.

A second transmission to Anton was going to be really dangerous, especially if it lasted longer than the first. Best to get much further away from camp this time, even if it meant that the rendezvous with Chrys had to be put off for an extra day. The Jays would approve of her caution.

Besides, another day here at the camp was no great hardship for Ellen. She was beginning to appreciate life out in the countryside – for a start, the food was much better than anything the Jays were able to produce – and she was learning a lot about the Blues, in spite of Seven's taciturn ways.

Like all Not-Blues, Ellen had been taught to fear and detest the Blues. She knew now that much of what she had learned – perhaps every single thing – was a lie. The Blues had far more reason to fear Ellen's kind than she had to fear them. Blues were different, certainly, but Ellen did not see why the state viewed them as such a threat.

Maybe Blue3 would tell her what it was all about? Their meeting would be today, Seven had said, and Ellen was planning to ask all the questions buzzing around in her head. Would Blue3 provide the answers?

No point in wasting energy over that. More important to focus on how Ellen would handle herself in the meeting with Blue3. She must not do anything to antagonise the Blues; and that included not allowing her frustrations to show. Without the Blues' help, she would not be able to return to the Jays. So far, the Blues had been kind, but would they provide the practical help she was going to need? It would mean putting at least one Blue in danger. It might even put their whole camp at risk.

Helping Ellen made absolutely no sense at all.

• • • • •

Ellen gazed round at the camp as Seven led her to the meeting place. There were fewer huts than she had expected, and they were a lot bigger than the one Ellen and Seven had been sharing. So Blues – or these Blues, at least – lived together in largish groups. Perhaps extended families? One or two of the female Blues came up to give Seven a quick hug, but most of them kept their distance. Ellen assumed that she, the Not-Blue, was the problem. There were very few people about in any case – and no sign of any male Blues, or children – which made the camp feel rather exposed. How could they defend it if there was no one around to fight?

They don't defend it. Of course they don't. They have no weapons to speak of. They rely on hiding. And running, probably, if they have to. If I'm going to deal with these people, I have to stop thinking like a warrior and start thinking like them.

"Where is everyone?" Ellen asked blandly.

"The children are in school," Seven said over her shoulder, answering a direct question for once. She said nothing about the missing men, though.

Ellen guessed that the men were off hunting. She would have loved to find out more about that, about the skills they had developed, and the weapons they used, but she knew there was no point in asking.

Seven led her deep into the tree cover, to a long hut with a wide doorway and several window openings. Even though the trees were bare, it was gloomy inside. And very cold. Glancing quickly round, Ellen decided this was probably the Blues' meeting house. Or perhaps a church? There were no religious symbols to be seen, but that proved nothing. She had no idea what the Blues believed in, apart from survival.

"Welcome, Ellen. Come closer." The voice was deep, and beautiful. Even with those few words, it felt reassuring.

Seven stopped by the door and gestured to Ellen to go ahead. The far end of the meeting house had no windows, but in the semi-darkness Ellen could just make out a single figure sitting on a high-backed chair.

"Come. Sit." A woman's voice. Reassuring, yes, but also very firm. She was used to having her orders obeyed. She did have status, whatever Seven had said.

Ellen went forward on silent feet and took the single low stool opposite the chair. It gave the other woman the advantage of height, but Ellen ignored the prickle of warning. Here, alone, with no means of escape, she was at a disadvantage all the time.

The two women sat in silence for several seconds, assessing each other. Ellen drew herself up a little straighter and lifted her chin. Blue3 did not move at all. She was a tall deep-bosomed woman with an air of wisdom. Was it the long grey hair streaked with white that did it? Plus the fact that she looked so calm and relaxed, almost serene? She sat with her slim hands clasped loosely in her lap. They were incredibly clean, soft hands, with beautiful almond-shaped nails that had been buffed to a shine.

Blue3 fixed her light eyes on Ellen's face and smiled a little. She did not blink. "Tell me about yourself."

Ellen was not sure if the words had been spoken aloud, but she heard them quite distinctly, inside her head. They made her eager to respond. She had such a long story to tell. She found herself wondering where she should start.

NO! Stop! Don't let her take control!

The warning slammed through Ellen's mind, coming from somewhere deep and very primitive, somewhere that piercing blue gaze had not quite managed to reach. With a huge effort, and using all her mental skills, Ellen forced herself to shut out the siren call. And then, at last, she was back in control.

Breathe. Watch. Beware.

Blue3 blinked and her smile widened. "Ah, I see," she said softly, nodding to herself. "We are two of a kind. That *will* make life interesting."

• • • • •

Inhaling deeply, K gazed round at his refurbished office. "Computer?"

READY.

The computer's disembodied voice was still tinny and grating. What had he expected? Upgrading the computer's voice was about the last thing the state would have paid for, even if K had thought to demand it. His antique desk, on the other hand...

He crossed to the corner of the room where the debris lay, carefully piled up on a large plastic sheet. Since the desk was beyond repair, K had insisted that the remains be gathered up and left in his office. What had he been hoping to achieve? He glanced over his shoulder at the state's ugly replacement and grimaced.

You owe me one antique desk, Greenland lady. With tactile curves and centuries of patina.

He bent to drag out the largest piece from the wreckage. It had once been part of his desktop. One corner was undamaged, still with its sensuous lines and polished surface, but the bulk of it was just a series of shards, as spiky as the profile of a young mountain range. In fact, there was something decidedly sculptural about the shape, and the contrast between polished and broken surfaces, especially when he upended it. He would have it mounted like that, spikes uppermost, on a heavy metal plinth. It could stand on the floor, a striking reminder of the need to be vigilant at all times. Eventually, he might move it out to his secret bolthole on the outskirts of the city. He could display it there along with his other hidden treasures, and enjoy it in private. But he would have to deal with the present crisis first. It would probably be a long while before he could risk taking any time for himself. He shrugged philosophically. His art collection wasn't going anywhere. It could wait.

He gave his orders to the computer, specifying exactly how the finished piece should look. Human hands might have to do some of the actual work, but the computer would oversee every step. "This other debris is to be disposed of," he said, pointing to the rest of the shattered wood. One reminder was enough.

The computer announced that his visitor had arrived.

"Send her in." K lifted his soon-to-be sculpture – carefully, since the exotic wood was heavy and the spikes were dangerously sharp – and crossed the floor to lean it against the far wall, ready for collection.

"You sent for me, sir?"

K turned round. Delta was standing to attention, and saluting smartly. When she registered the huge chunk of shattered wood, her eyes grew round. She was speculating about it, he realised, and she might be indiscreet enough to mention it to some of the other hounds. He couldn't tell her not to. That would simply arouse her female curiosity even more.

"This is the latest addition to my armoury," he said, improvising rapidly. He touched a fingertip to the point of the tallest of the shards. "Once it's on the right base, it'll be strong enough to go straight through a body."

Delta's eyes widened even more. In horror. Her skin had a greenish tinge.

What had possessed him? Delta was a potential ally, and well on the way to hero-worship. Now he would be firmly fixed in her mind as the new Vlad the Impaler.

Idiotic thing to do! Totally counterproductive with a woman like Delta. Three days of "rest and recuperation" has healed my leg, but it's turned my brain to mush.

The damage could not be undone. But perhaps news of his latest innovation on the torture front might divert attention from the rumours around Ellen's escape? The hounds were no doubt convinced that K had made an amateurish mistake over her – it was what he'd intended them to think, after all – but it was high time their gossip was choked off. Above all, the foot-soldiers must not lose their abiding fear of what K would do to them, if they ever failed in their duty.

If a reputation as "K the Impaler" achieved that, he would become the Impaler.

It hardly mattered whether Delta obeyed him out of hero-worship or out of fear, as long as she did obey. "Now, Delta," he said, sitting down at the replacement desk and steepling his fingers, "I have some questions for you. About Linden."

She was not green any more. She was grey. Her hands were starting to shake. Once she even glanced across at the shard sculpture.

After fifteen minutes of close questioning, K was satisfied that Delta had had no contact with Linden since his defection and that she had no idea where he was. Pity. Delta had been K's best hope of getting to Linden before Marujn did.

He frowned at the terrified woman standing to attention in front of him, and racked his brains for ideas. Delta did not move, but she seemed to shrink as the seconds ticked by and K continued to stare.

Ah yes! Why didn't I think of that before? Mush and double mush.

He smiled at Delta. She did not look reassured. He leaned

forward and made an effort to sound unthreatening. "At ease, Delta." She obeyed, looking puzzled. "I need a volunteer for a dangerous mission. If it succeeds, the volunteer will be promoted."

Her expression changed. She was not exactly eager, but she was interested. No doubt she wanted to regain the status she had lost.

"You know that Linden has defected?" He waited for her to nod before he went on. "He has been sentenced to death for treason, but we can't just shoot him on sight. That order has been countermanded. We need to interrogate him first, to find out what he knows about the terrorist cell he's joined up with." K made his tone even more confiding. He really needed this to work. "If we're going to take Linden alive, we have to set a trap for him. You know his weaknesses – for a start, he is always chivalrous, especially to women. So how do you think he will react when he finds out that a woman is about to be executed for failing to shoot him when she had the chance?"

"He'll try to save her," Delta replied instantly. "Bound to." Then her chin came up and her jaw clenched.

She had decided which side she was on. At last!

Delta straightened her back and stood to attention. She had recovered all her old confidence. "You need a volunteer, sir? You've found her. We both know that Linden will feel honour-bound to try to save *me*."

FORTY

"SO, TELL ME, ELLEN Not-Blue. You have mind-control skills, but you have not used them since you arrived here. Why is that?" Blue3's voice was still reassuringly soft, almost like a caressing hand, but Ellen was armoured against it now. Blue3 knew it; she was not really trying to reach into Ellen's mind. She would recognise a lie at once, though, so Ellen had only two options: tell the truth, or stay silent.

Ellen shrugged, trying to look relaxed and unconcerned. She risked a quick glance over her shoulder. Seven was well out of earshot, standing in the doorway with her back towards them, apparently on guard. "Because I had no idea whether it would work on Blues. I have enough enemies. I didn't want to risk making more here."

"So you believe we are not your enemies?"

Careful. This could be a test. Stick to facts. "Blue7 rescued me and cared for me. With gentleness and compassion. For an enemy, that would be...er... unusual behaviour." Blue3 did not respond. She sat motionless, solid as a graven image.

Ellen waited several moments and decided to risk a question of her own. In her most unthreatening voice. "*Are* you my enemy?"

Blue3 narrowed her eyes a tiny fraction. "You presume on your skills, Ellen Not-Blue. But I will humour you. We have been waiting for an opportunity to contact your group. You provided it and so we brought you here. Why? *My enemy's enemy is my friend.* Is that enough of an answer for you?"

Ellen was not at all sure that it was a valid reason – she had read enough history to know that it had often come unstuck – but she wasn't about to argue. It had saved her, hadn't it? And there was no doubt that the state did want to exterminate the Blues, just as it wanted to destroy the Jays.

"Yes, thank you," Ellen said slowly. "I understand now." Some, but not much.

Now what do I say? She gets prickly if she thinks I'm "presuming".

"You have other questions, I see. That is to be expected. You may ask them. I will choose which will receive answers." Blue3's manner had turned stately, almost regal. Was she queen here? With such strong mind-control skills – almost certainly better honed than Ellen's – Blue3 could easily make the whole clan believe that their decisions were all their own. Seven might not have been deliberately lying when she said there was no hierarchy. She could have been saying what she believed to be true.

Ellen had been imagining all sorts of dangerous assignments that the Blues might give her, but now she began to wonder if their purpose was simply to set up a conduit to the Jays. On reflection, she had to admit that, in spite of Blue3's scary mind-control skills, an alliance might benefit both sides.

Especially as Anton had devised those clever contacts to stop mind control from working! Ellen was beginning to see that the obnoxious little geek had his uses after all.

"I understand why your camp is not close to…er… urban centres," Ellen began, carefully avoiding any suggestion that cities equalled civilisation, "but why so far out? It's a long way to London for your scouts." She was avoiding the word "spies", too.

Blue3 unbent a little. She became gracious. And condescending. "I can see that you are very much a city dweller. You would not survive long out here."

Ellen nodded, ignoring the haughty tone. Not-Blues were very much an urban race nowadays. When Not-Blues did trees, or grass, it was always carefully controlled and manicured. Nature, in the raw, was dangerously unpredictable.

"Blues do not settle anywhere near your industrial farming," Blue3 went on. "Wherever you people are, you contaminate everything, for miles around. So we have to be a long way from your cities, too. We go to areas that reverted to the wild long ago, with dense tree cover. And safe clean running water, of course."

Startled, Ellen realised that the water in the camp tasted wonderfully clean and sweet, nothing at all like the piped water in the cities. She was going to miss it. "Your scouts must hate the water in London," she said, thinking aloud.

"No. They do not drink it."

"What, never?" Everyone had to drink when they were thirsty, surely?

Blue3 blanked Ellen's question. Clearly she was not about to volunteer any more information on that subject. Ellen did not need it anyway. She understood. Blue3 could easily hypnotise her spies into believing that they were never thirsty when they were away from camp. They might die of thirst as a result, of course, but they would not know it. Ellen felt a tiny shiver running down her spine. She was no longer sure that her mental armour was strong enough to keep withstanding Blue3's skills. She needed to get away. The sooner the better.

"Blue3, will you permit me to return to the Jays?" she asked humbly, avoiding the other woman's eyes.

"Yes."

Relief flooded through Ellen, washing away days of tension. She felt her body relax. A second later, she regretted her loss of control. Blue3 would be reading her.

"Thank you, Blue3," Ellen said slowly, desperately struggling to work out how to play the rest of this encounter. Humble had been good. She would go with that. "We...er... that is, the Jays will be very grateful to you. Is there anything you need that the Jays can provide?" She waited, holding her breath, for Blue3's reaction.

The older woman relaxed back into her throne-like chair. She took several long, easy breaths, staring down at Ellen all the while. "We will take their payment. In due time." Blue3 smiled, but it was no longer warm or reassuring. "Blue7 will take charge of arranging your return to your friends. Before you leave, you and she will agree methods of communication between your group and ours. You are to make sure that nothing, now or in the future, puts any of this community at risk. That is your first priority. Are we agreed?"

What am I agreeing to? She can't think that I'm writing a blank cheque here, surely? Once I'm back with the Jays, the Blues will have no hold over me. I could renege on anything I promise her.

"You hesitate. I see that you are wiser than your years, Ellen Not-Blue. You know the importance of a debt of honour. We are honour-bound to keep your secrets, just as you are honour-bound to repay us for rescuing you."

Oh hell! Secrets. That's how she means to do it.

"I cannot bind the Jays, Blue3. I am not their leader."

Blue3 looked distinctly sceptical. Ellen guessed that Blue spies had probably been watching the Jays for years. Had they learned all the Jays' secrets? "You have mind skills. They do not," Blue3 said flatly.

Ellen dropped her gaze to her feet. Blue3 must not see the truth. One day, the Jays might need Anton's protection against mind control. They certainly would, if they ever met Blue3 face to face. "I do not use my mind skills on the Jays," she said very firmly. It was the truth, though not the whole truth. "But I will put your proposal to them and I think they will agree to help you. I know they will be grateful to you for rescuing me."

"Very well. That will suffice. For now. No doubt you will take steps to ensure that your friends appreciate the importance of holding to your side of our bargain." She waved Ellen towards the door. The audience was over.

And the threat was all too clear. If the Jays failed to deliver whatever help Blue3 wanted, the Jays' secret hideouts would cease to be secret.

• • • • •

By the time Ellen and Blue7 got back from making the second transmission to the Jays, it was late and pitch dark. Ellen was incredibly tired. Not because of the distance, though they had trudged a very long way from camp before setting up the comms link, but because of the constant need to be on her guard. Seven had been her normal self all day, just as helpful and willing as before, but Ellen found herself suspecting that, back at camp, Blue3 would be waiting for Seven's report, demanding every single detail of what Ellen had said and done. So Ellen had spent the day minding every word and every gesture, and becoming mentally exhausted in the process.

She flung herself down on to her bunk as soon as they were back in the quarantine hut. If she could relax enough, she could will away her headache.

"Shall I take a look at your feet? Are you in pain?" Seven sounded concerned.

Seven did not have Blue3's mind-control skills. So Ellen decided she would risk a lie. It felt rather like a betrayal, but right now, she couldn't afford to listen to her conscience. She couldn't afford to *have* a conscience if she was going to get away from the Blues. Right now, she needed some kind of distraction, and sore feet would have to do. "Thanks, Seven. It's good of you. I don't think the skin is broken again, but I will admit that my feet ache. Quite a lot, actually." She groaned – just enough to sound convincing, she hoped – as Seven tugged off her boots and began a careful examination of her feet by the light of the precious solar lamp.

"Hmm. Skin looks a bit red in places. Only to be expected, I suppose. Rubber doesn't let the skin breathe. Best to leave the skin open to the air for a bit. Do you want me to get you some more of our painkilling tea?"

"No, it's not that bad," Ellen said quickly. "I'll be fine, really. I'll put my feet up for a while and let them cool off." The Blues' bitter painkilling tea had cured the pain that first day, but it had left her stomach feeling slightly queasy for a while. She could not afford to lose her edge. Not this close to getting away.

"Well, if you're sure." Seven stood Ellen's boots against the wall at the end of the bed. "I'll go and find us something to eat. Don't know about you, but I'm starving."

"Me too. But won't you be going back to your own place now? Quarantine's over, isn't it? I'm sure I can manage on my own. After all, I do know my way to the lepers' loo." She grinned across at Seven. *Keep it light. Keep it friendly.*

Seven grinned back. "But you don't know your way to the cookhouse, and I can't allow you to starve. You are our guest, remember? In any case, it's no hardship for me to stay with you for one more night. I'm enjoying your company."

Ellen gave in gracefully. "You are very kind, Seven." Seven was behaving like a good friend, but Ellen could not shake off the suspicion that Seven was also her guard.

By the time Seven came back with a pot of steaming hot food, Ellen had gone through her full relaxation technique, twice. Her headache was gone and her body felt re-energised. She reckoned she was ready for just about anything.

Seven has been away for ages. Plenty of time to brief Blue3 about my plans. What if she's changed her mind about letting me go?

Seven dumped the heavy dish on the table. "Come and eat," she said, waving a spoon encouragingly. "Your slippers are under your bunk, by the way."

Ellen rolled over on to her stomach and reached down under her bunk to retrieve the straw slippers. Somehow they had managed to get a long way from the edge of the bunk and she had to stretch almost to the back wall to haul them out. Now that her feet were no longer swollen, she had to curl her toes to keep them on. Still, it created the useful illusion that she was finding it difficult to walk because her feet were sore.

"Are you sure you'll be fit enough to go to the rendezvous

tomorrow?" Seven was sounding worried. "It's a long way, you know."

"I'll be fine once I've had a night's sleep," Ellen said. One question answered. Blue3 had not changed her mind. So Ellen would fulfil her side of the bargain. Part of it. "After we've eaten, I need to show you exactly how my comms kit works, and what to do if it starts playing up. I can almost guarantee that it will, I'm afraid. It's not exactly state-of-the-art." She shrugged. "I assume you'll be doing the comms?"

"I'm the one who will be listening, yes. Every other night, at the times we agreed. And a long way from camp." She ladled the food into bowls and pushed one across to Ellen. "Don't worry. I've got a very good memory. I won't forget the rules, or the codes you gave me. I won't acknowledge, and I won't do a send unless it's absolutely essential, but you can be sure I will be listening and that I'll relay your messages. You can rely on me."

"I know that, Seven." She ate a large spoonful of the stew. Not venison this time. Boar, maybe? The latest result of the young men's hunting skills? Ellen would have loved to follow the hunt – she'd have spied on it, given half a chance – but she was leaving in a few hours. She simply said, "This tastes fantastic," and meant it. "I'm really going to miss the food here. Nothing in the city is a patch on this."

Seven smiled. "Make the most of it, then. There's more if you'd like."

Seven's generosity made Ellen feel guiltier than ever. Seven trusted her, but Ellen could not trust Seven, because of the shadow of Blue3 at Seven's shoulder – listening, watching, plotting. Seven was a kind friend, but Blue3 owned Seven's mind.

Ellen ate in silence, thinking hard. There was one thing she could do for Seven. It was unlikely to be of much use, not while Blue3 was ruling the roost. On the other hand, anything could happen. And the risks to Seven were real.

Ellen put her spoon down and reached out to touch Seven's wrist. "This is a risky game we're all playing, Seven," she said. "Especially the regular comms link. It's pretty secure now, but in the future, who knows what the state will be able to do? All those codes I gave you to memorise… Let me add one more. If I send you this word, it means that it's not safe for you to come back here to Blue camp. It means you have to come to me in the city, because nowhere else is safe."

"It won't happen," Seven said quickly, but there was a flash of doubt in her eyes.

"I'm sure it won't. But just to humour me, eh? One friend to another?"

"One friend to another," Seven repeated in a whisper. "What's the code word?"

"Code word: Querca."

• • • • •

"You're a really fast learner, Seven," Ellen said, as Seven finished demonstrating that she understood how to manipulate Ellen's comms device. "Especially considering how little tech kit you have here."

Seven shrugged, but she had coloured a little at the compliment. "We have to be adaptable. You never know when knowledge, or resources, might come in useful."

Ellen nodded.

"Which reminds me..." Seven went on, delving deep into her robe. "We want you to have this back. You might need it." She held out her hand.

"My knife!" But it wasn't just the knife. The thin blade had been neatly fitted with a stitched leather scabbard. "How thoughtful of you. Thank you, Seven." Ellen ran a finger over the leather. It was soft and supple. The knife would sit much more comfortably inside her boot.

Seven grinned mischievously. "We're only returning a fraction of the leather you brought us, Ellen. It seemed fair. We are keeping all the rest."

"You mean this is the leather from my boots?" Ellen could hardly believe it. But it was bound to be true. Hadn't Seven said that the Blues were resourceful? Here was the evidence, in Ellen's hand. Evidence of Seven's kindness, too. One day, Ellen might be able to repay her, if only she could get Seven safely away from Blue3's malign influence. "Your skills are truly amazing, Seven."

Seven looked away, embarrassed. A moment later, she said briskly, "I'll pack up this stuff while you get your head down." She began to busy herself with Ellen's comms kit. "Don't worry about oversleeping. I'll wake you when it's time to leave."

Ellen could take a hint. She thanked Seven calmly and went across to her bunk to lie down. She had a long day ahead of her, first to reach the rendezvous point in the dark and then – provided everything went OK – to get all the way back to the city and the

Jays' new hideout, wherever that was. She would have Seven as a guide for the first part, which would help. After that, Ellen and Chrys would be on their own, trying to thread their way through the forest without being spotted. They could do it, Ellen was sure, but it wouldn't be easy. She was in for hours of trekking over difficult ground.

She wiggled her bare toes. Her feet were OK. She could make it all the way, no trouble, provided she had proper new boots. Even if she had to do every last step in the sweaty rubber boots, she would still make it. Mind over matter. She had the mind-control skills to shut out pain.

"Wake me in good time, will you? I have to—" Ellen caught herself. She needed time to go through her preparatory mind-control exercises, but it was probably best if Seven did not find out. Trusting Seven was the same as trusting Blue3, which could be suicidal. "Um, I don't suppose I'll have a chance to thank anyone before I leave?" she improvised. Any extra information she could glean might be useful.

Seven shook her head without turning round. "We get up early here, but not that early." Ellen could hear the smile in Seven's voice. "Blue3 will still be asleep."

"And I never did get to meet Blue1 and Blue2, did I?" Ellen asked, on impulse.

"No, it's forbidden." Seven gasped, and spun round to glare at Ellen. "That was unfair, Ellen. I thought we had an agreement?"

"Sorry, it slipped out." It was not a lie, though it was only partly true. "Blame it on my insatiable curiosity. My mind is always buzzing with questions and sometimes I say things I shouldn't. I won't forget again. Anyway, you'll be rid of me in a few hours."

The light clicked off. "Apology accepted," Seven said quietly into the darkness.

Was Seven mollified or not? Ellen did feel a bit guilty. If she'd taken the time to weigh her words, would she still have asked? Possibly not. On the other hand, she did need to find out all she could about the Blues. Blue3 had the power to betray the Jays, didn't she? Ellen could not bear to think about the revenge K would take if he pinpointed where the Jays were holed up. She had to prevent that, if she possibly could.

Her cheap trick had only proved that Blue1 and Blue2 existed. Who were they? Blue3's superiors? With the same mind-controlling skills? Truly scary, if so.

• • • • •

It was well after midnight. The Jays had been talking round and round their plans for what seemed like hours. Chrys was anxious to be off, but for the moment she was stuck. She couldn't leave until Jedda gave the word.

"One: we don't know where she's been since she escaped from K – assuming she *did* escape – though we do know she's not inside the city," Jedda said, counting off the facts on her fingers. "Two: she has managed to establish a comms link, somehow, though each transmission is very brief and from a different location well north of here. Three: we have a rendezvous point—"

"Which Ellen chose," Anton put in.

"Thank you, Anton," Jedda said, rather tartly. "I hadn't forgotten. We have a rendezvous point outside the city which Ellen chose. Four: we have a rendezvous time – pretty soon now – which she did *not* choose. Five: she has asked us to bring her clothes, and boots, and weapons." She sighed in frustration. "The rendezvous is in just a few hours and we still can't decide whether or not it's a trap."

"Jedda, if I leave now, I can make it to the rendezvous point with an hour to spare. I'll have time to recce all around. If I find anything suspicious, I'll come back without waiting for her."

"I know you're fit, Chrys," Anton said, "but even you would have to go some to cover the ground that quickly. In the dark." For once, he was not trying to be clever.

Chrys could tell that Anton was really worried for her safety. He was a good comrade. "Trust me, Anton," she replied quietly. "I wouldn't say it if I weren't sure."

Anton subsided. He still looked uneasy.

Jedda ran a hand through her hair. She looked frazzled. "We've got two options, both unpalatable. We pass up the chance of bringing Ellen in and using her skills. Fair enough, if it is a trap, but what if it's not? We'll have lost her skills. And betrayed her, too. The alternative is to let Chrys go out to bring her in. Great, if we win. But if it turns out to be a trap, we risk losing Chrys as well as Ellen. That's a hell of a risk."

Linden leaned forward into Jedda's eyeline. Until now, he had said hardly anything. "You're right, Jedda. It's a risk. Either way, we could lose. But we've got a lot to gain, too." He turned his head and looked directly into Jedda's face.

Chrys saw that he was smiling, though his smile was grim. "I know you're the leader, but it's Chrys's life on the line here," Linden said. "Maybe she could have the final say?"

Jedda sighed deeply and closed her eyes. Then she straightened, and turned to look at Chrys. "He's right, Chrys. Your life. Your decision."

Chrys had made up her mind ages before. "I'll go," she said immediately. If she was going to have that precious hour to recce the site, she needed to get a move on.

"Wait." Jedda hadn't finished. "Two things. First, you wear Ellen's slinky suit. You'll need separate IR goggles. Anton had to remove the integral headset when he was fitting the destruct kit. But otherwise it's good to go."

"Fine," Chrys said at once. Ellen's magic suit might well mean the difference between life and death if Chrys did come up against enemy forces.

"Second, if you have any suspicion that Ellen is leading you into a trap – the *slightest* suspicion, mind – you terminate her on the spot. That's an order, Chrys. Understood?"

Chrys was a professional assassin, wasn't she? Death to order was what she did. Even if the target was Ellen.

She nodded. "Termination. On the spot. Understood." But her voice sounded unconvincing in her own ears.

FORTY-ONE

IT WAS A LONG time since Chrys had been out in the forest in the dark. She was an urban warrior, always had been. In the city, there was hardly any animal life, apart from the rats and other vermin. The forest felt spooky, full of rustles and murmurs, especially at night. She knew there were plenty of woodland animals lurking in the shadows, like deer and wild boar, plus the feral dogs and other predators that hunted them, but there were bound to be smaller creatures too, snuffling through the undergrowth, turning over the dead leaves to search for food. There was lots of life here, and she must not alert it to her presence. A single pheasant, barking its alarm call as it rose from its tree roost, could be the death of her. And of Ellen, too.

She stopped yet again, and listened intently. Only the background whispering of the trees, which might be nothing more than a flicker of passing breeze. She was still behind schedule. When she first entered the forest, the unfamiliar surroundings had slowed her progress more than she expected, though she had made up some of the lost time over the last few kilometres, thanks to her infrared goggles and Anton. He could see everything Chrys could see – sometimes a lot more, since his kit back at HQ had much more processing power than Chrys's goggles – and it allowed him to check her position and give her occasional advice through her implant. It was a huge plus that it was not raining. Rain would have blocked out all the other noises and made her trek both more difficult and more dangerous. She needed to see any enemy, human or animal, before they saw her. Her slinky suit might not protect her against a pack of feral dogs or – if they really did exist – the big cats that were said to survive out here. She did not want to put the suit to that test.

Chrys hummed very softly: a low sustained note, deep in her throat. It would be inaudible from more than a metre away, but the implant would pick it up without trouble. It was the agreed signal to

Anton that she was calling for an update. Speaking aloud was absolutely a last resort.

He replied almost instantly. "Bravo one, hold course. Keep moving due north. Four hundred metres to rendezvous site."

Chrys hummed again, a broken repeated note this time, acknowledging Anton's transmission. Testing each step before she transferred her weight, she moved forward. She had hoped to have a full hour to recce the clearing where they were to meet, but now she had barely thirty minutes. She would be pushed to check the whole area in that time. It couldn't be helped. She would have to do her best in the time she had. Even in a forest, the likely enemy hiding-places should be pretty obvious, shouldn't they?

There was more to it than that. The whole area could be booby-trapped, with mines or other explosives. Much more difficult to spot than ambushes. Still, the sensors in her goggles should alert her to trip wires and hidden pressure pads. *Should.* Unfortunately, the sensors were calibrated for urban environments, not for a forest full of huge tree trunks, dark shrubberies, and hidden dips and hollows in the ground.

"Bravo one. Liveware at rendezvous. I say again. Liveware at rendezvous!" Chrys heard the edge of panic in Anton's voice. He was trying to hide it. And failing.

Someone's there already, waiting for me. Shee-it! I must have missed a heat signal. At least Anton's kit could see it. But where are they? And how many? Anton, you useless geek, why didn't you tell me how MANY?

She dare not break silence to ask. That could give away her position. She would have to go in blind. She would have to assume that the watchers were hostile.

She slithered the pack off her shoulders and placed it carefully on the ground. She would be able to move faster without it. And squeeze through tighter gaps.

She took a precious few seconds to check her main weapon. On kill. Good. She dug out her spare and checked it was still on default. Also good. With a weapon in each hand, and different settings, she had options.

She sucked in a long silent breath, filling her lungs. Her heart was pounding. Every sense was on full alert. This was her body's fight or flight response.

Chrys was not about to do flight.

• • • • •

Ellen had insisted that Seven stay a long way from the clearing, and keep her heat signal masked by tree trunks. It was not ideal, but at least Seven was probably out of earshot. When they said goodbye, Ellen had tried, and failed, to persuade Seven to return to camp. Although it was the safe and logical thing to do, Seven had refused point blank.

Arguing was a waste of time. Seven would be under instructions from Blue3 to report back on everything that happened. She would not leave until Ellen did.

Ellen herself was lying on her back in a deep hollow in the ground, covered with a thick blanket of dead leaves. They could not hide her from infrared detection, but the hole was deep enough to hide her heat signal from any sensors until they were almost on top of her. She had strewn more dead leaves all around the area. They were her early warning system, so crisp and dry they would shatter if trodden on. The most careful attacker would not reach Ellen's hideout without betraying herself.

Ellen's pulse rate was slow, totally under control. Even though her only weapon was K's knife, she was not afraid. She had the advantage of surprise. She was sure that only one of the Jays would come to the rendezvous. They could not afford to risk more. So it would be one on one, if it turned out to be a hostile encounter.

It almost certainly would. Ellen would have to ensure she had the upper hand from the outset, even against a warrior like Chrys. The Jays were permanently suspicious, and they needed to be. Caution was what kept them safe. In Jedda's place, Ellen would not have risked sending anyone to the rendezvous. But someone was going to be there, according to Anton.

Could it be a trap of some kind? Anton would enjoy arranging a trap for Ellen.

Surely that made no sense? Why risk sending someone to the rendezvous unless the Jays were prepared to take Ellen back into the fold? If they thought Ellen was set to betray them, they would leave her out here to rot, wouldn't they?

Not necessarily. They might be wondering how Ellen had escaped, how she had managed to get hold of comms kit, what information she had given to K. They might be worrying that she could identify them all and set them up for assassination, one by one. Or that she could betray their precious tech secrets. Ellen was a threat. Like an unexploded bomb. Jedda might be sending Chrys to eliminate the threat.

Bluff and double-bluff. What if they thought—?

It doesn't matter what their plans are. I'll never work it out anyway. Whether it's Jedda or Chrys who comes, I have to overpower her. I have to deal with the Jays from a position of strength. I can only go back to them once I'm sure I'll be safe.

With about thirty minutes still to go, Ellen forced her body to relax even further into the cold ground and focused all her mental powers on her hearing. She had to be alert for the smallest sound. It could come at any time now.

Silence. No wind. Not even a rustle of leaves. The trees seemed to be holding their breath.

Long minutes passed.

A tiny crackle.

Someone or something had shattered a leaf. Close by. Three metres, max. In Ellen's nine o'clock position. Whoever it was, they would pick up Ellen's heat signal any second. And they would have better weapons than a knife.

Ellen launched herself out of her hiding place. She crashed into the invisible body at about knee level, bringing it down with a thump. A satisfying grunt of exhaled breath. And a groan of pain. But Ellen was too busy grappling to pay attention to that. Her assailant would not be winded for long. Ellen needed to pin her to the ground. She needed to get rid of the infrared goggles. Otherwise, she could never win this fight.

Then she had them. Pure luck. Her finger caught in the strap as they fought. Ellen wrenched the goggles off and threw them across the clearing.

Now they were equal! The two bodies tussled and rolled around in the blackness, trying for holds, and failing. For a second, Ellen had a handful of hair. Then she lost her grip as her opponent wrenched herself free. Ellen felt a hand on her own throat. Fingers searching for the pressure point that would have her unconscious in seconds. Desperate to escape, Ellen feinted to the left. She gained just enough space to ram a fist into her opponent's kidney. Another groan of pain. Ellen instantly moved the other way and was free, rolling up on to her feet. She kicked out viciously at the body on the ground. Not fast enough. Her foot met thin air.

Sod it! In the dark, she did not know where the other woman was.

She could hear panting. The other woman's. Her own. Loud. Then both muffled.

357

Ellen crouched and listened hard. Nothing. Not a breath. Where was she?

Another leaf shattered underfoot. Then a shot!

She'll get the drop on me. I have to get that weapon!

Knife in hand, Ellen threw herself along the ground to the source of the noise. She missed. But her free arm scraped along the side of a boot. It was enough. She grabbed at the leg and felled her opponent again before she could escape.

This time, Ellen would use her knife. She reached for her opponent's neck. One touch of the knife there would end it. Her opponent was bound to yield.

The woman had rolled her upper body away, flexible as a snake. Ellen's hand found nothing. The knife blade sank into soft earth. She still had the leg, though. She jerked it. Hard. She had to bring their bodies back together. To keep things hand-to-hand so the woman could not shoot.

It began to work. Ellen was using every trick she knew. Knees and elbows and nails. She grappled, she punched, she feinted. She used holds she'd learned in the backstreets. Waiting for that single second's advantage to grab her knife and end this.

But her opponent was reading her every move. They continued to wrestle but neither of them was winning. Stalemate.

There must be something I can do! But what?

That tiny lapse of concentration was all it took. Ellen felt the smooth profile of a weapon touching the side of neck. A voice – Chrys's voice – said, "Surrender. Or I'll shoot."

Most of Chrys's weight was on Ellen's left shoulder. Ellen's legs were still free. She kicked across with her right leg. Chrys's weapon didn't move but her body did. Just enough. Just as Ellen had intended. She snatched up her knife.

"Surrender," she said, pushing the point against Chrys's unprotected belly. "Or I'll gut you where you lie."

"Will you?" Chrys wasn't afraid. She didn't even sound worried. "I can shoot you before you have time to move."

Ellen pushed the knife in a little further. Making her point. "Even if you kill me, Chrys, my reflexes will gut you. Mind control, remember? My arm will do what I've willed it to do." It was a lie, but how was Chrys to know?

Silence. Then Chrys laughed. The bloody woman actually laughed.

"If you don't believe me, try pulling the trigger," Ellen said fiercely. It was her last throw of the dice. And it looked like she was going to lose.

Silence. Much longer this time. Then, "Look, Ellen, we don't have time for this. We need to get back to the city while it's still dark. If you want to take me on, let's do it in the holo suite. Later." There was still a tiny hint of laughter in her voice.

It made no sense. This was Chrys, professional assassin. She didn't do laughter.

If I relax my guard, even a fraction, she can kill me. If that's what she's planning. If. She's forcing me to take a punt on whether I can trust her or not.

Ellen couldn't make up her mind. She tightened her grip on the knife. Steeled herself. She didn't do trust, did she? Even for Chrys?

Chrys smoothed the weapon down the side of Ellen's neck and dropped her arm to her side. Without another word. While Ellen's knife was still resting ominously against Chrys's vulnerable flesh.

"If you'll just remove the knife, we can get up and get going." Chrys rolled her weight off Ellen's shoulder. All the front of her body was open to Ellen's knife. As far as Ellen could tell in the dark, Chrys's weapon was no longer pointing at her.

Ellen might not do trust, but it looked as though Chrys did.

"I could kill you now," Ellen whispered, stunned. "You seem very sure I won't."

"Yup." Chrys lay perfectly still, waiting.

Ellen could not think of anything to say. She pushed the knife back into her boot and started to get up.

Chrys was ahead of her, leaping to her feet. She even gave Ellen a helping hand. Then she rooted around on the ground until she found her goggles and put them back on. "Now I can see what's going on. I've got a spare pair for you. This way." She tugged at Ellen's arm. "Don't you want the new boots? I've lugged that pack across half of England tonight. The least you can do is put the kit on and carry it back."

"You'd have had me to carry back if your shot hadn't missed," Ellen muttered darkly, standing her ground.

"I didn't miss. I was shooting in the air. You're no good to me wounded. I'm taking you back whole or I'm leaving you here dead. So shall we go?"

Brutally frank, but eminently logical. Ellen shrugged and allowed herself to be led into the trees.

Chrys started to unpack her supplies: infrared goggles, combat kit, boots. Within minutes, Ellen had shed K's stolen uniform and the sweaty rubber boots. She stowed the uniform carefully in Chrys's backpack, but she left the rubber boots on the ground behind a tree. With luck, Seven would retrieve them. Let them go back where they belonged.

With the goggles, she could see properly. Fantastic. And it was wonderful to be wearing decent clothes again, with really comfortable boots. She wiggled her toes appreciatively as she slid the leather scabbard into the top of her right boot. Its weight was reassuring against her leg. Would Chrys give her a weapon as well?

"That's the second test you've passed."

"I thought it was only Anton who talked in riddles," Ellen bit back. She didn't understand what Chrys was talking about and she was tired enough already, without this sort of idiocy on top.

"You passed the test at the New Barrier. Now you've passed the test here, too." When Ellen frowned crossly, Chrys replied with that mirthless thin-lipped smile of hers, "You had me under your knife and you didn't use it. Even Anton might accept you now."

Ellen was shocked into laughter. Anton would never accept her. Besides… "What if I *had* used it? You'd be dead. That's a hell of a risk to take, just to test whether I can be trusted. I thought Jedda was a better tactician than that."

"She is." Chrys pushed a weapon into Ellen's hand. "I'm wearing your armoured suit."

• • • • •

It had taken hours, but they had made it safely back to the city, and then to the new bunker. It was surprisingly spacious and the Jays had set everything up with amazing speed. There was even a holo suite. So Chrys might have been serious when she issued that challenge. Provided Ellen survived long enough to take it up.

Ellen found herself sitting in central control, surrounded by Jays. Chrys had stripped her, and searched her again. Minutely. She had found nothing except one lethal, narrow-bladed knife in a newly-fashioned but harmless leather scabbard. The knife now lay on the table in front of Ellen, its blade pointing directly at her heart. She did not need to be told what it meant. She was on trial here. Again. So much for passing their tests.

They questioned her for what seemed like hours. She told them how she had escaped from K's clutches. Including the sex. It was embarrassing, but without that part of it, there was no chance they would believe her story. She explained how she had deliberately led the man on, playing on his sexual desire, in order to get the drop on him. And then to escape. She made sure her actions sounded cold and calculated.

Chrys smiled thoughtfully when they learned that K was human after all, in the most basic way. But that was it.

None of the Jays asked her how it had *felt*. No one seemed to be wondering whether she might have feelings for K.

And I don't. I DON'T.

She swallowed hard, hoping she did not look as unsettled as she was beginning to feel.

"Tell us about your comms kit, Ellen." Anton leaned forward to stare at her. "Did you steal that from K as well? Or did he give it to you so you could inform on us?"

Ellen choked back a gasp as the full horror of that hit home. Now she understood why she was still being treated like the enemy. They suspected she was a double agent for K. She would die first, but protesting her innocence wouldn't convince the Jays. If she couldn't prove them wrong, she really would be dead. Before the day was out.

All that effort. All those miles of trudging. For nothing?

Coldly furious, she drew herself up very straight and stared right back at her accuser. "OK, Anton. You think I'm K's double agent. Even you aren't suggesting I'd do it for money, I imagine?" His instant change of expression told her she was right. "OK, not for money, at least. So, make your case. Tell me why. Tell me *how*."

He blinked. Then he blustered. "I don't have to prove anything. You're the one who's—" He stopped, colouring.

"The one who's on trial here?" Ellen snapped. "Don't I know it? It seems it doesn't matter how many of your sodding tests I pass. There's always another one, isn't there?" She whipped round to the women. "Isn't there, Jedda?"

Jedda ignored the jibe and said, simply, "I need to be sure, Ellen. In my place, you would do the same." Then she waited.

Angry though she was, Ellen had to accept that Jedda was right. In theory, Ellen could have been turned. In theory...

She had to take the accusation head on. "So the allegation is that K turned me into his double agent in return for my freedom. Great theory, Anton, but crap in practice. What happened to your logic? I could have done any deal with K and reneged on it the moment I was free. If I'm K's double agent, he has to have a hold over me, something that will keep me in line, keep me feeding back the information he wants. I challenge you to find it. I can assure you it doesn't exist."

Anton shrank a little, avoiding her fierce stare.

"I'm a loner. There's nothing, and no one, that K can use to control me. Think about it. You've done the research into my background, I'm sure, so even you must see that the case doesn't stack up." Out of the corner of her eye, Ellen saw that Jedda was starting to frown. Ah. "Didn't you share your findings with the others, Anton? Naughty." His eyes widened as her vicious shot hit home. She had him.

No, he wasn't giving up so easily. "It's not what I do that matters here, Ellen. You're the one who's avoiding the question. Did K let you go? Did he give you the comms kit?"

"No, Anton. I escaped. Just as I said. And I made the comms kit. I can, you know. It wasn't difficult, though the result was primitive. I had to make do with what was lying around in the old bunker."

"You went back there? Alone? After we'd gone? I don't believe you."

Now that Ellen knew she was winning, she could afford to let her temper show. "Where else was there?" she said, almost spitting the syllables into his face. "London's not exactly full of people wanting to welcome me with open arms, is it?"

Jedda leant forward to intervene. "You aren't K's double-agent. OK, Ellen, I accept that. You made your comms kit from the rubbish left at the bunker. I'll buy that, too. But we didn't find you at the bunker." Her voice was low but firm. She was clearly determined to get to the bottom of everything. "You were hours away from London, right out in the country. You'd managed to get out of the city unseen, and to survive out there, for days on end, without weapons or food. All on your own. Explain to us how you did that, Ellen. All of it, please."

Ellen took a deep breath. She was going to have to tell them. "I wasn't on my own. I never said I was. I was rescued at the old bunker and taken north, to a place of safety. I was given tools to make the comms kit out of the bits I salvaged."

Anton made a sound half-way between a sigh and a snort. Ellen guessed he'd been itching to point out that she would not have found any tools in the old bunker. He'd wanted to imply she was lying. Well, tough. One more point to Ellen.

"You were *rescued*? Come on, Ellen. Give!" Even Jedda was losing her cool.

"I was rescued and taken north to a hidden camp, in the oak forest." Ellen turned to look Jedda in the eye. "It's a commune. Of Blues."

"You went to the Blues?" Anton's voice was almost a scream. His face was purple with fury. "Are you out of your mind? Do you know what they are?"

"I know that the Blues rescued me, and looked after me, and helped me to make contact with you. Without the Blues, I'd never have got back here. I owe them." Ellen refused to say anything more. There was no point in trying to keep arguing with Anton around.

"You owe them," Jedda repeated quietly, nodding to herself. "Yes, you probably do. And what is their price for returning you to us? There *is* one, I assume?"

Ellen sighed. "Yes. They want an alliance. Against the state. They want us to help each other. I thought it could make sense. The state hunts us. The state hunts the Blues. 'My enemy's enemy is my friend.' That's what the Blues said to me."

"You're mad, Ellen," Anton burst out. "We can't have Blues as allies. They're— You don't know what they're like."

"I've seen enough to know that they might be useful allies. Also that when it comes to Blues, you're really not rational, Anton. What is it with you?"

He gave her a death stare. Then he clamped his jaws together and refused to say another word. He reminded her of a sulky child. What was it with him, indeed?

"Enough for now!" Jedda gazed round, making eye contact with each of them in turn. "We're all tired. We'll finish the debrief in the morning. Chrys and Anton, go and get your heads down. Linden, you take the first watch. I'll do the second." Everyone rose and made for the door without a word. Chrys looked relieved it was over. She was a warrior, yet she hated drama. She was a strange mixture. Unfathomable.

Ellen waited in her seat. Her turn next. Was it to be that freezing cell again?

To Ellen's surprise, Jedda smiled at her. "You've had a tough time, Ellen. And you're a tough cookie. We're glad to have you back. Come to my office for ten minutes, will you? I've got a few questions that can't wait till the morning."

FORTY-TWO

JEDDA WAS NOT SURE how to begin. Finally, she broke the awkward silence by talking about Anton. Ellen needed to know about his background. Especially if she—

No. Wrong time. If I ask her tonight, she'll refuse point blank.

Ellen had sunk into Jedda's spare chair. She looked exhausted. "OK. What do you want to know? And why is it so important it can't wait?" She sounded prickly.

"That's wasn't...um... exactly why I wanted to see you," Jedda began. She sounded lame. She started again. "I wanted to tell you about Anton. In private. I don't want the two of you going head-to-head over the Blues."

Ellen's shoulders sank. "Don't see how we can avoid it. He's not exactly rational when it comes to the Blues, is he?"

"He has cause, Ellen." Jedda waited for that to sink in. Ellen frowned, but said nothing, so Jedda went on, "Anton's father was a Blue. His mother wasn't, obviously, or he'd be a Blue, too. But his mother had the recessive Blue gene. Mating with a Blue man, she could have had Blue children. Fifty-fifty chance."

Ellen shot up straight. She looked shocked. "But Not-Blue women with the recessive gene are forbidden to breed. I thought they were all sterilised."

"They're supposed to be. But some manage to avoid it. Anton's mother did. She wanted children of her own, so desperately that she was prepared to risk her life. She fled to a Blue commune where there was a chance of finding a fertile man."

"She succeeded. Obviously," Ellen said tartly.

"Yes. Anton was brought up in the commune for a while. It didn't work out. The father died in some kind of hunting accident. Not that he'd been much of a father to Anton, anyway. He couldn't cope with the fact that his son was Not-Blue, apparently."

Ellen didn't react to that at all.

"It was tough for Anton. He was showing signs of interest in tech stuff and the commune didn't approve. He's never said exactly what they did to him, but I think he was probably beaten up by the Blue kids. Maybe by the adults as well. He'd be an obvious target: first, he wasn't a Blue; second, he was a geek. Whatever happened, he ended up hating the commune and everything to do with it. After his mother drowned – an accident, they said, though I'm not sure Anton believes it – he ran away to the city. He was luckier than most runaways. He was picked up by a member of the Jays – there were a lot more of us back then – and settled with a foster family."

"How old was he? When he ran away, I mean?"

"Not sure. He never told me. I'd guess about twelve. Why?"

"I was wondering when he acquired all his tech skills. And where."

"The Jays arranged his education. Before my time, so I can't tell you much. I think a lot of what he knows is self-taught."

"He's got the right kind of mind for that. He really is very good, you know."

Jedda was glad to hear Ellen admit that, though she would lay money that Ellen would never say it in Anton's hearing. "Yes, he is good, isn't he? But so are you. From what I've seen, your skills are complementary. If you could be persuaded to work together, the Jays would gain a lot. The old saying about the whole being greater than the sum of its parts, you know?"

"Why are you telling me all this, Jedda?"

"You know why, Ellen. I want you to stop baiting Anton, and to start working with him. You're one of the Jays now. And so is he. We all have to work as a team."

Ellen pursed her lips and frowned. "I'm one of the Jays, now? Really? You never trusted me before. So why now?"

"Because you've passed all the tests. Because we need your skills. You're a tech, and a warrior as well. That's quite a combination. No, we didn't trust you, but you went out of your way to seem hostile, didn't you? You were pretty much demanding *not* to be trusted." Jedda waited a beat. "Or did I read you wrong?"

Ellen made a face. "Look, the thing is that I'm a loner. I rely on my own skills. I guard my own back. It's better than—" She exhaled sharply. "What I mean is, if I don't trust anyone, I can't be betrayed."

Jedda found she was shaking her head automatically. She and Ellen were more alike than Ellen knew. Jedda was a loner, too, as all leaders had to be. She recognised instinctively that Ellen was not telling the whole truth, even if she thought she was. Time to shake her out of her comfort zone. "It's not betrayal you fear, it's the pain that comes with it. You're afraid of getting close to anyone, because you're afraid of getting hurt. It's happened to you before, hasn't it?"

Ellen dropped her head to stare at the floor. When she looked up again, her eyes were blazing. "You know what, Jedda? It's none of your business. I don't need an amateur shrink to sort me out. I know what I want. And what I don't want."

Jedda had provoked the emotional reaction she wanted. She held up a hand to stop the furious tirade. "OK, OK. If your past is private, that's fine by me." She waited a second and went in for the kill. "But I do need to know if you're prepared to join us. For real. I did ask you before, remember?"

Ellen seemed to shrink in her skin. She groaned. It sounded like a mixture of exhaustion and exasperation. The fire went out of her eyes, and she pushed a hand through her ragged hair. After a moment, she shrugged. Was she going to give in at last? It was the only logical solution, surely?

"I don't belong here. But then—" she sighed again "—I don't belong anywhere else either. So... OK, I'll join you." As if the words were being dragged out of her.

Yes! Jedda opened her mouth to say something positive, but Ellen wasn't finished. She wasn't beaten, either. "For now, at least," she said, in a voice more like her old, snarky self. The fire of challenge was back in her eyes.

Goaded, Jedda lost it. "That's not good enough. I can't afford to have a team member who might disappear at any second. Probably just when we need her."

"I won't do that. I don't promise to stay permanently, but I won't leave you in the lurch. I'll give you advance warning if I'm planning to leave. A few weeks, at least. Will that do?"

Jedda nodded. It was a great deal better than nothing. "I'll settle for that. Now, you'd better go and get your head down." She waited until Ellen had started to get up, before adding, "I should warn you, though, that we'll be trying to work on your itchy feet. It would be great – for all of us, *including* you – if you stayed for good."

An extraordinary shadow flashed across Ellen's face as Jedda spoke. Anxiety? No, it looked more like real fear. But Ellen was never afraid. At least, she'd never shown it. What could she be afraid of? The Blues? Or something here in London? It made no sense. There was no reason for a warrior like Ellen to be afraid of staying with the Jays long term. Short term OK, permanent terrifying? No, it made no sense at all.

It certainly wasn't a good omen for the success of Jedda's other plan.

· · · · ·

It was mid-morning when Linden was called in to see Jedda.

Looking strained, she crossed her tiny office to close the door behind him. He was guessing this had to be important. She had not allowed Linden to be alone with her since their first night in the new bunker, the night when she had flatly refused to go away with him. The thought of her rejection still caught him on the raw. He resolved not to mention it. Let her think he didn't care.

She clearly wanted to talk to him – and in private – but she was avoiding his eyes. Her first words came out in a rush. "Now that Ellen's back, there's a chance she might take over as leader."

"What?" Linden sat down with a thump and blew out a long breath. Since when was Jedda looking for a replacement? Hadn't she made clear she was staying? "But I thought... Surely, if anyone, it would be Chrys?" It was the wrong question, but it was the one that tumbled out of his scrambled brain.

"No, not Chrys. I asked her a...a while back and she refused. Not a strategic thinker, she said."

"A while back? You mean, *before* I asked you to come away with me?"

"Um... Yes." Jedda was blushing.

He swore under his breath. He had misread everything. She'd known Linden had to leave London and she'd been trying to find a new leader. So that she could go with him? Possibly. But she wasn't rejecting him. She hadn't rejected him!

He only just stopped himself from giving a whoop of delight. He started to get up, to take her in his arms, but what was left of his rational mind kicked in, and kicked him back down again. Right now, sex was not the answer.

Once he began to think properly, he realised it was going to take him a while to get his head round it. Being here with Jedda, alone in a confined space – within caressing distance – was absolutely not the best way to do that. When she was blushing she was just too desirable. The last thing he needed was for his body to start responding in ways he couldn't control.

One glance across at Jedda told him that his own problems came a poor second here. Jedda was really troubled over the Jays. Over everything. Poor Jedda. She'd been trying to do her duty as leader, even at the cost of her own desires. She was a heroine. It was one of the things he loved about her.

Linden was going to have to tread very carefully now. Jedda was embarrassed by how much she had already revealed. He must not make things worse. He got up slowly, being careful not to close the space between them. "Ellen," he began thoughtfully. "Yes, she probably does have what it takes. Amazing mix of skills, that's for sure. Er... what does Chrys think?"

"Chrys doesn't know. And nothing's settled. I haven't even asked Ellen yet. I've only got as far as asking her to join the Jays."

"But she agreed? She's got no other options, surely?"

"Yes and no. She'll join, but she hasn't agreed to stay for good. She probably won't want to be leader." Jedda, the leader who was always positive and always up for the next challenge, was sounding rather demoralised. She'd never let her mask slip before, not even with Linden, and it wrenched at his gut to see her so down.

Linden was not going to allow it. Not when they had a chance of winning on this. "I bet she will do it if you frame it right. Make it a challenge. Let her suspect you don't really think she's up to it. She'll do it just to prove you wrong. That's the kind of woman she is."

Jedda raised her eyebrows and said nothing.

Linden had the bit between his teeth now. He could see the answer. He was going to make sure Jedda saw it, too. "Ellen only needs to be leader short-term. You could sell it to her as a stop-gap solution until the new guys arrive from South America. One of them could take over, once they've worked out the lie of the land here. Then Ellen could go off and do her own thing, whatever that is. On the other hand, she might find she likes being leader. She might decide to stay. Either way, you get to leave."

It was difficult to read her face. He couldn't tell if he was getting through or not.

In for a penny...

He took a step towards her and reached out a hand, tentatively, waiting for a reaction. She didn't take it, but she didn't move away either. For a long time, the two of them stood there, motionless. When she looked up at him, at last, her eyes had softened. He dared to slide his arm round her shoulders. "Either way, we win. It's our chance, Jedda. Isn't it?"

She came into his arms, without a word. Then she kissed him, long and slow, and full of passion. Nothing between them had changed. They belonged together. They both knew it.

"Will you come to me tonight?" His voice was hoarse. Given half a chance, he would take her right now, on the bare floor. And he was sure she felt the same.

With a sigh, she pushed his arms away, and stepped back from him. "You know I can't do that, Linden. Not as long as I'm leader. If Ellen agrees to take over, then maybe…" She shook her head so hard, her loose hair whipped her face.

He tried to picture himself diving into ice-cold water. It helped. A bit. *Focus, Linden! Jedda needs your help here.* "I can wait until she agrees," he said, trying to sound encouraging. "Which she will. I'm sure of it. When are you going to ask her?"

Jedda swallowed. "It might as well be today. No time like the present, eh?"

Bless her. She was amazing. He managed to grin back at her. "No time like the present. And, just at present, if you've no more use for me, ma'am…?" She said nothing, so he put on his best, most cheering voice, to say, "Right then, see you later. I'm off to take a long, cold shower."

· · · · ·

As soon as she opened her eyes, Ellen knew that Jedda had let her oversleep. Deliberately. It was the kind of thing Jedda did. As leader, she took care of her troops. If Ellen stayed – no, *while* Ellen stayed, she would be valued, and cared for. In a way, it was better than being with the Blues. No one here was trying to mess with Ellen's head. Besides, she was half-warrior, half-geek. Neither of those could fit in with the Blues. No wonder Anton had run away.

All that stuff about Anton's childhood. Weird. It didn't sit with what Ellen knew of Seven's commune. She could not imagine Seven, or any of those little children, as bullies. They all seemed so gentle, in tune with the land and with each other.

There was nothing gentle about Blue3. Pure steel. And apart from Seven, I didn't get to know any of them. They could be raving child-molesters for all I know.

She forced herself to assess her evidence more rationally. She had seen one Blue commune, and bits of it were seriously scary. Other communes might be worse. On balance, there was no reason to disbelieve Anton. His visceral hatred must have come from somewhere.

Food for thought. Ellen did think that an alliance with Seven's commune could be useful – and given Blue3's threats, the Jays had no choice, really – but Anton would have to be brought round to the idea. Perhaps he would accept that it was a logical step, provided the Jays kept the Blues at arm's length? Anton had a good brain. He must be open to logical persuasion.

If he found out about Blue3's threats, he would probably lose it completely. Better not to let him find out. But, in fairness, Ellen would have to tell Jedda. The leader had a right to know.

Ellen continued to ruminate about the Blues while she showered and dressed. She pulled on her new boots with real pleasure, and smiled as she slid Seven's scabbard – with K's knife – down the side. She smiled even more at the memory of K, standing stark naked, while she threatened to cut off his balls. Next time, she really would do it.

Next time? There isn't going to be a next time.

A quick knock on the door was followed by Jedda. She had not waited to be invited in. She looked even more serious than on the previous night.

"Ellen, I need to talk to you. About the future. Are you OK to do that now?"

"I thought we'd sorted that last night. I said I would stay. I won't break my word." Ellen finished buckling her belt and straightened her jacket.

"I'm not going to beat about the bush here." Jedda gestured towards the single chair and, when Ellen nodded, sat down. Ellen perched on the edge of her bunk and swung one leg up, leaving the other dangling. She wanted to look the picture of relaxation for whatever was coming now.

"I want to leave the Jays, Ellen, but I can't go unless I can find a new leader. It could be you."

That was absolutely the last thing Ellen had expected Jedda to say. She felt as if she'd been propelled into a solid wall at top speed. She swallowed. "Bit of a change from wanting to blow me up, isn't it?" Yes, it was flippant, but she couldn't think of anything sensible to say. She needed time to digest this.

"Be serious, Ellen. You know why I played that trick with the killsuits. You'd have done the same in my place. You know why I ordered your termination, too. It's the deal we all make. None of us can afford to be taken alive."

It was all true. But it didn't help one bit. Was Chrys going too? If not, she should take over as leader, surely? Or was Jedda planning some kind of stitch-up with Ellen as the fall guy? It wouldn't be the first time a leader had dropped a nasty problem in someone else's lap and scarpered, sharpish, before the shit hit the fan. Though that didn't sound like upright Jedda.

Ellen needed time to think. Plus a lot more information. "Chrys is the obvious choice," she said flatly. "Not me. How could I possibly do it? Chrys doesn't trust me. Anton hates my guts, so I could never trust *him*. Besides, what makes you think I'm prepared to stay with the Jays for long enough to be leader?" That last bit was an afterthought, and Ellen knew it should have come first. Crap tactics. She was not handling this discussion at all well.

Jedda had coloured a bit. Clearly she was having difficulty, too. "Chrys won't do it. Says she's not leader material."

Oh. Interesting. Ellen decided Chrys was probably right. Whatever else she was, the Jays' quiet assassin was clear-eyed about her own limitations. "OK. Got that. Not Chrys, clearly not Anton... Linden's leaving, so I'm all you're left with. Great vote of confidence. Thanks a bunch."

"Cut it out, Ellen," Jedda bit back savagely. "You know the score. You know you can do it. Unless you're afraid to take it on? Too much of a challenge, is it?"

That was a nasty dig. Ellen had never backed down from a challenge in her life. But she knew when someone was trying to manipulate her. She said nothing. She just stared at Jedda. If Jedda wanted to take that as another challenge, then fine.

Jedda held Ellen's gaze for a long while. Then she shrugged, as if conceding defeat in their battle of wills. When she spoke, the sarcastic tone had gone. She was deadly serious. "It wouldn't have to be permanent. But you know you're the best choice. Out of all of us."

"*All* of us?" Ellen echoed, shocked. She'd thought she was winning here, but now she hadn't a clue what to do or say. She certainly didn't believe for a second that her leadership skills were in Jedda's league.

"Yes, *all* of us. That's part of the reason I need to leave. Since Linden... I've been losing my edge, Ellen, making mistakes. We can't afford that. All our lives are at stake here. Even after Linden goes, I can't guarantee that I'll be able to do what I did before. I can't take the chance that I could fail, big time. Even if I stay, I don't think I can be leader any more."

"Are you really suggesting that I take over as leader and you *stay*?" Flabbergasted wasn't a strong enough word for how Ellen felt.

"I could do. If you want. For a while, at least. Maybe until the new team has settled? But it's your decision."

"Only if I take the job. And it's a bloody big if." Ellen ran a hand through her hair. Was this really happening? She'd thought Chrys was clear-eyed, but Jedda was something else. After a long pause in which she failed to collect her thoughts, Ellen fell back on her old, safe mantra. "Look, I've always been a loner, you know that. You accepted it last night. Taking on the Jays – leading the Jays – would be… Hell, I don't know what it would be, but I do know it wouldn't be what I planned. I came to London to escape. I intended to shift for myself. *By* myself. It's what I'm best at."

"That's why you're the right choice. Leadership is a loner's role," Jedda said quietly.

That hit home, because it was true. Ellen had watched Jedda and seen how alone she was. Jedda had taken on the role and all its burdens and she had never tried to shift the load onto anyone else's shoulders. So maybe Ellen *was* a good fit for the job, just as Jedda said? And it would be a real challenge, something she could get her teeth into. With a trusted team at her back. It would be almost like having friends.

Bloody hell! Three days with Seven and I'm totally contaminated. Friends?

The idea was seductive, in ways Ellen had not imagined.

"*If* I took it," she said slowly, weighing her words, "there would be conditions."

"Leader's privilege."

"Even if my conditions involved the Blues?"

Jedda's eyes widened. She took a deep breath. "Leader's privilege."

Ellen waited, but Jedda didn't say anything more. The discussion was over. It was decision time. Right now, Ellen couldn't begin to think straight. "You can't expect me to decide here, on the spot. I'll need time. And there are other things I really have to sort out, before I can think about what you're offering."

Understatement of the year. Jedda didn't know the half of it. She didn't know about K. And Ellen could never tell her.

Ellen swung her legs down to the floor and stood up. "I should warn you that I may need to go out. Alone. And it'll have to be soon. I'll give you my final answer after that."

Jedda did not try to argue. "Take an earwig if you go out. Or get Anton to do you an implant. You may need his help. You never know. And don't forget, you're still wearing a killsuit." Jedda smiled, a little ruefully, Ellen thought. "Standard issue," Jedda went on in that same crisp voice. "Leader's orders. *Current* leader's orders, that is." Her smile widened a fraction. Then she turned on her heel and left, without a word.

Ellen sighed out a long slow breath and closed her eyes. *Things I really have to sort out. Too right. And the first of them is how I cope with K.*

Ellen had always assumed that she would get away from the Jays eventually. But if she became leader, she would be here in London for the long haul, possibly for years. She would be head of the main resistance group in the province and K – the man who turned her insides to a puddle of lust almost every time she looked at him – would be The Enemy. There was desire on both sides, Ellen was sure of that, but K seemed to be able to put his lust into a neat little compartment and lock the door on it. Most of the time, anyway. She, on the other hand...

She had already given in to hers once. Right now, she was seriously thinking about how she could do it again.

I'd be out of my mind to become leader, or even to stay in London long term. How could I begin to fight K? He really wants to kill me and he won't let sex get in the way. Though he might well reckon on a quick bout of horizontal combat before he puts the killshot between my eyes.

Could I do the same, in his place? Even without the sex, do I have what it takes to look him in the eye and take the shot?

She really, really didn't know.

She couldn't possibly make any decisions until she found out.

FORTY-THREE

JEDDA SPENT A LONG time alone, mulling things over. Then she went to find Anton. She had not told him she was hoping to go and she could not leave him in the dark any longer.

She found him with Chrys in the food preparation area. Both of them had their backs to the door. They were cleaning and chopping some of the Jays' precious supply of fresh vegetables. Jedda stood in the doorway, watching. Every so often, Anton was popping a chunk into his mouth, and chewing with relish. He would!

"Hi, guys," Jedda said.

Chrys glanced over her shoulder. Anton turned round and grinned, still chewing. Then he went back to his chopping.

"I need to talk to you, while Ellen's on watch," Jedda said. "It's important."

Anton stole another chunk.

"Hey," Jedda said automatically, "that's for all of us, remember?"

"Don't worry, Jedda," Chrys said. "When it comes to dishing-up time, I dock his portion. He thinks I haven't noticed, but I've been counting every one."

"Quite right, too," Anton said, flashing a grin.

"Sit down a minute, guys." Once they had done so, Jedda joined them at the table. "Chrys knows some of this already, but I need to tell you both that I've decided to give up being leader. If I can find someone to take my place before Linden leaves, I'll go with him. If not, I'll stay on, for a bit, until things are sorted. But I want you both to know that I will definitely be going, sooner or later."

There was a long pause. Chrys was staring at the table, her fingers playing with her chopping knife. Anton sat as though struck dumb, occasionally glancing sideways at Chrys and then back to Jedda. Eventually he took a deep breath and said, "What have you decided about who'll take over?" He glanced at Chrys again.

"I've already told Jedda I won't do it," Chrys put in quickly, before Jedda could respond.

Anton bristled. "But you—"

"I'm not—" Chrys stopped, shaking her head. "I don't have what it takes, Anton. It's not enough to be a warrior. I would be the wrong choice," she finished flatly.

"Oh." Anton looked uncertainly at Jedda and then back at Chrys. Neither reacted. "OK. Right. Not Chrys. One of the South Americans, I presume?"

Time for Jedda to drop her bombshell. "No. Ellen."

"*Ellen*? But—"

Jedda cut him off with a gesture. "Ellen," she repeated firmly. "She's the right kind of thinker to lead. And she knows how to fight. The tech stuff is a bonus. Or it will be, if she takes the job."

"You mean she might not…?"

Jedda sighed. "She wants a day or so to consider it. She's interested. She couldn't hide that. If she takes it on, there will probably be conditions."

"Huh!" Anton glowered and hunched his shoulders. "I bet I can guess what those are. The first of them will be to dispose of the existing tech."

"Anton, if I didn't know better, I'd say you'd been frying your logic circuits. She talked about possible conditions and none of them involved getting rid of you. She rates you highly."

"Ho yus?" he chortled.

"She does. And if you applied that sharp little brain of yours to the facts, you would see that your skills are complementary. You *could* work really well together. If you would bin the silly one-upmanship." That knocked him back. Jedda could see that he was beginning to think seriously about Ellen and her skills. At last.

"What do you want us to do?" Chrys asked in her quiet, practical way.

"First, accept Ellen into the team. Properly. We all know she's proved her loyalty. And her worth. If she asks questions, answer her frankly. She needs to know how we do things, what resources we have, that sort of stuff. Don't push her about her decision. She's promised me an answer and I've said I'll wait."

Chrys nodded. "Seems fair."

"Anton?"

"Um." He was still hunched and he was avoiding Jedda's eye.

"Is that a yes-grunt or a no-grunt?"

"Look, Jedda, I'm part of the team and I'll go with what the team decides. I don't have to like it, but I'm a professional too, you know.

If Ellen's the right choice as leader – *if* – I'll work as hard for her as I work for you. I don't have to like her, though."

"But you *do* have to trust her," Jedda countered quickly.

"Cuts both ways," he bit back.

He was right. Ellen and Anton would have to learn to trust each other. It could not be done overnight and it could not be imposed, by Jedda or anyone else. She took a deep breath. "Yes, you're right. You'll both have to put aside your differences. All I'm asking, Anton, is that you give her a fair crack of the whip. OK?"

He said nothing, but he did give a tiny nod. For Jedda, that was good enough.

• • • • •

When Chrys came back into central control after their meal, she found Jedda sitting at one workstation, and Ellen at another. Both women seemed to be busy. Linden was not there. He was on watch again, so he was probably doing his rounds. Anton would arrive eventually, once he'd finished clearing up and snaffling any spare goodies he could find. For the moment, everything was calm and peaceful.

Ellen looked up. "Chrys, can you give me a hand here?"

Chrys went across to Ellen's desk and tried to see what she was working on. Whatever it was, it was too small to make out.

"I've been doing some comms mods on my latest computer design. It works best implanted under the skin, against the skull, but I've found it works pretty well between the teeth as well. Makes it easier to remove, too, if it goes wrong. I want to run some tests, but I need two people for that." She produced a pair of thin tweezers holding what seemed to be a tiny chip. "The idea is that I put one between your teeth, and one between mine. Then we communicate."

"But we can already do that using Anton's implants," Chrys protested. She noticed that Jedda was listening, too.

Ellen smiled rather smugly. "With Anton's implants, you get incoming comms on silent, but outgoing messages have to be spoken aloud. This kit doesn't do noise. At least, it won't if I've managed to finalise the mods properly."

Chrys blew out a long breath. It sounded more like magic than tech. Or an elaborate joke. But unlike Anton, Ellen didn't do practical jokes. "So how does it work, then?"

"Basically, it works by the power of concentrated thought. You tell it, in your mind, to turn itself on and you tell it what messages to send. In your mind. No sound."

"You're kidding!" Jedda put in, getting up and coming over. "So with one of these, Anton would know every thought in my head? I'm sure it's incredibly clever, Ellen, but I'm equally sure I wouldn't want to go there. My thoughts are my own."

"Couldn't agree more," Ellen said, with feeling. "Don't worry, it's more sophisticated than that. You need a code word to start and end every single transmission. Let's say, for example, that your code word is 'lobster'. You think, very deliberately, 'lobster, computer, wake up, lobster." That puts it in listening mode. If it receives messages, you will hear them. To send, you think something like, 'lobster, leaving Point Foxtrot now, lobster,' and the message will be transmitted. If you go on to think, 'Sod it, I'm outnumbered,' that won't be sent, because you didn't use the code word to top and tail the thought."

Jedda's eyes widened. "Does it really work?"

"Can't be sure. Until now, I've never used it for external comms." She shrugged and almost smiled. "No need, when there was only me. It used to receive and act accurately enough on my thought instructions. Which of you wants to have a go?"

Both Jedda and Chrys nodded eagerly.

"Fair enough. In fact, having three makes it easier for me, because I'll be able to concentrate on monitoring the experiment. Here's what we do. Once we've installed the computers and got them working, I'll give you messages in writing. I want each of you to read the written message and transmit it to the other via thought comms. The receiver is please to write down the message she hears in her head. No one is to speak at all during the test. OK?"

Both women readily agreed. Jedda looked as excited as Chrys felt.

"Right. Chrys first. Open wide and I'll install it. Your code word, by the way, really is 'lobster'." Chrys laughed but sat down obediently and opened her mouth for Ellen to insert the tiny wafer between her molars and push it into contact with her gum.

"Feels like I've got something stuck between my teeth," Chrys said, working her jaw and tongue a little.

"That's because you have! Don't poke at it too much. Jedda? Your turn. Your code word is 'strawberry'. I thought it best to use words that didn't come up often in normal conversation." She chuckled. "When was the last time you had a strawberry?"

"Or a lobster," Chrys said with a hollow laugh. "I'm not even sure they still exist, actually."

"Oh, believe me, they do. Buttered lobster is delicious," Ellen said airily and busied herself with fixing Jedda's mouth.

Chrys was surprised, then very curious. It sounded as if Ellen had actually eaten lobster, possibly more than once. She was a bit of a mystery; there might be all kinds of exotic episodes in her background. Chrys made a mental note to find out more.

A minute later, she had forgotten everything but Ellen's experiment. All three were immersed in it. It took Jedda and Chrys a few goes to concentrate enough and to remember to top and tail their thoughts every time, but they got the hang of it in the end. Chrys couldn't wait to discover whether the messages Jedda had jotted down were the messages she had sent. It was such a weird sensation, nothing and yet something.

"Yes!" Ellen shouted, after the third silent exchange was over. "That last time, you made it work. You've done it. Brilliant! It works. It actually bloody works!" She danced round the control centre, waving her scraps of paper.

Jedda threw a seriously meaningful look at Chrys and Chrys nodded in reply. For a woman who had still to decide whether she was going to take on the job of leader, Ellen was donating an awful lot of her skills, and her secrets, to the Jays' operations. Chrys was sure that Jedda had made the right choice. And she was beginning to think that the Jays might just persuade Ellen to stay. For good.

• • • • •

It was the middle of the night.

In Linden's bedspace, it was almost pitch dark, but the slight change in the air woke him. All his warrior's senses were instantly on alert. Someone had opened the door to creep in. His gut clenched. An assassin? Sent by Marujn?

Never mind how an assassin could have got into the bunker. He had to prepare to meet an attack. His muscles tensed. His heart began to race. His breathing got faster, shallower. But he didn't have a weapon within reach. Bugger! And his arms and legs were hampered by the bedclothes. He started to ease them off, desperate to make no sound.

And then he recognised her. Somehow he knew, even in the dark, that it could only be Jedda, there by the door. She had come to join him. Because she wanted to. Not – he fervently hoped – to discuss Jay business. In fact, not to *discuss* anything at all.

Free of the covers at last, he was tempted to lunge across the room to grab her and kiss her senseless – and then to do all the things he'd stopped himself from doing when they'd been together earlier.

A wicked thought struck him. She'd had her reasons, but she'd been making him suffer, keeping her distance for what seemed like ages. Ever since that one night they'd spent together. Maybe it was payback time? Subtle payback... but still payback.

Grinning into the darkness, he slid his bare feet off the bed, sank silently to the floor and rolled under his bunk. His wound did not give him even a twinge. Thanks to Chrys's skill, his leg was almost as good as new. It was no trouble to push himself right back against the far wall and wait. Unless Jedda knelt down to peer under the bunk, she almost certainly wouldn't see him under there. His grin widened. Hide-and-seek for lovers. Why not? Could lead to very interesting surprises.

"Linden?" Jedda's voice was barely a whisper. "Linden, are you awake?"

He did not make a sound. He even held his breath.

Unlike him, she was not barefoot. He heard her cautious footsteps as she crossed the floor to the bed. She would be reaching out, expected to touch him. What kind of warrior did she think he was, that he'd still be out for the count when a potential assassin was standing over him? He'd pay her back for that, too. Slowly. And in a way they would both find deeply satisfying.

She muttered something he couldn't quite make out. Probably frustration. Excellent. Then she whirled round and left in a rush, without stopping to look for him, and without bothering any more about how much noise she was making. She seemed exasperated. Or maybe she was concerned? That thought fed and warmed his senses, and he relaxed quite happily where he lay, basking in the glow. It was more than pleasant to know that Jedda might be concerned for his welfare. Being a logical and methodical woman, she would search the bunker for him. When she failed to find him...

Shit, what if she raised the alarm? That would screw up everything. The whole team would discover exactly where she'd been and they wouldn't need to be told why.

He was about to get out of his idiot's hiding-place and go after her, when the door opened again. He breathed a silent prayer of thanks for her sharp tactical brain. Of course she wouldn't raise the alarm unless she was absolutely sure he was missing. She had come back to double-check.

The light clicked on. "Linden?" she said again, louder than

before. "Where the hell are you, you rotten bastard?" Louder still, and with feeling.

He'd pushed his luck far enough on the hide-and-seek front. He moved just enough to stretch out a hand to grab her ankle. And jerk her off balance.

Jedda hit the deck with a thump and a gasp of outrage. "You're not just a bastard," she spat instantly. "You're a lousy, underhand, conniving, devious—"

It was an inventive line in abuse, but he could think of better uses for her mouth. He dragged her to him and there, on the floor under the bed, he stopped her tirade by kissing her. When she eventually caught a breath and began to protest, he kissed her again, harder. This time she responded with the same passion they had shared before. A moment later he was tearing off her clothes. And she was helping him.

Their joining was fast, and furious. Yet utterly fulfilling. And then it was over and they were lying in each other's arms, panting quietly, totally spent.

For a long moment, they were both still, and silent, bemused by the wonder of it. Then Jedda began to laugh. Lying on top of her, skin to skin, joined from breast to knee, Linden could feel the helpless hiccupping of her ribcage against him. "Did we... D...did I just do what I *think* I did?" she wheezed. "On the floor? *UNDER the bed?*" She gave another gasp of gusty laughter. It was such a joyous sound – carefree, in a way Jedda had not been since the first day they had found each other. "It's ridiculous. And I'm the serious leader who doesn't *do* ridiculous."

"You do now," he said huskily into her ear, blowing against her skin. He needed to lift his head from her shoulder. He needed to see her face. "Argh!" Bad move. His head cracked on the underside of the bunk. His head might be hard, but the bunk base was harder. As he'd just learnt the hard way. *The hard wa—?*

Linden started laughing, too. Because his brain was creating infantile puns all by itself. And because laughing with Jedda – together – was nearly the most glorious thing in the world.

"Maybe we might...er... migrate to somewhere a little more conventional?" she said when she could speak again. It was gloomy under the bunk, but he could see that she was still laughing in fits and starts. She was a wonderful woman. She deserved better than a dusty floor and a lover with a swelling lump on the back of his head.

"If you want conventional, dear leader, I can do conventional."

He tried to make an elegant gesture in the direction of the room. "After you, ma'am."

"Idiot," she said lovingly, planting a kiss on his neck. "You know what? I'm a bit pushed to move, right at the moment, on account of a great heavy oaf on top of me. And— Ow! Can you put your elbow somewhere else, please?" She started to giggle.

Linden had never seen her like this before. He had never imagined she could *be* like this. And he loved it all.

Jedda, giggling or not, wanted to move. She gave a huge heave of her hips – she was strong for a woman – and Linden's bare backside hit the bunk above.

"Hey!" he protested. "That hurt."

"Nah! You've got plenty of padding. Now get off me, you great lardbucket."

"Lard—! I'll have you know, woman, that there's not an ounce of fat on me." But he slid off her, all the same, grinning fit to burst. He was still grinning as he helped her out and on to her feet.

She was a mess. Her hair was tangled, her body was powdered with patches of dust and half her clothes were bunched round her ankles. From the knees up, she was naked. Linden decided she looked scrumptious, but he could tell from her suddenly heightened colour that she did not think so. No time for words. He grabbed her round the waist and plonked her naked bottom onto his bunk, so that he could kneel at her feet and pull off her boots and her trousers. As he finished, he looked up at her slyly. "I've heard of *dying* with your boots on," he began, "but this adds a whole new dimension."

She swung a foot at him. It connected, but it was bare. He caught it and began to stroke his fingers down the length of the fragile bones. She shivered at his touch. "If you dare to tickle my feet, I'll kill you," she threatened hoarsely. "I swear I will."

"Don't worry, love. I can tickle you in much better places than that. Would you like me to try? I think I've had enough of hide and seek." He picked up her legs and swung them onto the bed, before flicking the switch to return the room to darkness. "Better," he said softly. He pulled the covers over her and climbed in to join her. "Cosy," he said against her cheek and began to nuzzle her ear lobe. It tasted of dust – a little. Mostly, it tasted of Jedda. And he wanted to taste much, much more.

He started to kiss his way down her neck to her vulnerable throat, and her breast. She moaned a little, and put a hand to his hair, stroking it away from his forehead, avoiding the tender spot where he had hit the bed. When he started to kiss and suckle her nipple in earnest, she did another one of those incredible hip heaves. In seconds, he was lying on his back, and Jedda was on top of him.

"My turn," she said huskily. "I didn't move under the bed, so you mustn't move on top of it. Got that?"

His eyes were accustomed to the deep gloom now. He could just see she was grinning wickedly. He grinned back. "Yes, ma'am," he said, in his best platoon soldier's voice. "Anything you say, ma'am."

"Anything?" she said, with a definite catch in her voice. "Now that, soldier, is an offer I am definitely not going to refuse." Slowly, she began to push her naked body down his, skin sliding over skin, until her mouth was kissing his ribcage and her loose hair was tickling his nipples. And then she was kissing his belly button. And then his stomach. And then...

He groaned. He couldn't help it.

"Groaning is fine," she said against his burning skin. "Moving is off limits, but groaning is fine. Now a little lower..."

FORTY-FOUR

JEDDA AND LINDEN WERE snuggled together, spoon fashion, relishing the cocoon of darkness and the freedom of being alone.

"I'll have to go soon," Jedda sighed. She made no move. A few minutes more would not hurt.

Linden put his mouth to the back of her left ear and nibbled.

"You're a very bad influence, Linden. You know I have to go, and you're trying to make me forget my duty."

"Don't worry. I'll make sure you leave before you can be embarrassed by meeting any of the others. I may lust after you something rotten, but there's a tiny part of my rational brain that still works." He nuzzled harder. "Most of the time."

She felt a bubble of laughter trying to expand in her middle. Linden really was impossible. Hadn't she read somewhere, in an old, old book, that the most successful Casanovas laughed their conquests into bed?

Linden planted a lingering kiss on her ear, and another on the back of her neck. "One thing I do have to ask you, Jedda. Sorry to go all serious on you, but you told me we couldn't be together until you had confirmed your successor. Yet you're here. So has Ellen actually agreed to do it?"

Jedda took a deep breath. Her bottom pushed into his loins in the most distracting way. She tried to ignore it. She hoped Linden could, too.

"Well, she hasn't actually agreed. But she didn't say no. If you'd been in the control centre this afternoon – you were out on your rounds at the time – you'd have seen her doing the most amazing things with comms tech and, basically, handing all of it over to us. Why do that if she didn't plant to stay?"

"At least for a while," he murmured against her skull.

"I think she might actually stay for good. She likes being in command. She was bossing me around this afternoon, and Chrys, and she was really enjoying herself."

"So you took a punt? And came to my bed?"

"When you put it that way, it sounds a little... sordid."

"No, I didn't mean it like that. You weighed up the risks and the potential outcomes, the way you always do – it's one of the reasons you're such a terrific leader – and you decided the odds were definitely in your favour. So you decided to take pity on a poor, sex-starved playboy."

"Sex-starved?"

"Well, I was. Then. At the moment..." He snuggled closer. "At the moment, I'm pretty satisfied. But if you felt like a little more...um... *nourishment*?"

She laughed and shook her head. Her hair wafted all over his face and made him sneeze. "I think I'd better go, before we do something we'll regret. It's getting late."

"You mean, it's getting early?"

"Whatever. Chrys will be going off watch soon and I don't want her to catch me sneaking out of your room. She knows what's going on, but there's no need to slap her in the face with it." She sighed. "And Anton. He'll be on watch after Chrys. I can never be really sure which way Anton will jump. He's loyal, no doubt about that, and he's probably even willing to make a go of working with Ellen, but sometimes he does lose his cool. I think it's because of his childhood with the Blues."

"Anton was brought up with the *Blues*?"

"Shit! Sorry. Forget I told you that. If Anton wants you to know, he'll tell you himself. I only know because... Well, a leader has to know some things about where her team have come from, what pushes their buttons. With Anton, the Blue button definitely produces massive explosions."

Linden chuckled. "Yup. I noticed."

"Let's not talk about Anton, or Ellen. Or anyone else. Just us." She turned in his arms and kissed him deeply. It was a kiss of passion and of commitment. Her decision was made. "We *are* going to be together. But now I must go."

She pushed out of the bed, snapped on the light and began to pull on her clothes. "Where's my bra? No, don't get up. I really can't deal with seeing you naked, not at the moment. But where the hell's my bra?"

"Um. Try *under* the bed?" He had stayed beneath the covers – obediently – but his wicked smile said it all.

"Ratbag." She punched him hard on the upper arm. Then she

knelt on the floor and started rootling around in the dust under the bed until she found it.

"You know what?" she said thoughtfully, a few minutes later, as she finished doing up her clothes. "When we get to wherever we're going, I want there to be sunshine, and fresh fruit that I can eat with the juice dripping down my chin. And I want there to be clean floors!"

"I'll second that," he said from the bed. But she had already gone.

• • • • •

"Guys, listen to this!"

Jedda jerked round, struck by the excitement in Anton's voice.

"You won't believe it," Anton said with a knowing smirk, once he had everyone's attention. "Put out over the public network. One of the hounds is to be put on trial for dereliction of duty, something to do with failing to take down a known fugitive. They're saying she had a clear shot and didn't take it. If she's found guilty – they mean *when*, of course – she's to be put in front of a firing squad. In the public arena. They're saying it'll be a week tomorrow. Incredible, isn't it? Apparently it's the state's latest wheeze for Dark Days entertainment."

Linden jumped to his feet. He was ashen. "It's Delta. It must be. She was the one who let me—"

"No! Don't be stupid. It's a trap!" Ellen was on her feet too, confronting Linden. "Can't you see?" She was beyond exasperated.

Jedda saw shock on Anton's face, and even on Chrys's. Jedda was feeling it herself, as well. What was it with Linden?

"I don't care," Linden went on doggedly. "I can't leave Delta to die for me."

Jedda's gut tightened as his words hit home. *Please, no! I can't deal with this. Not now. Not Linden.* Out of the corner of her eye, she caught Chrys's worried glance. She was looking to Jedda to intervene, but for this Jedda needed time to think.

Grasping at straws, Jedda signed quickly to Chrys to stay out of it. Then she gave a tiny nod in Ellen's direction. Let Chrys think Jedda actually *wanted* Ellen to take the lead here, to give Ellen a chance to prove herself. *Please don't let her think it's because the problem is Linden.*

Ellen was too focused on Linden to have noticed the byplay. She had curled her fingers into claws and was shaking them in his face. "Can't you see a trap when it's right in front of your nose, Linden?

Do I need to remind you that, the last time you did *impulsive*, you got yourself shot?"

"I'm not being impulsive. I'm doing the only thing I *can* do. The honourable thing."

"Oh, for fu—!" Ellen clamped her jaws together and dropped her hands.

Linden kept on arguing, determined to make his point. "Even if it *is* a trap – and you don't know for sure that it is – I can't let Delta be executed because of what she did for me. I *won't*. It's up to me to get her out. Even if I have to do it on my own." He spat the final words in Ellen's face. Then he turned a fraction and fixed hard eyes on Jedda. It was a clear challenge. Would she support him?

Jedda knew when she was cornered. She straightened and took half a pace forward. Anton's shoulders relaxed. Chrys's worried frown disappeared.

Oh, great! I'm expected to work miracles, too. Jedda swallowed and raised a hand. "Cool it, guys," she began automatically. "We need to think this through. We—"

"There's nothing to think about!" Linden shot back. "I *owe* Delta. So I have to rescue her. What kind of man would I be if I left her to die?" There was real anguish in his voice and in his face. This was no petty squabble. This ran very deep indeed.

Everyone felt it. No one spoke. In the strained silence, everyone was avoiding eye contact, especially with Linden.

Jedda took a deep breath and gathered her strength. She couldn't shirk her responsibility here. So she would have to take on Linden, even though it probably meant the end of their relationship. *Why did it have to come so soon? Didn't we deserve just a little bit longer?* Her insides felt hollow.

"Jedda." Linden's voice had lost that edge of desperate pleading; it was threaded with steel. When he spoke, it was as if she were the only other person in the room. "Jedda, I have to do this. You *know* I do. It's a debt of honour."

He was staring at Jedda. Such determined eyes, willing her to go with him on this. What could she possibly say? She didn't have the words.

She was still hesitating when bloody Ellen jumped in again. "This is K's doing. With Marujn at his back. If K had been going to execute Delta for dereliction of duty, he'd have done it days ago." She started ticking off points on her fingers. "You all know his reputation for summary justice, so why would he be planning a trial now? Or a public execution? That's the real give-away. When was the last time they had one of those? Anton?"

Put on the spot, Anton muttered, "No idea. Not in my time, anyway."

"Quite," Ellen said, with satisfaction. "It's not a dead hound they want; it's you, Linden. Delta will be marched out to be shot, but the shooting party will be waiting for *you*, Linden." She poked him in the chest. *"YOU."* She glared at him, daring him to keep on arguing.

Linden glared back. Trap or no trap, he was clearly not backing down.

Jedda swallowed. *How did I let it get this far? I've lost my touch. And then some.* She needed to get back to being detached and cool and rational. She mustn't allow her emotions to play any part in this, especially as they were urging her to cheer for Linden. Because… because his honour was the key to who he was. It was one of the things she loved him for. But Jedda had to be more than a lover. She had to safeguard the future of the Jays. She had made a bad mistake over the Barrier attack. Her decision there could have finished them all. She had to get this one right.

She made herself focus on the immediate crisis. First, she broke up the standoff. She put one firm hand on Linden's shoulder and one on Ellen's, forcing them apart. Then she pushed her way between them to take centre stage. What mattered was to take the heat out of their exchange. Deciding what to do about the Delta trap could come later. "The trick with traps," she said slowly, articulating each word in a deliberately calm voice, "is first to spot them, and then to spring them. Preferably from a safe distance." She took the time to make eye contact with each of the Jays in turn. She held Linden's gaze; and finally Ellen's. She could feel the drop in tension all round. Linden was starting to look a bit less belligerent.

Progress. Of a kind.

"So that is what we will do," Jedda went on. She paused, searching for a diversion. "Don't worry, Linden. I promise you'll be in at the death."

Chrys's strangled gasp proved that Jedda's shock tactics had worked.

"At the death?" Ellen repeated angrily. "You're mad, Jedda, if you—"

"You've had your say, Ellen," Jedda snapped. "Now sit down." She pointed to one of the chairs by their makeshift conference table. Ellen glowered, but eventually did as she was told. "You, too,

Linden. No, not next to Ellen. Here." Jedda nodded to Chrys to take the vacant seat between the warring pair.

Anton took the seat on Jedda's other side. He put a tiny portable computer on the vacant chair beside him and kept glancing sideways at the screen. Whatever he was doing, he didn't want anyone else to see. Jedda resisted the impulse to tell him to shut it down. If Anton was working in the middle of all this, it must be important.

Jedda herself remained standing in the middle of the semi-circle of chairs. "OK, guys," she began, looking round at her troops and trying to sound more confident than she felt. "We have to work out what we're going to do. We'll start by assuming that the execution is a trap. Ellen's right about that."

"But—"

Jedda cut off Linden's interruption with a sharp gesture. She could not be seen to be playing favourites here. "I'm not making any decisions yet about what we *do*, Linden. But Ellen's analysis was bang on the money as far as a public execution is concerned. It's very odd. We can be pretty sure it's not just to provide the underclass with extra amusement over the Dark Days."

Chrys and Anton nodded thoughtfully. Ellen had straightened her back and lifted her chin. So she thought Jedda was taking her side. In a moment, if Jedda was not careful, Ellen would be trying to lay down the law again.

Jedda knew what she had to say. "We can't mount a rescue at the execution," she began crisply. "That would be suicide for the Jays. K's kill-squads would be waiting for us and they would cut us down. So we are left with two questions. Do we try to rescue Delta? And, if so, when and how do we do it?"

"I don't think she's worth—" Ellen began.

"We have to rescue Delta." Linden shouted so loudly that Ellen's voice was drowned out. "*I* have to rescue Delta. I'll go against the kill-squads by myself, if the rest of you don't have the guts to do it. I can—"

"No, Linden, you can't." Jedda slammed the flat of her hand on to the table in front of him. Accusing the other Jays of cowardice was definitely not the way to enlist potential allies. "You can't go in alone," she said in a more normal voice, pulling out her chair and sitting down between him and Anton. "A lone attacker puts us all at risk. Think what would happen if you were captured." She shook her head firmly. "The Jays mount a rescue as a team, or no one does. That's how it has to be." Leader's decision. No argument allowed.

Surely Linden could understand why it had to be that way?

He turned his head and stared at her. He said nothing. But his expression said everything. He thought Jedda was going to betray him. And he was going to detest her for it.

Jedda hauled in a ragged breath. He didn't understand. He wasn't *trying* to understand what it meant to be leader of the Jays.

To fill the silence, Jedda asked the first question that came into her head. "Do we know where they're holding her?"

"She'll be in the cells in the barracks," Linden said at once, eager all over again.

How changeable he was. He hadn't stopped to think. He had taken Jedda's question as a positive sign. And now he was gazing at her in a way that had her insides in ferment.

He thought she was going to give him what he wanted, just because she had asked one basic question. He thought she should be ready to risk everything, the future of the Jays, their very survival, to help him save his honour. If she could have found a way, she would have, but Jedda would not gamble with everyone's lives, no matter how much it meant to Linden.

He was going to hate her when she told him so. That glow in his eyes… She would not risk the Jays to keep it there. She did not have the right.

Jedda realised that everyone was staring at her. She hadn't spoken out loud, had she? No, she couldn't have. Though it was perfectly possible that her face had given her away. She glanced quickly at Linden. Yes, the glow was fading, being replaced by uncertainty and the beginnings of deep hurt.

Jedda felt it. And her own pain too, burning and clawing at her insides. Whether he meant to or not, Linden was pitting his sense of honour squarely against Jedda's sense of duty. The gulf was unbridgeable. Jedda saw it stretching between them now, stark and black. In that moment, she ached for what they had lost.

She sat tight, even while her stomach churned. She had to get through this somehow. For the sake of the group, she had to find a way to let Linden down gently. All sorts of ideas began thrashing around in her brain, all of them useless. "Linden," she began slowly, not quite knowing where she was going with this, "you must understand that the Jays can't—"

"Delta's not in the military barracks," Anton put in sharply, his eyes fixed on his little screen.

"What?" Linden's head jerked round. "She must be."

Anton frowned angrily. If it had been anyone else but Linden, Anton would have snapped their head off for daring to suggest he could be wrong. But Anton was obviously reading Linden's pain, too, and he responded with uncharacteristic patience. "Believe me, Linden, I *have* checked. She's not there."

"Then where the hell is she?" Linden burst out accusingly, as if it were Anton's fault that Linden's assumptions were wrong.

Anton bristled.

"Try the military prison, Anton," Jedda said quickly, before he had a chance to start a vicious argument.

"I've already done that," Anton snapped. "It's next door to the barracks. I told you. She's *not there*." No signs of patience now. There was venom in every word.

"Then *find* her," Linden bit back. "Or is that beyond your fancy fingering?"

"That's enough!" Jedda had had it with massaging male egos. And this was all going in the wrong direction. Linden was assuming that the Jays would try to rescue Delta. Anton might even be assuming it, too. Jedda had to stamp on that idea before it took hold. "If we don't know where she is, we can't try to get her out," she said quickly, in an attempt to close down the discussion.

Jedda heard her own words too late. She'd made it sound as if there would definitely be a rescue attempt, that it was just a question of finding where Delta was being held. "What I mean is—"

Anton interrupted again before she could get the words out. "I've found her," he announced triumphantly, waving his little screen in the air.

Jedda's world turned grey. How had it come to this? Her fault. Again.

"Not that it's much help," Anton went on, without a pause. "She's in the cells under K's HQ. You're on a loser there, Linden."

"It makes no sense," Linden muttered, almost to himself. "Why would they be holding her there?"

"Why wouldn't they?" Ellen put in sharply. "A cell's a cell. You can hold a prisoner anywhere."

"That's not the way it works. There are systems. Processes." Linden shook his head. "The cells under HQ aren't prison cells. They're... they're interrogation cells. There are only a few of them anyway. It's where we— It's where K holds important prisoners for interrogation, people who have information he needs to extract."

Ellen went up like a rocket. "*Torture* cells, you mean? Then why not say so? Or are you ashamed to use the right word for the obscenities you used to be part of?"

Linden shrugged. "Torture cells? Yes, if you like." Torture was a fact of life. Everyone used it, including the Jays. "That's why it makes no sense for Delta to be there. She doesn't know anything, so there's no point in interrogating her. She's just a hound. OK, she's sometimes too loyal for her own good. But she doesn't know *anything*," he said again. Guilt and distress and desperation were obvious in every word he spoke. Then he paled even more and whispered, "It could be for revenge. On me."

Without thinking, Jedda started to reach out to him. She stopped herself just in time, a moment before their fingers touched. But Linden saw. He threw her a look that burned like acid. She knew she flinched. And he saw that, too.

After a moment, Anton said evenly, "It doesn't matter why K's holding her in his nasty little cells." He was back in control of himself, staring pointedly at Ellen with an effortlessly superior look on his face. "We can't rescue her at the execution site. Jedda's right about that. It would be suicide. We can't rescue her from K's HQ either. No one can get in there."

"Who says so?" Ellen snapped.

"I do," Anton said, supremely confident. "K's got state-of-the-art security on that building. It's been reinforced even more since we blew up his office. Cameras and sensors everywhere. Physical guards, too. Squads of 'em. No one could get in there and survive."

"You're wrong, Anton. Again." Ellen smiled coldly, enjoying her moment in the limelight. "You think no one can get in there and survive. *You* certainly couldn't. But *I* can."

FORTY-FIVE

"SO NOW YOU'VE GOT the run of K's HQ, have you, Ellen? You and whose army?"

Ellen threw Anton a withering look. "Me. On my own. Just me." If he'd been close enough, she would have punched him.

"You'll just walk back in through the front door, will you? Pull the other one. You got out by the skin of your teeth last time, remember? You'd never be able to fool the guards a second time."

"Who says I fooled the guards the first time?"

"Wha—? *You* did. You said you'd—"

"No, I didn't. I didn't *say* anything. *You* assumed I'd got out through the main entrance. You were so sure you were right," she added airily, "that I didn't have the heart to disillusion you." She flashed him a saccharine smile.

Anton took all of half a second to latch on. "Yeah, right," he said through gritted teeth. "Ellen is all heart. And we love her for that, don't we, guys?"

"But you really *can* get in there?" Linden put in eagerly. "Then we could—"

"There's no 'we' about it, Linden." Ellen was not going to involve Linden in anything she might do. The man was a liability. He didn't *think*. "*I* can get in there." In case he hadn't got the message, she repeated it. "On my own. Just me."

"No." Jedda leant forward and rapped the table to get everyone's attention. "Weren't you listening earlier, Ellen? I'll say it again, so no one is any doubt. *No solo heroics.* If there's to be a rescue – *IF* – it will be a team effort."

No one spoke. Chrys nodded her agreement. Ellen did not move a muscle.

"We screwed up at the Barrier," Jedda went on. "We should have – *I* should have aborted the op when Ellen came out that first time. We have to learn from our mistakes. We thought we were mounting a surprise attack, but it turned out to be a trap. This time, we already *know* it's a trap. Surprise is impossible."

"Except that K will expect us to attack next week, when they're taking Delta to the execution. Or maybe at the execution itself." Linden was sounding hopeful again.

Jedda shook her head. "We daren't assume that. We assumed that K wouldn't be expecting an attack at the Barrier, remember? Look where that got us. We mustn't underestimate him. He's dangerous. And devious with it."

Ellen did nod at that.

"So, on the assumption that K is setting a trap for us," Jedda went on, "what are the arguments *for* trying to rescue Delta?"

"Apart from salving Linden's precious conscience, you mean?" Ellen put in, before any of the others could say a word. If this mad rescue idea had come from anyone but Linden, Jedda would have slapped it down at the outset. Jedda was right about one thing, though – post-Linden, she was definitely losing her edge.

Linden had coloured and was starting to bluster about honour again.

For once, Jedda ignored him. "Chrys? Where do you stand on this?"

Chrys thought for a moment. "Delta is an experienced hound. We could use her fighting skills. She's got that scenting ability, too. She could teach us first-hand how it works." She paused again, then shook her head. "That's about it, I'd say."

"No, it's not," Linden protested. "Delta's a brave and loyal comrade. She put her life on the line for me!"

"And now you're asking the rest of us to do it, too," Anton muttered.

Ellen only just managed not to laugh. Sarky Anton was right on the button.

Jedda was pretending she hadn't heard. "We could use Delta as an extra fighter. That's true. I'm not sure about the scenting thing, though. Anton's already dealt with it. Thanks to him, it's not a threat any more."

Anton preened.

"It could become a threat," Linden objected. "Delta's is only the basic version. The pack leader you put in intensive care was trialling a later model. More sensitive. And the system's still being developed. In Warsaw," he added, as if that were the clincher.

Jedda frowned inquiringly at Anton.

"Our scent bots are still fooling the system, no problem. So far, the hounds seem to be learning to detect smaller and smaller traces of the *same* smell, not smells that keep changing." Anton sat back in his chair and sighed out a long breath. "But Warsaw is good. Better than good. Once K cottons on to what we're doing – if he hasn't already – he'll have Warsaw trying to develop countermeasures. They might manage it, too. They've got specialist gene manipulators there. I'm not in the same league."

Anton's admission took Ellen by surprise. He could actually be serious. And even modest. One up to Anton.

Strangely, a little of Jedda's tension seemed to leave her. "We've got help coming on that front," she said, smiling proudly. "Inez – one of the South American reinforcements – is a gene specialist, too."

"Great, we can use her. But Warsaw has dozens of them," Anton said, still sounding worried. "We can't be sure they won't get the better of us. If they did, we'd be screwed. They'd sniff us out. We'd have nowhere to hide."

"Am I reading you right, Anton? Are you saying you want to have Delta here, to study their basic scenting system in the flesh, so to speak?"

"Well, we could manage without. But on balance, I think it might help. It certainly wouldn't hurt. So, yes, Jedda. Yes, I am."

"Oh." Jedda looked as if she'd been poleaxed.

Ellen could see why. Jedda had been psyching herself up for a confrontation with Linden, preparing to tell him she wouldn't risk the lives of the Jays for his precious honour. She'd obviously been dreading it, since it would kill their relationship stone dead. Now she had that horrid little know-all telling her, in all seriousness, that there were rational arguments for going along with Linden's rescue plan after all.

Ellen looked at Linden, wondering how he would react when he realised where this was all heading. He was already looking dangerously excited.

Ellen swore under her breath. The last thing the Jays needed was more impulsive heroics.

Jedda straightened her shoulders and looked sternly round the group. It had taken her only seconds to recover. She was back in control of herself and back in leader mode. Ellen felt like applauding. Jedda really would be a hard act to follow.

For someone.

"Right, guys," Jedda said crisply. "Let's take stock. Anton thinks

Delta is probably worth rescuing. So does Linden, obviously. What about you, Chrys?"

"I'm not saying Anton's wrong about the smell thing, but I don't like the odds."

Jedda nodded slowly. "That's a no, then. Ellen?"

"I don't like the odds either. If we could find a way of tilting them in our favour, I'd side with Anton. Otherwise, I'm with Chrys. It's clearly a trap. Too risky." It was a totally honest reply, for once, but careful enough not to commit her to anything.

"Two for, two against. Yeah, it would be." Jedda threw her hands in the air and grimaced theatrically. No one laughed. "OK. Let's leave that for the moment. Let's think about the *how*. We'd obviously be relying on Ellen's magic wand to get us into K's HQ, and Anton on the comms, to close down the spy systems inside." She ploughed straight on, without giving Ellen or Anton a chance to agree or disagree. "Assuming we could do all that, we'd still need a diversion while we mounted the main attack on K's HQ building. Probably several diversions. And they'd need to be a lot better than the ones we used at the Barrier. Suggestions?"

"What about another shop attack?" Linden said. "The last one worked."

Jedda shook her head. "They've stepped up security at all the fancy stores. No, it has to be something off-the-wall, that K's devious brain can't figure out in advance."

"Bomb attacks on the road network?" Chrys said. "Could work if we picked a time when there are lots of limos about."

"Hang on a minute!" Anton sounded excited. He was working on his little screen again. "Yes! I should've thought of it before! There's to be a grand party at the Museum of Council Achievements, on Sunday night. Marujn's paying. Part of his contribution to the celebrations. It's to be the biggest event of the Dark Days, apparently. The President has even been strong-armed into ordering a guard of honour. And get this. There's to be some kind of vast military display, by torchlight."

Ellen grinned. The odds had just shifted. "So, two days from now, most of K's HQ guards will be out on a parade ground, in the dark, strutting their stuff?"

"Yup." Anton was grinning, too.

"OK," Jedda said thoughtfully. "So we're thinking our diversions could be bombs on the roads, and attacks on the limos bringing in all those VIPs."

"No," Ellen said firmly. "The VIPs have far too many guards in tow. After they've delivered their precious cargo, on the other hand..." She caught a wicked gleam in Anton's eye. Was he thinking what Ellen was thinking? "No one bothers to guard the limos once they're empty and operating on autopilot. We could attack then."

Chrys was looking puzzled. "I'm not following you."

"Neither am I," Jedda said. "Can one of you explain?"

Anton chuckled. "Sure," he said. He actually winked at Ellen. "Any of you ever seen pictures of an old-fashioned fairground?"

Even Ellen was surprised at that. *Fairground?* She'd been thinking explosives. Then she twigged what he was on about and burst out laughing. "You know what, Anton? I take it all back. As ideas go, that is bloody brilliant."

For once, Jedda's astonishing leadership skills were not helping her at all. She did not join in the laughter. She looked utterly bewildered.

· · · · ·

Delta gasped and sprang to attention the moment K appeared outside her cell.

K did not return her smart salute. Instead he frowned her down. After a second, she seemed to get the message and sank back onto her bench. A prisoner facing probable death by firing squad should not be responding eagerly when her chief tormentor appeared. Especially when there was another prisoner in the cell opposite, watching every move.

His own mistake, K told himself crossly. He should have checked before coming down. It was always a risk with these ancient barred cells. Prisoners could see far too much, not that they ever lived to talk about it. Still, one day, he'd have solid doors installed. When he could spare the resources.

He glanced at the huddled figure in the second cell. She was the real deal – dirty, dishevelled, and brooding. Murderous, too, judging by the way she was eyeing him. Tauber should have disposed of her long before this.

"Hound Delta?" K signed to her to stay where she was. "This is a formal military inspection visit. Do you have any complaints about your treatment here?" It was a bit lame – and he wasn't military, in spite of the uniform – but it would do. Provided Delta was sharp enough to play along.

He risked another glance behind him. The second prisoner had slumped down on her bench. She seemed to be trying to sleep. And his own body was now masking most of Delta's cell entrance.

"My complaint is that I'm innocent," Delta protested.

"Tell that to the trial judge," K snapped back. "It's of no interest to me." He was pleased that his judgement of the hound had been right. She was a useful plant, and sharp and feisty with it. "Do you have enough food and water? Blankets?"

"Suppose so," Delta muttered, staring at the floor.

"Your trial is set for Monday."

"And my execution?" she retorted bitterly. "You've fixed that too, I suppose?"

Very quick-witted. "That is a matter for the trial judge." When Delta choked on a very convincing sob, K decided he needed to sound a little sorry for her. "You might as well be prepared," he said quietly. "You could be taken from here at any time after the trial. At any time," he repeated. "Even directly from the trial itself."

She nodded miserably, not looking at him.

"Your advocate sent you these notes. Part of your trial preparation, she said." K pulled out the package and pushed it through the bars. It would look realistic enough from a distance.

Delta reached out to grab it, without getting up. Covering her actions with her body, she explored the parcel with eager fingers.

K saw her slight start when she felt the shape of the weapon inside. He nodded meaningfully at her. "Your preparation starts with that package, according to your advocate. She warns you to take good care of the contents. There is only *one* set. Understood?"

Delta had slipped the weapon out and was hugging it to her middle, checking it as he spoke. She frowned when she saw that the kill setting had been permanently disabled. "One set. Yes, I get it. Tell her I'll do my best."

There was nothing more to be said. K nodded curtly and started for the exit.

"What about me?" the second prisoner whined. "I've got complaints. I—"

"Your complaints don't count. You're a civilian. Complain to Commissar Tauber. If you dare."

K marched out, with the second prisoner's curses ringing in his ears.

• • • • •

It had taken over an hour of tense discussion to work up a coherent plan of attack. Ellen saw the moment when Jedda was finally convinced it could work. Jedda had asked for something off-the-wall and the plan was certainly that. Ellen was proud of her part in it.

Jedda leaned back in her chair and worked her shoulders, trying to release some of the knots. She smiled encouragingly at each of her troops in turn. "We're going to have to keep a lot of plates spinning, but we've got a whole forty-eight hours to prepare. Let's make the most of it. Anton, you're the lynchpin here. You've got to penetrate the comms shields round K's HQ. Without comms between you and the away team, an attack is dead in the water. So...?"

"I'll give it my best shot," Anton said, nodding seriously for once.

"How long?"

Anton shrugged unhappily. Ellen felt a twinge of sympathy.

Jedda must have realised her mistake, for she leaned forward again and said, "Sorry, Anton, that came out wrong. I know you can't predict how long it'll take you to get into K's HQ systems. But, once you're in, how long will you need to work up the programs to piggyback on his comms during an attack?"

"Oh. I see. Well, at least twelve hours. Twenty-four would be safer. It will depend on how many subsystems I need to keep running so I can use them. I won't know the answer to that until after I've got in."

Anton did not add, "*If* I get in," but Ellen knew that everyone was thinking it.

"So you need a minimum of twenty-four hours after you're in. In other words, if we don't achieve the initial breakthrough within the next twenty-four hours, we're probably not going to be able to mount the attack at all. Right?" All Jedda's attention was fixed on Anton who took a slow breath and grimaced. Then he nodded reluctantly.

Ellen caught the hostile look that Linden flashed at Anton. Frustration and anger were beginning to come off Linden in waves. As soon as Jedda turned back from Anton, she would see. And Linden would probably start another argument about honour and duty. That was the last thing the Jays needed right now.

"I might be able to help," Ellen said quickly, leaning forward to attract Jedda's attention to herself. "I can't guarantee that the HQ systems have anything in common with K's private security, but it must be a possibility. And I know how to penetrate that." Out of the corner of her eye, she saw with relief that Linden's fury was subsiding.

Jedda had not turned her head. She was still focused on Anton. She spoke in a carefully neutral voice. "Anton?"

"Um, well…" Anton looked across at Ellen. Eventually he nodded, very slowly and deliberately. Was that respect? "I'll need a few hours to scope it out," he went on, "to get a better idea of where the vulnerabilities are. Ellen's experience could be useful then, if she's got the time."

"I'll make time," Ellen said firmly. She would get well ahead with her own preparations while Anton was doing his initial probing of K's systems. He would have to tread incredibly carefully to ensure he did not alert K to what the Jays were planning. Every step would have to be erased as Anton went along. That kind of invisible stalking was definitely a one-man job. Anton was right there.

Ellen had plenty on her own plate. She had agreed to design the fairground device. Like Anton, she had no idea how long it would take her to get to first base, but once she had a working prototype, Chrys and Jedda could produce the copies while Ellen concentrated on making another tooth computer. There wasn't time to do a major mod to give it the range for comms to Anton, so its use would be limited. Even so, the op would be much more secure if she and Jedda and Chrys could communicate with one another in silence.

Anton was eager to get on. "If you don't need me here any more, Jedda, I'll get started." At Jedda's nod, he got up and made for his main workstation.

That was when Ellen remembered yet another thing she needed to do. Luckily, this one would not take long at all. "Can I have the cloudburst, Anton?" she called.

"What do you want that for?" Linden asked sharply, before Anton could answer.

Ellen made herself smile encouragingly at Linden. He had guts. And he'd been badly used by people he'd thought he could trust. No harm in stroking his bruised ego a little. "To get back at Marujn, Linden. That was your big idea, wasn't it? We know he's probably planning a very painful end for you – you're his grandson, after all, and you've humiliated him by defecting – but what he really wants is the information you're carrying on the cloudburst. Or rather, the information he *thinks* you're carrying. So let's give Marujn – and K – something else to occupy their nasty little minds."

Ellen gave Linden a few seconds to react. A grin spread slowly across his face. Very satisfactory.

She turned back to Anton. "I'll need some of your specialist tools, Anton. *If* I may borrow them, that is," she finished, with the utmost politeness.

For a second, Anton was visibly taken aback, but then he grinned. "If you're planning to make Marujn's day, Ellen, you can borrow every tool I possess."

Chrys's eyebrows shot up. Jedda was surprised into a laugh, though she tried to disguise it as a cough.

"Thanks, Anton." Ellen smiled at him. Genuinely. "Now, let's see what mischief we can do with Marujn's little cloudburst, shall we? Shrinking balls, wasn't it, Linden?"

• • • • •

Chrys and Jedda were working together in silence, making copy after copy of Ellen's fairground device. Linden didn't have the tech skills to take part, but he was a very willing gopher. In the corner, Anton was still hunched over his computer. He hadn't said a word for hours.

Ellen looked up from the part-finished tooth computer and glanced across at him. It took a second for her eyes to refocus. Ah. Not good. Anton's body language was not encouraging. Soon they would be right up against their deadline.

At least the cloudburst was primed and ready. Ellen had tucked it into a plain white envelope and sealed it. According to Linden, Marujn was going to have a seizure once he heard the message about shrinking balls. Taking no chances, Ellen had written a carefully worded note on the outside. For K *and* Marujn. It would do the trick, she was sure. But only if they could leave it *inside* K's HQ.

Everything depended on Anton.

There was nothing she could do to hurry him. She went back to work. The tooth computer needed just a few more tweaks.

Barely five minutes later, Anton gave a yell of triumph. *"YES! I'm in!"*

The Jays' tension dissolved into a huge, ecstatic cheer.

FORTY-SIX

THE NIGHT AIR WAS deliciously crisp. Chrys sucked it deep into her lungs. Ready.

She sprang out from the shadows, rolled across the ground and stuck her last device to the underside of the empty limo as it purred idly past. Seconds later, she was back in her hiding place, invisible in the darkness. "Control, bravo one. Bombs away."

"Roger." A pause. Anton would be checking with the others. Then, "All units. Commence phase two."

So Jedda, Linden and Ellen had finished planting all their devices, too. The rest of the fairground phase was now up to Anton and his clever programs. Chrys grinned briefly – the have-nots were going to have a whale of a time, and part of her was sorry to miss the show – but she had a mission to fulfil. She checked again for infrared signals in the narrow street. Clear. She loped off towards the rendezvous.

The others were already there, two shadows crouching in the lee of a building and the third as lookout at the far end of the alley. Chrys heard Jedda's brisk orders inside her head, via the tooth computer. "Bravo one. Maintain current position. Transport in five."

Chrys acknowledged the order, remembering to bracket her thought with her code word. It still felt weird. But it worked. And silent comms was so much safer than speaking aloud for Anton's implants.

She turned her back on her comrades and sank down onto one knee, weapon in hand, scanning the darkness for enemy movement.

Barely five minutes later, an enormous silver limo slowed just long enough for Chrys to leap inside to join the others. The door slid shut behind her and the limo began to gather speed. Chrys's jaw dropped as she looked round the interior. She had never seen the inside of one of these before; the one-way glass made it impossible.

"Quite a pad, isn't it?" Ellen said chirpily. "You could live for a week in here."

Linden had opened one of the small doors in the upholstery. Behind was chilled champagne, crystal glasses and what looked like caviar. "My gr—" He grimaced. "Marujn doesn't stint himself when he's travelling. No matter how short the distance."

"This is Marujn's limo?" Chrys gasped. "Um. Right."

Ellen was grinning. "It seemed…er… appropriate."

"Actually," Jedda put in firmly, "I chose it because it's by far the biggest. When we get Delta away, we may be dealing with a stretcher case. We need the space."

"Oh." As ever, Jedda's logic was impeccable.

"All units." Anton's taut voice came through their implants. "K's limo is not responding to the device. I say again. Controller's limo is not responding."

"Shit!" Then, more calmly, Jedda said, "Control, can you terminate his limo?"

"Negative. Tried and failed. Limo is ultrashielded."

"Roger."

"He *would*!" Ellen spat. "Somehow his limo has to be different."

"And no doubt he can still call it, and still use it to get back to HQ," Jedda said. "OK, guys. We'll just need to work faster. K's still at the Marujn reception. The fairground won't start until we give the word. That's when he'll be alerted. So we'll leave it as late as possible." She gave Anton her revised instructions.

No one else spoke for several minutes. Their op had just become a great deal more dicey. None of them was stupid enough to underestimate what K might do.

"All units. Drop point for bravo one, one minute."

Chrys checked her weapons one last time. She was ready.

"Good luck. Keep safe." That was Linden, with a warm smile.

"You forget, Linden. I'm the one wearing Ellen's slinky suit. I'm safer than any of you." Chrys still didn't understand why Ellen had insisted on giving her the armoured suit. Chrys would be operating alone and out in the open, but still…

"Since you wore it in the forest, you're obviously used to fighting in it," Ellen said, with a dismissive wave of the hand. "Why change a winning combination?"

"Ready, Chrys?" Jedda said quietly.

Chrys nodded as the door slid open. In seconds, she was out and on her way.

• • • • •

"All units. Second drop point, one minute."

Jedda took a deep breath. "Right. Recap. Ellen, you're leading this first phase, until we split up. All comms will be silent, via the tooth computers. Linden, you're with me. You and I are using hand signals only." She waited for Linden's brief nod. "Control, messages to our implants only if absolutely essential. We won't respond unless we have vital info to pass."

"Roger."

"Control, update on bravo one?"

"Bravo one is in position, waiting for the signal to start her attack. Ten seconds to second drop point. Good luck, guys. Out."

• • • • •

Watching the limo glide away, Ellen swallowed her excitement and shrank down into the shadows. Anton would ensure that the limo cruised the streets until the team needed it again. Behind her, Jedda and Linden were almost invisible. They would wait here until Ellen gave them the word to move.

She checked the approach was clear and pulled down the makeshift black cap that Chrys had provided. Combined with K's black uniform, it would help her to pass for a state officer. Underneath, she was wearing standard body armour. She hadn't dared to wear the slinky suit to enter K's den. He had got the drop on her before, and she was enough of a realist to know it could happen again. K must *not* get his hands on the suit. But it should be safe enough on Chrys. Chrys was staying outside.

Ellen gave Jedda the thumbs-up. Jedda nodded. Good to go. Ellen marched off down the middle of the street, the picture of an arrogant state officer.

She knew how big a gamble she was taking. It was possible – highly unlikely, but possible – that K had discovered how she had corrupted the computer system in his private basement when she'd escaped last time. His secret entrance might be barred.

No, he's too cunning for that. If he's sussed it – IF – he'll have realised it was me. He'll have rigged some kind of alarm, to catch me the next time I use it. We both know this contest is personal now. He wants the pleasure of killing me himself.

So the entrance should still be open to her. Even if K had turned it into a trap.

She smiled. She could do traps. Especially when she knew they were coming.

She told herself she could do duels to the death, too.

• • • • •

403

Ellen played the uniformed state flunkey, marching around as if she owned the place, until she reached the hidden corner where K's escape hatch was.

It was deserted. There would be no security cameras around. K would have seen to that. He would not want his secret comings and goings to be recorded.

The high wall was dark and shadowed. She slithered along to the concealed entrance, keeping her back against the stone and all her senses on alert. She had not drawn a weapon yet. That would attract far too much attention, if anyone should come round the corner. Once she was inside, it would be different.

She opened the hidden control pad and spoke into it, in her normal voice. It was the agreed signal for Jedda and Linden to move closer. For Ellen, surrounded by silence, it sounded dangerously loud, but she had to be sure the computer would obey her commands, at the first time of asking. It probably had some kind of failsafe, to sound an alarm if alien voices gave it instructions. At least, that was how Ellen would have programmed it.

I have to remember that K is not a tech. He can't do what I can do. I think.

The lock clicked and the door opened. The internal doors would be unlocked, too, if the computer was obeying commands properly. So far so good.

Ellen peered inside and checked the passageway. Empty. Time to bring in reinforcements. "Alpha one," she signalled via the tooth computer, "rendezvous clear."

Jedda's response came almost at once. "With you in two minutes, max."

Ellen drew a weapon. It was set on kill. She didn't have to check. She knew.

Jedda and Linden made it in less than ninety seconds. Ellen smiled with relief. She waved them in and locked the entrance again. Now their backs were protected. No enemy could get in behind them. Except K, of course. And he was safely on the other side of the city.

Slowly, Ellen led the way down the long passage to the basement and K's personal playground. The walls were bare and flat, so there was nowhere for an enemy to lie in wait. Not that she expected there to be any foot soldiers here, inside K's basement domain. Surely he would never allow that, especially when he was not in the building himself? There might be cameras watching them, but they would not matter. Even if there was a feed, there was unlikely to be anyone in K's apartment to watch it. And Ellen planned to erase the records in any case.

They reached the door to the basement.

If K had set a trap for Ellen, it would be now. She shrugged. She had got them this far. No point in delaying. She signalled to the other two to stay where they were.

Weapon in hand, she opened the door and slid through to the other side.

• • • • •

K sat immobile in his place, watching the military manoeuvres in the flickering torchlight. Tauber's big idea, intended to impress the Council members. As an idea, it wasn't even original. Tauber had cribbed it from a twentieth-century dictator whose twilight rallies had been a great deal slicker than these.

K was thoroughly bored by the whole business, but he refused to fidget. He kept his face suitably blank, too, while his mind went over his plans, checking for flaws. Would Linden take the bait? His precious honour was bound to drive him to rescue Delta, surely? Would he be able to persuade the Jay and his warrior women to mount a joint attack? Or would Linden be left to go it alone? K very much wanted to take them all, but he would settle for Linden alone. Linden was the vital one.

K had made some very detailed, and very secret plans for what was to happen to Linden. *After* he was captured and *before* he was delivered to his grandfather. Linden had to be carrying some kind of specialised bug in his body. There was no other way that devious old swine could have eavesdropped on what was being said in K's inner sanctum. It had to be the answer, even though K's office systems screened all his visitors for bugs and Linden had been passed as clean, over and over again. The screening must have been fooled. Which meant it was a really clever bug. It had to be retrieved and neutralised, but only after K had found out precisely how it worked.

Marujn would be furious when he discovered that his bug was missing. But what could he do? He couldn't accuse K of stealing it. He couldn't say anything at all, without betraying the fact that he was the one who had planted it. Poor old Marujn. So very frustrating for him! Admittedly, he might complain about injuries to Linden if the bug had to be cut out, but K would simply deny all knowledge and blame the terrorists. He might even enquire, very politely, if there was some particular reason why Marujn was so anxious about minor injuries to a defector's body. That should shut the Baron up in double quick time.

Yup, it was a pretty foolproof plan. And if the bug was a recording device, it might give K a lot of information about the terrorists, too. Better and better.

• • • • •

Jedda waited behind the door. She could feel her heart thumping.

And she could feel Linden's breathing against the back of her neck, steady but a little too fast. His body was almost touching hers. They were both staring through the gap in the door, watching Ellen's every move.

Ellen had edged through the doorway, just enough to put her back against the wall alongside the steps and slip down them. If K had set up an infrared beam, there was a chance she would not break it. She was being very careful indeed.

After a few seconds she was at the bottom and out of sight. Now it was up to her. Jedda and Linden had to stay in the passage until Ellen sent the signal to move.

It seemed to take an age.

How much longer? Jedda resisted the temptation to message Ellen. She could not stop her own thoughts, though. *Come on, Ellen. What's happening?*

The answer came through the tooth computer. "Computer systems neutralised. Basement secure. Safe to enter."

Jedda was so relieved that she let out a long sigh. Mistake! Too much noise! She flashed Linden a quick grin and a thumbs-up, before leading the way through the door into K's private domain.

She had to swallow a betraying gasp of astonishment when she saw the swimming pool and its pristine surroundings – grey and white tiling, its austerity softened by subtle hints of marble. K surely wasn't stinting himself here. She looked a question at Linden. The answer was in his face. He looked as flabbergasted as she felt.

"Alpha one. We're wasting time."

Ellen was right. They could not afford to dawdle here, gawping.

Ellen beckoned them across to a spiral staircase in one corner, signalling that they had to make as little noise as possible. They did not know what they would find upstairs. Ellen began to climb with exaggerated care, testing each tread before she transferred her weight and hugging the rail for good measure. Jedda followed her example. Behind her, Linden could be relied on to do the same. At the top of the stairs, they emerged into a dark space, but before Jedda could reach for a torch, low ambient lighting came on automatically. Responding to their body heat? She assumed so.

They were in a neat hallway with various doors leading off it. Only one was open. Ellen signalled to Jedda and Linden to stay put while she went in.

Jedda could see a sparsely furnished room beyond the open doorway. Ellen was hovering over a wooden desk, her fingers working furiously at something. A touchscreen? The only other furniture seemed to be an arrangement of elegant pale-grey leather chairs and sofas by the fireplace. The walls were decorated in shades of grey so that they appeared to merge with the matching window hangings, in heavy, opulent fabrics. The whole room was like a muted display case for the huge abstract painting above the fireplace. Jedda felt transfixed by it. It glowed in the half light. The vibrant colours seemed to shift, and merge, and flow. As if they were alive. And hungry. She shivered.

In no time, Ellen was beside them again. She touched Jedda on the arm, bringing her back to the moment. "I've disengaged the apartment's surveillance systems," she whispered. "There's no one here. We can talk, provided we keep it down. The official surveillance systems are still working in the main part of the building and we don't know how far they can reach. So back to silence once we're beyond that door." She nodded towards what looked like the entrance to the apartment.

"What's through there?" Linden whispered.

"Private corridor. Best to assume it has surveillance. It leads to K's main office and the rest of HQ," Ellen explained.

Linden nodded. "Right. I can guide us from there. Getting down to the cells from the main entrance is easy enough but, from K's office, it's a bit like threading a maze. Jedda will need me for that. I'll leave markers for you, too, Ellen."

"We've got to do the ambush first," Jedda put in quickly. He was very keen to get to Delta. Too keen? And he was interrupting Ellen's briefing. "Ellen?"

"When we leave this apartment, its records will be wiped and the normal surveillance will come back on line. K won't know we've been here at all." Ellen sounded very sure of herself, Jedda thought. But it was a bit late to start questioning Ellen's tech skills. The whole plan was based on them.

"Stay here, both of you," Ellen went on. "Don't leave any traces.

I'll signal Jedda once I've made it to K's main office and turned off the surveillance systems in the rest of the building. Get to the ambush point as fast as you can. I can't issue the summons until you're in position. OK? Right. Back to silent comms. Good luck."

Ellen motioned to the others to move tight against the wall. Then she opened the door and walked smartly into the corridor beyond, closing the door quietly behind her.

· · · · ·

Ellen made her way along the corridor that led to K's main office. She kept her head down so that the cap shadowed her face. Any surveillance cameras would register the uniform more than the person inside it. It shouldn't trigger an alarm.

She still held her breath until she reached the main door to K's office. Bound to be cameras there. So she stopped on the threshold and pulled her uniform straight and her shoulders back. She knocked and stood to attention, as if waiting for an order to enter. She gave it five seconds and went in.

A rapid glance round told her that K's office was more or less restored to normal. Obviously, for a man like K, all sorts of things could be done in double-quick time. There was no sign of smoke or water damage, and certainly no obnoxious smell.

First things first. The wall unit near the door. The panel inside controlled the flow of signals to and from K's office systems. It should house the voice recognition protocols as well. She prised the cover off and subtly modified the settings. "Computer?"

READY.

Good, it was obeying her voice now. She instructed the computer to turn off surveillance throughout HQ and to wipe the record of everything she had done since she left his apartment. She wanted K to know that she had been here – by the time she was finished, he certainly would – but she did not want him to discover how she was getting in and out of his secret lair.

She sent the *go* signal to Jedda's tooth computer. Less than two minutes later, she had the confirmation she needed. Jedda and Linden were ready.

"Computer. Instruction to main entrance. Senior door guard is to report to this office. At the double."

Next moment, the computer's disembodied voice was relaying the order over the building's PA system. Ellen was shocked. Why use such primitive technology? Then again, it was great for the Jays. Ellen didn't need to tell Jedda and Linden what was happening.

They would hear it for themselves, anywhere in the building.

Ellen signalled silently to Chrys. "Bravo one. Senior guard leaving post. Go when ready."

Ellen stood behind K's closed door, listening, ready to intervene. She heard the sound of running feet. Boots skidding to a stop. A pause. A deep breath. A knock on the door. "Come," Ellen ordered, not bothering to disguise her voice.

The door did not open.

Ellen heard a slight scuffle, followed by a strangled gasp. The sound of a body being dragged across the bare floor. All over in seconds. She grinned. Very efficient. In a couple of minutes, all traces of the guard would have vanished.

And Jedda and Linden would be on their way down to the cells to find Delta.

FORTY-SEVEN

CHRYS TOOK THREE CAREFUL steps through the shadows and flattened herself against the wall. The next step would take her into the light, and possible discovery. The next step had to be her full-on attack.

She waited, watching for her moment. The one remaining door guard looked rather dozy, but she was patrolling the entrance, after a fashion. Six steps, turn. Six steps, turn. Yes, it would be enough. Six steps—

Chrys sprang out from the shadows the moment the woman turned. Her left arm went tight round the guard's mouth from behind, choking off any sound. Her right hand jabbed the trank syringe against the side of the woman's unprotected throat. One second's delay. Two. Chrys took the weight as the guard crumpled. She pulled the body back into the shadowed sentry post.

Stripping an unconscious body was never easy, but Chrys, as a medic, had had plenty of practice. Within just a few minutes, the guard was trussed up and stowed in a locked cupboard. Chrys emerged as the new door guard, tugging her stolen uniform jacket into place as she resumed the patrol, much more alert than the real thing. Six steps, stop, check, turn. Six steps, stop, check, turn.

No one around to raise the alarm. No one to notice that the entrance had ever been unguarded or that anything had changed. And the surveillance systems were blind.

Chrys was alone in charge of the main entrance to K's HQ. She could risk speaking out loud to send her one vital message. "Control, activate fairground."

• • • • •

Ellen had several more things to do before she could follow the others down to the cells. Now that she had disabled the surveillance systems, she had a little more time. She had to be sure that every last detail was done right.

She looked round the office again. Hmm. One thing was very

different. His flashy antique desk was gone. Destroyed in the blast? The replacement was bigger, and uglier, and K would hate it. Good.

And then she noticed the strangest thing. Over in the corner, there was some kind of sculpture. She took a closer look. And gasped.

Sculpture, my ass! It's the top of his precious desk. And he's had it mounted.

The piece of flat wood was attached to a polished steel support; the shattered edge stuck up like crazy, clawing fingers. To cap it all, the pseudo-sculpture had a title plaque. She read it. And read it again. "WHAT IS OWED SHALL BE PAID."

It was not a title. It was a message. So that everyone would be afraid of him.

Pretty much everyone already is. But not me. Not any more.

Smiling grimly, she took the envelope from inside her jacket. For one mad moment, she was tempted to impale it on his swaggering sculpture. *No. Childish. Besides, he might not notice it immediately and I daren't risk that. Timing is crucial.*

Sticking to the agreed plan, she laid the envelope on K's new desk. Since the paper was a bit crumpled, she even smoothed it with the flat of her hand. The wording on it was incendiary enough. "For onward transmission to His Excellency, Baron Marujn – Linden's cloudburst device."

K was no fool. He would find out what a cloudburst was and he would suspect the Baron of all sorts of nefarious dealings with it. K would be very reluctant to hand the cloudburst over until he had deciphered its contents. The Baron, of course, would be desperate to stop him.

Ellen congratulated herself. And Linden.

As a method of sowing enmity between K and Marujn, it was foolproof.

She still had one final set of tasks to perform.

• • • • •

Linden led the way through the maze of corridors at a fast trot. He sensed Jedda's presence, barely a pace behind him. At every corner, Linden stopped just long enough to mark a tiny arrow, low down on the wall. Crude, but effective. Ellen would know where to look for them. Others were unlikely to notice anything at all.

As expected, the main hall was empty and silent. Since K's HQ was closed to visitors at this time of night, there were no internal guards. The Jays were running little risk of being interrupted.

Especially as, by now, Chrys should have dealt with the lone woman on the door.

Linden led the way across the bare floor. Speed mattered here. He scrawled a mark on the wall at the head of the stairs and started to race down the steps, with Jedda hard on his heels. Delta would be right at the bottom, in the basement torture cells. He had to be in time to save her. He had to.

There would be guards at the entrance to the cells. Not more than two, surely? Together, he and Jedda would certainly be a match for any two of K's foot soldiers.

• • • • •

Ellen parked her backside against the edge of K's new desk as if she owned it. She was going to enjoy this. K would hate it.

"Computer, issue a statement over the public network. In two hours from now. Authorised by K himself." She grinned to herself. "Network statement begins: 'The public execution announced as part of the Dark Days festivities has been cancelled. The guilty party died in prison before she could be brought to trial. The gap in the programme of festivities will be filled by an extra distribution of food in the main square. And a free open-air pantomime.' End of statement. Computer, organise the extra food distribution and the pantomime to take place on the planned execution day. Charge the costs to K's personal account. Acknowledge."

The computer repeated its instructions.

Ellen grinned even more widely. Another cat among K's pigeons. And K would never be able to admit he had been manipulated.

Finally, there was Marujn. "Computer?"

READY.

"Send a message to Baron Marujn, personal, his eyes only. Two hours after K returns to this office. The message is to be anonymous and to appear to come from the barracks. Message starts: 'Linden has escaped from the province. Linden's cloudburst device has been retrieved. K is investigating it.' End of message. Acknowledge."

The computer did so.

Excellent. Time to tidy up the loose ends. And leave.

She instructed the computer to wipe all record of her instructions from its memory as soon as they had been executed. Surveillance systems were to remain disabled. Let K try to puzzle out who had done that, and how.

Ellen then crossed to the control panel by the door and restored its settings to normal. All but one. K's precious systems would still respond to Ellen's voice as well as his. And hers would always have priority. Satisfied, she gave the computer its final instruction. Deep concealment. K would never be able to find out what she had done.

A bubble of glee rose in her throat. That would teach K to use advanced computers that he was not savvy enough to control. Always a risky business. Always a chance that someone more savvy would come along and subvert the system. She chortled. She had done it twice now, and she fully intended to do it again in the future.

In ways that he would never discover.

• • • • •

K felt a twitch on his sleeve. He did not react. Out of the corner of his eye, he caught a gleam of gold braid. It would be one of the museum's gaudily uniformed servants. Marujn flaunting his wealth again. The man was utterly crass. And puerile. K swallowed his distaste and kept his expression impassive.

A voice hissed by his ear. "Sir, sir! An emergency. You must come."

Without visible haste, K slid out of his place. He disturbed no one. His seat had been carefully chosen so that he could make a discreet exit as soon as protocol allowed. He followed the servant's gold-and-green livery out of the arena and into the museum itself. The building seemed deserted. Presumably, the rest of the staff had sneaked outside, under cover of the darkness, to watch the military display.

Once inside the building, the servant speeded up, almost running along the corridor ahead of him. K lengthened his stride to keep up. He would not be seen to run.

The servant led K down two flights of stairs and along a short passage to the museum's surveillance room. She flung open the door and pointed to the monitors on the far wall. Even from the doorway, K could see that they were showing a composite picture of New Piccadilly Circus.

K dismissed the servant with a wave of his hand and strode across for a closer look. Two female operatives sprang to attention at the sight of him. He ignored them. He stopped in front of the monitors, hands on hips, staring up at the scene. The Piccadilly area should have been full of London's underclass, watching the military display on the huge public viewscreen above their heads. There should have been awed expressions on their faces.

The viewscreen in Piccadilly was doing its job as programmed, but no one was watching it. Piccadilly itself was full of driverless limousines in gleaming kaleidoscope colours – brights, darks, metallics – and they appeared to be fighting!

At first, it was more of a dance than a fight. The limos advanced and retreated, almost bowing to each other. Then a pair went too far. They advanced, at the gallop, straight into each other. They attempted to reverse, but they were stuck fast. They started to push instead. Another pair did the same. And another. Until there was an immovable jumble of pounding, pushing cars. Finally, a single silver limo sped in and crashed broadside into the huge heap of metal. It worked. Some of the graunching wrecks were pushed apart again.

It was as if a hidden hand had fired a starting pistol. K could hardly believe his eyes. More limos powered in, at all sorts of angles. Cars were hit amidships, or with glancing blows on their rear ends so that they spun out and away, open for further assault on front and side. None of the limos was immune. One moment they would be the aggressor, the next, they would be the victim, sometimes three or four against one. A midnight blue limo, under attack from all sides at once, was squashed almost flat. At the same moment, a bright red car managed to reverse a few metres and launch itself back into the tangle of mindless machines. It crunched into the buckling heap, reared up on its back end and stuck fast.

No more sullen silence after that. The spectators cheered, raggedly at first and then louder, with full-throated glee.

K swore like a trooper. Behind him, a watcher gasped, then tried to disguise it as a cough. Those blasted women had clocked his moment of weakness. They would tell the world. K swore again. Silently this time.

The Piccadilly chaos was another successful blow against the state. It had to be the Jay's doing. K knew he was becoming obsessed with the man, but he also knew he was right. Who else would provide such subversive entertainment for the masses? Who else was this inventive? The Jay had turned Piccadilly into a melee of empty limousines, crashing and bashing into each other like fairground dodgem cars.

Few of these limos would be in a fit state to ferry the guests away from Marujn's grand reception. The old man would lose face. Big time. So he would be out for blood. Unless K could retrieve the situation.

K scanned the mass of crumpled metal and plastic. No black. That was hopeful. He reached into his pocket and pressed his call button. He needed to get to his HQ. He needed to find out what was really going on. Would his vehicle respond? Or was it already on the way to Piccadilly to join the limos' amazing death dance?

As K watched the scene in unwilling fascination, the doors of three of the limos slid open. Their opulent interiors were exposed and inviting. A second later, all the other doors slid open, too. K heard a gasp from the watching crowd.

A new kind of movement caught his eye. The underclass were not just cheering from the sidelines any more. A small figure – a child? – dashed out of the crowd and leapt into one of the stalled, helpless limos. A moment later, the child emerged again, carrying a bottle of champagne in one hand and some kind of fur wrap in the other. Shrieking with delighted laughter, the child waved its booty in the air. The effect on the crowd was like sounding the advance. They stopped being spectators. Dozens of figures dived for the open doors and began to plunder, stripping everything movable from the limos' interiors.

Another twitch at K's sleeve. "Sir. Your car is waiting."

K allowed himself a moment of deep satisfaction. Sometimes austerity paid off. He had been right to invest his limited funds in security rather than luxury for his official transport. His pared-down, ultrashielded black car was apparently immune to the Jay's underhand tricks. And it was very, very fast.

K started for the door. He would soon be back in his HQ, and back in control of events. It was time for this nonsense to stop.

• • • • •

Weapon in hand, Linden skidded to a halt on the stone floor at the bottom of the stairs. No one in sight. No sounds of movement. Odd. Where were they all?

He motioned to Jedda to get his back. They would move forward together, hugging the blank wall. If the opposition appeared in the passage ahead, she would be shielded by his body. If the attack came from above, she would have a clear shot at their legs before they could get a bead on her. It was the best he could do to protect her.

He crept forward, listening intently. Still nothing. Thirty seconds. Sixty.

A shot scorched past his ear.

Automatically, he ducked. In the same instant, Jedda fired from behind him.

A sharp cry of pain. Then the sound of a body falling.

"Good shot," he said.

"One down. Any more?" She motioned him forward. Closer to the doorway, they'd have a better line of sight. For the defenders, it would be worse.

They ran forward and took cover. Tense seconds passed. Nothing. If they stayed where they were, it could be stalemate. And they were losing precious time.

"I'll go in," Linden said. "Cover me. Ready?"

Jedda nodded and ducked down with her back to the wall. She had a weapon in each hand. "OK. Go!"

He sprang forward and burst through the entrance to the cells. He almost tripped over the uniformed body on the floor. Probably dead, but no time to check. He grabbed her weapon – just in case – and pushed the body against the wall.

Need to keep the escape route clear. Need to keep moving.

Half a dozen rapid steps and he was in the cells. A guard wouldn't fight from in here, surely? There was no decent cover. Apart from inside individual cells.

He was right. The cell block was empty. Except for the inmates. Two of them.

"Delta!" She was in the cell on the left. And conscious. Relief flowed over him. He could still save her. Amazingly, she looked whole -- no broken limbs, no visible bruises, no glazed eyes. "Delta, we've come to get you out. Can you walk? Do you need help?"

"Only to get this door open," she replied.

"I can do that." Jedda. With one of Anton's clever decoders in her hand. "What about the other one?" She nodded towards the prisoner in the second cell.

"Let her go, too," Linden said quickly. "*My enemy's enemy*, remember?"

Jedda pinged the decoder twice and both cell doors opened. The unknown woman was out in a flash and running for freedom. Delta was nothing like as fast. She started gathering up stuff in her cell.

"Get a move on, Delta," Jedda snapped. "Remember, there's only one way out. It's a potential death trap down here."

Delta had her back to them. "Is it?" she said.

· · · · ·

A little of K's tension left him as his personal vehicle set off, responding to his order for maximum speed. Everything appeared to be working normally, even the comms. Excellent. He would work during the journey across the city.

He could do nothing about Linden, or about the Jay's dodgem cars, until he was back at his HQ, so he concentrated on the one problem he could solve – Marujn's. Alternative transport would have to be waiting outside the museum, as soon as Marujn's illustrious guests demanded their limos. K reckoned he could provide that. He also reckoned the Baron would not be too embarrassed as long as his guests were able to leave in good order. One limo more or less meant nothing to people of such wealth. They would shrug it off. Marujn would still be furious at the breach of elite security, but the eruption should be containable.

"Computer, urgent message to Commissar Tauber."

READY.

"Message starts. 'Priority One instructions. Effective immediately. Organise alternative departure transport for all museum guests. No driverless vehicles are to be used. Commandeer military vehicles and drivers if necessary. Confirm to HQ when complete. Second instruction: issue all points warning. Private or driverless transport is deemed a security risk until further notice. The state will no longer guarantee the safety of users of such vehicles.' Message ends. Computer, acknowledge."

The computer repeated its instructions. A few seconds later, it confirmed that the message had been successfully relayed.

Now it was all Tauber's problem. Was the man up to that kind of instant action and decision? K was not sure, but he would soon find out. As a test of Tauber's abilities to operate effectively in a crisis, this was not bad at all.

Peripheral movement caught K's eye. A huge limo, driving sedately down a side street. It turned a corner and was gone. K was almost sure it was Marujn's vehicle. No one else used a silver monster like Marujn's. Was the old man's limo ultrashielded too? It certainly didn't seem to be going berserk like most of the others.

Food for thought. Perhaps the Jay's tech skills only gave him control of the unshielded limos? Perhaps some of the others were still responding to their owners? With luck, the problem was only in Piccadilly.

Wrong! Two marauding limos were speeding towards him right now, side by side, taking up the full width of the street. They were aiming to crush him. "Computer, I have control!" K shouted, grabbing for the levers. He wrenched his car right into a tiny lane and shot along it. The attackers were too wide to follow. Weren't they?

A quick glance at the feed from the rear-view camera. Nothing behind. But in front? Was the Jay out to kill him? Or just to capture him? Would there be an ambush up ahead?

"Computer. Plot a route to HQ using narrow lanes wherever possible. Display."

The head-up display appeared immediately. Yes, there was a way. It would take twice as long. And there would be moments of real danger. He wasn't out of the woods yet.

K shrugged the tension out of his shoulders. He had enjoyed manual driving once. And he'd been good at it. Time to prove he could still do it.

FORTY-EIGHT

ANTON WAS USING SEVERAL screens at once. He ignored the Piccadilly screen. His dodgem program was running things there and the real excitement was over. Manually battling K's little black limo through the streets was proving to be much more fun. Anton had seen K climbing into it. By himself. So it was one on one. Almost like being a real warrior. Any moment now—

Anton stared at the main screen in disbelief. His clever two-car attack had just failed! K's car had taken a very tight corner on two wheels. Autodrive limos would never do that. So had K taken over the controls himself? At that speed? Anton blew out a long breath. He hadn't bargained for that. Somewhere in K's mysterious past, he must have learnt manual driving skills.

Anton had to up his game here. What now? He forced himself to take the time to reason it out. The normal limitations on an autodrive car would not apply. It would be much more difficult to predict what the vehicle might do. Or where it would go.

He separated his two attacking limos. He sent the green one to follow K, quickly setting up the reserve program to report K's progress and choose the best interception route. K could use narrow twisting alleys where the green limo couldn't go, but the green machine would be much faster on the wider roads. It would always catch up in the end. Crucially, it would stop K from reversing out of trouble.

Anton concentrated on his faster blue limo. He would need to outthink K. And to go on controlling this limo manually. He called up a map on a side screen, highlighting all the narrow lanes. K would use those. But they wouldn't get him all the way back to his HQ. He'd need to come out in the open some of the time. Crossing major intersections. Yes. There! And there! Anton touched his screen and sent the blue car racing round a long loop to get to the first potential ambush point.

If only he had more vehicles to attack with. Maybe he could use the Marujn limo? That would make it three against one. Much better odds.

No. What kind of warrior would I be if I screwed up Jedda's chances of escape just to beat K in a car chase? There isn't time to do both unless— No. I can't risk it.

Anton forced himself to concentrate on his blue car. Nearly there. Anton pulled it to a screeching halt, a few metres from the intersection. It would be hidden by the grand department store on the corner. K was still a fair distance away, speeding along an alley. He'd have to turn into the main street for a short section. One minute to get there, maybe? Fifty metres more to the intersection. Where the blue limo was waiting.

Anton's reserve program was doing its stuff, too. The green limo was catching up again, speeding up the main street towards the department store. K's small black vehicle would be no match for the two big beasts. He'd be the meat in a very squashed sandwich.

Anton held his breath. His finger was poised to send his blue limo out to fight.

Wait... Wait... Yes. Now!

Anton's finger stabbed. The blue limo shot out. Straight across the front of K's vehicle. They must crash. Black into blue. Broadside.

It didn't happen that way.

K's reactions were lightning. He wrenched his vehicle left, aiming it at the blue limo's rear end. He even seemed to think to accelerate.

Black crashed into blue. Bits everywhere. Blue bits. Anton's limo spun round through ninety degrees and ended up facing down the main street. Mangled, but still accelerating. In the wrong direction. Before Anton could react, the green limo ploughed straight into it, head on, at top speed. A sandwich with no filling at all.

Anton swore with all the worst words he knew. He had run out of cars. Both his weapons were a write-off. And all the spares were already wrecks in Piccadilly.

K's tough little black job seemed to shrug off the impact. It sped off into more dark alleys. So K had won this round. He was probably laughing, too. Nothing now to stop him getting back to his HQ.

Chrys would have to be warned. She had nine minutes, at most.

• • • • •

Ellen followed Linden's trail of tiny arrows to the end of the maze of passages. She reached the main hall at last. One last corner. She risked a quick look. The hall was empty. At the far end, she glimpsed the huge double entrance doors, flanked by mythical stone figures holding up the roof. No sign of Linden's arrow that way. Chrys would be out there, on the far side, in the cold. She would hold the fort, single-handed. Whether by guile or by force, she would deal with anyone who appeared. Even K.

Ellen risked another peek. Both directions, scanning the walls. She needed to find out where to go next, and how to get there without being caught. Loads of rooms and corridors and staircases opened onto this vast hall. Soldiers might appear at any moment. From anywhere.

Ah yes. Got it. Well done, Linden.

He had made the final arrow bigger and easier to spot from a distance. There was a set of stairs diagonally opposite Ellen's hiding place. Down only. That had to be the way to the cells.

If the enemy came up the stairs, they would see Ellen before she saw them.

She shrugged off the risk. At least she'd have a wall at her back while she was going down. She dropped to one knee, checked the hall once more and launched herself across it, at full pelt. She didn't stop until she had reached the stairs and gone down to the first half-landing. She flattened herself against the wall, looking up to the hall and then down into the relative gloom below. No sound of movement in the hall above. Anyone passing was unlikely to notice her now.

And down below? She heard steps. Faint. Light-footed. One person. Probably a woman. Hurrying, then hesitating. Someone trying not to be seen. A potential attacker?

There was no decent cover where Ellen was. A blank wall on the outside of the stairs and a solid waist-level wall on the inside, guarding the drop to the stairwell. If Ellen used a weapon here, the noise would give her away. Every spare soldier in the building above would be after her. No. There were other ways. She shoved one of her weapons into her pocket and pulled K's knife from her boot. She could shoot left-handed if she had to, but she needed her right to throw a knife. And to guarantee a hit, she needed to get a lot closer to her target.

Keeping her back against the blank wall, she stole soundlessly down the stairs. A full flight. Stop. Listen.

Silence. Half a flight more. This time she heard the scuff of a shoe on a stair. The attacker was on the next flight. Coming up. Close now. In seconds, whoever it was would be visible and Ellen would have a clear target.

Ducking down, Ellen crept across the width of the step so that she was hidden by the low wall overlooking the stairwell. The attacker would have to come right round the half-landing to see Ellen crouching there. Ellen would be able to throw her knife long before her attacker could sight and shoot. There should be no noise.

Provided Ellen's knife hit home.

• • • • •

When Delta finally turned round, Jedda saw that she was clutching some kind of package to her middle. Strange. Prisoners weren't allowed possessions, surely?

Linden was still talking. Too much and too fast. "We'll get you out, Delta, don't worry. And then you can join us."

He holstered his weapon and moved forward to help her. "You'll be a great asset, you know. And we'll take care of you. We'll—"

"So why'd you do it, Linden?" Delta cut in sharply. "Become a traitor, I mean."

Linden seemed to stop in his tracks. The back of his neck turned bright red.

Delta took two steps towards him. She was standing plumb in the open door of her cell, hands still at her middle, almost all of her body shadowed by Linden's. "You betrayed everything you stood for – state, family, colleagues. You're a gullible fool, Linden." She sounded hurt. Then angry. "But you're a typical man, aren't you? With a cock for a compass. You took one look at a woman and your brain went south."

Jedda gripped her weapon and started to edge round Linden. She could guess where this was going, even if Linden could not. She needed to get a clear shot.

"Stay where you are, woman!" Delta ordered instantly. "If you move again, I'll kill him."

Jedda gasped out Linden's name.

"She's got a weapon." Linden's voice sounded breathy, unreal. Then it steadied. "Stay right behind me." He moved half a pace closer to Delta, near enough to ensure that his body was masking Jedda's completely. "I'm sorry, Jedda. It's my fault. I'll deal with this. Get yourself out."

"Don't be even more of a fool, Linden," Delta snapped. "She'll never get out of here alive. They're waiting for her. Give up. You can save yourself."

Linden snorted. He didn't move. Stalemate.

• • • • •

The silence was lasting too long. Ellen's attacker must have stopped moving. Did the woman sense that death could be waiting for her round the corner?

For a moment, Ellen was in a quandary – move down to the landing and take the fight to her attacker, or sit tight and wait for the woman to expose herself? Ellen glanced up the staircase behind her. Nothing. No sound above, either. As long as there was no second attacker coming down, Ellen could afford to wait. A little longer.

A sound. It was so low, and so fleeting, that Ellen barely heard it above the thudding of her own pulse. A single soft-footed step. Her attacker was coming up at last. Knife poised, Ellen focused on the point where the woman's torso would appear.

"Don't shoot!"

Too late. Ellen had thrown her knife.

But the attacker had been slithering round the landing on her belly. The knife missed. It struck the wall and clattered harmlessly to the ground. In the same instant, Ellen flipped her weapon into her right hand. She would not miss with that.

"Don't shoot!" cried the woman again. "I'm unarmed."

"Stand up then, and prove it."

The woman got cautiously to her feet, holding her arms out wide and spreading filthy, empty hands. She was dressed in the layers of drab clothing that most of the have-nots wore to keep warm in winter. She looked ordinary. Unthreatening. Was she one of K's guards in disguise? Was she hiding a weapon under all those layers?

"Put your hands on your head." As the woman obeyed, Ellen barked out her next question: "Now, who are you?"

"A prisoner. From down there." The woman glanced towards the stairs leading to the torture cells. There was fear in her eyes. "Your friends let me go."

"What makes you think they're my friends?" Ellen retorted.

"Well, they killed the guard, so they're not part of K's machine. And neither are you, or you'd have sounded the alarm. So will you let me go?"

There could easily have been a second prisoner in the cells, though there had been no thought message from Jedda about one. An oversight? Possibly. This woman's story could be true. In any case, Ellen could not afford to be lumbered with prisoners. She had to shoot the woman or let her go.

"Ellen?"

Wha—? How does she know my name?

"Ellen, Blue3 will be grateful."

The words struck home like a blow to the gut. Ellen felt winded. But only for a second. Her fighting instincts kicked straight back in. "OK. Go. Quickly. Up the stairs and out through the main entrance. The guard there is a friend. I'll tell her not to stop you."

The woman – another one of Blue3's spies, of course – was half-way up the flight before Ellen had finished speaking. Then she was gone.

Ellen sent a silent message to Chrys and put the Blue woman out of her mind. She had to find Jedda and Linden. They should have been out long before this. The rescue plan must have gone wrong.

Ellen retrieved her knife from the landing, put her back against the outer wall and kept going down.

• • • • •

K leapt out of his vehicle. The danger was over, now he was back at HQ. He could breathe easily again. Not that he really wanted to. He had been enjoying the car chase. Winning was very sweet.

He made for the main entrance and took the steps three at a time. He was shocked, and then infuriated, to see there was only one guard on duty. There should have been two. And this woman was scruffy with it. Her uniform was a mess: wrinkled and poorly-fitting, as if it had shrunk.

She jerked to attention and saluted as he reached her.

"Where's the other one?" he snapped.

"She's…um… she had to go for a bathroom break, sir. Sorry, sir. She was having…er… women's problems. But everything was quiet, so we thought… She'll be back any minute, I'm sure, sir. Sorry, sir."

The woman was gabbling. And staring at the ground, too nervous to look K in the face. She was right about that. Both women would suffer for their dereliction of duty. "You're both on a charge. Report to my office first thing in the morning. And make sure your uniform is in order before you show your face to me again."

He strode through the entrance before the woman could move a muscle. What kind of officers were running this detail? He'd give them women's problems! He'd have someone's head on a platter for this.

Out of sight of the woman, he began to run.

Chrys signalled as she watched him disappear. She could see why his minions were terrified of him, but she was glad to have met him face-to-face at last. Not that he had actually looked at her face, of course. To him, she was just another piece of anonymous cannon fodder. She allowed herself a wry smile. He had been so very easy to fool. Pity she would miss the fireworks when he discovered the truth.

• • • • •

The stalemate in the cells froze time. No one moved or spoke.

In the end, it was Delta who broke the silence. "OK. We'll do it the hard way," she said. "Drop your weapons, woman! Or I'll drop Linden where he stands. You have three seconds. One…"

Jedda closed her eyes, trying to force her brain to work.

"Two…" Delta counted. She was starting to sound pleased with herself. Why?

Jedda's brain was startled into working again. If Delta shot Linden, his body would be blasted backwards on to Jedda. She'd be flattened, with no chance to shoot back. So Delta would probably get Jedda as well. Yeah, right. That was why she sounded so smug.

Jedda grimaced and dropped her weapons.

"Kick them over into the far corner," Delta ordered. "No funny business."

Jedda took a deep breath and obeyed. She had a knife in her boot. Linden's big body was still covering hers. If she slid her hand down her leg, very slowly, she could—

"Now, move to the side, woman, so I can see you."

"No, Jedda! Stay close behind me!"

"Same deal," Delta said. "Do as I say, or I'll shoot him. One…"

Jedda didn't hesitate. She took two long steps to the side. She had to put as much distance as possible between herself and Linden so that Delta couldn't keep them both covered. It was half a chance.

Delta was too experienced to be caught that way. "Back off, Linden." She waved her weapon. "Stand next to your ladybird. Closer. Closer. That's better. I want to be able to fell you both with one shot."

Jedda's world was turning grey and bleak. Then she saw red. Strawberry red.

Chrys's report of K's arrival buzzed into Jedda's brain. How could she have forgotten about silent messaging? Concentrating hard, she sent the distress call that she should have sent when Delta first produced her weapon. Even though it was probably too late.

• • • • •

K raced down the last passage and threw open his office door. "Computer."

READY.

At least one thing was dependable in this place. "Lock down HQ building, immediately." Was that overkill? Probably. The Jay was a classic guerrilla warrior. He would never risk a direct attack on K's HQ. His target had to be a long way from that distraction in Piccadilly. Maybe the Barrier again? But a lockdown was still a sensible and rational precaution. It meant K could concentrate on assembling his counterattack forces without worrying about whether his back was exposed.

The computer made the formal announcement over the PA system. The building was secured in less than twenty seconds. Textbook stuff.

"Computer, order all off-duty personnel to assemble in the top-floor ops room, with weapons. I will brief them there myself. In three minutes."

Another PA announcement. That would light the blue touch paper under the idle women in the mess hall. They'd better have sharpened up their act by the time they went into action. Otherwise, the Jay's warriors would eat them for breakfast.

K went to his safe to collect his own weapons. Pity there was no time to change out of his stiff dress uniform. It was definitely not designed for fighting. He threw two weapons onto the desk behind him while he struggled with both hands to stuff a third into the front pocket of his close-fitting trousers. Insurance. He'd keep the other two in his hands, set on kill. And—

There was a white envelope on his desk. With writing on it.

• • • • •

Linden was frozen with terror. Not for himself, but for Jedda. And for the others. He had led them into a trap. He had insisted on following his chivalrous instincts – his *arrogant* instincts – and they had been dead wrong. Dead! Yeah.

Delta's weapon was covering them both. She was too far away for Linden to jump her, but she was too close to miss.

Linden had misread her completely. She was K's creature, body and soul. Unless... "Delta," he began, trying to sound like her pack leader again, "you could—"

"Shut it, traitor!" Delta moved her weapon so that it was clearly trained on Jedda. "One more word out of you and she dies. One move, and she dies. Got it?"

Linden swallowed. And nodded.

Think! Come on, think! Jedda has no weapons but I've still got mine. If I can do something to distract Delta, just for a second, I might have time to draw and shoot.

What kind of distraction? If he moved, or spoke, Delta would shoot Jedda before Linden could get a hand to his weapon. He risked a sideways glance at Jedda. There was concentration in her face. Odd. Why was she…?

He couldn't waste energy on that. He had to devise a distraction. But what?

The distraction came. Not from Linden. Not from Jedda.

The door burst open behind them. Firing. "Take cover!" in the same moment.

Ellen! Firing at the ceiling until she sussed out who was where.

For Linden, time slowed. He saw Delta's face harden. He saw the moment when she decided to shoot. He saw that her target was Jedda, not Ellen.

He threw himself at Jedda, hauling out his own weapon as he sprang. His weight knocked Jedda down. And his shot felled Delta. But not before she'd fired.

"Any more of them?" Ellen barked, looking round for new targets.

"No," Linden gasped automatically, dropping to the floor beside Jedda's body. "Jedda. Jedda, speak to me!" Was she dead? She was not responding. Her eyes were closed. Then she shivered. Wounded, not dead, then. Her body armour must have saved her. Delta had been too close to miss, even with a moving target. He cursed himself as he ripped open Jedda's jacket and slapped on a field dressing. He should have been quicker to shield her. It should have been him lying there. He touched her face and spoke gently. "Jedda. Open your eyes. Come on. You can do it."

He was vaguely aware that Ellen was kneeling over Delta's motionless body. "You missed," Ellen said tartly, throwing Delta's weapon into the cell opposite. "She may lose her arm, but she won't die. Pity. She was K's bait. Bait should get eaten."

The accusation was clear in her voice. They were all in K's trap. Linden had led them there. "I'm sorry." He kept his eyes on Jedda's face. This was for her. "It was my fault. All of it. K set a trap for me and I walked straight into it. I—"

"Save it for later," Ellen snapped, frowning across at him. "Right now, we need to get out of here." She stood up and came over to them. "Jedda, can you move?" Her voice was suddenly very sharp and penetrating.

Jedda's eyes fluttered open. "Ellen. Leader," she whispered. And passed out.

The PA system sounded, every word clearly audible in the cells. Lockdown. No mention of a target, but mustering forces for a counter-attack.

"Good. He's panicking," Ellen said acidly.

"He never panics," Linden said automatically. He put his arms under Jedda's inert body and began to lift her.

"He's locked down the building. He probably thinks we're still outside. It means reinforcements can't get in, though. Basic mistake. He can't take us on without them."

"But it means we can't get out, doesn't it?" Unless Linden could get Jedda out, she could die here. Along with everyone else.

"Nope," Ellen said. "I can override the lockdown. Trust me. Can you carry Jedda? Right then. Get her up the stairs and through the main door. I'll make sure it's open. You've got five minutes, tops. As soon as Chrys gives me the all clear, I'll sound the alarm down here. K and his troops are bound to respond. They won't think to check the main door. Not in lockdown. So they won't see you."

"But you—"

"Just get the hell out of here!" She waved him towards the door. "Control, alpha one injured. Alpha two taking command. Transport to main door soonest. Warn bravo one to be ready. She's to take alpha one and bravo two back to base. Out."

• • • • •

K grabbed the strange white envelope from his desk. Someone had been in here. How had they bypassed HQ security? It was supposed to be the best in the province.

"Computer. Review surveillance data. Visitors to this office since I left it. On screen."

NO DATA AVAILABLE FOR REQUESTED PERIOD. SURVEILLANCE SYSTEMS NON-OPERATIONAL.

Non-operational? Disabled? "Computer, check that all HQ surveillance systems are operating normally."

CHECKS COMPLETE. ALL HQ SURVEILLANCE SYSTEMS ARE DISABLED FOR TWELVE HOURS.

K's gut clenched. That was impossible. "Computer, override that order. Controller's authority. Bring surveillance systems back on line immediately."

NEGATIVE. ALL HQ SURVEILLANCE SYSTEMS ARE DISABLED FOR TWELVE HOURS.

K's fist struck the desk so hard that both weapons bounced into the air. He was beginning to realise he was really up against it here. The Jay was one truly devious bastard. First the ridiculous dodgems in Piccadilly. Then the car chase. And now this. K wouldn't be able to see what was going on anywhere else in the building. Which meant the Jays must already be inside. He had underestimated them, big time. Now he wouldn't be able to find out where they were. And there was absolutely nothing he could do about it. He was flying blind.

No. No, he wasn't. He knew exactly where he would find them. They would be down in the cells, trying to rescue Delta.

And falling into K's neat little trap.

He stuffed the envelope into his pocket, grabbed his weapons and ran for the stairs to the ops room. This time, the odds were definitely on his side.

He reached the assembly point in record time and threw open the door.

The ops room was empty.

FORTY-NINE

THEY FELT LIKE THE longest minutes of Ellen's life. Once she'd overridden the lockdown on the main entrance, there was nothing else for her to do.

C'mon, Chrys. C'mon! Haven't you got away yet?

She thought it, but she knew better than to send it. She waited, pacing up and down between the cells. Chrys was a pro. She would signal the instant they were out.

Ellen made herself focus on her own escape. The moment she set off the alarm, she would sprint up the stairs. She had to be out through the main door before K reached the hall. It would be tight. It helped that he would be in his ops room on the top floor, with however many soldiers he'd been able to muster. But as soon as K heard the alarm, he would know where the enemy was. He'd still have to brief his troops, though – even if it was just "Follow me!" – and then get back down to the main hall. Elapsed time? Two minutes, surely? Maybe longer. Long enough for Ellen to get out. Unlike Linden, Ellen wouldn't have to carry an inert body up the stairs.

She continued to pace.

$\bullet\ \bullet\ \bullet\ \bullet\ \bullet$

K wasted no time at the ops room. If he had to take the Jays on by himself, he would.

He raced for the stairs. He would gather up any soldiers he found on the way, but he couldn't waste a second looking for reinforcements. The basement cells were a dead end. Only one way out. He needed to get down to the main hall before the Jay and his women had a chance to break out from the cell level. If they got to the hall, they could go anywhere. And with no surveillance, it might take half a regiment to flush them out. But if they didn't make it back to the hall, one well-armed man could pin them down.

He wanted to be that man.

$\bullet\ \bullet\ \bullet\ \bullet\ \bullet$

Chrys's thought message came through to Ellen at last. "Cargo despatched."

Ellen didn't waste time on a response. She banged the alarm and legged it out to the stairs. She was halfway up the first flight before the PA system's siren echoed round the building.

INTRUDERS IN BASEMENT CELLS. INTRUDERS IN BASEMENT CELLS.

• • • • •

K was only one floor from the main hall when the PA broadcast the alarm from the cells. He grinned as he started down the last flight of stairs. His quarry was still in the basement. He was going to spring his trap. It was going to work.

Moments later, K clattered down the last few steps into the hall. It was empty, too. No Jays. But no soldiers either. Where were they all?

That stupid prick Tauber! So keen to suck up to Marujn that he sent all my troops to be part of the old man's bleeding parade. I'll have his guts for this.

That pleasure would have to wait. For now, he had to decide what to do. Could he be sure the Jay and his women were still trapped down below?

K marched over to the top of the stairs and listened hard.

• • • • •

Only one flight left. I'm going to make it.

Ellen was panting fit to burst and her leg muscles were screaming, but she would not slow down. She had to make it out of this building.

Movement up above! Bugger, bugger, bugger!

She stopped dead. For a second, she doubled up over the half-wall, gasping for breath, trying to swallow the noise she was making. Then she heard movement again. Boots on bare floor. She hadn't been quick enough. She was trapped.

She started to scramble back the way she had come. Back to the basement.

Now what? Where can I hide? There's no cover down there.

Her brain was working even faster than her legs. Should she try hiding under the stairs in the basement hallway? No, too risky. K's people would find her easily and there was no way out. She'd be a sitting duck. It would have to be the cell block. There was no way out from there, either, but at least there was some cover in the cells. She could put up a fight from there.

Her left boot skidded on the edge of a tread and she went up in the air, arms flailing. An instant later, she landed hard on the stairs. One weapon flew out of her hand. She tried to grab for it, but she was already bumping down the stairs on her backside. It took all her efforts to stop and get back on her feet. No time to go looking for the weapon. No need, anyway. She still had one good weapon. And a knife.

· · · · ·

For half a second, K thought he heard heavy breathing. Followed by silence. Was he hearing things? No. More sounds. Definite sounds. Feet on the stairs, but not many. Scrambling down. Falling? Then scrambling again. So at least some of the Jays were down there.

K could really do with some reinforcements. Clearly there was no off-duty backup. His only option was to pull people out of operational surveillance teams. Very risky, leaving whole sectors of London vulnerable. What if the Jay was setting a trap for him? A diversion for another major attack, like the one on the New Barrier?

No, that wasn't it. K was sure of it now. His gut was telling him the Jay was *here*. The Jay had swallowed K's bait and he was trying to rescue Delta.

"Computer, make announcement. 'All code red personnel to remain at post. All code amber personnel to basement cells with weapons. At the double.' Message ends."

The computer's tinny response came instantly. *NO CODE AMBER PERSONNEL AVAILABLE IN HQ. ONLY CODE RED STAFF AVAILABLE.*

K was so shocked, he swore aloud. Only code red? Available, yes, but deployable? Not a chance. Even K couldn't pull code red staff from their posts and get away with it. Tauber had screwed things up, big time. K was on his own.

He had two choices. Stay where he was and try to keep the terrorists pinned down in the basement, or go down and take them on. Logic said it would be suicide to go down there. He had weapons, yes, and body armour in the fabric of his dress uniform, but he had never tested it. He suspected it was pretty flimsy. Besides, he had no idea how many of the enemy were down there. The Jay had at least three warrior women, including Ellen, so it could be four against one. What if they came charging up the stairs, guns blazing, as soon as they realised no one was coming for them? What then? They would only need one lucky shot.

He had to go down or he had to retreat.

K straightened his shoulders and gripped his weapons. Where the Jay was concerned, K didn't do retreat.

When Ellen reached the basement hallway, she took one precious second to stop and listen. Yes, she could hear boots a long way above, but not many. Maybe only a couple of people? And going more carefully now.

Of course they're being careful. They don't know it's only me down here.

She ran through into the cell block, ignoring the dead guard. Delta was still lying motionless on the floor, blocking the way to the cells. She hadn't been unconscious all the time, though. She'd clearly come round for long enough to put a field dressing on her injured arm. Bully for her.

Ellen checked round for cover. Yup, she'd remembered it right. The only real cover was in the cells, behind the sleeping benches. Not great, but better than nothing. Fair shooting angles. And her attackers would have very little cover at all.

She didn't bother to push Delta out of the way. Let her lie there and provide another obstacle for the attackers to deal with.

She stepped over Delta's inert body to get to the empty cells beyond.

Mistake!

Strong fingers grabbed her ankle. Wrenched. Twisted. And twisted again.

Ellen cried out in pain. Then all the breath was slammed out of her body as she hit the deck. Her weapon rattled across the floor and was gone.

They'll be here any minute. They mustn't find me out in the open. I have to get into cover.

Ellen kicked out viciously with her free leg. The contact jarred through her whole body. She heard the crunch of boot into bone and gristle. Groans of agony. She kept right on kicking. More groans. The death grip on her ankle slackened at last. She pulled free.

She lurched to her feet but her injured leg almost gave way under her. Great. Just what she needed to run up all those stairs when this was done.

Using the wall for support, Ellen gave Delta one last solid kick in the head. Enough to knock her out for hours. Or worse. She wouldn't be able to tell anyone what had happened or how the Jays had escaped. It might give Ellen slightly more of a chance but she would need help. With all the others gone, she'd have to rely on Anton.

"Control, alpha two," she managed, gasping to get the words out. "Am pinned down in basement cells. Opposition small. Will fight my way out. Send transport to main door soonest. How long? Over."

"Transport still en route to base. Turnround time, plus time back to HQ, at least twenty-three minutes. Will reach you soonest. Good luck, alpha two. Control out."

Twenty-three minutes? AT LEAST? Thanks a bunch, Anton.

Noise in the hallway, beyond the doors. They were there, getting ready to burst in. They'd be on her any second. And she was definitely on her own.

She dived for the empty cell where she'd thrown Delta's weapon. She wouldn't be defenceless after all. And she still had her knife.

She found Delta's weapon on the floor in the far corner. Yes!

Weird. It's still on default. So that's why Jedda isn't dead.

No time to wonder why Delta had done something so stupid. Ellen simply clicked the setting through to kill and slid down behind the sleeping bench, trying to make the most of the cover. Pain shot up her leg when she felt for her knife, but she forced herself to ignore it. Pity there was no time for mind control. But once the shooting started in earnest, a crocked ankle would be the least of her worries.

• • • • •

K flattened himself against the wall in the basement hallway and used one weapon to push open the door to the cells. Just a crack. If the Jays were on alert, they would see the movement and shoot at the gap. He waited, pulse thudding.

Nothing.

The thudding got faster and louder. He was going to have to go through that door, not knowing what was on the other side. Burst through, firing at random? No. Bad odds. They'd get him before he got them and he might hit the guard, or Delta. They were in there, somewhere, probably prisoners. Or dead? Whichever, he was on his own.

He'd done this kind of thing before, in the holo suite. And he'd got away with it. So maybe the same tactics would work against real terrorists?

He didn't stop to consider the risks of his new idea. He simply kicked open the door and launched himself through it at ground level, skidding across the floor on his belly with both weapons poised to fire.

The place was empty. Apart from one body on the floor by the wall, clearly dead, and another by the cells. The second one looked like Delta's.

He checked all round. Nowhere for anyone to hide. Except in the cells. That was when he realised that both cell doors were wide open. From where he was, they both looked empty. No sound, no movement. He knew that was a dangerous illusion. He *knew* the Jays were down here.

He inched forward. Yes, the second body was Delta's. She was flat on her back. One arm was badly injured. Someone had bound it up, roughly. Her head and upper body were a mass of blood and bruises. Her good arm was stretched out across the floor. As if she were beckoning to him. He managed to reach her wrist. A faint pulse. Delta was not dead. But without a medic, she soon could be.

He needed to be able to see into the cells. But he wasn't close enough and he'd be exposed if he crawled over Delta's body.

He looked round again. Yes, that would do it. He pushed himself back towards the door. When he was absolutely sure he couldn't be seen from either cell, he jumped to his feet and flattened himself against the right-hand wall. Right? Left? What did it matter? He had no means of guessing which cell the enemy was in. Maybe both.

If they were in both, he was dead meat.

He forced himself to concentrate harder, edging along the blank wall, with careful, soundless footsteps. Two more steps, three at most, and he would be able to risk a quick look across into Delta's cell. Anyone inside would probably see him, too. He mustn't give them a chance to shoot.

He took a deep breath, holding it, focusing on physical control. Step one. Weapons at the ready. Step two. Not there yet. Step three.

Delta's cell was empty!

K closed his eyes for a full second and breathed out. He felt his shoulders begin to slump against the wall as relief flooded through him. *No! Stay alert!* He jerked himself back to all-too-dangerous reality. OK, there was no risk of crossfire. The Jays were all in the cell opposite Delta's. Even if it was four against one, he should be able to hold them there until reinforcements arrived. If his troops brought stun grenades with them, it would all be over in seconds. Otherwise, it could be a full-on firefight.

He retreated rapidly along the wall to the entrance. He stopped to listen at the door for a second, hoping to hear the sound of soldiers' boots on the stairs. Nothing.

He was still on his own. He had to stay here, to keep the Jays

435

pinned down in that one cell. He knew where they were, but he didn't know how many he was up against. Numbers mattered. Especially once the shooting started.

He had options now. He could creep forward again, on the other wall, and try to see how many were in the cell. He might even try to pick off one or two of the terrorists before they could get a shot in. Risky, though. He might get himself shot in the process. If the Jays worked out that he was alone, they might rush him and break out.

The other option was to play for time. Bluff.

"Stay back, you men," he ordered loudly in the direction of the doorway. "We don't want a bloodbath. No shooting until I give the word."

Silence from the cell. No reaction. No movement.

"You in there. You can't escape. Throw out your weapons and come out with your hands on your heads." He waited another beat. Nothing. "Have it your way," he snarled. "You want to be martyrs. Believe me, that can be arranged."

A single shot rang out. It hit the wall above Delta's cell door and dislodged a tiny piece of masonry. A pitiful gesture of defiance. All noise and no substance.

Just what I'd expect from a man who hides behind women. So there's a good chance he's in there with them.

As the echo died away, K allowed himself a thin, cold smile. He was winning at last. This time, he was going to finish the Jay.

• • • • •

So K plans to make martyrs of the Jays, does he? Not on my watch.

Ellen's pain was more or less under control now and she was moving almost normally. She slid across to the far wall and sighted more carefully across the corner of the cell opening and into the space beyond. This second shot would land much nearer the enemy. With luck, some debris might hit someone.

Preferably that arrogant swine, K.

She fired and slid back into cover in a single swift movement. She listened. No cry of pain. Pity. But if she kept firing that kind of shot, sometimes at torso level, sometimes higher or lower, she should be able to keep the enemy at bay. K didn't know she was alone. He probably wouldn't risk a full frontal assault, even with a squad of soldiers at his back.

Hang on a minute. That's garbage. K doesn't care how many soldiers die for him. Of course he'll send them against me. Probably any second now.

436

She readied herself for action. Waited. Nothing. She loosed off another shot at knee level. Still no response.

Ellen's antennae twitched. What if he was bluffing? What if he had no one at his back? She listened even harder. No sound at all. If there was a squad of goons out there, surely there would be some kind of sound, even if it was only heavy breathing? She couldn't be sure. Not without putting her head above the parapet.

She fired twice more on autopilot, while she struggled to find an answer. If he was alone, she could take him on. If he had company, it could be suicide.

The solution was simple enough once it came to her. It had its downsides, but so did everything. Decision made.

She drew her knife, leapt up and threw it with all the force of her arm. It lodged in the outside wall of Delta's cell and hung there in no-man's land, quivering like a live thing. Ellen grinned and ducked back down into cover.

Your move, K. It's your knife.

• • • • •

"Control from bravo two." Linden knew the limo would have to be ditched soon, or it could betray where their base was. He was still cradling Jedda's unconscious body against his own. Apart from a few desperate words to Chrys when she started to work on the wound, Jedda had neither moved nor spoken since he slid her onto Marujn's cushioned seat. She was barely breathing. She would have to be carried for the last leg back to base. "How long till drop point? We're getting too close." He could hear the edge of panic in his own voice.

"Under control, bravo two. Stopping in eighty metres. Be ready for quick exit. Sitrep on alpha one?"

"Alpha one needs urgent medical attention. Get your kit ready, Control."

"Bravo one can do that when you get here. I'm needed in central. Alpha two is in a firefight. She needs the limo back at HQ, soonest."

Linden swallowed hard. Anton clearly wasn't coping. Too many variables? For Linden, as well. The limo was slowing. He had to concentrate on getting Jedda out. Safely. And covering the ground at top speed. Nothing else mattered. "With you soon as we can, Control. Get your kit ready. Out."

• • • • •

K's response to the knife was almost instant. "So it's you, Ellen? How delightful. We meet again." K sounded very, very sure of

437

himself. "Seems that this time I've got the upper hand, though, doesn't it? And talking of hands, how is yours? I'd hate to think I'd done any permanent damage."

Lying sod!

She knew better than to respond. She needed to keep alert. Let him make the next move. Let him come within range for one single second...

He didn't.

Instead he spoke to her as if they were at some social gathering. "You want to kill me, don't you, Ellen?" he asked smoothly. A long pause while he waited for the response that did not come. "Don't you?" he said again, louder this time. It was a clear challenge.

He knew she was in the cell, though he didn't know she was alone. She'd wanted him to know she was there, to bait him into making a mistake. So why not reply? She had to break this standoff somehow. The frustration was starting to get to her.

"The feeling is mutual, K."

"Then why didn't you finish the job last time?" he flashed back. "Couldn't bring yourself to cut a man's balls off, eh? Not when you and he had just—"

"You flatter yourself, K," she barked, before he could get the word out. How *dare* he? "The light was bad. But this time I'll see exactly what I'm aiming at. And I won't miss." The fit of fury kept her words flooding out. "I'm going to finish the fat cats' puppet. That's you, K. You! A soulless villain with a black heart. How many innocents have you killed?"

"About the same number as you, I'd imagine," he cut in coolly.

Was that laughter in his voice? *Damn the man!*

"We're two of a kind, you know, Ellen, though I don't suppose you're honest enough to admit it." He was taking his time. Relishing this. Sure he was winning.

She clamped her jaws shut. She'd already said far too much, letting him goad her into that angry outburst. She had to stay in control. She had to stay calm until he showed himself. A hair's breadth would do.

"You and I, dear Ellen," he went on, so softly that she had to strain to hear the words, "are twins in the shadows. We tell ourselves that we serve a higher cause. We stalk the dark. And in the dark, all cats are grey."

A shiver ran down her spine. Was it his words? Or that sinister, caressing voice?

His snort of laughter shattered the silence. "So now you kill me. Or I kill you. *Get it over with.* That's what you once said to me, remember? You were my prisoner then…" He let the words hang.

And she understood. All of it. That's why there had been no alarm, no lockdown. The streets should have been crawling with hound packs, but K hadn't sent them out. He had let her get away. Deliberately. Because he wanted to take her on himself. Because it was a private duel. One on one. To the death.

"Show yourself," he urged again. "Forget the Jay. *You're* not a coward. Come out and face me. A good death brings sweet dreams, Greenland lady."

Sweet dr—? The shock of the memory vaporised the last of her anger. She was back in control. Her logical mind reasserted its chilly grip and began to dissect K's every move.

In his arrogance, the man had blown it. No way would K ever mention all those betraying details in front of common soldiers. So it was a bluff. Had to be. There was no one out there with him.

He didn't know it yet, but it was just the two of them. Ellen and K. One on one. To the death.

FIFTY

WAS HE GETTING TO her at last? *Yes!* The silence proved it. She wasn't talking but she wasn't firing either. Typical woman. Her emotions were getting in the way of her fighting skills. So maybe he had a chance to creep up on her? If he could keep her attention diverted for long enough…

He started to edge along the left-hand wall. "Come on, Ellen," he urged. He could make it, he reckoned, as long as she didn't detect where his voice was coming from. "Your precious Jay is too much of a coward to come out and fight." Nearly there. One more step would do it. If he kept talking. Kept taunting. "But *you'll* come out, won't you? Or are you becoming as gutless as he is?" He ducked forward.

And saw.

He jerked back out of shot. A fraction of a second later, the wall exploded where his head had been. Man, had he misjudged her! Her fighting skills were as sharp as ever.

He had seen the truth now. His insides were churning with it. She was all by herself in there. At his mercy? Her precious Jay had chickened out again and sent his women in alone. "Gutless" didn't begin to describe the man. Shooting would be much too good for him.

K couldn't kill the Jay after all, but Ellen was another story. She had no way out. She would have to die in the end, of course. Pity. She was quite a woman. But if K could take her hostage, he'd have the whip hand over the Jay. He'd have options.

Yes. He needed her alive. And when it was over, he'd give her a quick death. She wouldn't suffer much.

He clicked both his weapons back to default and readied himself to attack.

He was glad he was doing this on his own, one on one. It would make for a very sweet victory.

• • • • •

Ellen wasn't going to show herself. She wasn't stupid enough to let him needle her into making that kind of a mistake. Let him make the first move. She crouched down behind the solid sleeping bench, trying to ensure that as much as possible of her body was protected. The top half of her head was vulnerable, but she couldn't help that. She had to watch for the attack. She had to keep her weapon up. Ready to fire.

K's attack came quickly. It was frenzied. Dozens and dozens of shots, all round the cell. Like an old-fashioned machine gun out of control.

Ellen instantly abandoned any thought of firing back and flattened her body on the floor behind the bench, as close as possible to the wall. How many weapons did he have? It felt as if a whole regiment was attacking her.

It stopped as suddenly as it had started.

Phew! She began to breathe again. She'd been lucky to come out of that unscathed. He'd been firing at random, hoping for a lucky hit, knowing that she would automatically duck for cover. Against such an onslaught of rapid fire, and in such a confined space, she'd had no chance to shoot back. But she would have found a way, eventually. He would know that. So he had retreated. He was no fool.

"Enjoy that, did you, Ellen?" He was back at the far end of the cell block. He sounded downright pleased with himself. "There's plenty of weaponry out here. I can keep it up until you surrender. So why don't you? *Get it over with.*"

She ground her teeth. She said nothing.

"On your own head be it, then," he said sadly. He was even pretending to be sorry for her.

Two-faced bastard!

This time she knew what was coming. She made herself as small as possible behind the bench, head well down. If he could fire at random, so could she.

Once he started shooting, she would stick her weapon out round the side of the bench and fire back. She wouldn't risk looking out to aim. But luck might just be on her side.

His second attack was even more ferocious than the first. With no spare weapons, Ellen couldn't afford to fire at anything like the same rate as K.

She let him have his head for a few seconds. Then she loosed off a couple of single shots. Another few seconds. Then one more. He stopped shooting quite soon after.

In the echoing silence, she heard his laboured breathing. Exertion? Certainly not pain. He hadn't been hit. Maybe next time?

"You've got guts. I'll give you that, Ellen." His voice had changed. Very subtly. Was he a fraction less sure of himself now? "But you're going to lose eventually. We both know that. And then you'll be *mine*."

He was savouring the word. She heard his breathing getting faster. In that instant, she read him.

She shuddered, to her core. *Please, let me be imagining this.* She tried to push it away, but her insight would not be denied. He would overpower her in the end. Control her. And the prospect was turning him on.

She was going to die here. K was going to keep attacking until her weapon ran out of charge. Then he was going to kill her – himself – to prove that he had won their duel. But that would not be the final humiliation. To show that he was master, he was going to fuck her first.

Her stomach heaved. She controlled it. Just.

I can fight him. To my last breath. I CAN!

But what if I don't? What if he gets me to respond to him again? He'll know. And then he'll kill me, knowing.

Her stomach heaved again. She threw up.

• • • • •

K knew it was just a matter of time. She was using the cover well, but it couldn't last much longer. Either she would run out of charge, or one of his random crippleshots would take her down. He'd promised himself he wouldn't let her suffer, but in the end it was her own choice. She still had the option of surrender, didn't she?

She would rather kill herself than surrender to me. We both know that. From before.

He made himself check his weapons. Time for another attack. Third time lucky?

A noise stopped him dead. Movement behind him. Another enemy?

He spun on his heel, weapons at the ready. It was just a blessedly familiar uniform. Reinforcements at last. About time!

"Have you brought stun grenades?" he snapped.

The soldier's jaw dropped. "N–no," the woman stammered.

"You're no use to me then. Stay where you are. Don't interfere." The woman looked baffled by his unexpected orders. So K barked them out again. Word for word. He refused to explain himself to a scruffy foot soldier.

• • • • •

Ellen's mouth tasted vile. Her body ached and her head was buzzing. She was even hearing voices. Out there? Or in her head? No, impossible. Her tooth computers couldn't possibly carry all the way back to base.

It must be K. His reinforcements must have arrived at last. So this was truly the end.

The buzz resolved into words. "…and I'm here in the cells. Right behind K. He thinks I'm one of his guards. Shall I shoot him?"

Chrys? Here? Never mind how or why. The odds had just turned.

Ellen sent a desperate thought message. "Don't touch him. He's *mine*!"

• • • • •

K started to edge forward to the point where he could start shooting again.

"Hold your fire. I'm coming out." Ellen. She sounded…odd. He couldn't quite put his finger on it, but there was something different about her voice.

He kept his weapons at the ready. There was no knowing what kind of trick she might play. But she must know she'd lost, surely?

She walked slowly out of the cell, her arms dangling loosely at her sides. She stepped over Delta's body and started towards him.

"Drop it!" he yelled, seeing the weapon still in her hand. "Drop it, or I'll drop you!"

She shrugged. "Look behind you, K."

"I don't need to. I know who's there." He'd give her one more second to obey his order. Then he would shoot her.

"Bad mistake. Look again." She sounded almost triumphant.

Her confidence rattled him. He risked a quick glance over his shoulder. As he expected, there was only that single scruffy soldier.

Her weapon was trained on the middle of his back!

"Clearer now? So drop your weapons. Or she'll fire."

He turned back to face Ellen squarely. She looked utterly determined and very sure of herself. Helped by the fact that her weapon was pointing directly at his gut! So this was it. He was trapped between two of the Jay's warrior women. He was going to die.

He shrugged and let his weapons fall. "Get it over with, then."

K C ABBOTT

Surprised at his own choice of words, he almost laughed. And discovered that he had more to say. "Tell your precious Jay that at least one man has the guts to take on the enemy, face to face, even though he doesn't."

Ellen took a step closer. Her eyes narrowed. "You really don't get it, do you, K? In your book, a war leader has to be a man. The *Jay* has to be a man. Time to take your blinkers off. The Jay's standing right in front of you. *Female. ME.* And this Jay is the last thing you're ever going to see."

He saw the hard light of decision in her eyes. She raised her weapon a notch so that it was pointing at his heart. It was the final round. And he'd lost.

She almost smiled. "Sweet dreams, sunshine."

Pain seared through him and he felt himself falling.

· · · · ·

Ellen squatted down beside the body. Her injured ankle protested at the strain, but she gritted her teeth and focused on her task. Too good an opportunity to miss, though she'd have to be quick. She started patting down K's uniform tunic.

It was skin tight. No chance that anything was tucked inside. No room for any layers underneath, either.

"No body armour, eh? Too vain to spoil the line of your fancy suit, I suppose. Never mind. Probably wouldn't have saved you anyway."

"Ellen, what are you playing at? We need to get out of here."

"I need to find the call button for his limo." She kept on searching. "I can use it to— Yes! Found it!" It was in his trouser pocket. She tried to get at it but she couldn't. The trousers were almost as form-fitting as the tunic and the dead weight of his body was pulling the pocket tightly closed.

There was a simple solution to that. She jumped to her feet and went to retrieve her knife. It was a struggle to pull it out of the wall and bits of masonry came with it. But it was just what she needed.

She bent down and slashed the fabric open. The call button fell out onto the floor. Along with a white envelope. Her own white envelope.

She had forgotten about that.

What was she to do with it now? Take it back? There was no need to sow enmity between Marujn and a dead man, but Marujn still had to get the message. It was vital to frighten him into giving up on his pursuit of Linden.

444

Besides, it would do no harm to let K's successors know that the Jays were thinkers as well as warriors. She jammed the call button into her pocket. Grabbing the envelope, she smoothed it against the wall and wrote. Yup, that should do it. Perhaps, as a final message to Marujn and his Council, she should impale the envelope on K's dead body? The final indignity. She speared the knife through the envelope and went back to stand over him. Dead, he didn't look threatening at all. He looked quite peaceful.

"Stop wasting time, Ellen. Come *on*!" Chrys was already making for the door.

Ellen slammed the knife down and ran for the stairs without looking back.

$$\bullet \bullet \bullet \bullet \bullet$$

By the time they'd raced up two flights of stairs, Ellen's ankle was threatening to give way completely. She'd forced it to work on the level, but it couldn't cope with stairs. She grabbed for the half-wall with her free hand. Its support might be enough to get her back to ground level. Up ahead of her, Chrys had almost disappeared.

Ellen followed as fast as she could. Not too much further. She could make it. She would. She couldn't give up now.

Sheer bloody-mindedness kept her hobbling upwards, though the stairs seemed to go on for ever. She was almost glad to be distracted by the sight of her missing weapon, the one she had lost when she skidded earlier. Without a moment's hesitation, she stowed Delta's half-depleted weapon away and grabbed her own, relishing its familiar weight in her hand. It was still on kill. Good.

"All units from Control." Anton's agitated voice came through their implants. "State troopers will arrive outside HQ in just over four minutes. Get yourselves out. I say again. Get out of there! *NOW!*"

Chrys's reaction was instant. And unbelievably calm. "Control, update on transport?"

"Transport not close enough, bravo one. Get out on foot. I'll guide you to rendezvous with transport."

"Wilco. Out," Chrys said. "Come on, Ellen. If your mind control can make that ankle work properly, use it now! We're going to have to sprint. *Come ON!*" Without giving Ellen time to reply, Chrys started racing up the remaining stairs.

Ellen followed as fast as her injured leg would let her. She might get out, but could she outrun a posse of K's guards? Her mind started calculating at top speed, sharpened by the stabbing pain.

Yes, there was just time. "The call button for K's limo," she gasped. "It'll get us access. Once we're inside, I can take it over."

Chrys didn't break stride. "Are you sure?" she called over her shoulder.

They had less than four minutes left. Ellen's leg would fail long before their time was up. "Of course I'm sure," she snapped.

She wasn't. But she'd weighed the odds. Chrys could escape on foot. If it came to it, Ellen would order Chrys to go. But for Ellen, K's limo was the only chance.

• • • • •

Chrys looked behind her to check again. She was ready to go back for Ellen, even to half-carry her. But she wouldn't have to. Willpower, or something, was keeping Ellen going. She was climbing pretty fast, too, faster than Chrys would have thought possible with a crocked ankle. Ellen would make it. So Chrys had to stay on point.

Reaching the top of the stairs, Chrys crouched down, weapons in hand, scanning round for danger. The hall was still empty but the clock was ticking.

Come on, Ellen. You can do it. We can get out of here.

It took another thirty precious seconds, but Ellen made it to the hall. "Let's go," she gasped. "Through the main entrance and into K's car. Come on!" She was so determined, she was leading the way. She made it through the door and down the steps. Chrys followed, marvelling that Ellen even remembered to reset the lockdown on the main door as she came through. No sign of the opposition yet. But it wouldn't be long.

Ellen hauled out the call button and pinged the car. The door slid open. "Get in," she ordered. "I'll fix it from inside."

They dashed across and climbed in. The door slid closed behind them. Ellen started fiddling with the controls. Chrys held her breath, checking around for the arrival of the troopers. Nothing yet. Of course, when they did arrive, they wouldn't be able to see through the one-way glass. That would give Ellen a little longer to work her magic.

Sixty seconds passed. Ninety. Still no troopers. But the limo wasn't responding.

"It's not working. I can't do it. Save yourself, Chrys. If you leg it now, you can still make it."

Chrys knew better than to argue. She reached for the door control.

"No. Wait! *I've done it! EU-bloody-REKA!*"

The limo started to move. Ellen was exultant, laughing till she almost cried.

Chrys started laughing, too, just as the troopers came into view, racing across the square towards the entrance to K's HQ. One of them stopped in her tracks when she recognised the Controller's blacked-out limo. She sprang to attention. And saluted.

Chrys laughed so much it hurt.

• • • • •

They were clear of all possible pursuit and halfway back to base when Ellen remembered. She was grateful, but she knew she mustn't let it go.

"You disobeyed my direct order, Chrys. You're the medic. I told you to go back to base with Jedda. She needed you."

Chrys went very still. Her eyes narrowed angrily as she held Ellen's gaze. "I don't flout orders." Her voice was very clipped. She was breathing hard. "Jedda ordered me to go back to get you out. Her last order as leader, she said." She stopped, chest heaving, long enough for Ellen to digest the new information. She let out a long jagged breath and said, "I know why she gave that order. And so do you. She believes in you, Ellen. She knows you won't let us down." Chrys turned abruptly and stared out of the window, apparently searching the streets for enemy forces. Then, in a half-voice, she said, almost to herself, "I believe in you, too."

Ellen was stunned into silence. And humbled. Jedda had risked her recovery, maybe her life, to give the Jays the chance of a new leader. Jedda was in a league of her own and Ellen could never match her. Did she want to try?

• • • • •

Chrys was surprised when Ellen ordered the limo to stop well short of base.

"You could go closer," Chrys suggested. "Less strain on your bad leg."

"No. This is quite close enough for this little beauty. I've got plans for it and I don't want it caught on any cameras. I'll be able to make it back to base when I'm done."

Ellen grinned. "We've won. K is dead and I'm not. Thanks to you, Chrys."

Chrys felt the start of a glow. She stamped on it. "What are you going to do?"

For once, Ellen seemed ready to share. Was she learning to trust

Chrys? "I'm going to subvert the limo's systems so that I can override its controls. It'll be a waste of effort if the next Controller doesn't take over K's limo, of course, but there's a fair chance he will. At least at the start. With luck, the new man won't be savvy enough to look for the kind of fix that I'm going to do. It's worth a try, anyway."

Chrys nodded, marvelling yet again at Ellen's skill.

"You go on ahead." It was said in Ellen's normal voice, but it was an order. "Anton will have done his best for Jedda, but I'm sure she could do with the real medic. Don't bother about me. I'll be there soon as I can. I'm not about to get caught now."

Chrys didn't doubt it. She nodded and reached for the door control.

• • • • •

In spite of her ankle, Ellen had a spring in her step when she finally got back.

She'd fixed the limo and sent it on its way with the door unlocked and the call button inside. It would stop right outside K's HQ, exactly where she had stolen it from, ready to be found by its new owners. With luck, the soldiers would be too busy chasing around to report having seen it drive away. The new Controller would assume the Jays had failed to start it and thrown down the call button in disgust. She was particularly proud of that neat little wrinkle. She almost bounced into the bunker. And she was smiling.

"Hey, Ellen, you found the crock of gold?" Anton, of course. Typical.

"Something like that," Ellen said, trying to hide her smile. It didn't quite work, until she took in the picture in front of her. Everyone was in the control centre. Her arrival seemed to have frozen them into some kind of tableau. Jedda, white-faced and bandaged, but clearly recovering. Linden, standing protectively beside her stretcher, not quite touching, but much too close to be a mere colleague. Chrys, half in the shadow, alone again, her face showing signs of strain. Only Anton was moving. He was sitting at his screen, working – no, playing – with his precious computers. But then, Anton didn't have a horse in the leadership race.

No one spoke. No one was prepared to ask the question.

Ellen shrugged and stepped into the middle of the open space, where Jedda had so often stood to give out orders in that crisp, quiet way she had. "You'll be a hard act to follow, Jedda," Ellen began, fixing her eyes on each of them in turn and coming to rest, finally, on Chrys, "but if that's what you want – what you *all* want…"

Chrys gave a tiny nod. She did not take her eyes off Ellen.

"OK then, guys." Ellen nodded, twice. This was a serious commitment she was making here. "You've got yourselves a new leader."

Anton – Anton, of all people! – gave a whoop of triumph and jumped to his feet, hand raised as if for a toast. "Our new leader! And all who sail in her!"

END OF BOOK ONE
The story continues in Book Two of
the *GENERATION OF VIPERS* series:
AT THE SONJA HOTEL

Generation of Vipers Book 2

AT THE SONJA HOTEL
~ a dystopian thriller ~
Book 2 of the
GENERATION OF VIPERS series

Ellen, the leader of the Jays, is on a high. She's dealt with K and now she plans to take on the real oppressors – the shadowy Council – via their soft underbelly, a luxurious prison where beautiful women entertain the men who rule the planet.

When the Jays' first attack fails, they discover that the Sonja Hotel is much more than a high-class brothel. It's a danger to the future of the world.

It has to be destroyed.

But the Sonja Hotel is not Ellen's only challenge. In the totally networked world, London Province's Central Lab has a strange new cell with no external comms at all. There's only one way to find out what secret research is being done there. One of the Jays will have to be planted on the inside.

Coming Soon

A Last Word From The Author

I hope you enjoyed **ALL CATS ARE GREY** and were not too disappointed by the absence of cats!

Yes, that was intended as a joke. Typical Brit humour, I guess. It's one joke that has rebounded on me, though, because somehow a cat has slithered its way into the second book of the series, **AT THE SONJA HOTEL**, and the wily feline is skulking in the shadows. It appears to have decided that it's going to make a home in my *GOV* world. In other words, cats and cat lovers appear to be winning. So far...

Book 2 of *GENERATION OF VIPERS* is currently in the process of completion – though it's taking much longer than I planned, I admit – and it will be out soon. In the meantime, you can read a prequel to **ALL CATS ARE GREY** in my short story collection, **VIPER VENOM**, available as a free Smashwords download via my website or from Amazon. The prequel story is called – bad pun alert! – *Birth of the Blues*.

If you'd like to be the first to know about forthcoming publication dates and the latest developments in the series, visit my website at kcabbott.com or follow me on Twitter @KCAbbottVipers. I'm also using them to share some of the secrets of the *GOV* world and how its sinister power brokers conspire to keep control.

Finally, if you enjoyed **ALL CATS ARE GREY**, I'd be really grateful if you would leave a review on Amazon to say so. Your reviews help other readers to choose what to read and they help me to reach more readers with my stories. Thank you.

Casey Abbott
March 2019

Free download via kcabbott.com

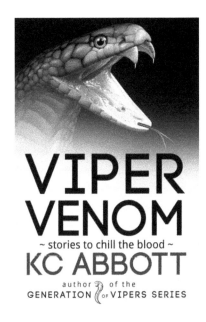

VIPER
VENOM
~ stories to chill the blood ~
KC ABBOTT
author of the
GENERATION of VIPERS SERIES

The VIPER VENOM free story collection
includes a prequel to the Generation of Vipers series :
Birth of the Blues

Enjoy!

Lightning Source UK Ltd.
Milton Keynes UK
UKHW012109080419

340685UK00001B/25/P